A Green Flash

A Green Flash

Winston Graham

Random House New York

Library of Congress Cataloging-in-Publication Data

Graham, Winston.
A green flash.

I. Title.
PR6013.R24G7   1987   823'.912   87-12711
ISBN 0-394-56392-1

Manufactured in the United States of America

24689753

Book design and calligraphy
by Carole Lowenstein

To
My friend
Desmond Brand

A Green Flash

I

When he killed his father they sent him to a psychiatrist called Meiss in Wimpole Street. Meiss was a Swiss of late middle age who sometimes did work for the Home Office.

The boy came in that first afternoon in a gray flannel suit, with a scarlet and azure school tie, a small faded carnation in his buttonhole. Hair matted and needing a clip and a brush. He had a Renaissance look. You could see him among the frescoes in some dark Italian church. He looked Dr. Meiss in the eye.

"David," said Dr. Meiss. "David, please sit down. No, over there, it will be more comfortable. Did your mother bring you?"

"We came together, sir," the boy said.

"Just so. She is in the waiting room? I will see her later."

The boy sat down, pulled at the knees of his trousers as if unaccustomed to their being long.

"I will see her later," said Dr. Meiss. "So far we have only spoken on the telephone. The arrangements, you will understand, were made by her solicitors."

"Yes."

Meiss had a hawklike, sad face, as if rivers of other people's troubles had run down his cheeks and left them furrowed and worn. His graying hair, thin on top, curled over elfin ears; his suit was shiny at the elbows.

"How old are you, David?"

The boy bit the skin round his thumb. "Don't you . . . won't they have told you?"

"I like to hear it for myself."

"Eleven."

"When were you eleven?"

"Last May."

"And you are at school at . . . ?"

"Hartford Grammar School, sir."

"Is that a day school or boarding?"

"Day school in Leeds."

"So you live at home."

"Yes, sir."

"I understand you have been enrolled for Loretto when you are thirteen."

"Well, yes. I suppose so."

"How d'you mean, you suppose so?"

"Well, it will depend if I pass my Common Entrance Examination, won't it? I shouldn't think I've much chance of that now."

"Who knows? In two years much may have changed."

Meiss began to reread the report on his desk. For this he put on half-moon spectacles.

"What I wish to do, just to begin, is to have a friendly talk."

David had been looking round the room. "Are those ivory, those elephants, sir?"

Meiss glanced at the two ornaments on the mantelpiece. "They're ebony, with ivory tusks."

"Are they yours, sir?"

"Yes, I brought them back from Nigeria."

"Ah." The boy thrust his hands into his trouser pockets, feeling for the bit of cord, the stone, the handkerchief, the four pennies.

"Talking," said Meiss presently, "you may think it is all talking. But sometimes, I assure you, it does help. If nothing else it will enable us to get to know each other. And that is the most necessary preliminary if I am able to help you."

When there was no reply Meiss said, "What do you think?"

"I don't know, do I, sir?"

"You don't know and neither do I. We can only try together. And first perhaps before we go any further, you should stop calling me 'sir.' "

"Should I, sir? All right."

There was another silence. "I know how tired you must be of answering questions." Although the doctor's English was very good he pronounced it "kervestions." "Many, many times you will have been asked about the night your father met with his accident and I am sure that many, many times you have tried to answer. So I don't think there is any need to pursue that further at present. I'd like you first to tell me about your life before all this happened."

There was a long pause. "I don't know what you want me to say."

"I don't *want* you to say anything. I'd like you to volunteer any information you would like to tell me."

After a few minutes the boy said, "Did you live in Nigeria?"

"My brother does. I have visited him there."

"What's it like, sir?"

"Pleasant for a holiday, David. I will tell you about it when we get to know each other better. Would you like to travel?"

"Yes, I think so."

"Do you like your school?"

"My school? . . . Oh, so-so. Not much."

"What is wrong with it?"

The boy shrugged.

"Are you bullied?"

"No. Not much anyway."

"You're tall for your age, so that's a good thing. Do you bully others?"

"No. Not much."

"Do you dislike the masters?"

"Oh . . . more or less. They're not bad. I don't like being— pushed around."

"You mean doing what you're told or *really* pushed around?"

"I don't like pettifogging rules—that sort of thing."

"Discipline?"

"Maybe."

"Are you good at games?"

"Average."

"What do you like playing?"

"Oh . . . swimming, fencing, boxing."

"Football? Cricket?"

"No."

"Perhaps not team sports, eh?"

"I don't know."

"And as to your lessons? You have been good at them?"

"No."

"Yet you do not seem like a dull boy, David. I would have thought you had a high intelligence."

The boy looked out of the window. It was just beginning to rain. A taxi with its light on went past. He said, "Is your brother a doctor in Nigeria?"

"No, a sort of chemist. I will tell you about that sometime too . . . Are you—er—slow to learn?"

"I don't know."

"Don't you?"

"Well, sometimes I'm not interested."

"But when you *are* interested?"

"Yes. OK, I suppose."

"The purpose of discipline is to be able to work at things which do *not* appeal to you. Do you have many friends?"

After thinking, David shook his head.

"At home? At school? Not one?"

"Oh, yes. A few. Some are all right."

"Do you like coming to London?"

"Yes . . . But not—"

"Not coming here, eh? That is understandable. Yet you have nothing to fear from me. If I send an unfavorable report it will be more a reflection on me than on you."

"Why?"

"Why? Because it will mean I have been unable to help you. And that would be a pity, wouldn't it?"

Dr. Meiss was wearing old-fashioned gold cuff links. Like Cartwright, the headmaster. Only Cart's cuffs were not so clean. Cart's fingers were stained with chalk. Cart's moustache was yellow under the nose but gray at the sides.

"My wish is to help you, David, if I can. You may not feel that you need it. You may not feel that I can help you, even if you should need it. But one thing is clear—quite certain: I cannot be of the least assistance to you or to your mother or to Mr. Kingsley if you are not willing to cooperate with me. You do see that, don't you?"

"Yes."

"And you are willing to cooperate?"

A hesitation. "I haven't much choice, have I?"

"You have every choice. If I find I am unable to obtain your cooperation I shall quickly give the case up. I do not wish to waste my time."

"What'll happen then?"

"Nothing very much, I should think. Probably nothing at all. So far as the law is concerned, the matter is closed. But I think I can say that if you cooperate it will be a help and comfort to your mother. That at least is not in doubt. And I presume you would wish that."

The boy picked at a tooth and then sucked his finger. He gave the psychiatrist an assaying look that seemed too old for his years.

"I'd like you to tell me about Nigeria," he said.

 The afternoon had darkened. A steady rain had set in and low clouds crouched over the street.

Dr. Meiss said, "Tell me about your mother."

"She's my father's wife, isn't she. Was."

"Do you talk to her?"

"Oh—yes."

"You are fond of her?"

"Oh, yes." This casually.

"I know in some quarters it is not done to express affection, but do you not love her?"

"I've just said so."

"Good. And does she love you?"

"I think so."

"You only think so?"

"No, I'm sure she does."

"You have no brothers or sisters?"

"No."

"But was it a happy home? Was it? Just your mother and your father?"

There was a long silence.

The boy said, "You couldn't help but wonder, could you, when he came in drunk."

"Wonder what?"

"You couldn't help thinking of it. My father and my mother. Could you. It's not natural, is it?"

"Isn't it? I would have thought so."

"They should have had separate rooms. She wanted it but he never would. He was—pretty awful to her at times. And I couldn't do anything right when he was in that mood. I'm not . . ."

"What were you going to say?"

"It doesn't matter."

"It's good to be able to say exactly how you feel."

For the first time the boy had flushed. "Of course I didn't mean to do him any *harm*! Not really. He was the sort of man who'll get you in a corner . . . It was just the way it happened, wasn't it?"

"Yes. Just the way it happened."

There was another long silence. Somewhere a clock chimed.

"Can I go now?"

"Of course. You are never compelled to stay here. I will see your mother before you leave. But is there anything else you wanted to say?"

"About what?"

"About anything that comes into your mind. For instance, did you *never* like your father? Did you not ever have any companionship with him?"

"Oh, sometimes. He *could* be quite jolly. You know. He was a great one for fast cars. He used to take me out sometimes and drive like the wind. We had an open Alvis. He was fun then."

Meiss watched his patient, but there was no moisture, no evidence of sentiment in the boy's candid eyes.

"But even then you could never quite rely on him, trust his mood," the boy said.

"How do you mean?"

"You'd be giggling with him and maybe say the wrong thing —there'd be a closedown, a freeze-up, finish to the fun. So that after a while being with him was scary."

The boy swallowed the rest of his words, as if aware that he had said more than he had intended.

"Your father was often away, though?"

"Sometimes."

"Did you enjoy the times when he was away?"

"I suppose so."

"Wasn't there a suggestion that you might be sent away to school—to what is called a preparatory school?"

"Oh, yes. They argued about it."

"Your mother and father did? How did they argue?"

"He wanted it. She didn't."

"Why did your mother not want it?"

"I don't know."

"And how did you feel?"

"Oh." Another shrug. "Not too keen."

"Any reason?"

"It would have been the same as day school, wouldn't it? Only more so. At least, that's what I should expect."

"So you were comfortable at home?"

"More or less. More comfortable than going away."

Meiss nodded understandingly. "Did your father say he wanted you to go away?"

"Yes, sir. They were the schools he'd been to. He thought I ought to go to the same ones."

Meiss tapped his teeth with a pencil. "Are you fond of flowers, David?"

"What? I don't know. Why?"

"Your buttonhole."

"Oh that." He peered down. "I picked it in the garden."

"Today?"

"Yesterday."

"Now it is faded you do not throw it away?"

"No, it seems a pity."

"Are you specially fond of carnations?"

"They're all right. This isn't a real carnation, you know."

"Isn't it? What is it then?"

"A pink."

"Oh. Is that some sort of garden carnation?"

"Yes."

"Yorkshire is not your county, is it? Are you not Scottish?"

"My father is—was. I was born in Yorkshire."

"Are you fond of Scotland?"

"I've never been there."

Dr. Meiss looked down at his notes.

"I see."

III Mrs. Abden was a pretty, bone-pale, dark woman of thirty-five, with gratuitous lines on her forehead and flared, oval-shaped, dignified nostrils. You could see where the boy got his looks from. She was above average height, willowy, hatless, in a fawn frock of impeccable simplicity, stockings a shade darker, tan shoes, the skirt a bit short.

Dr. Meiss said, "I believe I can be of use to him but it will take perhaps two more meetings to be sure. There are obvious areas of resistance, yet often he has responded willingly and well. He has a directness of gaze which is unusual in such cases. It is a good sign."

Mrs. Abden crossed her legs, carefully pulling down her skirt as she did so. It looked as if she was just beginning to put on weight.

"When do you wish to see us again?"

"If I take this case on, I think it will have to be a minimum of three times a week."

She drew in her breath. "It's so *far* from Leeds. And I have so much to see to. Mr. Kingsley has been so kind and helpful but . . ."

"When he came to see me he explained the position fully. I think it was his suggestion that David should come to me in the first place."

"Yes; his and that children's social worker, or whatever she was."

"But I understand there was no pressure applied to you from any other source?"

"No, no."

"I really feel that three times a week is the satisfactory minimum." Dr. Meiss picked up a letter from his desk. "This that has happened—this tragedy—has tended to obscure everything else. But it is fairly clear, is it not, that there was something before?"

"Before?"

"In your son's—in David's—general behavior, which was not quite running to a normal pattern."

"I'm afraid I don't know what you mean."

"Well, this letter from his headmaster. This was with his school report last year. You know what it says, of course?"

"Oh, that . . . I do *remember* it."

Dr. Meiss read out: " 'David has a variety of talents, but a clear determination not to make use of them in school time. He refuses discipline whenever he can, makes few friends, and appears to want to live in a world of his own. He seems to have a disregard for proper restraint where his own urges are concerned. I am coming to have grave doubts about his willingness to shoulder the responsibilities of growing up.' "

"Oh, yes, that's Mr. Cartwright; but I shouldn't pay much attention to him, doctor. He's well known for his prejudices. David will probably tell you all about *him*."

"He talks freely about his school, then? I mean, to you?"

"Yes, yes. When I ask him he tells me. He's always very frank and very honest with me."

"I understand from David that there was some disagreement between you and your husband as to whether he should be sent to a normal preparatory school—away from home, I mean."

Mrs. Abden fingered the short pearl necklace around her throat, slowly, individually, like prayer beads.

"I have never felt David was strong enough for the rough and tumble of boarding-school life."

"Why? Is he delicate? He's well developed. Tall for his age. Looks strong."

"We nearly lost him with rheumatic fever when he was seven. And he catches cold very easily. And gets quickly tired. Believe me, Dr. Meiss, I should know."

The psychiatrist made a note or two. They were of no importance but they helped him to think. One trod delicately.

"Do you think still to keep David at his day school? I mean, when he restarts next term."

"Why not?"

"He is clearly not very happy there."

"Where else would he be more happy? Though in fact Kenneth . . ."

"Kenneth?"

"Mr. Kingsley. Our solicitor, as you know, and a great personal friend. I can't imagine how I should have got through this time without him. He has advised on so many things."

"And he thinks?"

Mrs. Abden blinked. "He thinks it might be a good thing if David went away. At least for a time."

"Perhaps I shall be able to advise you on this in a month or so."

"Kenneth thinks David should go to Loretto, as planned. That's if they will still have him."

"Why should they not? After the coroner's verdict no stigma should attach to your son."

"It was in the papers, you know. 'Baronet's nephew dies in kitchen brawl.' These things stick. People will go on talking."

Dr. Meiss coughed into his hand. Time was overrunning and another patient was almost due.

"Far more important, Mrs. Abden, is to get David into the frame of mind when he will study to pass the Common Entrance. He looks to me the sort of boy who should profit from the education such a school provides. But I will know better after a few more meetings."

"I hope it helps. As I say, it was Mr. Kingsley's idea. He felt that it had all been a terrible shock for the boy, and that if he came to you it might help to clear up any anxieties or fears . . ."

"Is he greatly attached to you?"

"Who?"

"David, of course."

The lines on Mrs. Abden's forehead sharply deepened. "David and I have always thought the world of each other."

"I'm glad of that."

She hesitated and then went on, "Only last year, when my husband was away, I was laid low with tonsilitis. David did everything. He'd—he would even come in and tuck me up before saying good night."

"So he will cooperate with me more completely if you encourage him to do so, if you let him know that you want him to come."

Mrs. Abden opened her bag, took out a compact, peered at herself, then, reassured, snapped it shut.

"Where is David now?"

"In my small sitting room. With my receptionist."

Mrs. Abden said rapidly, "It's difficult for an outsider like you—I don't wish to be impolite, Dr. Meiss—but it's hard for someone outside to understand what has happened. We were . . . a happy family, really. You can't know what I felt for Stewart. I *cared* for him . . ."

Meiss nodded. "Yes, yes."

"He was hard to manage at times, I know. My husband, I mean. And when he was worried about money matters he would drink too much. Without that he would have been very different . . . But then, who hasn't little crosses to bear? Even if a man *is* difficult it does not stop you from caring. Are you married?"

"Yes."

"Well, in this, I've been in hell. I mean! The two people I love most, they do this to each other! How do you feel at the end of it? How *do* you? Whose *fault* was it?"

"At the inquest, Mrs. Abden, you said that your husband bullied David."

"That's true."

"You said that that evening he even threatened to kill him."

Rachel Abden fingered her pearls confidentially. "It was nearly true. By then I could do nothing to help Stewart. He was—gone. I could only try to make things easier for David."

Meiss nodded again. "What you tell me will, of course, go no further. The tragedy is over. Your son is in no danger from the law. It is simply that I am trying to find out why this quarrel between them went farther than any had gone before. You—I presume you did not say anything to either of them that might have provoked the quarrel?"

"For God's sake, why *should* I? What are you accusing me of?"

"Nothing at all, believe me . . . Did your *son* say anything to his father especially to provoke his anger on this occasion?"

"He . . . well, no."

She looked at the psychiatrist. Her umber-dark eyes were full of the emotional tears her son's had lacked.

"You don't want to speak of this?"

She said, "David called his father a particularly foul name. His father said, 'I'll have the hide off you for that!' "

"He did not actually threaten to kill David?"

"No . . . I don't think so."

"You added it to help David?"

"Mr. Kingsley advised me to say that."

"I see."

After a minute she said, "I don't think I'll ever forgive David —properly, that is, altogether."

"You must try not to think that."

"Oh, I know, I know. It's easy to say, but hard . . ."

"Did he push his father, as you said at the inquest?"

"Yes."

"Was that not something Mr. Kingsley also advised you to say?"

"Of *course* not! He—he thrust at him hard in the chest and Stewart sort of lost his balance and turned and fell and struck his head on the fireplace . . ."

Meiss thought over carefully what Kingsley had told him, but decided not to confront her with it. He said, "You will forgive me for being so persistent. All this you will have been asked before, and you may think my insistence is an impertinence. Believe me, it is not meant so. But if I can begin to find from you any cause of this quarrel this particular night . . ."

"How does *any* quarrel begin? They were—jealous of each other—I believe. The slightest thing would start them off."

"It's not unusual, of course. When a son grows up it is a commonplace for him and his father to have a resentment of each other. We have all heard of Oedipus."

She said, "I don't think it was quite like that. David was really quite *fond* of his father. That was the *strange* thing. That made it *worse*." She wiped her eyes. "Really. I suppose in a way they were a little jealous about *me*. They both—*wanted* me, wanted to be first in my attention, my love. I suppose you're right in a way. Sometimes I blame myself."

"Oh?"

"Couldn't I—shouldn't I—have stopped it?"

"Stopped what?"

"This jealousy, this rivalry. I should have been able to do *something*."

"Perhaps subconsciously you were flattered."

She blinked her tears angrily away. "What sort of a wife and mother do you think I am?"

"I did say subconsciously, Mrs. Abden. After all, this also is not uncommon. Everyone wishes to be popular, to be desired."

"I've not slept properly since it happened, except with Nembutal. Even now I take Valium every day. It's been terrible. A nightmare. Mr. Kingsley says he does not know how I have come through it."

Another pause. Eventually Dr. Meiss said, "Will next Thursday be convenient? For me to see David again?"

"I suppose we could manage the afternoon."

"At three, then?"

She wiped her eyes, again, on her dignity now.

Meiss said, "Has David not ever been to Scotland?"

"Oh, yes. His father took him last year to see Loretto."

"Strange."

"What's strange about that?"

"He told me he had never been. Does he not like it, I wonder?"

"It may be. I don't know. Of course his father had quarreled with his relatives up there. They never met or corresponded in any way."

"You are not Scottish, Mrs. Abden?"

"No."

CHAPTER ONE

I It was fairly well on in the swinging sixties that I met her. I had just missed the worldwide celebrations for my twenty-fourth birthday.

The party was at Lady Rowton's. Maud Rowton, being the wife of a recently created life peer, was not sure of her way in society, and was trying to launch her daughter Caroline into the whirlpool of a Season. From my experience of the two previous years, when I had escorted any number of girls on any number of occasions, I knew better than she did the intricacies of getting "in," the concentric circles which exist of which only the inner two or three are anything but hell. Every year around these inner circles runs a pack of yelping girls who at the end of the summer have done all the proper and expected and expensive things, without ever having achieved the accolade of acceptance.

Caroline Rowton was a bright kid who unfortunately had inherited her father's lantern jaw. It was not this, however, that would mar her chances. Some of the girls in the very center of things had faces like starving horses. It was just that her mother had not been to school with enough mothers of the right sort.

So I felt sorry for her in a detached way, and when Jerry Dawson, who had brought me, said would I stay behind and go to a dinner party after, I said of course, hardly listening to him, wondering why I had come. Was this the life I really wanted to lead: all this inhaling of other people's hot breath—bangles, jangles, cigarette smoke, high voices, high heels, fractured conversations, sweat, assessing eyes, polite masks, smeared lipstick, alcohol, flip, flap, standing about holding a glass, all a strain on legs, on shoulders, on bellies, on buttocks, on one's *patience*. But then I often asked myself questions like this. What life did I want to lead—if any?

"Where did you say?"

"It'll be at the Savoy. One of their chaps has stood them up."

"Fine," I said. "Who's that woman by the window?"

"The one in black? With the sleeves? Mme. Shona."

"Who?"

"My dear chap, you ought to know."

"Why?"

"Well . . . our line of business."

"What—d'you mean the one who makes . . . Well, well, rather a surprise, isn't she? I always imagine these women as well-preserved old dragons of seventy-five."

"She'll get like that in her own time. Want to meet her?"

Did I? It might make a change.

"Yes, I think so. She looks interesting."

Jerry chuckled. "Oh, interesting is quite the word. But take care. She has a reputation."

The reply that came to my lips seemed a trifle malapert, so I said nothing. It's strange what repression of the sort I'd just experienced will do to the frankest of men.

In a while I found myself going up to the throne. At the time I reckoned her about thirty-five, though a closer look added a year or two. No beauty, and I didn't think ever had been; and pretty wasn't a word you could ever use about her. Five feet seven inches tall, I was told much later, and weighed 117 pounds. Skin pale to dusky; hair black and a bit lank but capable, I was also to learn, of being disciplined, like many other things, to the order of its owner: Two or three twists of the long fingers and it would be changed from low life to haute couture. Really handsome dark eyes, equable brows, big clever mouth. An air. Certainly a smashing-looking woman, I said to myself. It was a word you used in those days.

When Jerry Dawson had gone off I casually helped to refill her glass and she nodded her thanks, but Caroline Rowton was speaking to her so I had this minute or so to sum her up and to listen for the first time to the tenor bell of her voice, the too perfect English fretted with a lisp of accent.

"You work for Yardley's?" Suddenly I was in the firing line. I met her brooding candescent stare for the first time.

"I joined them earlier this year."

"Ah." She nodded as if this explained something.

"Not quite in your league, ma'am."

"Oh." She shrugged, taking it without hesitation as a compliment. "They are *far* bigger than we are—and far older—longer established. But I agree, I do not look on them as rivals. I should not have thought . . ."

People came between us. "What would you not have thought?" I prompted when they had gone.

"That you were in the business."

"Should it show? Like a shoulder strap?"

"A shoulder . . . ah, no." A flicker of her thin lips. "But you know how it is: Certain professions tend to attract types, certain businesses."

"In what way don't I fit the slot?"

She looked at me soberly. "Now you are asking for compliments."

"Not necessarily."

"No? . . . But you were expecting that."

"I never," I said, "ask for anything."

"That I believe. Instead of asking, you would try to take."

This was a little near the bone in more ways than one. "You read me well, Mme. Shona."

"All right. All right . . . First, there are no such things as slots. Are there. I was wrong in that. What did you do before you joined Yardley?"

"For a while I was not gainfully employed. Jerry stepped in and offered me this job."

"And what is *this job*? What position?"

"Assistant sales director."

"You're young for that, Mr.—er—"

"David Abden. I don't think age should come into it, do you?"

She breathed out through her nose. On a cold day you could imagine fine visible discharges of smoky breath as from the nostrils of a thoroughbred mare.

She said, "Age has no privileges. Youth no virtue. It is what one does that matters."

We were apart for a bit. I kept looking across at her, slim and straight in one of those black sheath things; this one with dazzling gold sleeves. I began to figure if there was anything in it for me. I hadn't had the least intention of staying in the perfumery business longer than it took to find something better or to rediscover one of the easier ways of making money, but I had to keep an open mind in all these things.

I couldn't get hold of Jerry, who was the center of a crowd, but I saw Patrick Favill in a corner. Patrick was a television writer and sometimes worked for the press.

"Shona?" he said. "I know her. Everybody knows her; but nobody gets *close*, as it were. What d'you want to know? She's Russian, of course. You know the legend, I suppose."

"If I've heard it I wasn't listening."

"They say she was picked up by American troops when they were invading Germany at the end of the war."

"So?"

"They found her in rags, they say, barefoot, starving, but with books by Schopenhauer and Goethe clutched under one skinny arm. That's the story anyhow."

"What happened?"

"Well, she claimed she'd walked all the way from—was it?— Kharkov or Lvov, begging, stealing, living off the land, sleeping under hedges, dodging the retreating armies. The American commandant didn't know quite what to make of her—thought she was some kind of 'plant' at first, but she convinced him she was on the level and only keen to put as much territory as she could between herself and Uncle Joe."

I waited. He glanced at me, lifted an eyebrow. "So she ended up in Paris—lived there a few years—married, came over to England and a bit later started this business that everyone has heard about."

"Is she still married?"

"I think so. But one doesn't hear much of him." Favill's nose quivered at the sight of another drink approaching. "Thanks, darling." He sipped. "One can't of course get much personal corroboration of the story from her. I've asked her and she just shrugs and smiles. One can understand."

"Why?"

"It dates her."

I began to calculate. "She could have been in her teens."

"Who knows? They say she studied for the ballet and took it up again in Paris. But it's all very vague. We've tried to persuade her to let us do a profile, but no dice."

When she came to leave I happened to be by the door.

"Mme. Shona."

"Yes?"

"You left something," I said, "unexplained."

"In what way?"

"Certain professions, you said, attracted certain types and that I didn't look a type you would have expected to find in our business."

She half smiled. "Later I withdrew it. Don't you remember?"

"All the same . . ."

She considered me, then shrugged as if shrugging away an unwelcome familiarity. "In our business as in all there are the professional men who run our affairs with talk of sales, of cash flow, of balance sheets and the like. I did not think you looked one of those."

"Too much of the amateur?"

"No, I wouldn't have said that either."

"Actually, I *am* one of your dull professionals—"

"But aside from professionalism there is the need for flair. It is what distinguishes us from many other 'gainful employments.' "

She had remembered and had turned my words against me.

"That I'm still learning," I said. "The novice has to begin somewhere."

"You plan to stay in our trade?"

I glanced toward Jerry Dawson. "It depends."

"On what?"

"On what it has to offer."

"I doubt if there is *that* much."

She said this with a sort of sly good temper.

"Well, it remains to be seen."

An attractive female of indeterminate age with a peaches and cream complexion was holding out a sable cape for Mme. Shona to put on.

"Ours is a small world, Mr. Abden."

"Indeed. I should like to continue our conversation sometime."

The woman beside her opened her eyes at me as if I'd been guilty of a remark beyond my proper station.

Mme. Shona inclined her head. "Of course."

But it was said so noncommittally that it could have been interpreted in many ways, one of them being the snub her acolyte clearly thought I had asked for. But when she had gone Jerry Dawson said, "You've made a mark there. Take care. She might even fancy you."

"I might even fancy her," I said.

"That'll be the day," he replied.

II Going straight is a strain—not just on the finances, but on something inside yourself that isn't satisfied. Sometimes the need to break out is like lust: Without it the world is monochrome; you don't get your lungs open deeply enough.

But, like it or leave it, enough is enough: The last thing I wanted was a repeat show of last year. So I toed the line—nearly, anyway. The only thing I got involved in was a sharp switch of cars on a fire insurance claim at a garage; that brought me in about a thousand pounds.

Actually it had been a pretty lousy year, and I marked up my obligations to the two or three characters who had stood by me. Chiefly Jerry Dawson, who had found me this job in Yardley's. I'd scraped in simply as a junior salesman, but then somebody quite early on discovered that I'd got a "nose." It turned out that I could pick out scents, unexpected essences or what have you, give an enlightened opinion as to whether something they had blended with pine oil was likely to be heavy or light and what it actually smelled of—the definitive smell, that is. So though my occupation was still mainly to sell the damned stuff I was shoved up the ladder. Jerry was delighted and I certainly hadn't objected since they upped my salary at the same time.

The other individual who'd done me a good turn was this Derek Jones whose flat I was sharing. I'd known him on and off for about four years, a tall thin chap with bright wicked blue eyes and as bent as they come. As soon as he heard I was on my uppers he insisted on offering me a bed in his flat and I'd been there ever since. Terribly good company, and in the early weeks, when I was not going on all cylinders, he'd expected, and got, more than friendship. But I'm not really that way at all, and it hadn't worked out the way he wanted. I stayed on because I genuinely liked him—rare in me—and the place was cheap and convenient and I didn't have the incentive to find anything else.

In the months following my first meeting with the Shona woman I caught sight of her here and there, but never got into the sort of contact that enabled me to exchange more than a word. Then one day I met her shopping in Harrods and she was without her usual entourage of well-preserved milk-complexioned, middle-aged peahens. We stopped, and to keep her I asked her advice about the quality of a scent I said I was buying for a girl. She advised me, looking more feline than feminine.

"Have you seen our new product?" I asked.

"Of course. It is widely advertised and very popular. Congratulations."

"Thank you. In the main I only help to sell the package. Our chemists . . ."

"Oh, yes, oh, yes." She made a little dismissive gesture. "But I am sure that by now you understand our business too well not to know where most of the credit for a success lies."

"I'd go along with that . . ." I stopped. "Sorry. I thought you were serious."

"Half serious, perhaps . . . So I take it your directors are pleased with you."

"They don't say so in so many words."

"But you are happy there?"

"I have no complaints."

"What position has Mr. Dawson in the firm?"

"Administration. He's the son of one of the directors."

"Ah . . . So that is how you came into the firm."

"I was with another a year or so before . . . But yes."

"And do you still think of making it your career?"

I smiled. "I don't know. It's too early to say. Mme. Shona . . ."

"Yes?"

"Will you have lunch with me one day?"

She looked toward the door. "I never lunch with men."

"I'm sorry."

"Sometimes men lunch with *me*. But then I have to ask them."

"Sorry again."

"It's of no moment."

"It is to me."

"Why?" she asked suddenly, sharply, as if the answer meant something to her.

"I'm afraid I don't always analyze my reasons."

"You should. It is a valuable exercise."

I smiled again. "Shot down in flames. But thank you for the flak."

As I moved to go she said, "I have an appointment at the Mirabelle tomorrow and my guest is unable to come."

I waited, did not utter.

"What?" she said. "No pretty speeches?"

"With you I have to beware of them," I said. "My only safety is in silence."

"Of course . . . I am too blunt. It is a tendency. I am always trying to curb it."

"And failing?"

"And failing. Well . . . pretty speeches or not, it is twelve-forty if you wish to come."

III It was a long luncheon. She ate very little, toyed with her food, using a fork almost all the time, held and poised in long fine-skinned fingers. Like crabs, I thought, smooth elegant crabs. For a woman who made a fortune out of it, she seemed to use a relatively small amount of makeup, and scent was not pervasive.

She asked me about myself. I gave her a potted biography. My father had married against his family's wishes, had taken to the bottle and died when I was eleven. My mother Rachel had remarried when I was twelve. My stepfather was a wealthy solicitor in Leeds. Nothing in common, he and I, they and I. Left home as soon as I left school. Got a job as a rep for a paperback publisher; changed to a TV-rental firm. Worked in a London hotel, then a wine firm.

"You have seldom stayed long in one place," she said. "But you said this was not your first position in the perfumery world."

So, as before, she listened.

"Actually it was in soap. You've heard of Langton's?"

"Yes. Bath essence."

"That's what it came down to in the end. They advertised for a 'dynamic young man' to take over the marketing. I went along, lied about my age, and was taken on. I found they had nothing to market. Everything was too out of date to be true; the place was creaking into bankruptcy."

"So?"

"I said this to John Langton, and after a bit of hedging he agreed. But what was he to do, he asked. Sell the factory for site value? I said I thought we should concentrate on the one line that showed tiny signs of life and ax everything else. We did. It was a bit of a shambles, and a lot of people got fired. But I think they're in profit now."

"They are . . . But you didn't stay even there?"

"I—was tempted to move away."

"By Yardley's?"

"No. This was before Yardley."

"What did you do in between?"

"I was out of work when Jerry offered me this job."

She turned her wineglass round by the stem. "Taking the air at Pentonville?"

I was very still, could feel myself getting mad. There were fewer people in the restaurant now and the noise level had dropped. For a few seconds I was very annoyed. Then I took a grip of myself.

"Should I see that as a compliment?"

"Should you?"

"Well . . . the great Mme. Shona is interested enough to pay a private inquiry agent to delve into my past."

She was watching me. "I paid nobody. A few—yes, a few inquiries were made."

"Why?"

"Why? Because I *was* interested—if only slightly. You seem to me to have flair. Good looks, of course, as you well know. And some ability, we hear." She shook her head as the waiter hovered with the coffeepot. "I am a little vain and pretend to myself that I have an aptitude, do you call it, to judge men. I think you have drive, determination—what one might call unrealized potential. So to that extent I was interested."

"And the result of those inquiries, no doubt, has put you right off."

"Not quite. Not altogether."

The annoyance was passing out of my fingertips. After all, what the hell? But I would not pick up my coffee cup in case it shook.

"And did your friends tell you why I was taking the air of Pentonville?"

"Some sort of fraud, they said. Was it passing bad checks?"

"That I haven't tried yet . . . No. An old schoolmate called Tom Martin came to London from Greenock. I and one or two of my colleagues creamed the dough off him; it isn't difficult with a Scotsman who wants to be shown the town. This time, because of the stupidity of one of my friends, it all misfired. That's all."

"This time," she said. "So there have been other times?"

"Oh, yes. I made a fair thing out of it."

She began to play with her wineglass. "You regret it now?"

"That I was caught, yes."

"Not otherwise?"

"Would you expect that?"

"I expect nothing. I am just asking. You make a good thing out of cheating your friends?"

"Tom Martin was never my friend—though maybe he thought he was. Even as a boy he was a clumsy oaf."

"And the others?"

"Arrogant, conceited Scotsmen who were all the better for being taken down a peg."

"But you told me you were Scottish yourself."

"On my father's side, yes."

She gave me a look of a sort of benevolent irony. Clearly she wasn't all that shocked by what she had heard. But then, I guessed, she was probably unshockable. You got the message of such general sophistication that life had few surprises for her. Her eyelids drooped.

"Do Yardley's know about this?"

"About what?"

"Your time in prison, of course."

"Not the board. Jerry Dawson's father does."

We were silent for a time. I beckoned to the waiter that I wanted the bill.

"So," I said, "you can probably get me chucked out of Yardley's, if that's on your mind."

She ran a finger along the edge of the table.

"I suppose honesty is a relative term. Is it not? In my business for instance. Of course one is honest in putting into one's perfumes only the finest ingredients, the most scrupulous chemistry, the most genuine research. But after that there is more than a suggestion of a confidence trick about the way it is marketed. Not so, of course, within the—how do you say?—the legal definition of the term. I do not think I run any risk of going to Pentonville—or is it Holloway for women? I do not defraud trusting schoolfriends."

"Only trusting shoppers who fall for the sales talk."

She brooded a moment. "Last year de Luxembourg spent three hundred thousand pounds in promoting a new line: Incognito—you know it, of course. A clever idea. It was pushed, and it caught on. In fact it became the success of the season."

"A chypre basis," I said. "A bit sultry, I thought."

"Well, it caught the mood. It was not just the perfume but the end products which took off. Yet the essence contained nothing new, nothing *originally* new which was of particular special benefit to the skin. Women bought it because they were persuaded, hypnotized into buying it." She paused to nod at someone passing by. "Within a week of its coming into the shops it had, of course, been taken and analyzed by its rivals."

"I've tried this GLC," I said. "Gas liquid chromatography. It approximates but it can't get it exactly right."

She looked at me. "So you are a chemist as well."

"Far from it. But if you're in a business you want to know the tools."

She nodded. "Good . . . All the same the mass-market perfumers will buy every new perfume as it comes from the exclusive houses and have it analyzed and have it copied. Well, before Christmas last year Incognito had been copied and was on the market under other names and selling at a fifth of the price. The copies lack the exact quality and subtlety of the original but does that matter so much? How many women can *really* tell? No; what matters is that the copiers cannot steal the name. Women buy Incognito, and will continue to buy it because it comes from a high-class house

—and because it *costs* so much. Price in our world is paramount. Price and styling and the indefinable element of class."

"Which you have," I said.

She inclined her head.

"For instance in Dryad," I said, turning the edge away a bit.

"Dryad in its various forms has been on the market for seven years now—ever since I began. It still accounts for forty percent of our total sales."

"I gather it's a Russian formula brought to England when you came over, and long in your aristocratic family."

She breathed gently through her nose. "Yes. You see. That is the sort of thing. But it is still not as bad as cheating an old schoolfriend."

"I've turned over a new leaf."

"For how long?"

"I don't know. The deterrent effect of jail is still quite strong."

"It did not make you bitter?"

"Oh, yes. But to what end? One takes stock. One weighs the advantages against the risks. I didn't like being locked up and am at present doing my best to avoid it."

"I think, Mr. Abden, if you are to work for me you will have to give me an undertaking not to—what is it?—backslide."

So there it was, what I had been angling for.

I said with an assumption of modesty, "I didn't know there was any question that I might work for you."

"At present it is no more than a suggestion. But you really cannot pretend that the idea never occurred to you. Can you? In this there must be a sort of honesty—*this* sort of honesty on both sides?"

I pursed my lips. "Are there two sorts of honesty?"

Her face for a moment looked very Russian: the lidded eyes, the slant of the cheekbones. "Degrees perhaps."

"And you do not think twice about—engaging a jailbird."

"Of course I shall think twice, and more than twice, about engaging *you*. And not for that reason only."

There was a long silence, as if all that could be said at this meeting had now been said.

I asked, "D'you know a man called Roger Manpole?"

"Who does not?"

"Well, I don't think he'd wish to be all that widely known."

"I know him well by repute, though little personally. His repute is—not good. Though I understand he operates always within the law."

I laughed. "You could say that."

After a minute she said, "Why do you ask?"

"I met him first when I was at Langton's. Later, when I came out, before I joined Yardley's, he offered me a job."

"And you refused it?"

"Yes."

"I think that may be the best reference you can offer me."

"Why?"

"If you wished to continue in the half light of your previous operations I would have thought the offer perfectly judged."

"So did he."

"May I ask why you refused?"

"I wish I could say it was an attack of the little Lord Fauntleroy. Alas not. Simply that he makes my back hair stand up."

"Ah. Another honest answer. Perhaps we shall get somewhere even yet."

"I rather hope so."

"How long does your present contract run?"

"Monthly. But it was understood it should last at least until the end of the year. I may stay on longer."

"Well, this is for you to choose, isn't it?" She glanced up. "And please do not gesture to the waiter again; he will take no notice because the *conto* will automatically be sent to me at the end of the month. Does that offend your male pride?"

I said, "Not in the least. I am sorry to have been guilty of an act of *lèse majesté*."

"The Latin," she said, "is *laesa majestas*, and it was first used in the fourth century. I forget by whom. That is a piece of useless knowledge in the profession where I find myself. Or its only use is to impress. Like my Russian background. In my efforts to leave the Soviet Union, as I am sure you will be aware, I have little time or attention—or even the interest—to bring away the secret formulas for the preservation of the skin."

Perhaps anything else *ought* to be left for a second meeting. Yet I was never one to wait.

I said, "You've taken a fairly good look into my background. I know only the superficial things about yours."

"All backgrounds are superficial," she said, "if that is not a contradiction of the words. It is the present that matters."

"What strikes me, Mme. Shona, about your house, as you call it—your business—is its remarkable reputation with so small an output."

She ignored this. "Are you married?"

"No."

"Girlfriends?"

"A few."

"Boys."

"Not really in that way. Perhaps if I were a pansy you might think it better."

"For whom?"

I shrugged. "Forget I spoke."

She said after a moment, "Pansies, as you call them, are sensitive people; imaginative—far more so than most women. *And* creative. Of course bitchy. But who is not on occasion? If one were lunching here with me today he would be little different from you—wishing to play the host, touchy, prickly, on his mettle . . . In our trade there are many such. Of course we are not an *art*, as you well know; but there is an element of finesse, of grace, of elegance about the beautifying of women, in any aspect, which attracts them, even though they admire women and seek their company on a different level. If I am meeting you on a social basis it makes not the slightest difference to me how your tastes incline. If I am considering employing you, then it is of some importance."

I had hoped it mattered to her how my tastes inclined.

She moved slightly, and instantly a waiter came forward and took her chair.

I said, "Is this some new position you're thinking up for me?"

"Why do you ask that?"

"It occurred to me that you might be looking to expand."

"Why should I?"

"You've just mentioned that de Luxembourg spent three hundred thousand pounds on promoting Incognito. Your advertising can never approach that."

"De Luxembourg is international. We are largely British. Except for a few outlets in Canada and Australia."

"That's what I mean. You could never justify that sort of promotion."

"There is something a little vulgar in pressing one's wares too hard."

"Oh, I know how subtly you've put the things over up to now. But I don't see that *size* necessarily renders something unacceptable. You've moved from the corner shop—using that figuratively of course—and created a business that—although still so small—for sheer class is the envy of your competitors. To promote on a larger scale doesn't necessarily alter the quality of the approach. One doesn't need to shout louder—only more often."

She was thoughtful as she straightened the panels of her frock. "Yes, you can certainly express yourself—put over a point, one might say."

"The gift of the gab, one might say."

She smiled slightly. "An ability to persuade, one might say . . ."

I knew then that I was on my way. "May I ring you sometime?"

"Leave it till October. Let me know what your feelings are then. I should be the last to press."

"Thank you for my lunch. It has been an experience."

As we were moving out of the restaurant she said, "Yes, I have had the thought of creating a new position. For some time I have been looking in a desultory way . . . In fact I brought a man to lunch here last month."

"Was he not suitable?"

"No."

"In what way, may I ask?"

"For one thing he lit a cigarette in the middle of the meal. People who behave like that are savages."

CHAPTER TWO

I Perhaps I ought to say a bit more about Roger Manpole at this stage, and about Derek too.

Manpole, I suppose, was about forty when I first met him, which was at the Cellini Club in St. George Street, quite near the fashionable church. I'd joined soon after I came to London so that I could take my Scottish friends there to gamble. (Joining that sort of club, of course, is nothing. Any two members who've never even seen you before will sign the proposal form; you pay your dues and you walk right in.) Naturally it was Derek who introduced us. But whereas Derek looked more untrustworthy than he ever really was—something maybe about his bookmaker's smile—Roger Manpole was always the picture of rectitude and clean living. Suntanned, soft-spoken, candid gray eyes, hair a bit long and nicely waved, clothes with a hint of the countryman about them; as far as I knew he was entirely English, with a good pedigree, his father an ex-ambassador, his mother a shipowner's daughter (though the shipowner had gone bankrupt).

At that time, in the early days, I was doing honest work trying to pull Langton's together, and went to the club in the evening only for a game of bridge and to relax. Roger, I gathered from Derek, ran a company from behind the scenes called Mancat, which did big business in toiletries and the cheaper end of the perfumery trade. He also had a printing company called Henry Gervase Ltd., which had a factory in Hackney for turning out soft-porn magazines by the thousand. In those days, of course, if you printed color pictures of nude women in revealing postures you came up against the Obscene Publications Act. Now soft porn of that sort, and a lot more explicit, is on every station bookstall; and a fat lot of no good it does to some people. But Gervase were always liable in those days to be raided, so infra-red warning rays were installed by the door and the magazines stacked on chutes so that, when the police called, while the door was being unlocked, the magazines were tipped down the chutes into a room in the house next door owned by one of Manpole's nominees.

Derek and Manpole were old chums, though Roger was as hetero as they come, being on his second wife and always on the lookout for a new bit. After meeting him a couple of times, when we talked about talcs and lip salves and bath essences and when he went out of his way to be friendly, I came to realize that he fancied himself as the associate of young men he could patronize and manipulate. That wasn't for me, and when I made it plain that it wasn't for me he ticked my name off with a black mark in the little book he kept in his memory.

All the same, as I'd told Mme. Shona, when I ran into trouble and served four months and came out and stayed with Derek, Manpole did have another shot and offered me a job with Mancat. And although I was down in the mouth then and feeling at an all-time low, I still said no. So we weren't on the best of terms.

Of course we met at the Cellini from time to time and played bridge now and then. Derek was no go as a bridge player—he just didn't have card sense—but Roger was quite good and knew I was better, so we did keep on terms that way.

One evening after we'd met coming from the roulette table he said in his low soft agreeable cultured easy voice, "I think I should congratulate you, David."

"What on?"

"Your coming move."

"What move?"

"Oh, you know it's very hard in this business to keep a secret. It's a very small world, the cosmetic world. We live in each other's pockets."

"Tell me what you think you've picked out of my pocket."

The smile became a bit less amiable. "You're going to work for Shona."

"Oh," I said, "reports of my death have been much exaggerated."

"Death? A fate worse than? I doubt it. She's a tremendous personality. You should do well."

We passed on. As always after a meeting with Manpole I felt rubbed up the wrong way. I suppose you can't explain it, this allergy you have for some people. If he was served for lunch, I'd come out in spots. His offer of a job—though a pretty queer one—when I came out of prison had been quite well meant within his own terms. It wasn't a matter of principle on my part, for God's sake, just an antipathy.

I knew of course where he'd picked up this rumor. I didn't tackle Derek with it, but quietly I began to look for a pad of my own. I'd sponged on him, spacewise, for too long anyway, and our relationship wasn't ever going to continue or develop along the line of his ambitions. I knew that in my guts now—or wherever it is appropriate to know these things.

After my father did himself in by getting bibulous and cracking his skull on a fender, I'd gone away to a prep school for a couple of years and been crammed to pass the Common Entrance. Kenneth Kingsley, who became more and more important in our lives, insisted it was the Right Thing for me, and persuaded my mother to agree to this, where my father hadn't been able to. I'd always been close to my mother, but after his death things changed. She was more distant, less concerned, less demanding. And when the next year she married Kingsley, that drift away from me put on skids.

I'd not seen my mother for upward of three years. She knew all about the big event of last year, of course, and she'd written a couple of fairly pathetic letters when I was inside, but I think she'd persuaded herself that I was coming to a bad end anyhow and there was nothing much she could do about it. In one letter she said, "You should have told us about it when you were first charged; Kenneth might have been able to do something to help you." Privately I thought Kenneth had written me off more comprehensively than she had. And why not? They had two kids of their own now—I was only a pain in the neck to him.

As I'd said to the Shona lady, the four months inside had left a taste. In fact (since this is supposed to be a candid account) it had left a hell of a taste. Apart from what you'd expect—the gray faced, hard-nosed lags trooping like zombies, their talk and their grunts and their belchings, like a Tannhauser chorus in Z flat minor; and the screws, domineering, tight-mouthed, insufferably superior; and the locked doors, the clang of keys, the drab, flat uneatable food—apart from these that you'd expect, I was knocked right out of my groove by claustrophobia. It was the jim-jams all right. That last door shutting for the night: the panic clutched at your bowels; you wanted to bloody your fists on the bars, to struggle for breath, for air that wasn't there, to scream at the top of your pipes till you ruptured something. Honestly.

And it was still too just round the corner to be ignored. Of course you wisecrack about it, it's all over and done with, isn't it? But as for the future, the memory nudges at your elbow like a tout in a pub. The deterrent. Too bad. Also it was clear from what the delightful old boy in the judge's chair had said that it would be much tougher if I was caught doing the same thing again.

"I listen to many cases in this court in which the accused comes from a broken home or has an underprivileged background, or one in which circumstances have combined against him and made his behavior, if not excusable, at least understandable in the framework of his life. But you come of an excellent and a distinguished family. You have been well educated. You have lived all your life in a comfortable, genteel environment. No extenuating circumstances have been put before me by your counsel for your deliberate and callous fraud upon an old friend, so I can only assume none exists. I therefore have no alternative, having regard to your previous convictions, but to sentence you to a term of imprisonment. You will go to prison for six months."

Much as I dislike to think of the trembling old nerk, or pay any attention to his humbug homily, I continued to do so from time to time.

And anyway I'd rather meet *him* behind bars than one or two of the types I did. That sort of contact hardens you up and softens you up at the same time.

The deterrent. Well . . .

So I looked at the idea of working for La Shona with a divided mind. On spotting her at that party it had occurred to me that an affair might pay off one way or another. It seemed probable that, apart from any personal pleasures involved, such a woman if she found herself financially out of pocket for her acquaintance would, as a foreigner and intensely proud of her firm's reputation, be likely to write off any loss to experience. But since then I had revised my views. From such slight knowledge as I now had of her, I thought I would have to get up very early in the morning to pull off any profitable exercise in which she was the loser.

So you look at the job purely on its merits. I was getting sick of Yardley's. I'd been there nine months, which was an all-time record for me. I'd no real desire to be selling lip salve all my life, and if some other bandwagon came along I'd be quick to hop on. But in the meantime . . .

There was also the question of the small dent this woman had created in my protective skin. That's a stylish way of saying that I fancied her for her own sake.

I'd never become involved in my life; my girlfriends frequently complained. But detachment is all. Well, it might be more difficult to stay detached from this lady, always supposing that one ever got near enough to her to exchange small-arms fire.

Her husband, John Carreros, supervised the factory at Isleworth. He had, it seemed, been a research chemist for Rochas in Paris, and it was likely that he was more responsible than she was for the formulas they had first sprung on an unsuspecting world seven or eight years ago. Nobody seemed to know whether the marriage worked as a marriage. They had a flat in South Audley Street and a small house on the Green at Richmond. No children. Their shop and offices were in Wigmore Street.

It was plain enough that in a handful of years she'd become a rich woman; and yet compared to the giants she was still small-time. Why did she want me? Did she fancy me as I fancied her? Did she have a succession of handsome lapdogs following her around while she continued to keep her grip on her small, highly lucrative, top-class market? (So far I had heard, no other boyfriends, current or discarded.) Or was she really looking for someone who would help her to expand and take on the Avons and the Ardens on their own ground? And did I even remotely want to be that someone? I certainly wanted money, but not at any price, not at the price of some boring old job trying to expand a business I wasn't interested in. There were other and better things in the world.

I went to her flat in November.

It was in a block, with the conventional lift approach to the two-bedroom apartment, long living room and tiny kitchen. Inside this one were pink-striped wallpapers and Aubusson carpets with lots of small drawings and pictures. And gilded wood caryatids and cherubs straining their infant muscles to support bookshelves and ornate console tables. Plenty of books, and color in cushions and chairs. And a baby grand. All a bit overlush.

She said, "There's a lot about you I still don't know, David, and a lot I do not understand. Some day perhaps you will tell me what is this chip on your shoulder, what it is all about. You are educated, so good-looking, intelligent, enterprising; but there is a worm in the bud. All right, that is your affair so long as it does not affect your work. I think you may be good for this firm, that you may have strong new ideas—what John, my husband, lacks. You will meet him soon. We are the best of friends. But he has come to the limit of his ideas; and I do not think firms such as ours can stand still. I do not think so."

I rubbed my chin, looked at her ankles in their beige stockings and black mules. "I'm replacing no one?"

"Alice Huntington will look after you. She's an outstanding woman, and if you are tactful she will not resent this."

"You mean you want me to do her work?"

"That will depend on you."

"No, surely on you, Mme. Shona."

"Well, let us see in three months. If you are still doing Alice's work in three months I shall know my hunch has been wrong."

II   I found a small flat in Fulham. It wasn't much to write home about but it was the move I needed. All my life I've been against having people too close to me. I put on this front of being a good mixer—have a reputation for it— but when you've finished with your day it's good to end up by yourself. That shrink I went to once might have said it came from an inverted sense of superiority. Me, I just think that if you depend only on yourself there's no one else to let you down. Even as a boy I remember thinking that. There's no one to care anymore so there's no one to let you down.

Derek, when I told him, was sulky and waspish by turns. I explained to him it was nothing personal, and that made it worse. If he had been able to look on it as a lover's tiff he would have understood better. "Of course, David was *too* difficult, so we went our separate ways." This just walking out from a preference for being *alone*.

"Believe me," I said, "I do appreciate the way you made room at short notice, took me in when I was in a crummy state, made things better. But I've been in your hair long enough. And I'm OK now, standing without support, don't need a crutch. We can still meet at times. Any objection to that?"

"Is it because of my friendship with Roger Manpole?" he asked. "You've not the least need to resent it, I assure you. Anyway, as you know, he's strictly machismo . . ."

"My dear old fink," I said, "stop trying to see it in those terms."

"Fink yourself. But you don't like Roger, do you?"

"I don't trust him. I've a feeling in my lower guts that he helped to put the finger on me in the Tom Martin case."

"How could he? That's ridiculous."

"I don't know. Does he have an interest in the Cellini Club?"

"Not to my knowledge. Anyway if it's choosing betwixt the twain I'll choose my old buddy boy, Abden."

"Don't do anything of the sort," I said. "Stick with us both. See us through to the end. Be thou our link and guide."

"Go to hell."

Instead I went to Fulham.

At first it had amused me when people, seeing me with Derek, automatically assumed I had the same tastes as he had; but then I'd begun to get uptight. It was good for me to move for that reason. All the same, with considerable perception, Derek had seen through to the deeper cause.

III It was the Saturday following the move that I played golf with Jerry Dawson. We went down to Cooden and played in a foursome he'd arranged with two friends of his. At that time I owned a clapped-out Mini, so Jerry drove us in his Jaguar.

On the way down I broke the news that I was leaving his company in the New Year.

He smiled. "Are you going to Shona's?"

"Is that obvious?"

"I know you better than most . . . It was on the cards, wasn't it?"

"Suppose so. Anyway I'm just going to try it for size."

"The firm won't be pleased; don't tell them until the last minute; otherwise you'll be out on your ear . . . Pronto. In a way *I'm* pleased."

"Glad to be rid of me, eh?"

"Not really, no. Though at times you have been rather the square marble, haven't you. A firm like ours has its set ways, its go-ahead but conservative approach. At Shona's you'll probably fit in like—like the missing piece of a jigsaw . . . But that wasn't mainly what I meant. I meant that if this really takes your fancy it'll keep you out of mischief."

"Don't rely on it."

"Oh, I'd never rely on anything with you. But if you're working for Shona—and she'll make you work, believe me—you're bound to have less time for your other nonsense . . . particularly for taking it out on your fellow Scotsmen." I didn't speak, so he added, "And if she pays you well—as she probably will—there'll be less *need* for it."

I said, "It wasn't really ever that sort of need."

He glanced at me a bit uneasily, took a firmer grip of the steering wheel. "I suppose not. Or if you tell me not I have to believe you . . . well, good luck, that's all I say."

"Thanks . . . But why not tell the firm? They've treated me well. It's proper to give them fair notice."

"Not in this business, it isn't. We don't operate that way. It wouldn't matter so much if you were going off to sell motorcars or something, but you're moving to a rival firm and taking some of our expertise and knowledge with you."

"Precious little."

"Well, you've been making rapid strides. We'll be sorry to lose you for that reason too."

I grunted. "I don't *feel* this is my mission in life. It's just selling smells, for God's sake."

"Not for God's sake—our own. And, incidentally, keep a look-out for John Carreros."

"Why?"

"They say he's a difficult man."

"In what way?"

"You'll find out."

It was a fine day and for once at Cooden the southeaster was not blowing.

I've an eighteen handicap at golf, and even that is flattering. I never have had any organized approach to the game, and never much cared about winning. The nearer the play gets to the hole the less interested I become, so that my short irons and putter chronically let me down. My chief pleasure is squaring up on the tee and trying to blast the bloody little white ball into the next county. The result is when I do connect properly a drive of over 300 yards is not uncommon; when I don't connect properly the ball goes droning off at an angle of forty-five degrees into the neighboring churchyard or the local housing.

Jerry's friends were called Armitage and Foster. I hadn't met them before, and I took a dislike to Armitage. He was shaped like a hyacinth bulb, and was hair-scanty, self-satisfied and middle-aged. He had just bought his first smart car, a BMW, and he talked about it too much, and smirked his pleasure whenever anyone mentioned it. In spite of his waistline, he also thought highly of his golf, and I suppose he was reasonably good in a steady, dependable, rhythmic, flat-footed, cautious kind of way. So, to annoy him, I buckled down and tried my hardest. I was able to cheat once by dabbing my ball out of a rut when the others weren't looking, but otherwise we won fair and square. Two and one.

"Well done," said Jerry with a grin, "such restraint must have cost you dear."

This character Armitage was a property developer by profession, and you could imagine all the shopping precincts and the ghastly urban sprawl that he and his like were responsible for.

After the game was over we had drinks and then lunch together, but I turned down the opportunity of a second round; another chap was waiting to mix in, and I told Jerry there was a girl I wanted to see in Bexhill, which is only a couple of miles away. If he could take my gear home I could telephone for a taxi, and later on get the train back to London. He grinned understandably.

"The old dark horse as usual. Where did you meet her?"

"In Bexhill."

"You don't say. Well, good luck with her too."

"She's always welcoming," I said.

Before I telephoned for a taxi I carried my things out to Jerry's car. A couple of places away was a splendid new BMW. Armitage had left the keys in the car. I suppose he thought it was a private park and no one would touch it.

I put my clubs and bag in Jerry's car and then got into the BMW. It started easily and I drove it slowly out of the park.

I must say it handled well—you have to hand it to the Germans; they make a good machine. I drove through St. Leonards and Hastings and then turned up to Battle before making a circuit back to Bexhill. Of course there was too much traffic to try the car out properly. I've inherited my family's consuming passion for good fast cars, and I parted from it with regret. I parked it in a busy street on a double yellow line, and thought it would be nice to see what happened.

The street where Essie Morris lived was only three minutes away, and she was in. A great beam split her ugly face when she saw me.

"Why, David! You should've told me! Isn't that grand!"

"Put your bonnet on," I said, "and we'll go out to tea."

Essie Morris was the mother of Crack Morris, the chap I'd shared a cell with in Pentonville. He'd done me favors while I was a new boy, advising me what to do and what not to do, and generally restraining me from getting too much at cross with the screws. And from getting too much at cross with the bully-boys inside. Though he never knew how near I was to some sort of scary breakup, his company was what had got me through the worst patches. Since I came out I'd taken Essie Morris to tea once a month, because Crack was in for another year yet.

She loved to have tea at the Pavilion; I thought it dire, but it was her outing and she drank cup after cup of tea and ate hot buttered scones while she prattled away about this and that. Chiefly it was to do with Arthur and what a good lad he really was if he could only learn to go straight, and how she'd been to see him last week and what he'd said about full remission, and she hoped, she really hoped, when he came out I would still come to see them, and maybe my influence would be a help to him to start afresh.

I said yes and no, and don't be too damned sure about the good influence, and shall I order more scones, and no, I never take sugar; and I gaped around at all the people quietly guzzling tea at the other tables and thought, my God, they're *all* old, the women have all got short crimped hair like wigs, brown and gray and white stubble, and the men—but there aren't so many men because they usually pop off first—are small and tubby and white-pated, or tall and creak-jointed and bald, with crumpled suits and scraggy pullovers; and I bet they wear long underpants down to their ankles, and my God, they're all just sitting around waiting for Death. *All* of them. They've retired down here from Preston and Pontefract and Peterborough and Purley, living in their little quiet houses—often as not cut off from their old friends, never quite making enough new ones—nourishing their arthritis and their diabetes and their minor coronaries, and just waiting for It. And I thought, Christ, human beings are a sorry lot, a common lot, a job lot, a dull lot, and wouldn't a bomb do a bit of good around here—and yet, Christ, why've they any *reason* to be anything but sorry and common and dull: that's all life has ever had to *offer* them, any of them—the treadmill, the old one-two from cradle to grave. And who's to blame for getting off the treadmill?

"What's the matter, love?" Essie said.

"Nothing. What should be?"

"You're looking grim, like."

"Sometimes I feel grim, like."

"I never understood, you've never told me, why a gent like you ever got into trouble."

"It's a long story, Ma. I wouldn't want to make you cry."

"Go on, I never know when you're teasing."

"I'm always teasing," I said, "that's the only way you can get through life."

"I don't want to get through life," she said. "I'm happy enough. Or will be when Arthur gets out."

"It's something special to be happy."

"Aren't you happy, love?"

"I don't know what it means."

"Go on. You're teasing again."

"I know a state of non-unhappiness," I said. "Maybe it's the same thing seen through a dark window."

Afterward I walked back with her but said there wasn't time to go in. By now dusk was falling, and when I left her I strolled back to the street where I'd parked the BMW. It was gone. I'd left the keys in the ignition so maybe the police had taken it away. Unless someone else had stolen it. That would be a joke.

There were a lot of cars parked in the side streets off the promenade. I walked along till I saw one with a quarter light that looked easy to open. It was. The car was a Rover 2000, about a year old. I hadn't any string so I took off my tie and lowered it through the quarter light in a loop till it caught on the door handle. The handle came up and I was in.

A few people were going past, but the important thing is not to look around in any surreptitious or apprehensive way. I tried the cubbyhole and the pockets and the ashtray just in case the ignition key—or a spare—should be to hand, but it was not. I got out and opened the hood in a casual way. I hadn't come prepared for anything like this, but my folding penknife did have sharp clippers which would cut wire.

I went round to the road side and cut the wire connecting the offside headlamp. I got a piece about three feet long which was enough to connect the battery to the coil, then shut the hood and climbed in. The police will sometimes stop you if the headlamp on the driver's side is not working, seldom or never if it's the inside light.

Then I couldn't find the solenoid button, which operates the starter. Or maybe the car was too new a model.

A couple of lolloping teenagers were passing. I got out and offered them a pound note.

"My starter seems to have jammed. Think you could give me a push?"

"Right, mate. Come on, Ern."

With their help, I nosed gently forward and engaged the gear. The motor fired and I waved my thanks and eased out into the traffic.

I drove the car back to London, finding standards of comparison with Armitage's BMW. They were both 2000s; and there were minuses and pluses on both sides. Patriotism will not allow me to say which I found the better.

I left the car about a quarter of a mile from my new pad in Fulham and walked home. It was not until I got in and switched on the light and made myself a coffee that I began to ask myself why I had behaved like this. It wasn't even logical. If you're going to bend the law you surely have to calculate the percentages. Any sensible man does. So I hadn't behaved like a sensible man today. Was I batty, I asked myself? Probably a bit. But sometimes the temptation really is too great. Maybe my father had had a bit of the same complaint, same need to get the blood going. But he had taken to drink. Drink was never my problem, not even my solace.

CHAPTER THREE

I John Carreros was a square-faced chap with leathery cheeks ravined on each side of a sensitive mouth. Eyebrows and ears sprouted gray hair, and horn-rimmed spectacles hung loosely over a hawk nose. He was old, and not as tall as he looked sitting down. He grabbed my outstretched hand.

"Mr. Abden. I have been hearing things about you. Welcome to our little firm. I hope we shall be happy with you."

Apart from one or two racing drivers, he had the hardest hands of any man I'd met. Not that he tried to emphasize his masculinity by gripping too hard. But you couldn't miss the inversion of the last sentence.

"Thank you," I said, "I'll do my best to fit in."

"I understand you have a nose."

"They tell me I can smell better than most people."

"I would like to test it. Perhaps you will come down to Isleworth."

"Surely. But of course I'm not a chemist, you know."

"Who needs a chemist? Do you play bridge?"

"What? The card game? Not in office hours!"

He laughed. "But out of them?"

"Yes, a little." I had once thought of trying to make my living by it.

"Good. Good. My wife—she will not play. She calls it systematized frittering."

"Most of life is, one way or another, isn't it?"

"Ah, the philosopher." He shoved his heavy spectacles up his nose. "A philosopher and a pessimist in one so young. I like that. I was a pessimist at your age."

"And now, Mr. Carreros?"

"Ah, now I am a fatalist. What will be will be. It saves a lot of worry, eh?"

"It's a rich man's indulgence," I said.

He gave me a sharp look. "Perhaps more truly an old man's. When one looks back on one's life and observes the fine threads of chance and mischance which have shaped one's destiny . . . It is impossible to suppose one is in personal control. Do you play Acol?"

It was the new thing just then, superseding many of the old systems. "Yes."

"We must have a game sometime."

I wondered what stakes he played for, and thought of introducing him to one or two of my friends; but that might queer my pitch before I began. That would have been even stupider than joyriding in other people's cars just for the hell of it.

II

Jerry told me of this mishap that had befallen his friend Armitage. They were all drinking in the bar after their second round at Cooden when the police rang him. They accused him of having parked illegally in Bexhill, and said they had driven his car away. They had found his address and telephoned his wife, who gave them the Cooden number. They seemed reluctant at first to believe his story that he had parked at the Cooden Golf Club, their view being that no one would steal the car for so short a trip.

Jerry said, "Did you find your girl in Bexhill, David?"

"Yes. She was there."

He grunted and fingered his tie. "Did you—er—take a taxi?"

"Of course. It was too far to walk."

"I just wondered."

"Wondered what? Oh . . ." My eyes opened. "Do you think I would be that much of a screwball? What would be the point?"

"No, no. I see that. It was just the odd coincidence."

"What coincidence?"

He looked uncomfortable. "Well. You know."

"No, I don't know. I'll bet there were plenty of golfers at the club who live in Bexhill."

"Ah, yes, I'm sure."

"But we don't know who did it, do we? Some passing hitchhiker maybe. Anyway Armitage left his keys in the car, didn't you say? Must have been an ass to do that."

"Yes," said Jerry. "Yes."

III

When I actually joined the firm in the first week in January, Alice Huntington was delegated to show me round. She was this crone of about forty-five who had the skin of a girl of twenty. Yet somehow she looked no younger for it. She dressed in frocks of heavy silk and was always gracious and smiling, as if someone had cut her out to be the Queen Mother. Clearly she didn't like me and suspected me of being groomed to take over her job. I went out of my way to be genuinely nice to her: butter wouldn't-melt, etc.; ingenuous questions; holding open the door; handsome young man escorting handsome young woman. Perhaps the thing that annoyed me most about her was the way things dangled and jangled, bracelets, earrings, brooches.

The firm was amazingly compact after Yardley's. Exclusiveness on a shoestring. The laboratory wasn't bad, but any other machinery or gadgetry in the factory was well worn and out of date. Two nice new delivery vans tastefully advertising Shona. Really not much else.

Although I saw the Isleworth factory right away it was not until March that John Carreros had me over for a day and "tried me out," as he called it.

As I suppose most people know, no "house" makes its own perfume entirely. Not only the ingredients but usually the almost finished product comes from the great chemical firms. You don't exactly scream for a ton of Dolly Dream or whatever the perfume is called; but you order a ton of the already blended essences that make it up. What you do in your own laboratory is really quite little; but in a way it just puts the finishing touches on what is supplied to you.

In "our" laboratory there were two bathrooms, two lavatories, two washing machines and a variety of other gadgets that helped our chemists to test out their new ideas. Beyond these quarters were a couple of small smelling rooms, empty except for a table and a couple of chairs and a few Shona photos. John Carreros installed me in one of these, and a girl brought in a collection of smelling papers, each one prepared with a 1 percent solution of different aromatics, and I was invited to identify them or describe them. I said one smelled of chocolate, another of spice, a third of lemonade, a fourth of margarine, a fifth of machine oil, a sixth of lavender, etc. It was all nonsense really. If I was going to be of any genuine use to this successful but one-horse firm it was in the realm of expansion and advertising and total sales, not just because my nose was above average sensitive.

However, it seemed to please old Carreros. He grunted his way through his notes, like a heavy dog scratching for a bone, and then he asked me if I could identify what the perfumes were. I got three: Vanillin for the chocolate, Citral for the lemonade, oil of lavender for the lavender.

"Good," he said. "Good. Number two you said was spicy. What sort of spicy? Meat—soup—cake?"

"More like cinnamon."

"That is what it is. Now tell me, does any one of the others remind you of fresh green leaves that you have just rubbed in the fingers?"

"Number five maybe."

"Right. Hydroxycitronellal. Interesting that you should think of machine oil. The margarine smell, as you called it, was methyl heptine carbonate. Now let us try some more difficult ones."

We went on to balsam of Peru, oil of vertivert, geraniol, oil of bergamot. I had a shot at comparing the two lots of smelling papers, arranging them into groups.

Then he said, "Now we must stop for a while. I will have some water brought for you to drink. The sense of smell gets tired far more quickly than any other sense. Do you smoke?"

"Thanks."

"No, no, I am not offering you one now. I mean you would do well to give up smoking; it destroys the finer senses."

He began to talk. I sat back and sipped water and thought how difficult it must be for him to shave, with all those nooks and crannies about his mouth and chin.

"I am sure, David, you will have learned to take no notice of trade journals, textbooks, published formulas; because no good firm will ever divulge the whole of its knowledge to an inquirer. The most essential ingredient of all is secrecy."

"And at the end of it all," I said, "more than half of a success is not content but psychology."

Carreros shoved up his thick glasses. "Madame, I think, tends to underrate the chemists' work at times. It is an inescapable fact that it is from the small laboratories such as ours that there have issued some of the finest perfumes on sale in Europe today."

It was time for lunch, but he didn't seem to notice. I was hungry. I began to perceive that, whatever Mme. Shona thought about her business, John Carreros was the dedicated technician.

He was going boringly on about Dryad, the research, the experimentation, the fine ingredients, etc. I interrupted him by saying, "Yes, I'm sure. But you have to face facts. I've been working them out. A half ounce bottle of Dryad perfume costs £14. How much of that is ingredients? You know as well as I do: probably about seventy pence. It's not a large part for your chemists to play, is it."

He stiffened. "You think it overpriced? But, David, you know well that that sort of percentage is the norm. For every pound the public pays for Dryad, how does it go?"

"You tell me."

"Do I need to? Of every one hundred pence the retailer takes forty-five. That I agree with you is excessive, but we cannot change that without a total upheaval of the retail world. So we are left with fifty-five pence. Is that it?"

"That is it."

"Of that, thirty or thirty-one pence goes in advertising, promotion, overheads, administration, particularly the great cost of maintaining and paying the girls in the big public stores. Fourteen pence is roughly the cost of the making of the perfume, of which about ninepence is spent on the packaging and, as you truly remark, only fivepence on the ingredients. Shocking! On every pound the woman buyer lays down she only receives five-pennyworth of perfume. But what is our profit? Tenpence. That is correct, is it not?"

"About that, I'd reckon."

"And is a ten percent profit before tax so much? And without the skill of the chemists, without their strict quality control, their extraordinary care, it can quickly turn into a heavy loss. Let me tell you, five years ago a mistake was made in our laboratory in the blending. When that is done there is nothing to save the consignment, nothing to do with it but pour it away. We made a sixty thousand pounds loss on that one consignment—half our profits for the year were gone."

John Carreros, I decided, was a man without humor, and a man with a mission—the mission being to please women, to enhance their beauty, to preserve their skin; to be a public benefactor—at a price—to half the human race.

Even now, for heaven's sake, he was not done. He rang the bell and the girl came in again with a new set of smelling papers.

"Just tell me what you think of these, David." He stretched his legs indulgently and sat back in his chair. "Take your time."

I held the first paper up and sniffed it. "Jasmine. But something else."

"It's benzyl alcohol. Very good. It is a delicate scent, is it not?"

I tried the second. "Dog dirt," I said.

There was silence. He adjusted his spectacles again.

"That is musk," he said. "Or a composition of musk . . . Go on."

I took the next paper and smelled gently. "Cat's piss," I said.

Another silence. John Carreros was looking at me. "And number four?"

I tried again. "Lavatory paper after use."

After a few moments he climbed to his feet. "I think you have done enough for today. It is time for lunch. I cannot unfortunately lunch with you as I have another appointment."

IV It was two or three days after this that Shona called me into her office on some unimportant routine question. After a couple of minutes she said, "I hear you have been to the factory with John."

"Yes."

"He is pleased with your nose. But not so pleased with your general attitude."

"Oh?"

"Why did you try to—what is the vulgar phrase?—to take the mickey out of him?"

"Is that how he sees it?"

"Oh, come. Don't fence with me, David."

"At the time I happened to be getting hungry."

"Rubbish."

After a minute I said, "He takes it all too seriously. The sermon began to drag."

"So you just felt like being offensive."

"Not at all. If you ask silly questions you get silly answers."

"It is not your business here to be silly."

"Oh, for God's sake," I said. "You must know that many of these basic smells are pretty rank. That third thing he gave me at the end. What did he think he was playing at? I knew at once it was civet resinoid. If that doesn't smell like cat's pee, I don't know what does!"

She went to the window, looked out at the traffic. She was in working clothes today: tailored slacks and an expensively casual V-neck shirt, flat leisure shoes, a ponytail. Moving as she usually did with the speed of a Force Seven wind, she gave the impression of being about twenty-five.

"And you are upsetting Alice Huntington. By being too clever, too sarcastic."

"Alice Huntington is ready to break out in a rash at anything that might seem to threaten her place in the firm."

"Maybe. Maybe you *are* too clever, though, too arrogant . . . But tell me—you have now been here more than two months. If you despise Alice Huntington, whom else do you despise? Everyone? What is your view of the staff as a whole?"

"Dedicated. Old-fashioned. Totally reliable. Totally unlike me."

"At least you know your faults. And how do you see the firm generally?"

I hesitated. "Fine, as far as it goes."

"And how far do you think it goes?"

"Well, you're like a manufacturer of hand-built motorcars, aren't you?"

"Pray go on."

"You've recognized it yourself. You don't need me to spell it out."

"I don't *need* it, maybe. But yours is a fresh eye."

"Look at the factory at Isleworth. Apart from the little laboratory and the testing room, just one big room, the size of a women's institute. Apart from your husband and young Parker, there are eighteen employees, aren't there, who do all the labeling, the packaging. What do they turn out in a year? I'd guess a million pounds' worth of perfumes, soaps, creams, lipsticks. It's fantastic. What are your net profits?—well over a hundred thousand a year? You've got a gold mine!"

She was still standing, slim and tall, frowning out at the day. Nobody spoke for a while. Then I went on, "But it's what you said in November: You have to choose between carrying on at the present level, with demand always exceeding supply, living regally but pretty well unknown outside this country and in the second division here—and expanding into an international business, able to challenge the biggest and the best . . . But I rather assume you wouldn't have engaged me if you hadn't that idea in mind."

"To have it in mind is not to act on it," she said indifferently.

"Too true. Well, there's no half way, is there?"

She looked at me then. "Isn't there?"

"How can there be? It's in the nature of the problem that you have to go the whole hog or not at all. I haven't seen your balance sheets yet—or anything else . . ."

"You may do so. There's nothing secret."

"I know of course that you're a private company."

"Yes, John and I own ninety percent of the business."

"What's your overdraft limit?"

She lit a cigarette, considering if the question were impertinent, if the questioner had this right.

"A hundred thousand."

"Which you probably don't use."

"No."

"Well, to expand in any substantial way you'd need vastly more than that."

"I've no doubt."

"A million at least—and that just to begin."

She waved the cigarette smoke away from her face as if it displeased her.

"You would have to say all this to John."

"If he'll take it from me. After all he's twice my age and I'm the intrusive new boy."

"We would both have to consider your intrusiveness."

What was the use, I thought? Why not get out at this stage? But she still interested me.

"Well, if you want me to look at it more closely I'll have a shot. Of course the best way of raising the money would be to go public."

"I don't think John would ever consider that. It might lead to a takeover."

Sometimes this morning she seemed to be bringing in the name John deliberately. In the short time I'd been around I'd come to the conclusion that he didn't count for a lot when it came to major decisions made by the firm. Perhaps she was paying me out for my flippances.

"It wouldn't lead to a takeover," I said, "if you kept sixty percent of the shares."

"Ah, well, I prefer to borrow from the bank, David."

I shrugged. "You wanted my views . . ."

She said, "The more you borrow from a bank, the more concerned they become for your welfare. It is one of the paradoxical facts of financial life." Her lips moved in a brief smile. "I have no doubt I could get finance if we decided to proceed. My reputation over eight years. And the name of Shona."

"Oh, they'd welcome a sound investment, sure enough. But in the one case you'd be paying a hundred thousand pounds a year for the use of their money. In the other the new shareholders would pay you enough to expand free of any cost except only, say, a third share in your declared profits."

"Where did you learn all this, David, in your young life? I do not think it can have been so dissolute after all."

"You forget that I have a stepfather who is a lawyer."

"And you learned this from him?"

"Probably not."

"No, probably not. It is not that sort of knowledge that a boy usually gets from his stepfather. Let me see, how old were you when your own father died?"

"Eleven."

"And your mother remarried soon after?"

"The following year."

"Ah, so. I wonder if that explains anything?"

"What is it supposed to explain?" I said.

"I mean, that a fatherless boy is sometimes like a ship without a rudder . . . Perhaps ideally all fathers should die when their children are about twenty-five. By then the ship is launched and has taken its true course. After that you do not want two hands at the helm . . ."

"But I thought you said you had a father still alive."

"Indeed, yes. And I would not be without him. There are exceptions to the rule. Had he died when *I* was eleven . . ."

"You might have turned out the same sort of irresponsible miscreant that I am."

"Who knows? But we have wandered from the subject, have we not?" She put out her cigarette, which had only been to her lips twice. "I still have doubts as to the future of Shona, particularly in the small hours. For a huge expansion . . . There are still not enough people of taste in the world."

"Helena Rubinstein would have taken you up on that."

"Oh, I know. She created her own market. As others have."

"You have to educate people," I said. "Precious few can really judge for themselves what is absolutely the top, in anything. They get persuaded to *want* it. That's not so difficult." I stopped. "But look, it's up to you, isn't it? You're riding high as you are and nobody is going to push you into this unless you really want it. I'm certainly not. There are other slots in the business world I could slide into without running the risk of tangling with the fuzz again. After all, Roger Manpole did make me an offer."

She laughed.

"Perhaps," she said, "if I do decide to go ahead, you should come with me to talk to the bank manager."

"God forbid! You'll need to keep me under wraps for the time being. A man with a record is not likely to inspire the confidence you need."

She continued to stare me out.

"Tell me one thing. Was that your first conviction?"

"Oh, yes," I said. It was very unlikely that she could ever find out. Or that anyone could find out, unless I came up into the courts again. Anyway, the previous convictions had all been for very small things.

V Small things, but read out in court after the verdict as if the last trump had just sounded. A two-pound fine for stealing a horse; put on probation for attempted theft; a month's detention center for breaking a window "with intent to steal"; one day's imprisonment for "assaulting a police-man." All notably achieved before I was twenty-one. Petty as could be, but drawing a picture for the judge of a prime social delinquent. I wonder if Shona would have been shocked or amused if I told her.

CHAPTER FOUR

I There has never seemed any percentage to me in doing anything whatever that didn't take my immediate fancy, so I suppose I must have found some satisfaction in that first year doing my bit for Madame.

Not surprisingly, John Carreros was against the expansion; he dragged his feet in whatever way he could, and although Shona really ruled the roost, his hesitation and reservations held us up. But eventually the first fell steps were taken. At great expense a lease was bought on premises in Bond Street; the Wigmore Street shop given up. Isleworth was vacated and a much larger place bought in Stevenage, in the new town. The tiny output of Shona and Co. was increased tenfold, with only half the capacity utilized. The bank had financed the development: Neither Shona nor John would countenance going public.

I suppose the fact that I had never had this sort of responsibility before ministered to my vanity. It seemed likely that if I stayed in line and played the choirboy I was all set for a highly successful career in the perfumery trade. Did I want that? No. But I still wanted her.

And I saw a lot of her: The guard began to drop on both sides. But I made no other move yet, and she certainly did not invite one.

We had to engage new staff, and one day I said to her, "We need an extra van man. Somebody who knows London like a taxi driver and doesn't keep on picking up parking tickets. I think I have the man. Like me to engage him?"

"Of course. You do not need to ask me that."

"I thought I should. His name is Arthur Morris. Familiarly known as 'Crack.' "

" 'Crack'?"

"I shared a luxury flat with him in Pentonville."

She looked up. "You mean . . . So?"

"He's only just out and looking for a job. I promised his mother I'd try to do something for him."

"And what does the nickname 'Crack' mean?"

"What it says."

"Well, I do not think I want him here if he is going to come in and crack our old safe."

"I have a feeling he won't if I ask him not to."

She pursed her lips. "It is not very nice, David."

I said, "When I was in there he did a lot for me. Cushioning the shock to my genteel nature, as it were. Gratitude is not my strongest point, but I think this would be a moment to put a little on the line."

"At our expense?"

"No, my expense if it goes wrong. After all, if he starts filching the parcels, you'll throw the hatchet at me."

She hesitated again. "Well, the choice is yours, this time. But no more, please. I do not want our trademark to be changed to a broad arrow."

So Arthur Morris joined the firm. He was a thin, hard young man with too many lines on his cheeks. At my suggestion he dropped the nickname of "Crack" and became known as "Van."

Early in the second year Shona and I traveled by train to and from Birmingham together. There was a trade show in which I had pressed her to take part.

I'd also pressed her to book a whole first-class carriage—which one can do—with a bar at the end for entertaining journalists and publicity people on the way there and back; but she had refused.

"It is not the money, David; it is to me just a little vulgar."

"The other ladies in our profession—the Rubinsteins and the Ardens—would never consider traveling any other way."

"Ah, that I know. And ours is a business which demands— what is it you say?—the razzmatazz. Nevertheless I think I shall not follow them all the way. There is a discretion—there should be some dignity in it also."

As it happened, on the way back we were in one of those dreadful new British Rail first-class carriages—chairs obstructed by immovable tables, no control over heat or air, no privacy; anyone walking down the center of the carriage can cannon into your shoulder—and I made disparaging remarks about it.

She eyed me, then shrugged. "Maybe you are right. For me at least it is easier than traveling on the couplings."

"Come again?"

"Have you ever traveled on the couplings of a train, David? It is an interesting experience. Especially a train that stops with a jerk and starts with a jerk five or six times every hour; but you are afraid ever to let go lest someone else should steal your place. And more especially when you are starving hungry too."

She so seldom made any reference to her past that all this time I knew little more than I'd done at the kickoff.

"You mean, when you were leaving Russia?"

"That and other times."

"How *did* you eat on that journey across Europe? How did you even stay alive?"

Her eyes reflected the wintry sunlight outside. "It is surprising when you are young how far you can go on nothing, or next to nothing, with what little you can make do. Wild nuts, earth nuts, stray sheaves of unground wheat; and foods far less savory than these. I should dislike to upset your tender stomach."

"It must have upset yours."

"Ah, but then it is surprising how one becomes accustomed. In Moscow for three years before it had been black bread and cabbage soup . . . Tea—yes, there was usually tea. Though often it was hard to find the fuel to heat the water."

"How did you escape?"

"It was not so much a question of *escape*. My father was in prison for 'lack of revolutionary vigilance,' my mother had been dead a year; I had lost my place at the Bolshoi because of my father's disgrace. I simply stuffed a few things in a holdall and left. Walked out. At that time all Europe was in the pot—the melting pot. I simply directed myself west. There were no frontiers left."

"I've heard about your arrival in the West."

"Oh, stories. Whatever drips from the journalist's pen."

"You eat precious little now," I said. "If I had been like that I should have turned into a glutton."

She smiled. "Oh, I did. For a while I did. I grew so fat they thought I was with child."

"But you never were?"

"Were what?"

"With child."

"No. Ah no. Ah no . . . Now tell me your thoughts about America . . ."

This had been in our sights for some time. It was the biggest and riskiest market open to us but also the one most saturated with home products. But the top layers of the American market are peculiarly susceptible to European influence. Half is snob appeal, half's an atavistic tendency to look for what is best in the continent from which most Americans sprang. We'd talked a good lot about it, and there were plenty of people to warn us of the pitfalls. Without the right outlets you could fall flat on your face and lose a million.

Oddly enough, John Carreros was a bit more forthcoming about this. He had a number of relatives there who might be willing to help and advise. He thought in another twelve months the time would be ripe. Till then we could begin to prepare the way. Perhaps he would go over first, make his presence felt.

"You know," Shona said. "It may be that you are good for John. He has shown more initiative since you came than for years past."

"Perhaps he is a little jealous," I said.

"Jealous?"

"Of my influence in the firm."

"Ah." She breathed through her nose. "It could be. Perhaps you have been a—spur to us all."

"I believe," I said, "that's the first compliment you've ever paid me."

"Do not allow it to go to your head."

II The following day unexpectedly we had to go back to Birmingham, and as we were in Stevenage at the time I drove her up in the car I had just bought, a 1965 Austin Healey 3000. It had been in a garage most of its life and there was only five thousand miles on the clock, so it had been a snip at £600. After we had been on the motorway for a few miles she said, "Why do you drive at ninety miles an hour when the speed limit is seventy?"

"A family habit. But it's not excessive in so stable a car."

She said, "As usual, you do not answer my question."

"Why ninety in a seventy?"

"Yes. If the limit were eighty would you go a hundred?"

"I don't think I know the answer. Probably it depends how I feel."

"And whom you have as your passenger?"

I grinned. "That could be."

"Attempting to frighten? Or impress?"

"Aren't they both rather the same thing? Sorry." I slowed a bit.

"Oh, do not mind me," she said, "if it gives you a thrill."

By a coincidence on the way home we came on an accident. It was actually the first I'd ever seen and was a lousy one. The ambulance hadn't yet come and there was gore everywhere and vomit and a man unconscious and a woman dying. I had been all for being the bad Samaritan and gliding past, but Shona commanded me to stop and was out of the car before I put the handbrake on. She seemed to know more what to do than any of the other few people there, even for the woman who kept gasping for someone to take the weight off her chest when there was no weight there.

When it was over we were an hour late for our appointment and Shona had bloodstains on her skirt and a torn sleeve where the dying woman had been grasping at it, and her shoes and stockings were caked in pinkish mud. As soon as we were in the car again she sat back, lit a cigarette and began to talk about the forthcoming meeting as if we'd just come away from a garden party.

Feeling a bit sick myself, I said peevishly, "I suppose after your war experiences you take that sort of thing in your stride."

She sat there for a while like feminine whipcord, then she just said, "No."

We batted on a few miles, and she actually smoked the cigarette she had lit, which was unusual. As she put it out she said, "When the Germans were only twenty-five kilometers from Moscow I hitchhiked out to see my brother. He was one of the two who died in the end. It was not hard to get there, for there was such confusion, such chaos. It seemed nothing could save the city. In the end I think the cold did, that and our ski troops. Their armor froze—the Germans, I mean. What I saw then—well, yes—and since of course, and since, when I was less of a child, yes I suppose in a way you are right. That accident we have just left—it is not very important."

This was so often the same between us: much of it the evenly balanced to and fro between a man and a woman accepting each other as equals; then the little stone in the jam grating on the teeth; her superiority in talent, in judgment, in experience. Little boy, little boy . . .

III I moved houses again—to a top-floor flat in Red Place. It was vastly more expensive than I could afford, being in the heart of Mayfair, but it was convenient for work, and I had a feeling for a fashionable address.

The sticks of furniture that came from Fulham looked out of place in this new luxury, so it meant buying more and getting it on credit. I had changed my account to Shona's bank, though the overdraft on the flat soaked up all my goodwill with them. But I was earning a fair salary now and she worked me so hard I didn't have much time for squandering it in wild living.

Then one night, after I'd been in residence only three weeks and some bits and pieces of furniture still needed, who should be there but Derek Jones. I let myself in and the lights were on, and here he was in the sitting room in my pajamas, smoking one of my cheroots and playing one of my tapes.

"How the hell did you get in?"

"Picked the lock, old dear. Hope you didn't mind, but really you should have something better on the door than that old mortice. Simply not safe."

He looked up at me with his bright baby-blue eyes, so deceptively innocent. I laughed.

"Well, do make yourself at home. After all, it's late."

"Yes, I was wondering. Been on the tiles? I suspect so. Is that a smear on your lip? Or doesn't he use lipstick?"

"I use it myself now. Gives one a better look in artificial light."

"Oh, yes," he said, "how *is* the stench factory? Still pouring out the old viscous fluids?"

"Some, yes."

"I'll bet." He looked round speculatively. "Doing all right for yourself anyway. Bit better than the sty we shared. Seriously, David, I'm not here just for the thrill of sharing a bed with you . . ."

"I hope not, because you'll end up on the floor."

"Courteous, I must say."

I went to the cupboard he had already found, and gave myself a drink. The whiskey tasted bitter. In fact I'd been out playing bridge at the Hanover Club with John Carreros, who was a member there. It had been a waste of time. They played for a shilling a hundred, and more by good luck than good play I'd been the winner of a whole £1. Some of them barely understood the game, and their bidding was hairy.

"I'm here," said Derek, "because of an attractive little proposition that's cropped up. Wondered if you'd like to have a piece of it."

"You and who else?"

"Brad. Connie. Peter. Just the four of us. Cozy."

Bradley, O'Connor and Peter Jones had been in with me on the Tom Martin fiasco, but had been able to slide out from under the benevolence of the law. Only Muggins had copped it.

I looked at the clock. "It's late."

"Well, you were, dear. I think this little propo is rather up your alley. Know a chap called Vincent McArthur?"

"I knew him at one time."

"Can you listen without yawning?"

I listened. It was soon clear why they needed me. Without my name and connections McArthur would skip away from the speculation he was being invited to invest in. I remembered him from school. He'd been two terms junior to me but was big for his age and good at games. A natural bully. He'd been in London at some of the early dances, but I hadn't seen him for two or three years.

"He's a tough nut," I said. "And he'll be slow to part with his siller."

Not if it's put to him the right way, dear. The meaner they are, the keener they become to have a little flutter, if it's a flutter on cert.

After all, it's not the racecourse, it's the stock exchange. What could be more respectable?"

I didn't like McArthur. A clumsy, overconfident oaf. But no fool. His family were wealthy ironmongers in Glasgow. The connection with the Highland clan of Abden would tease him into taking the risk if anything did.

Afterward? Afterward, if the plan went to order, there would be nothing to complain of. On the face of it we should all have lost the same amount. It was not an ambitious plan either. They expected to relieve him of about £15,000. Divided among four, it was not exactly El Dorado, but it was quite a lot for those days, and it would certainly solve the problem of furnishing the rest of the flat. Worth the risk? If anything went wrong I'd be out of Shona and Co. on my backside without a penny. Worth the risk?

"No," I said.

"Why not?"

"God wouldn't like it."

"Seriously. It's money for old rope."

"Wake up," I said. "We're living in another world. It's only a couple of years since I went inside for pulling a con trick that went wrong. The name of Abden won't commend the scheme to McArthur. He'll double back and run for cover at the very sound of it."

Derek got up, lanky, loose-jointed, ambled to the cupboard and poured himself another two fingers of Grant's, shot an inch of soda in it.

"McArthur's been in Johannesburg for two years. He'll have heard nothing of it. Cheers, mate."

"Maybe not. Somebody's likely to tell him."

"You'd be surprised. Scarcely anyone *knows*. You were lucky because your trial coincided with that Welsh mine disaster. What was it? Aberfan. Amid all the commotion and the weep stories, you hardly rated a mention."

"My pajamas don't fit you," I said.

He came back, gazing into his glass. "Mind if I stay the night anyhow?"

"Not if you sleep on the couch."

He grinned. "Anyway after your orgy I expect you wouldn't be much use to me . . . Can we talk it over again in the morning?"

"What?"

"The Proposition McArthur."

"Is Roger Manpole involved in it?"

Derek shrugged. "There's not much wrong with Roger except what you imagine. By most standards he's the height of respectability."

"Tell him to stuff it," I said.

There was silence. Then Derek said, "Anyway, as you know, he's deep into your sort of business. If you really want to avoid him, you ought to go into aeronautics or something."

"Or emigrate."

"Or emigrate, darling. In the meantime it might be worth figuring the angles on this old scent business."

"How?"

"I don't know. Not off the cuff I don't know. It was just a thought. Might there not be profit for us both one way or another? Don't you think?"

"Actually I don't think much."

He watched me. "Who knows? Something might be worked up. Strictly *entre nous*. Keeping Roger out."

I stared back at him. "Maybe. I'll have to see."

"You're certainly on the inside now. And well in with a bird that's ripe for plucking . . . What time d'you like your coffee?"

"Seven-thirty."

He winced. "Oh, well. Derek will set his wrist alarm and do his best. And, dear . . ."

"Yes?"

"Do change that mortise. Someone might come in and rape you."

IV I usually sleep well, but there are times, have always been times, when something gets on my wick and I'm restless and pumped full of nightmare. Usually there's this sort of no-man's-land between the barbed wires of sleeping and waking, when all sorts of things back up round my bed like mourners at a funeral. People I've never seen and never want to see, pointing, glowering, staring; and even when I open my eyes they stick around, seem to be sitting on the bed, shaking the bed, gibbering—dead themselves and wanting me dead. It takes a real effort to force my eyes *really* open, and then the things dissolve into the arms and legs of windows and the bulbous noses of furniture.

This night, though—actually it was early morning—I had this old dream I'd had before. It always begins the same, with me staring at a chink of light coming through the curtains and knowing it is the split in the cupboard door where he's locked me in.

It's odd how drink takes different people. There's a legal definition of the four stages of drunkenness, isn't there: jocose, bellicose, lachrymose, comatose. He never got beyond the second stage.

I used to know as soon as he came in that I was for it. I used to know that whatever I said or did or didn't say or didn't do it would be wrong. For instance, he might come in and see that I was having my supper and hadn't changed my shoes. So I had to rush out *quickly* and change them. Then he'd swear that I'd banged the door in a temper, then that I didn't know how to eat because I was chewing too loudly. If I said anything in reply he'd say it was time he taught me a lesson for answering him back; if I said nothing he'd say it was time he taught me a lesson for being sulky. It was always the same lesson. In the cupboard for an hour or two; then, when he felt like it, the door would open and he'd be standing there with the strap.

A tall chap, my father, with aggravated eyebrows and a hot complexion. He'd the blue eyes of the Abdens that I didn't have, and they soon became bloodshot, especially when he was stoking up. He always dressed well, often wore his old school tie with a red carnation in his buttonhole. Tremendously good company, especially among strangers who didn't know the other side. The life and soul. But God help you if in the middle his mood should change, and he should suspect you were laughing at him instead of with. It could happen in ninety seconds flat—the time it took to drain a glass and dab his mouth with an Irish linen handkerchief. Wow. The laughter in his eyes would go suddenly sour. You couldn't have a worse example of the way the old hooch ran into a man's nature like poison.

Yet there was this terrific charm that worked part of the time even for his son. When I was nine he bought a marvelous new 3-liter convertible Alvis in dove gray. It was a great car, very hard sprung—like a bed of nails—and if you tried to do more than ninety-five in it it would begin to smell of oil. But it was about the fastest thing up to ninety that I've ever known. Or it seemed so; you slipped up to eighty without knowing you were moving. My mother would usually be beside him and I would be in the back seat, my nose pushed forward almost touching their shoulders as we beat it up. Those were good days.

But gradually the old bottle tipping grew more frequent. Once a month became once a week, then oftener. In the early days I used to be scared out of my wits, not only at being locked in the dark but knowing what came next, waiting for the sound of the footstep. But later I toughened up to it. I used to put on a deadpan look that would infuriate him; and I'd not open my mouth for anything; after all, I'd get the same lamming anyhow. He used to try to beat me harder, I suppose to see if I'd blub; but fortunately he was usually so far gassed by then that his strength was half spent when he began.

Half the time my mother was hypnotized by him, as I was, totally under his influence, under his thumb. If he said the sun shone, it shone; if he said not, not. Yet other times she really let go about him. When he wasn't there, when he was away for the night, she would whistle, and I'd slide out of my bed, cross the landing, and crawl in beside her. Then she'd say frightful things about him in the dark, whispering as if he might hear, though we both knew he was miles away. She'd stroke my face and arms, and I'd push against her nightdress, feeling the softness of her and the warmth. And we'd spend all night together in rich, comfortable sleep.

After he died it all changed. There was a sort of resentment even before she remarried—as if I'd done her an injury by being so loving to her. A lot changed after my father died.

Then we all went to live in Quemby and her belly swelled, and soon there were these two daughters, Edna and Marjorie; and when I went home from school I used to find four strangers waiting for me and living a life I was no part of.

As I say, this night that Derek came I had the old familiar dream, but somehow, as happened nowadays, it was all mixed up with the time I spent in jug and the slamming of the cell door. Anyway

I woke up eventually in a muck sweat and sat up and groped around as usual looking for reassurance: the table top, the telephone, the bedside light. When this came on I felt certain at last that this wasn't the cupboard, this wasn't the cell, this was the new bedroom in the new flat in Red Place; and the curtains were shabby and didn't match the furniture, and there were a couple of magazines on the floor where I'd dropped them last night, and a glass of water I'd nearly tipped over in my fumblings, and the clock said half past six.

I lay back breathing the muck out of my lungs. Somehow sleep still seemed vaguely threatening, so I opted for a cigarette.

I chewed over the significance of these nightmares. I tried to decide how much of it had actually happened to me. Certainly the cell; certainly the cupboard door. Of *course* it was all true! But how much of it did the nightmare exaggerate? Had it all happened exactly like that to me in the past, or had I partly been dreaming about a dream?

CHAPTER FIVE

I The day after Derek left—with no encouragement from me for any of his nefarious schemes—I took an hour off from work and went to Harrods to see about new curtain material. The present stuff was like old sackcloth; what I wanted was a good clear yellow, something lively. The new flat was light, but London gets its overload of gloomy days. I found some figured silk at a sky-high price per yard, but it looked just the job, so having fingered the material and held it to the light and made a swift guess at the hole it was going to make in my overdraft, I looked around for an assistant. In the distance was a trim young gent deep in conversation with a fat woman about some cushions. Nearer, a female assistant was on the telephone. Five or six other people milled about variously concerned with looking after themselves. I waited. I looked at my watch. Choosing this particular stuff, plus a holdup finding a parking place, had taken longer than expected. There was a brush I had to have with Shona when she got back—to do with marketing Faunus—and she was due at three-thirty. It was now three-fifteen.

Of course there was no great hurry. She would be there until four-thirty.

I walked into the next department and said to a personage, "Pardon me, can you help me over some curtain material I want to buy."

The personage looked at me. "I'm afraid that isn't my department, sir. I'm sure someone will be free in a few moments."

"I've been more than a few moments," I said.

"Yes, sir. I'm sorry. I'll try to find someone to attend to you."

I wandered back to the curtain material. The lady assistant was still on the telephone. The other one had changed his tack with the fat woman and seemed to be trying to interest her in a bed-spread. I fingered the material and let it fall back. It was about a quarter roll, a bit more than I should want. I looked at my watch. Three twenty-five. The assistant on the telephone had stopped bleeping but was holding the receiver to her ear, a hard-worked, patient expression on her face. With her free hand she tapped her order book.

It was three twenty-seven. I picked up the roll of material, put it under my arm and walked out of the department. It was long and quite heavy, and you certainly couldn't hide it. Two women were arguing about a linen ruffle but didn't raise their heads. I sidestepped them and walked past them, through the television department to the lift. No one took any notice. There were stairs just round the corner, but I waited for the lift. Presently it came. It was half full of shoppers but they were all concerned with their own affairs. One small boy did stare at me with a fair amount of interest but he made no comment.

The lift reached the ground floor and belched out its passengers. I walked through the various departments to the side door and went out. My car was just round the corner. I threw the curtain material into the passenger seat and drove off.

II As it happened I was in for a bigger brush with Shona than I expected. It began on the Faunus thing, of course, but halfway through she told me she was of the opinion that I was intent on cheapening the reputation of the firm.

Then it all came out. It was the talcum powder I'd ordered last week. I'd made it grade five instead of grade one, and only accidentally it had come to her notice. Certainly John Carreros could never have told the difference. But now that it had come to light, they were both furious.

I said, "You know as well as I do how many grades there are. Let's not deceive ourselves. If we'd changed from deep-mined talc to the open-cast, sterilized stuff you could say I wasn't playing fair by the customer; but first to fifth is really a distinction without a difference. And it saves us money. I am trying to save *you* money, not make money for myself. In bulk buying—"

"I know very well what it saves in bulk buying; but I will not have it. Please understand that. You know that some talc carries the spores of tetanus. Would you want—"

"Shona, don't wave that bogey in my face. Fifth grade is as safe as first. You want the best of both worlds—expansion, bigger sales, bigger profits, fine!—but you still expect to run the place as if it were a corner shop selling homemade toffee!"

She tapped her foot, but the thick-pile carpet soaked up the annoyance. "You argue like a crook, David. I told you from the beginning that if bulk manufacture meant lowered quality then, whatever the sales, you would have failed! So you want to fail, is that it? You can't do what you said you could do, not because it is impossible but because it is not in your character to do it!"

I knew I was in the wrong, but that doesn't make you any more reasonable at the time. The row made me forget altogether about the roll of stuff in my flat, and it was not until I got home late that evening that I saw it and stared at it with critical memory.

The following morning I put the material against the present curtains and up to the light. It was very grand. Too grand for a top-floor flat. It would have looked fine in Shona's lush drawing room. Derek would have loved it. I ate my breakfast and went off to Bond Street, where I was to spend most of the day, but at eleven returned to the flat. I picked up the roll and put it in my car and drove to Harrods.

Parking was even more difficult than yesterday, and I had to walk quite a way through the streets with the roll under my arm. Fortunately it wasn't raining.

Through the enormous food halls, find the lift, and up to the second floor. The state of play seemed very much the same as yesterday, except that the second assistant wasn't on the telephone; she was leafing in a depressed way through a pile of papers at the pay desk. I went across and put the roll of material back on the pile where I'd found it yesterday. It didn't seem the time to consider another choice, so I turned away.

"Excuse me, sir," said a voice. "Can I help you?"

It was the assistant who yesterday had been in spirited conversation with the fat old girl.

I said, "This material; afraid it isn't right. The color's too strong. I've just had it to the daylight to make sure."

He hesitated, his face a notable study.

"I thought . . . You brought it from the lift, sir?"

"Yes. I wanted to make quite certain. But I'm afraid it isn't right. Too bright for my flat."

"Ah." We both stood there a few seconds. I made no move to leave. "Can I interest you in something else, then?"

"Not this morning; I haven't the time. I shall come earlier to-morrow. If you'll give me your card I'll ask for you."

"Thank you, sir." A card was reluctantly offered. He was still flatulent with suspicion. It could be that someone had noticed the disappearance of the roll. But there was nothing he could do. No-one can be accused of *returning* a bolt of material.

I nodded and left him.

The next morning I was there at nine-thirty and bought something less high-society. I don't think he had ever expected to see me again, and it gave me a special pleasure to turn up.

All the same I was aware that I had been acting the juvenile delinquent again.

III

Somewhere along the line people began to speak of Shona and David. It began that year but it was more common the next. We were a couple working together in harness, building and expanding as we went. John got left behind.

He was a hard man to read, but most of the time he played along. Now and then I caught him looking at me over the top of his spectacles and I wondered if he was biding his time. I was helping to lead his firm in a direction he didn't really want it to go, and if I put a foot wrong he might kick the other out from under me. Particularly if I started making it with his wife. Late in the day I heard tales of two other young men who had been in the firm in the early years and had left. No one knew what had happened to them so I couldn't ask them for details. There was also a report that Shona had had an affair with some young marquess, but that had been over for a while.

An American called Barton was appointed as our potential representative in the States, and I went across a couple of times to see how he was getting on. Shona would not come with me, said she would fly over only when the project was fully ready to be launched. Once or twice I brought her back presents: terribly discreet things like a desk set in red morocco with "Shona" on it in gold leaf.

The con man with a dirk in his stocking had deteriorated into a sleek executive type expanding a business and initiating an export drive, flying to New York first class in his pinstripe.

I saw a bit of Caroline Rowton, who'd had a disastrous love affair and wanted someone's shoulder to weep on. And once or twice I had mild, brief affairs of my own. Insofar as I like any company I like the company of attractive women; I enjoy taking them out, giving them a good time, just talking to them and listening to them. But unfortunately there usually comes a point at a quiet dinner where a girl lets out a spark. If it doesn't ignite in you she isn't really happy to go on enjoying the dinner and leaving it platonic. She thinks there's been something disappointing in her, disappointing to you, that is. And it worries her. Or else she thinks there's something wrong with you. More than once in those years I've found myself sleeping with a girl more out of politeness than passion. I'd as soon have gone to bed with a good book.

For holidays I started popping off to Barbados. I hit on an excellent hotel first time and stuck to it. Good beach, just tolerable company, good sunshine, good food, and no temptation to gamble my salary away, as sometimes happened in London.

Shona and I talked and argued much more on a personal level now—and on a more or less equal basis that could register a disagreement without ill will. Although committed to the expansion she was still influenced by John, still kept turning her head to look over her shoulder at the old ways, the aristocratic advantages of scarcity, the principle of restricted supply and restricted outlets, the fact that when a woman opened her handbag and took out a Shona lipstick knowledgeable people would be aware that she could only have bought it at one of a few exclusive shops.

When we had disagreements they were hardly ever aired at the monthly get-togethers which took place in the new assembly room at the Stevenage factory; they'd brew up before or after in the semiprivacy of her own office. But because of the none-too-thick walls, these set-tos were conducted in the lowered voices of terrorists about to plant a bomb, and this made it all the more difficult to work up a temper over them. Once she hissed at me, "Go to hell, you stupid little man!" and then seeing how comic it was she burst out laughing.

She didn't have a nice laugh; not like the clear note of her voice—it was broken, like a twelve-year-old boy's. But it suited her.

When I came back from Barbados the second time she asked if I had enjoyed myself and then added, "Have you ever fenced, David?"

"Fenced? At school a bit. Centuries ago."

"That's at least five years. Well, I go once a week to the Sloan gymnasium. It is perhaps the nearest I can now get to ballet, and it is an aid to fitness. If you are doing nothing tomorrow night, possibly you would like to come with me?"

"OK," I said. It was the first sign of social friendliness in more than two years. Even John Carreros, with that one invitation to bridge at his club—which had never been repeated—had been more forthcoming.

So on the Tuesday I went. The fencing school was in this big hall, as big as a film studio, with the floor marked out in white paint to line out the fencing territories. A fair number of people turned up, some getting tuition, others practicing on their own or having mock contests. Those actually in contention had wires running from their backs to a control panel, so that every time a hit was scored a bell rang and a light showed on the board. That didn't stop them howling out in triumph as well—a sort of "gotcha!" without the consonants.

Shona was good, as I suppose you would have expected, and you could guess at her Bolshoi training by the way she used her feet. We did a bit of limbering up together, then I sat and watched while she had a couple of bouts with a slim fair pretty female who was better still. The girl won 9–1 and 9–2, and then Shona, breathing hard, took off her mask and sat beside me and introduced me to this girl, who was called Erica Lease.

Eighteen or nineteen: long narrow face, deepish voice, a cheeky way with her, sultry eyes which didn't quite match her comic style. They said she was among the top women fencers in the country.

After she had cooled off Shona said, "Come, David, let us try a little engagement."

We shoved on protective masks, got wired up and had a go. It was a casual bout without any formality except the bells, and of course she scored the first seven points over me more or less as it grabbed her. I was rusty. When she put on her mask there had been a glint in her eyes; now when I saw her sword flickering over my chest it seemed to me to be warlike behavior that went a bit beyond ordinary fencing. And the "Yah" she uttered every time she scored a point riled me. They hadn't shouted like that at Loretto. So I began to concentrate. I tried to recall in five minutes all I'd forgotten over the last decade. I scored two hits before she won 9–2.

"Thank you," she said, grasping my hand in the formal way. "You did well."

"Not well enough," I replied, rubbing my arm where her last point had been scored.

"You could be good, I think. You have quick reflexes. Do you not think so, Erica?"

"He *could* be good."

"I'll come again," I said, "after I've done a job on my reflexes."

Pupils a muddy gray, even though the whites were clear. Maybe they masked the mischief. "Come next Saturday," she said. "We have some good county trials. Shona, bring him then."

"I cannot," said Shona. "We shall be in the States."

"Ah. Then the week after. Or as soon as you come back."

"I will do that."

"Have you fenced for long?" I asked the girl.

"Oh, all my life." She pulled off her gauntlet and grinned at me. "Mine, they say, was a foil birth."

"The sport's on the increase," said a chap standing near. "There's a new school opening in Lambeth later this month."

"Yes, I put money into it," said Miss Lease. "Have you time for a drink, Shona? We're all going round the corner in a minute."

Eight of us went. It was a jolly party, and for once Shona seemed overshadowed by the others, who all chattered in loud voices and interrupted each other and yelped good-humoredly at their own jokes. After the stimulation of the sport she was in one of her quiescent moods, hair screwed back any way, small-boned and foreign in her camel-hair coat. Not the great lady for the time being.

She caught my eye, blinking her own through somebody else's cigarette smoke.

"I expect you do much of this in Barbados, David."

"Much of what?"

"Drinking in bars."

"To excess. It's Jerry Dawson's weakness."

"Does he go with you? I didn't know."

"This year, yes. Of course the whole island is a sink of vice."

"That is a funny joke; but who knows? Think of Haiti."

Talk of holidays had gone around, and it seemed Erica had recently been to Cap Ferrat. She had met the Gregory Pecks while she was there. And David Niven. And Trevor Howard.

As I drove Shona home I said, "A high-flying filly."

"Who, Erica? Yes. Lives a full life. If she concentrated on her fencing she would be a world beater."

"Married?"

"No."

"Lovers?"

"Why, are you interested?"

"No," I said. "Though I see she would be top of the milk for many a good man."

"Not for you? Oh, come now. Pray be honest."

"You know that's not my best policy."

She laughed, broken-voiced. "You've not stolen anything from the till yet, have you?"

"Not a bean. Disappointing."

"But you can still be honest about Erica?"

I pondered. "She's OK, yes, I could bed her. But she's not really my style."

"Who is?"

It was an incautious question. I said, "You, of course."

The lights went green and I edged forward. The car in front belonged to a driving school. The student driver was so nervous that even her brake lights were trembling.

Shona said, "I think I had better take that remark as unspoken."

"Why?"

"I was not looking for that answer."

"Well, now you have it."

We turned into South Audley Street.

"It would never do."

"Why not?"

"I need you still to remain in the firm."

"Of course. I don't see that the two ends are incompatible."

She patted my arm. "But I am afraid, David, that that is how it is."

CHAPTER SIX

I flew to New York on the Friday and was met at Kennedy by Jim Barton and by another man we'd engaged called Phil Grogam, a big hearty Jewish character who had been an executive with Estée Lauder. Shona reluctantly followed on the Monday. John would not come, so she arrived quite alone. She was met at the airport, of course, by a bandwagon of reporters and publicity men, and photographed and interviewed in the airport buildings, in the limousine, in the lobby of the Pierre. I was surprised to see how edgy she was; I suppose she realized she was now in the country of the big talkers, the big sellers and the big spenders. All the same in the end she had her way and insisted on a quiet luncheon with me. I explained to her about the party we had arranged at the hotel that evening; the fashion press would be there in even greater force, of course; the buyers for the major stores, a variety of people who counted in one way or another; and a few celebrities.

She said, "This is foreign territory for me, David. Essentially I am still a Russian—and very much a European. I feel quite at home in Paris or London. But New York—what is this food we are eating?"

"Long Island clams. Thought you might fancy them."

"Well, I do not. They are revolting. And those districts we drove through from the airport; they remind me of Moscow!"

I looked round the plush restaurant. "And this is the Lubyanka?"

"Do not joke about that," she said. "I once went to see my father in the Lubyanka, before he was sent away to a corrective camp."

"What was his error—your father's error? The reason why he was sent away?"

"He became friendly with an English girl secretary at the embassy. In Stalin's day it was considered treason."

"Well, there's no treason involved in becoming friendly with your secretary here. That makes a refreshing change."

She did not take me up on this. "You will make the necessary speech, David?"

"I'll say a word. But it's your big night. Above everyone else, you *are* Shona. Even if you make it quite short, you'll have to give it to them."

"I will speak. But briefly. You will draft something for me and I will amend it as I think necessary."

"I've made one or two notes."

"Good. We will discuss them after lunch."

We finished the meal. She had picked at a few pieces of under-cooked lamb, an elaborate iced sweet, sipped two vodkas and shared a half-bottle of Chablis.

"Now I am going to rest for an hour," she said. "The airplane has made my ears deaf."

I wondered how she'd dress for the evening, whether her cool dignity would fit well with the Americans, who were so used to a more free and easy way and had their own ideas—put over by other ladies of far greater flamboyance—of how a leading woman perfumer ought to court their attention.

I needn't have had a second thought. They seemed to see her as a friend at once. Her few words went well; she contrived to answer some rather bitchy questions, and answer them in a good-humored way which kept everyone in the right mood. It was I who splotched my copy book.

But this was later. The speeches were long over, the perfumes and beauty products had been displayed and samples pushed around. Then there was a move downstairs. Grogam had cunningly ar-ranged that our party should begin at 5:30, because on the same evening at the Pierre the Fragrance Foundation was holding its annual awards dinner, where presentations were being made for the best perfume of the year, the best advertising, etc. Tickets for this were highly sought after, and those of our guests who didn't have tickets could at least say they were at the Pierre that evening; those who did could join this other and more prestigious party where all the great names of the cosmetics business were in at-tendance.

Now among the press people was this tall blonde called Kathy Schwarzheim, with lots of obvious attractions in the right places.

She was on behalf of some insignificant rag in Philadelphia, but she'd somehow scraped an invitation for the Foundation dinner. She'd been around me ever since I landed last Friday, making rather a nuisance of herself.

When we were circulating at the gathering downstairs I found her next to me.

"Tell me, Mr. Abden," she said, "is it true that Mme. Shona is a ballet dancer?" I hesitated a moment, and she added, "Or *was*," and laughed.

I said, "She studied ballet."

"Where?"

"At the Bolshoi."

She whistled. "Wow! Isn't that something! And she's a concert pianist too?"

"Hardly. She plays Brubeck."

"What talent! . . . Tell me, how does it feel to be the Prince Consort?"

I looked across at Shona's lanky, distinguished figure. Then I looked at this Kathy Schwarzheim. "That implies a lot."

"Oh, surely not that much!"

"Well, since you ask, I think she makes a good Queen."

There was a laugh. Having tossed off her drink, Kathy Schwarzheim turned toward a waiter with a tray of full glasses and took another quick one before we were called for dinner. No doubt she would have come back to me for more sly questions, but her face annoyed me and I edged away. As I did so I heard a black-bearded, heavy, middle-aged character say to her in an amiable overtone: "I guess it's one queen to another."

Kathy Schwarzheim giggled so much she spilled champagne on her fingers, and I moved out of hearing. But not for long. Two minutes later I saw her bearded friend without a companion and sidled up to him. I clutched his velvet jacket by the lapel and gave it a violent wrench downward. There was the sound of threads breaking and he was nearly pulled over, dropped his glass with a clatter.

"You goddam fool! What d'you mean—"

I said, "Sorry, dear. The trouble with us queens is that we can't keep our hands off other men."

I suppose I must have looked ugly, because he slowly unclenched the fists he had raised.

A breaking glass always briefly stops talk, and people around cut off what they were saying and stared. Grogam came steering across, anxiety writ large. A waiter brought another glass while a second disappeared in search of a brush and tray. It was maybe a minute before the noise decibel in the room reached its previous level, like water rising in a cistern after someone has pulled the plug.

Marini, as I learned he was called, laughed and moved away, examining his torn lapel with fat nicotined fingers. Eventually he left the room, presumably for another jacket or a quick stitch. I could see Grogam looking daggers at me. Somebody spoke to him and he made a gesture toward me and shrugged. Then dinner was called. I sat next to a pretty young female who was the buyer for Tracey's of Fifth Avenue, and a not so pretty one high up in the Arden hierarchy. The dinner and the presentations seemed to go on for ever; and it was not until we met in the lobby much later that Grogam launched into a diatribe. Marini, it seemed, was the chief executive of de Luxembourg, one of the most powerful and successful of the newer cosmetic giants.

"It just happened that the hairy slob made a remark I didn't like," I said shortly. "He was lucky he didn't get his teeth knocked in."

"Maybe you'll be lucky if *you* don't," said Grogam.

"What's that supposed to mean? The fellow's a competitor. Teach him to mind his manners."

Grogam looked at me in a peculiar way. "You don't know about de Luxembourg, then."

"What about them?"

"They're financed by the Mafia."

 Shona said, "I will write a letter to Francesco, explaining that you are new to the United States and do not understand their ways. You must write too. A letter of apology will not hurt you."

"Yes, it will."

"Only your pride, isn't it? What else? Tell me what else?"

I grunted. "He sweats."

"Fat men can't help it. Thin men too sometimes."

We were in her suite. She had asked me to come in, and I had gone preparing for battle. But so far she had been calm.

"Tell me again," she said, "exactly what happened."

I told her. She sat back in a large divan chair and prodded her hands through her hair, loosening it from its severe fastenings. Then she laughed, harshly, unmelodiously, irritably.

I said, "I'm glad it amuses you."

"It does. In a way. It amuses and it annoys. It was all so trivial, so unnecessary."

"Maybe."

"Why should it worry you that you should be mistaken for one of them?"

"D'you think I often am mistaken?"

"By a few. It is not always easy to be sure about these things. I asked if it worried you?"

"Not worried, no. Riled."

"Clearly. To the extent that you allow yourself the luxury of incurring the enmity of a man like that?"

"I told you, I didn't know the fat slug was important at all."

"You must have known him to be important to be at such a dinner."

"Oh, well, I just felt like it."

"Were you given to violence before you joined us? Am I harboring a dangerous psychopath?"

"Yes, you can rely on me to shake the collar of any overweight Italian gangster who thinks he can call me a queer in his spare time."

She sighed. "You must become more *civilized*. Over such a little thing!"

"I have this aversion."

"So it seems."

"Some people can't stand cats. Others come out in spots if they eat lobster. You don't explain an allergy."

The sigh turned into a yawn—as cavernous as that of one of the cats some people could not stand. "Dear boy, you are not being so honest with me—or with yourself, is it? You know you get on very well with Jimmy and Fred . . . and even Bruce with all his tantrums. And also did you not *share a flat* with one? You do not have an allergy for queers, your allergy is for being thought one yourself."

"So what?"

"It is an occupational hazard in this business."

"Maybe."

There was a pause.

"Where is your room?" she asked.

"Five floors up. Why?"

"And cheaper than this?"

"Oh, much."

"This is too extravagant. I will stay until the publicity is over and then move."

I said, "When we first met—d'you recall you asked me which side of the road I was on."

"I did not. You volunteered the information—possibly to dispel any doubts in my mind."

I thought round this remark. I hadn't remembered it that way. "And were there?"

"What?"

"Doubts in your mind?"

"By then, no. But David, for all your petulance about this, you must remember you are a good-looking man . . . Sometimes you remind me of a handsome drawing by Delacroix in the Louvre."

"Don't know him. He a friend of yours?"

"At others you look like Lord Byron on one of his less agreeable days."

"Thanks a lot."

"Always you dress well. And that carnation you so often wear in your buttonhole . . . Even when I first met you and you had little money, you dressed well. I do not at all mind if I am attractive to women. Why should you resent it when it is the other way round?"

"Another drink?"

She hesitated. "Thank you. Scotch, please. I suppose one has to call it that here. The champagne at our party was good, though I drank very little of it."

She put a finger in the heel of her shoe and eased it. Her elegant silk legs were much to be seen.

"It was Spanish," I said.

"What?"

"The champagne. Half the price of the real thing."

"It is not always a good thing to economize on what may be noticed."

"The first six bottles were Moët, and when that was done the empty bottles were left at the back of the serving table. The waiters were told to keep the other bottles covered with their napkins."

She laughed. I carried her drink over.

"Take one yourself."

"Thanks, no. I have a skinful already."

"Is that one of your distasteful Scottish sayings?"

"Fu' as a lord. That's Scottish. Fu' as a tick, is another. I'm not sure about skinful . . . Incidentally, if you gave me the necessary alibi I should, no doubt, be far less sensitive about misunderstandings."

She looked up at me. "I am not quite sure I follow you."

"I hoped you would."

"Alibi? It is a word now often misused. It does not mean an excuse, you know."

"Do I need an excuse," I asked, "for wanting you?"

She sipped her drink, eyelids lowered.

"Perhaps yes. Perhaps no. We have spoken of this once before. Leave me now, David. I am tired."

"Whatever you say, Madame. But I may come back to the subject."

"Pray do not."

"What time d'you wish to see me in the morning?"

"You say our first appointment is ten?"

"Yes, at the General Motors building, that's Fifth Avenue at Fifty-ninth, so it won't be far from here."

She wrinkled her nose. "I do not think I like cities that have addresses which sound like crossword puzzles."

"Take it from me, it's much easier when you know how."

"So many things are . . . Nine-thirty in the lobby, then."

"Very good, Madame."

"Don't be silly, David," she said.

"Psychopaths," I said, "often are."

I bent and kissed her, near the corner of her imperious mouth. She made no move and no comment.

I went out.

III The next day was a madhouse, and I had no chance to speak to Shona alone until after dinner, when once again I whirred up to her suite and was joined there by Grogam and Barton for a last drink. After his dudgeon last night Grogam had said nothing more to me about the Marini affair. Everything had gone like a starburst today, and Barton had brought in clippings about us from the New York papers, and of the ads that had gone in. We were away to a good start. She rang John Carreros and read him the favorable bits. Presently Phil Grogam left, and then Jack Barton.

As soon as they had gone I said, "I haven't written to Marini."

"No . . . I have. So has Grogam."

"Is that enough?"

"Well, what can you say, personally? That you made a fool of yourself and happen to be unduly sensitive about your sex life?"

"I reckon."

She hesitated, thought it out, finger on lip. "Then do it tomorrow. Perhaps it is just worth doing as an overinsurance."

"Overinsurance against what?"

"Enmity where it will do you no good."

"I can look after myself."

"You think so? Well, maybe. Let us say, then, enmity where it will do *us* no good."

"Right. I'll make the necessary grovel. Shona . . ."

"Yes?"

"This pitch that Phil gave me about de Luxembourg. Is it true?"

"Being financed in the way he said? Oh, yes."

"By the Mafia?"

"Oh, yes. That and more."

"In what way more?"

She said, "*Mon Dieu*, these American meals! How do they make everything taste like sawdust?"

"I'll ask around tomorrow, try to find somewhere quieter, with wooden seats, where they'll serve you black bread and borsch."

She fingered her hair but did not let it loose tonight. "Have you a cigarette?"

I took her one. She fitted it into her black ivory cigarette holder, and I struck my lighter, held it to the cigarette. Her hand was rock steady.

She said, "It is strange to think—how many years ago?—I was with my mother and my brother in our rooms in Moscow, and we were eating just that, just what you said, when the music on the wireless stopped and an announcer came on and said in harsh tones—he said, 'In crude and uncivilized violation of the non-aggression pact which exists between our two countries, the German army has this afternoon invaded the sacred frontiers of our Russian fatherland.' I think it was June. I know the evenings were long. Over twenty-five years ago! I can hardly believe so much time has passed."

Nearer thirty, I thought, but didn't correct her. "We'd been at war two years then," I said. "Though I wasn't quite yet alive."

She looked at me, brooding. "Are you that young? . . . Well, it had been a false peace for Russia all along. Ribbentrop and his posturings . . . I do not know what the Politburo thought, but the ordinary Russian had no faith in Nazi promises . . . The same night—the night the war began for us—Stalin came on, uttered a stirring message. He was like a foreigner, you know, Stalin—a Georgian—he spoke Russian with such an ugly accent. But we rallied behind him. He spoke then for us all."

I took the chair beside her, patted her hand. "Let us talk of happier things. The Mafia, for instance."

There was a long silence. "You have never heard how the de Luxembourg firm began?"

"I'm ready for a Bible story."

"Well, a Bible story indeed . . . Some people must still remember . . . Though now they pretend it never was like that, that it is all just stupid calumny . . . Fifteen years ago they began. You recall the famous de Luxembourg lipstick? The eau de toilette? The first perfume—I have forgotten its name. To begin they did not catch on, any of them. Sometimes the trade has to be wooed, is more difficult than the public. We don't want any more, the trade said. Our shelves are full. Folk don't want your stuff. Sorry and all that. At the end of a year there was a meeting of the de Luxembourg directors and they agreed on a change of policy. The representative would go into a shop, 'Good morning, I represent de Luxembourg. Can I interest you in our range?' 'No thanks. Nothing doing. We have shelves full of all the best perfumes. We don't want any more.' The representative would be polite and say, 'Very sorry to hear it. I'll call in a few weeks.' An hour later a car will draw up outside the shop, two bullies go in, walk up to the shelves of perfumes and lipsticks and upset them all, smash them with clubs, crush them underfoot, then go out, drive away, leaving a pyramid of ruined scents and lipsticks, and a terrified proprietor is dialing the police. The next week the polite representative comes in to the shop, 'Good morning, I represent de Luxembourg. Can I interest you in our range?' "

I whistled. "That's a Bible story I *never* heard before!"

"That is how it happened. Of course for the bigger cities, the larger shops, this was not possible. But every buyer has a husband, a wife, a lover, or children. It soon got around that de Luxembourg had to be stocked—and given the top treatment. So they are now where they are."

I looked at her long tawny figure taking its ease in the chair beside me.

"And to think in my childlike way I used to imagine the perfumery business was a genteel profession."

"Nothing is genteel where big money is concerned."

"How did you come to know all this?"

"John told me."

"And how did he come to know it?"

"Through his relatives."

"*Oh.* Are his relatives—connected with the Mafia?"

She shrugged. "One or two."

"And are we making use of these connections to up our prospects in the States?"

"Of course. But not in an illegal way. That is all past. They are simply extending a helping hand, advising and helping on our outlets."

"So I don't need to feel that if that attractive young female from Tracey's doesn't order enough, her boyfriend may be run down by a taxi tomorrow?"

"Of course not! Don't be so silly."

"Don't you think I should have been told?"

"What is there to tell? That competition in the United States is so cutthroat that cooperation from an existing company is a great advantage?"

I got up and walked the quarterdeck. "Everything is relative, isn't it? Even honesty. No wonder there was alarm and despondency when I shook up Marini. I'm surprised at John."

"John? Why?"

"He has always seemed to me the idealist among us, more concerned for the principles than you or I."

"My dear David, idealism and realism do not mutually exclude each other. Nor are principles necessarily altogether lost in a conflict with the economic facts of life. I was reluctant to attempt the American market. But the attempt has now been made and it appears to be set on the road to success. There is little more to be said."

"Not much more to be said; a lot to be thought."

"As you please."

"Tell me, Shona, if this is a time for confession, what is your real relationship with John?"

The cigarette had smoldered away unsmoked. She often did this.

"John is a dear man. I like and respect him. From the beginning it was something of a *mariage de convenance*, because our abilities complemented so well. I cannot tell you there was ever *passion* between us, but we have played fair by each other. Once in a while he has had a little *affaire*; once or twice I have. He does not quite like that, I have to confess; but he accepts it."

"So that if you had an affair with, say, as an outside example, with me, for instance, there would be nothing too exceptionable about it."

"There might be."

"Nothing, at least, on your conscience so far as John is concerned."

"That is not the hindrance."

"What is, then?"

There was a pause. I was afraid she was going to ask me to take off. If she didn't I was making progress. Then she glanced up at me and I saw that I was making progress.

She said, "No woman is offended by being desired. But it is another matter to yield to that desire. Why do you want this affair, David?"

"I don't want this affair, I want *you*. Is it necessary to say more than that?"

"Try."

"In basic English you're the most exciting woman I've ever seen, and I've hankered after you since the day I met you."

"But you are my—employee. Is that an offensive word?"

"Out of context, yes. In context, no."

"But there, I think, is the danger."

"There's no danger that can't be overcome, Shona."

With long pointed nails she squeezed the cigarette end out of its holder, put the holder away. "We must not be facile, David. We must not use glib words to slide over a serious issue."

"Then say what's in your mind."

"In my mind is my belief that in a sex relationship it is the man who must dominate—or at least be the prime mover in any stable or reasonable variant of the sexual act. It is, as I say, a belief, and it may surprise you. But that is how I see it. But that does not, and never can, apply as far as this business is concerned. There could be no question now, or ever, *or ever*, of your being—dominant, the decider, even of your ever becoming an equal partner. There would therefore be a constant contradiction, an opposing role, to be played between us, one for the day, one for after the day is done. And contradictions are irritants; they cannot fail to be. There is obviously great danger in any such relationship."

"If the danger has been laid on the line, as you've stated it now, it should be much easier to avoid."

She shook her head. "You are not thinking, David. Or shall I say not thinking beyond the next half-hour. I don't believe you love me, even if you know what love is—which I doubt. I certainly do not love you. But when there is a double relationship such as you are proposing, there is no way, I assure you, of one life not coming to intrude upon the other. If things were to go sour for us at night, it would of a certainty affect the day. And vice versa. You have been working for me for well over two years, and although we have differed from time to time it has been easy to accommodate the differences. With this new element intruding it might not be possible to heal the differences, and then you would lose your job and I would lose a man I need and have come to rely on."

I sat beside her again. So close, finger's length, but mustn't touch. Have to face up to her rational mind before you can essay her irrational body.

"D'you realize one reason why everything has run on greased

rails is that all the time I've been in love with you? All right—call it what you fancy—but that's been there, on my side at least, a pressure on me to settle, to give way. Don't you think that if we become lovers it will be all the easier for me to concede—for us both to agree?"

"No," she said.

I laughed.

She sat up straighter, limbs folded, one hand at ease still within a few inches of mine. "I have to make this clear, David. About the business. With John's help in several vital particulars, *I* have created it. It is trivial, I know—as important as that fly on the wall, no more. But I fear it is all I shall ever create. I became too old for ballet; my fencing can never be like Erica Lease, it is just a sport; I am no writer; and only a very amateur pianist. So *this*, this Shona business is all. While I am here, and for a few years after I am gone, it will serve as a flimsy monument. And *while* I am here it shall be preserved to the best of my abilities."

"Who in hell is trying to touch it, to harm it? I'm not."

"Ah, no, but there are various ways of harming. As you know."

I felt she was at her most Russian. Although nearer to me sexually than ever before, she was at her most alien, giving me this grilling out of her deep emotions. It hit me.

"What do you want me to promise? What do you want me to concede now? Shona."

She looked up. "It is what *you* want *me* to concede. Perhaps I do not altogether trust you."

"I don't altogether trust myself," I said, "when you're around."

She shook her head at me sadly. "That came too easily. Not from the heart at all."

"I was told hearts were not going to come into this."

"Not hearts. But not a commitment that is only glib."

At last I put my hand on hers. First time ever. This way. It didn't stir. "I can't match you in argument. If you wanted to you could make John the Baptist sound superficial. But I can tell you, there's nothing glib in my wish to make love to you. I promise you if you'll let me into your bedroom there'll be no need for further talk."

She smiled, but with a downcurving of the mouth. "Sex without intellect? Isn't that for the apes?"

"Still trying to put me off?"

"Yes."

"You don't really fancy me; is that it?"

She looked at my hand on hers, then at me again. "The truth is that I am a little *afraid* of this involvement you suggest. If one jumps in, who knows how deep the water will be?"

"I'm not offering a lifebelt."

"No, I'm sure of that. But I am much older than you, wiser than you, isn't it? I pause to count the risks."

"You've already done that. You were never short on resolution."

"Nor you on persuasion. What are you selling this time, David?"

But I wouldn't be insulted. I put my hands in hers and gently hoisted her to her feet. The movement didn't stop, and the expensive Balmain frock covering the expensive body came along quite readily. We kissed properly for the first time. Her lips didn't feel thin to kiss.

Maybe I should have known better. At least, surprise, surprise, self-advancement wasn't one of my priorities just then. I'd got just a little beyond that.

CHAPTER SEVEN

I After New York, Boston, then Chicago, then San Francisco, then home. Of course everything was different between us, and yet above the board everything was just the same.

It was a wild two weeks in all senses. Insofar as it was in my nature to enjoy things I enjoyed that time. Hock-deep in work and play doesn't leave much time for the morbid stuff.

Maybe it's stretching things to say she was something quite new. All right, she was older than I was, which in some stages can be an advantage. Anyway she had a sort of ageless relish that never became mere lust. Not that I'd have cared at first. She taught me the difference. I thought one night it was like the first time I'd played first-class bridge. It raised your own game.

Coming now so close to her, I couldn't help but wonder more about her age. I guessed she was about fifteen years older than I was, which would make her forty-two. She never mentioned how old she was when she left Russia, or what year it was, and it was such an obvious ploy I wouldn't ask.

We never made love in bright light. She preferred it that way, and it didn't worry me. I've known twenty-year-olds with a similar preference and greater reason.

When we got home it was as if nothing at all had happened, except that John wouldn't speak to me. At first I thought he'd somehow latched on to what had been happening; then I realized it was altogether another set of misdemeanors he had in his craw. The Brotherhood had let him know that I had offended against one of the family. It was settled, of course. No more would be said. But there was a black mark against me. So when I went to the States again I would have to watch my step. Francesco Marini was one of their top men.

This I learned in bits from Shona. I was derisive.

"Feeling there were a few hoodlums looking for me would be stimulating. Helps you to breathe more deeply."

"Sometimes if you breathe too deeply you stop breathing altogether."

"Oh, come. You don't give them credit for a sense of proportion. Of course I know they can kill; it's all part of the legend. But grant them the virtue of common sense. Everything they do is done with a good reason. Or what appears to be a good reason to them."

"Quite. Well, I know you like taking risks, David."

"How?"

"How do I know it? I sense it. It is one of your more agreeable characteristics. But don't allow the temptation to go to your head. If you were to take on the Mafia in any way you would be the loser. Of money, of comfort, or of life."

"Perhaps I could join 'em," I said. "How does one become their favorite nephew?"

She did not reply to this, as if in her opinion it was beneath contempt.

Most Tuesday evenings we'd still go to the fencing together, then I'd take her home to my flat. Later, much later, I would take her to South Audley Street. It was less than half a mile.

Sometimes in the middle of a business spat at Stevenage, with me on one side of her and John Carreros on the other, and circled by the reps, the sales manager, the chemists, all with intent faces, considering the reactions of the average woman to a lip brush instead of a lipstick, or the kind of moisturizing cream best for those who live in central heating, I'd think of the way Shona had been with me the night before. You couldn't relate the person she was now to the naked woman lying twisted on the mat in front of the fire or involved in an octopus of limbs in the half-dark of my bedroom. So I'd got what I wanted, hadn't I? This was what I'd been going straight for three years for, wasn't it? Not a cash-catch this time. Just a woman-catch. Couldn't say I wasn't enjoying it. But on dark nights ugly specters came to tell me it was a letdown.

We were careful in office hours; but Erica Lease soon caught on. She said nothing we could pick up, but there was a knowing glint in her eyes, an acceptance of a situation nobody needed to spell out. Once or twice she picked on me specially for advice or a spot of tuition, as if to challenge Shona, not to fencing but to monopoly of a male.

One night we sat in a corner while Shona was fencing and she said, "So I suppose it's you and Shona now, is it?"

"Has been for a long time. We work well together."

"Oh, yes? That wasn't what I meant. Unless you call it work." She looked me over. "She's picked rather well this time."

"Doesn't she usually?"

"Well, it's a long time since she had a steady. I thought she was maybe giving it up in favor of eurythmics."

My mistress was weaving her way with elegance and grace through a compound riposte.

"Have you known her long?" I asked.

"About six years."

"So you won't have seen her through many steadies?"

"No . . . The only one was Eddie Ludgrove. You know, the Marquess of Ludgrove."

"What broke it up?"

"You'd better ask her! Rumor has it that the duke didn't like it. And sometimes *she* gets tired of her playmates too."

I said, "Do you know John Carreros?"

"I saw him once. Heavy man? That's it. You expecting a knife in the back?"

"Not particularly. Did Eddie Ludgate?"

"Ludgrove. No, he was too important."

"Well, thanks."

"I mean a peer, and all that. They wouldn't, would they?"

"Who's they?"

She was silent a moment, running her hands through her loose fair hair. "One thing I can promise you won't get, and that's a divorce petition."

"Why d'you say that?"

"Carreros would never break up the firm. Shona is his meal ticket."

"Isn't that a bit hard on him? He's done a lot on the laboratory side."

"Which any good chemist could do, I'm told. No, Shona's the magic."

"On that," I said, "I'm inclined to agree."

"I thought you would."

| | A couple of weeks later we went to dinner with Erica.
| II | She had a very big flat on the second floor of a block in
| | Kightsbridge overlooking Hyde Park.

In answer to my raised eyebrows Shona said, "Her father is a biscuit manufacturer. Have you not heard of Lease's Hardbake, Lease's Shortbread? She's his only daughter."

"And lets her have all her own way?"

"Pretty well."

There were ten of us for dinner, and as soon as I got in I saw a tall, craggy-looking chap whose face I vaguely knew. He was untidily dressed—looked as if everything had been thrown on in a fit of absence of mind—but his cultured dogmatic voice and bulbous brilliant eyes seemed to claim and get an immediate circle of attention for himself.

We took drinks and talked and then Erica, virginal in white satin, took me over and said, "Wonder if you two are related? Same name. Both from Scotland, I suppose? Or do you know each other already? Dr. Malcom Abden. Mr. David Abden."

We shook hands, and the man looked me up and down.

"Are you Uncle Stewart's son? Angels and ministers of grace! I think I see a faint resemblance! We're cousins germane, in that case."

His voice was not very cordial, and mine reflected the same warmth.

"*First* cousins?" said Erica. "Never to have *met*? How comical? Can you beat it?"

"I see your name in the papers a lot," I said.

"I see yours from time to time too," he said. "Is that all over now?"

"What all over?" asked Erica.

"A bit of trouble I was in," I explained. "Remind me to tell you about it sometime."

"Oh, I will—I will. Was it scandalous?"

"Ask Malcolm," I said. "He's the expert."

"Oh, I know all about Malcolm," said Erica. "You're the dark horse."

I could see my cousin switch on when he met Shona. A noted

womanizer, he at once gave her the full benefit of his charm. You could understand why he was a success on television, popping up on any program that invited him, so long as it was one that recognized his importance. Warm, witty, old-fashioned, eccentric, authoritative, highly prejudiced and often mildly gassed, he was good value on the screen, at a dinner party or in Parliament. I couldn't remember exactly about the last, but he was soon contradicting someone in the room and denying he was a member. At the recent general election he had lost his seat at North Banff to the SNP.

"SNP," he said, "stands for Scotsmen Never Pay. Never mind: I'm looking for another constituency to nurse. I'll be in again at the next general election."

He was probably forty-three or -four. I should have known, but in fact had kept few tags on my relatives in the Highlands. He talked all through dinner and seemed well informed on when the Americans were going to put another man on the moon, and whether Heath's twenty-odd majority would see him through a full five-year term (personally he hoped not!). He was dead against England going into the European Economic Community; he wanted to ban all future immigration, reintroduce hanging, and was in favor of Rhodesia's declaration of independence. All a fairly normal printout considering his background, but proclaimed with a sort of polemic good humor that took the sting away. Every now and then some turn of phrase got into my hair, but it was not his political opinions, for which I cared nothing either way.

I had to remember what else I knew about him. Like me he'd been to Loretto, and from there had gone on to St. Andrew's and taken a classics degree. Whispers had filtered down that he'd never actually got a doctorate anywhere but had adopted it for himself. A flamboyant marriage with some noble but impoverished laird's offspring; a big family; then some scandal or other and a divorce following on the other side; but his wife, in good Catholic fashion, had not taken her grievances to the courts. She'd died, I remembered, a few years ago and he had remarried, to another Scottish girl, but this time a rich one from the lowlands of Ayrshire.

After dinner somebody mentioned motorcars, and he and I discovered a common interest where the old animosities didn't show. He had owned a 4½-liter Bentley and swore with his usual zeal that it held the road better than any other car there ever was. We rattled on about Alfas and Astons and the like until the coffee and the brandy were done.

One other guest came as quite a surprise. He'd arrived late, just as we were going in to dinner. Derek Jones.

III

Though we broke up late we went straight back to my flat and made love. A sudden need, a crawling demand of the flesh. More than I'd ever felt before. It was heady and startling and not unbrutal.

Afterward I said, "I never knew before that sex was so addictive."

"Ah . . . That is when it is just right . . . You are joking?"

"No, this time I'm not joking. You ought to know."

"I do know. But you are so prone to the throwaway line."

After a pause, "Will John wonder where you are?"

"He's in Madrid. I did not tell you?"

"Think he tumbles?"

"Not yet . . . Tell me, who was that loose-jointed, shambling young man who was almost late for dinner?"

"Derek Jones. The chap I shared a flat with for a few months."

"My God, and you are angry if people take you for one of them? You couldn't have chosen a more obvious one!"

"Coming out of clink you're not too choosy, and he offered me a bed when things were pretty bleak. That adds up to more than a bag of beans."

"What is his background?"

"I don't think his name is Jones; he took it for a whim; says he likes to feel anonymous. He calls himself an underwriter. His father bought him a partnership, or whatever it's called, but I doubt if he ever puts in an appearance."

"What made you leave him? His peculiarity?"

"Not his sexual one. The peculiarity I took exception to was his friendship with Roger Manpole."

"So we are back with him . . . I saw him again only last

week—the first time for a year. Ever more respectable. If you did not know you would not think him crooked from his looks."

"I suppose it depends what you mean by crooked. He's never been into drug pushing or any of the really serious stuff, has he? He's just an off-color money-maker who runs his little companies through nominees."

"Derek Jones is one of them?"

"Not in a permanent sense. But he does the odd thing. They're very friendly and that's not on for me."

"But Roger Manpole offered you work when you came out?"

"D'you know what it was? Being secretary for a company called Saurus. Overseeing their reps."

"Saurus? That is in our line—but cheap."

"Yes. They've got three hundred reps. Suitcase men."

"They're the men who—"

"Yes. They stand in the street with their suitcases in front of the big stores with open copies of *Vogue* magazine showing a full-page color ad for Saurus perfume at fifteen pounds ninety-five a quarter-ounce bottle. And the men say, 'Ladies, here is the same perfume at five ninety-five, and for the first four ladies to buy, only five pounds a time. Exactly and in every way precisely as advertised!' "

"So, yes. So, yes. Tell me how it is a cheat?"

"It's a cheat because one of Roger's other companies, Henry Gervase Ltd., the one that turns out pornographic magazines, prints the advertisement, and clever men insert it into the current numbers of *Vogue* or *Homes and Gardens* or whatever, and the salesmen show it as if it had actually been put in and paid for."

"Surely the law can *stop* that! It is doubly illegal! The magazine can sue and the public can sue. I have always had a great faith in the English law because it is above politics."

"It's above politics, but first you have to catch the rabbit and then you have to skin him. Can you imagine a judge saying: 'Am I to understand this prosecution has been brought solely on the allegation that spurious pages were inserted in a certain magazine?' After all the public are getting five pounds' worth of perfume for every five pounds they pay."

Shona snorted. "And he offered you *this*?"

"Not to be a suitcase man but to be in charge of 'em—their boss. Good money. Not much less than you're paying me now."

"We will have to look into that . . . Anyway you behaved quite well tonight."

"I see; good for a raise."

"You did not clutch anybody by the throat, nor smash any glasses. *Almost* polite to your *cousin!* Can it be that you are really on the mend?"

"The mend from what?"

"I do not know. You will not tell me. At least on the mend."

"You're out of your tiny," I said.

"Maybe." She laughed—or coughed. "Well, tell me more about your cousin."

"Nothing I know."

"I thought he was delightful." She paused. "*How* does he come into the family? Is he a first cousin?"

"Oh yes. I've told you all I know."

"You've told me *nothing.*"

"What is there to say? My family—on my father's side—comes from the west coast of Scotland. Catholics, always have been, never changed. Lochfiern House. Far north. Near Ullapool. Nicholas Abden was made a baronet in the time of James II—of England, that is. It still goes on. The present one is Sir Charles Abden. My father was his younger brother, Stewart. There's a brood of 'em up there now. Stewart, my father, never conformed; God knows why. He went in for motor racing, won a few things, married my mother, ran through what money he had and then through hers. He became a real estate agent—quite successful— but took to drink. Or maybe it would be truer to say he went in for it more earnestly. He died when I was eleven—result of a fall."

"And Malcolm Abden is the heir to the baronetcy?"

"You have it."

"So that is what I have suspected. *You* are the true aristocrat, not I."

I grunted. "Maybe we should bring out a Scottish moisturizing cream which has been the closely guarded secret of the Abden clan since the days of Mary Queen of Scots. How was it Mary retained her beauty so long and was able to captivate the handsome and daring young men who came to visit her from Elizabeth's court? *Only* because of the secrets passed on to her in her captivity by Sir Nicholas Abden whose secret formula—"

Shona put her fingers on my lips. "What is it like, this area of England? I have not been north of Glasgow."

"No idea."

"D'you mean you have never been yourself?"

"That's right."

"Never met your other cousins? Surely that is a strange way to behave even in this coldhearted country."

I turned over against her. "I have to tell you, Shona, that the Abden family didn't at all approve of my mother; so when my father married her the family cut off all communication with him. He'd finally gone to the devil, they thought."

"Why, what is wrong with her?"

"First, she was English, which would have been a bitter pill anyway. But what put her right outside the gates was that she was a Jewess."

There was a long silence. Then Shona breathed out gently through her nose. "Is that true?"

"Certainly is."

"Incredible! Quite incredible. But when was this—a generation, two generations ago! What were they: Nazis?"

"Not quite. My uncle went through the war as a captain of the Argyll's. He got the Military Cross and bar. My other uncle, Robert, was killed at Arnhem. My father tried to enlist but was turned down . . . You don't latch on to some of the old families up there—particularly the Catholic ones. They take immense pride in having survived through everything: wars, persecutions, rebellions, the lot; so it's especially important, they think, when they marry to keep the strain pure, and to keep the religion pure."

"You're explaining very well."

"I'm not. It's crap. But I'm explaining how they think. For a Catholic Abden to marry a Jew was pretty much the end. He'd have been as popular if he'd married Gandhi's mother."

"And so you've never been to see them?"

"Nor ever will."

"But you met your cousin this evening for the first time! Must the prejudice endure even in this generation?"

"I would think so. My prejudice against *them* does. And yet . . ."

"Yet?"

"I might put him to some use."

"That sounds very calculating."

"So it is. You mentioned the other day about our never having supplied the Royal Household. I'm sure he'd have connections or will know someone who has. I'll ring him next week."

"I think from what he said that he had heard you had been in trouble. That may add to his—er—prejudices."

"No matter. I can overcome them."

"How?"

"Just by being persuasive."

"Yes, by God," she said, looking Russian. "You can be that!"

There was a long silence. She lit a cigarette.

"You know I have a father in Paris?"

"Yes, of course."

"Also a brother. I go over to see my father from time to time. When I came west, after I had begun to establish myself, my one aim was to have some of my family *rejoin* me. It was like the labor of Hercules to get them out. One. Then the other. Oh, the trouble! But I have run away from the Soviets and their prejudices, not expecting to find them here!"

"Don't pretend these are the first prejudices you've come across in the West . . . Anyway, if you are so family-minded, why don't you have your father in England?"

"He will not come. He speaks French—badly and laboriously, but he speaks it. He cannot master English at all. *And* he is deaf. And my brother has established a taxi service. Training to be a doctor in Russia . . . he began by driving a taxi in Paris. Now he owns a fleet and is well off. That is why they do not join me—not from absurd, infantile prejudices and resentments about *race*."

"All right," I said after a minute. "I told you my family is mad."

"No, you did not. But I have been seeking to find why you have this—what do you call it—chip."

"A chip off the old block," I said.

"Now you are only trying to confuse me. Is this—this family feud the reason why you dislike Scotsmen?"

"Not altogether. But perhaps, to some extent."

"But then you are disliking a part of yourself! You are half Highland Scottish. You are tearing yourself asunder!"

"Asunder," I said, "is not in colloquial use nowadays. You might say: 'split down the bleeding middle.' "

"However you describe it, that is the fact of the matter."

"Why should you worry?"

"Because I believe you would be a better human being if you came to terms with yourself."

"And better in bed?"

She sat up slowly, wiped her lips carefully with a tissue. "It depends how you mean the word. Not physically, of course. But if you were a more complete human being, then that must be so. Sometimes when we are making love—even tonight when it has been so special—I see a look on your face almost of hostility. Almost as if you disliked me—or disliked the act."

"Certainly not the last," I said. "Not even the first. But don't you think in sex there ought to be an element of conflict?"

"Conflict is another word. Not if there is something destructive in the conflict."

"You think I am destructive?"

"I think you're lonely. And you can't cure that except from within."

"David the old schizo," I said. "Abden and Hyde. What more d'you want? Two for the price of one?"

"No, it is not that *at all*," she said in vexation. "And you know it is not or you would not suggest it . . . I want to know, or to find out, if I can, why you dislike people."

"Who said I did? I can assure you—or reassure you if that's better—that in spite of the element of conflict you seem to detect in our lovemaking, I certainly do not dislike *you*."

She sighed. "That is something to know. You see—it is so dangerous—you have this infinite charm you can put on at will. I suppose you are going to essay it with your cousin—in whom, God help me, I detect some likeness! But there are few if any people you really *like*. A small number you tolerate; but as for the rest . . . Only someone who has come to know you as much as I do can have any idea what you think of the rest. Because the charm goes quite deep. It is hard to see through it. But when one does see through it . . . one shivers."

I kissed her. "Dangerous character."

"Yes . . . dangerous. And horr-ible. And since I am a person who in general is attached to the laws of cause and effect I am seeking, have been seeking . . ." She stopped and laughed. "No doubt I am out of my tiny. Is that what you said?"

"Like me to stretch out on a couch?"

"You are already stretched out."

"Carry on, Mrs. Freud."

"How can one carry on in the face of such—derision? Of course I am arguing in circles myself. But you don't *care* enough, you don't *feel* enough—perhaps not even for yourself. You—you are like a Buddhist, but for the wrong reasons!"

"Well, stone me," I said. "What trip are we off on now?"

She saw my eyes going over her and pulled the sheet to cover herself.

"A Buddhist cares little for this world because he believes, so long as his life here is based on good moral precepts, that what happens to him in it is unimportant. You care little for this world, care so little what *happens*, below a certain shallow level, *not* because you are developing and following your Karma but either because it does not exist or because it is hidden behind a wall, buried too deep to be got at!"

"It doesn't exist," I said. "Haven't you noticed I have no reflection in the mirror? Makes shaving difficult."

After a few moments she sighed. "Oh, well, that is how it is, I suppose. It just seems . . . such a waste."

"A waste of what?"

"A human being."

"Well, thanks a million."

"Perhaps," she said, "it shows I am beginning to care a little. And that is even more perilous."

CHAPTER EIGHT

I went to see Malcolm. I have as horny a sense of pride as any Highland Scot, but I can put it under wraps for the special occasion. This was the special occasion. He wasn't too hail-fellow when I rang, and still less so when I called. Looking as big, as disheveled and as impressive as ever, he said he'd had a busy day, there was a long evening ahead of him and he was traveling north tomorrow; but I managed to outflank the early pockets of resistance and got him talking about cars again and advising me what to buy. Then I persuaded him to walk round the corner to Claridge's, where I bought him a series of champagne cocktails and led him to tell me about himself and his family. Having got up to the right atmospheric pressure, and made it clear to him by a number of casual references to titled people that my present social standing was not despicable, I brought the subject round to the purpose of my visit.

He wasn't enthusiastic, to say the least, and his eyes, like unlit electric lightbulbs too big for their sockets, ranged round the ornate room for some subject more interesting than the one I'd brought up. He found it in a young blonde who had just come in in a dashing scarlet velvet cocktail frock with a split skirt and choker pearls.

"Damned good-looking girl," he muttered.

"Yes," I said. "I know her."

He looked at me doubtfully. "What? You do?"

I didn't, in fact, but I knew her by sight. I'd seen her somewhere before.

She took a table by herself, and a waiter brought her a drink. They exchanged a few words. She looked toward the door.

"Excuse me." I walked circuitously toward the restaurant and stopped the waiter. A five-pound note changed hands.

"Miss Adamson?" he said. "Miss Rona Adamson. She comes in quite frequent. I think she's a dancer."

That was it, of course. I went across to her.

"Miss Adamson. I wonder if you remember me? David Abden. We met at Lady Rowton's."

She looked at me, and her eyes, from being cold, became less so.

"Lady Rowton's?" she said. "I don't think I *know* Lady Rowton."

"Could I be mistaken? It's Miss Rona Adamson, isn't it? Would it be at the Bellevilles', then?"

"I *do* know Mary Belleville, but I don't remember—"

"I'm sure you're expecting a friend, Miss Adamson. But I wondered if you could make our day by sparing five minutes to meet my cousin first? Dr. Malcolm Abden. He was most anxious to meet you. Of course you'll have seen him on TV."

"Well . . . I *am* expecting someone. I don't think I should—"

"For five minutes only," I said. "Or less, if your friend arrives. It would give us so much pleasure."

After a bit more stop-go she rose and came across to our table. We had, I would guess, more than seven minutes of pleasant chitchat from which the sexual element was never entirely absent; then her friend—who looked like an American film producer—came in and bore her away.

We settled to our fifth cocktail.

Eventually Malcolm said grudgingly, "There's a fellow called Arthur, Gilbert Arthur, who's Controller of the Royal Household. Of course you could just write to him, impersonally, send samples of your products, ask for their patronage . . ."

"Or?"

"Or—if you wish—well, on the whole—you could write first to Sir Frederick Lukey—mentioning my name—it would help matters along. He's the man, as it were, who *oversees* all these things."

"I'll do that."

"But don't forget it will cost you something."

"Cost me something?"

"Your firm. Not money, of course. Nothing so vulgar. But gifts in kind. It's an accepted practice. After all, many of these people—controllers and the like—are very ill paid. The tradition has been long established. It can all be done very discreetly."

"Thank you, Malcolm. You've been very kind."

We separated with a degree of warmth hardly imaginable ninety minutes ago. He even said he thought his father, old Sir Charles, might be interested to meet me if I ever happened to be passing their way. I said I'd be delighted to do this sometime, not having the slightest intention of going near them.

"By the way," I said, signaling for the bill, "I've put a few things together. Some Dryad perfumes. And our latest, Faunus. We thought your wife might find them useful. I've left them in the cloakroom. I'll give them to you as you go."

"Thank you," said Malcolm, without blinking an eyelid. "My *new* wife, in fact," he added, with a little satisfied smile. "Yes, she'll be pleased to have them."

Within six months we were supplying soaps, bath essences and perfumes to the Royal Household. Whether they went to royal personages or were shared out among the staff didn't much matter. It was simply that we could claim the accolade. Shona was very pleased with me.

II In spite of all our teamwork in the shafts, sometimes out of step but generally jogging in the same direction, in spite of the success of what we did and the sense of getting somewhere that went with it, I never felt Shona's equal. It was the same old stone in the jam, the thorn in the shoe. One thing was that John and she still owned the business. I was an employee—decently paid but on a salary. (Having become her lover hadn't changed *that*.) But mainly it was the strength of her personality. She'd been in the business longer; everyone thought she was the tops. And I had this continuing old spur sticking in my flanks of knowing her intellectually that much ahead of me and no way of making up the ground. Her taste was better, her culture deeper rooted; nearly always it was her judgment that created a product with an appearance of higher quality than those of her rivals. It wasn't something she'd learned—I could have dealt with that; it was innate. Sometimes she put the stamp of her yes or no on a point at issue and wouldn't condescend to say why. Maybe she couldn't put it into words, but often and often she was shown to be right. I suppose you can't build up a business of that sort without a flair, a touch of genius. Well, she had it, but it didn't make me easy under the bit.

Yet our affair went on and continued to work. In fact just to say it worked would be the understatement of the year. When I saw her again after a break of a few days my mouth would go dry; and I knew she was pretty far gone down the same road herself. While it lasted like this the friction had to be smoothed over, the blue touch paper frizzled out with the firecracker unlit.

I saw Derek still occasionally, and out of one of my meetings with him came the notion to set up a little private limited company of my own, just to make a bit on the side. Kilclair Ltd. I called it, which is my middle name. I suppose you could say it all grew out of my adolescent resentment of her superiority, but I preferred to consider it as a perfectly legitimate and logical development of my position in the firm.

Every perfumery business has its unsuccessful lines from time to time, or overproduces on a successful one, or for one reason or another has surplus stock it wants to get rid of. In those days all the high-class producers simply ditched the stuff, so that nothing of theirs ever came on the market cheap. Ever since I knew about it this had distressed my Scottish-Jewish blood. I decided that Shona Ltd. should sell their surplus stuff to Kilclair Ltd. at a knockdown price and Kilclair Ltd. should sell it cheap in the north country factories where no one would ever notice. Result, profit for Kilclair Ltd., and much better than a total loss for Shona Ltd. I knew it wouldn't appeal to Shona, who had this frightful preoccupation with exclusiveness and cost. However, as far as I could see, she need never know the favor I was doing her.

I made Derek a director—I owed him something, and this was the sort of extra perk he would appreciate. The other director was Crack—now Van—Morris. Since he joined the firm he had been living an exemplary life—in office hours anyway—and he'd found himself a girlfriend from somewhere and was going steady. Since his hope of promotion in his present job was nil, this would be a

profitable side-shoot for him without extra work, except the occasional weekend driving stuff up north.

All this time I never knew Shona's age, which showed some
ingenuity on her part and some lowered eyelids on mine because,
traveling abroad as we sometimes did, it was a question of filling
up forms on aircraft, having your passport quizzed, sometimes
handing the passports in at the hotel and then these being casually
returned when you next collected the key to the rooms.

Except when away, she kept to the same routine: an hour at
the clinic every morning for face and body massage, and a week
every three months in a health hydro in Sussex; fencing one or
two evenings a week. She ate precious little but wasn't really thin
in a way that mattered. (Actually, in spite of being careful not to
be seen in bright lights, she always looked younger without her
clothes.)

When we went to Paris she took me to a tiny flat in Montparnasse
where her father lived with a middle-aged niece to look after him.
He was a tall bearded old boy, very deaf, and looked like Tolstoy.
The flat was chock with Russian books and furniture that looked
as if it had come from a stage set of *The Cherry Orchard*. He had
been a schoolteacher until he offended Beria's secret police. Because of her father's disgrace Shona Maraskaya Pantelevitch had
not been evacuated from Moscow with the Bolshoi—instead had
stayed on and seen the war through, losing her mother from
pneumonia and two brothers in Poland. Old Pantelevitch had a
small crackly fire burning, and she sat cross-legged before it warm-
ing her hands while the light danced on the skin of face and neck.
"That second year of our war," she said, "it was the coldest winter
ever, and my mother was ill. Of course the pipes had long since
frozen and burst. I brought in bricks and mortar and built a stove
in the middle of our living room. It was smoky but it was heat.
Fuel? Oh, the fuel was our furniture."

When I came back that year from my holiday in Barbados she
said, "David, do you find there sometimes younger women to
your taste?"

"I'm a lazy man. I can't be fished."

"You go so regularly I wonder if you have a special favorite
there."

"If I had, d'you think three weeks a year would keep the battery
charged?"

She slanted her eyes at me. "Maybe yes. Maybe no. In all your life you have calculation."

"Have me watched," I suggested. "Private eyes could go on business expenses."

"You stay at the same hotel always?"

"Yes. You get to know people who come each year."

"Sometime I should like to meet them."

"Of course," I said insincerely, and then, to duck the searching glance, I got up and lit a cigarette. "Sun and sea are what I look for, not conquests."

"But if you find one without looking? . . . No, don't answer. It is all private. I must not ask. Indeed, my question was a general one, not a particular one."

"I've forgotten what it was."

"No, you haven't."

"Well, then, the answer is no."

A day or two later she brought up the subject again.

"You must meet many women younger than I."

"How'm I supposed to answer that?"

She brooded a moment. "By saying yes."

"Then yes."

She said, "I think of all the pretty girls who represent us in the shops. Nubile young women—isn't that the fashionable phrase? You go among them often. I see their eyes follow you. You would only need to raise a finger. I heard two talking of you the other day. It was very naive but very sensuous."

"You're killing me."

She turned her head away. "Ah, well . . ."

"Well what?" I said. "Aren't you content? I am. Age is not as important as you think."

"Thank you. But in some ways it must be. Do you know, I have no fear of death at all. It means *nothing*. But I have the greatest fear of becoming old."

"Growing old like your father?"

"Oh, no . . . Not like that. When I am his age maybe I shall be reconciled. No, it is the growing old before that—in the next ten years, or whenever it may be. I know I am good-looking. All my life I have been good-looking. I remember the first time going into a restaurant with my father and mother when I was twelve: men stared. My mother was quite upset; she thought it was bad for me, me being so young. My father said, 'Are you surprised, Elena Maraskaya? I am not surprised.' Ever since then." Shona breathed through her nose. "Ever since then. When I go into any public place people look—not just men, people. I enjoy it! It is meat and drink to me. So I dread, as if it were the cholera, coming to a stage when that will no longer be. When I shall have all the emotions and desires of a woman and find my body has become a shell. If one could so regard it, it would be funny. As in a nightmare I dread the time when I shall walk into a restaurant and all the men will continue to eat their roast beef!"

"Well," I said, "you don't need to worry just yet. That is, if you can bear to take the opinion of one man."

She kissed me. "Do you know in France they call a nightmare a *cauchemar*? I often think it should be translated as bed-mare."

"I know one or two women like that," I said.

She laughed, comforted, and began to dress.

If I'd had a conscience this time, it was not about another woman. In fact, I'd had only ten days in Barbados. The previous ten had been taken up visiting various factories on behalf of Kilclair Ltd. and in getting the venture on the move. Derek didn't have the patience or the talent to go around, and Van Morris hadn't the appearance, though he was fine for delivering the goods. Once the thing got going it could be slotted into my ordinary routine.

For my ordinary routine meant a good bit of traveling, even just round England. At Shona's I now needed two more men, and we took them on. John Marks and Leo Longford were both young and eager, Marks having been in advertising, Longford with Elizabeth Arden.

In spite of our early success, the Shona line didn't really quite take off in America as we'd expected; it became a goodish market, and after a year or so it cleared the initial outlay; but the figures never went over the top. Shona never came up with any suggestion that my quarrel with Marini had a bearing on these results, and probably it didn't, because once a thing is in the shops it stands or falls by the quality of the stuff and the way it is put over in advertising. But sometimes peculiar things happened, and I wondered.

About this time I fell into the habit of spending one evening a week with Shona without the bedroom as the ultimate end in view. Sometimes we went to a foreign film but more often were just together in her flat. We'd eat a lazy meal and talk a bit or read, or she would play the piano, which she did well if you accepted that her range was limited. A bit of the simpler Bach or Scarlatti, or more often people like Scott Joplin, who was just then coming back into favor.

In my travels in England I'd been to Leeds a dozen times since I took on the job but had never gone to Quemby. There was nothing there for me. But one thing and another now made me think about a call. Meeting Shona's father. And meeting my own cousin; weakening of the old Abden resolve, so to speak. But the real reason—was it excuse?—was this fencing business.

I had been fretted to find myself outpointed by relative beginners, and particularly by people like Shona and Erica Lease, who were women and therefore should have been disadvantaged and yet could more or less pick me off at will. At Loretto I'd fancied my chances as a fencer. I suppose the problem in Kensington was that I was too big-headed to take lessons from the various experts there and thought I could get on without them. I couldn't—or I didn't quickly enough. I knew that in my old room in Burton House, Quemby, there should be three books on fencing I'd bought when I was about eighteen, all by a chap called Roger Crosnier, and called *Fencing with the Foil*, *Fencing with the Epée*, and *Fencing with the Sabre*. I'd tried to buy them in London recently and was told they were out of print. At the time—when I'd first bought them and read them—I'd thought them good. If it could be done, it would be nice to improve my style without lining up some tutor.

It was September when I was next in Leeds, and I thought whether to call when they were all out and bully a maid into letting me into my old room. But it was nearly eight years since I'd been back—in these days there might well not even *be* a maid—and anyway one did not have to act as if one were scared of the family. Chances were by the eighteenth of September the two lumpish girls would be back at their academies, and if I called in the early afternoon old Kingsley would be at his office in the city wrestling with contractual torts. That left only Mother. I could, I thought, face a brief and solitary encounter with Mother.

It was a showery day, and I drove out in my new Aston Martin DB6, a car I'd discussed with Malcolm and bought earlier in the year. It had the Vantage engine and a manual gearshift, which was so much faster as a car and sweeter to drive than the automatic version, except that it had a pig of a clutch. I wondered if Mother remembered the days when we used to have hairy cars. Old Kingsley, though rich enough, usually drove a Rover not much younger than himself.

Quemby is halfway between Leeds and Harrogate and just off the A658. The Kingsley house was about a mile from the village in a group of six large houses built probably in the twenties. The fat car tires crunched over the loose shingle of the drive as I drew up in front of the oak door with its stained-glass panels and hanging lantern. A feature of the house was a big fan window on the first floor which lit up the hall and staircase. It had stopped raining, but the heavy beech trees dripped into little pools formed in the drive. I saw there was a Volvo in the double garage, which was a hopeful sign.

I rang the bell, which went ding-dong. Somehow you would have thought they would have grown out of that. A dog barked.

A lady in her early fifties came to the door. A green-flowered apron over a pink silk and lace afternoon frock. She'd put on weight since I saw her last.

"Hullo, Mother," I said.

She swallowed a couple of pebbles, stared at me as if I were a ghoul.

"David!" she said, her expression tentative changing for the better. "What a *surprise*! Whatever brings you here?"

"Passing," I said. "Thought I'd call."

"Come *in*! You gave me quite a *shock*. I was expecting someone else. At least, I thought they were early but I thought it must be them." She stood aside and I went in.

I looked round the hall. Nothing much changed. I kissed her. She was using L'Interdit.

"Come in here," she said, leading the way into what I suppose Kingsley would call the lounge.

"Ah," I said, "you've had it redecorated. And that's a nice Georgian table."

"Yes, Kenneth and I picked it up near Knaresborough. Got it very cheap. Of course it was in bad condition. He put a lot of work in on it. Kenneth is very clever with his hands."

"And a new dog," I said, as a terrier came waggling in.

"Yes, that's Sandy," said Mother, standing cautiously in the doorway. "Perry got a canker in his ear."

Extra weight made her more Jewish-looking: it was in the flared nostrils, the eyelids, the curve of the lips. Still very handsome but no longer the woman I had once been in love with. And the expression in her fine eyes was not really the expression for a woman regarding her firstborn.

"Have I come at a bad time?"

"No, not really, David. Pleased to *see* you. As a matter of fact I have three ladies coming for bridge today, but they shouldn't be here for half an hour yet. I was just—cutting some sandwiches."

I said, "Do you still have a maid?"

"Only in the mornings."

"Then I'll come in the kitchen while you finish off."

"Oh, no, I couldn't let you do *that*! Are you staying long? You could stay the *night*. Kenneth will be back at six."

"I have to be on my way. Actually I came just to pick up one or two of my things."

"Things?" she said. "What things? There wasn't much . . . you didn't leave much behind."

"Chiefly books," I said, propelling her into the kitchen. "No, I didn't leave a lot behind. I don't gather much moss."

She stood over the table. Smoked salmon and brown bread and butter. She made a move or two to continue, but her fingers were a bit of a jumble. She looked at the pink carnation I was wearing.

"How are the girls?" I said.

"Oh, *fine*! Edna's the brainy one. We hope she'll get into Oxford and read Law. But of course it's early days yet. Marjorie is the pretty one, but—"

"Takes after you, I suppose."

She didn't smile. "I was going to say, but has no head for schooling. Perhaps she's like me in that too."

"And me," I said.

"Oh, you've a *good* head, David; always have had. The trouble was you wouldn't *use* it. Least, not in the—the ways you should have . . ."

I patted Sandy, who had followed us. "Thanks for the letters when I was in jail. Did I reply? I don't remember."

She seemed shocked that I could mention it so casually. "No."

"Sorry. It was just the feeling from what you wrote that you'd given me up as a bad job."

"There was no reason to think *that*! But Kenneth felt it was such a pity, with all your advantages . . ."

"Yes, I was never one you could make up a hard-luck story about. The judge thought the same."

She said, "This perfumery firm you're working for. Shona Ltd. Are you doing well?"

"Yes."

"I'm *glad*. I've read about this Mme. Shona. What is she like?"

"All right."

"I expect she's like Coco Chanel, isn't she? I once read a book about Coco Chanel. She was always philandering with some titled person or other."

"Well, it can happen."

"What's your position in the firm?"

"Sales manager."

"So you see something of her?"

"From time to time." I said, "Look, you want to finish those sandwiches, so, how about me going upstairs and seeing if I can find what I want while you fix them. You don't need to show me the way—"

"Oh, but I *do*," she said with a defensive look. "The—the girls often have people here, so we decided to turn your bedroom into a second guest room. We've—had it redecorated and refurnished. We didn't think it likely you'd want to come back . . ."

I said lightly, "And the bits and pieces? Were they thrown out?"

"Of *course* not! At least, nothing of any *value*. You know the loft?"

"Yes."

"Up there there's a tin box. It belonged to Kenneth's father. It's got J.K.K. on the outside. Everything of yours was put in there. Probably any of your books—"

"I'll go up and see while you're organizing the feast. Coming, boy?" I said to the dog, who was looking expectant.

"Don't forget," she called. "The ladder pulls down, you know. Perhaps I'd better show you—"

"Nonsense. I remember it."

"I can make you coffee if you want. The kettle's always hot on the Aga. Or a drink . . ."

"Coffee I'll have. In ten minutes."

The house had a peculiar smell; houses do; this one was reminiscent of those last years at home; furniture polish, new chintz, vacuumed dust, central heating; not at all like my first home in Leeds. Only the Aga stove was the same. Mother was a great believer in them. God knows, you'd think she might have changed her preferences. The ladder pulled down and I went up. Sandy whined at the bottom so I went back and carried him up with me. He scrabbled at the edge and then launched himself into the roof; more happily after I had found the light.

The metal trunk was a big one, and you wondered how many trees had been cut down to provide all the wills, the deeds and the rest of the legal wastepaper that had once been in there. The three books were at the top; I fished them out and put them on one side to carry down, fingered through the rest of my stuff. Mostly useless: a cricket bat, a tennis racket now warped, a certificate I'd won for—of all things—fencing; some other books, gym shoes, motoring gloves. I took the gloves.

There were things in it not mine—a photograph album which must have belonged to the Kingsley family. A thin folder with a flap—inside some newspaper cuttings. I began to read them, at first not realizing.

> The inquest was resumed yesterday on the death of Mr. Stewart Kilclair Abden, aged 43, of 121 Avenue Road, Horsforth, who died at his house on the third inst. Mrs. Rachel Abden (31), in describing the quarrel which had developed on the evening of that day, said her husband had been drinking before he came home and was worried about money. Their eleven-year-old son, David, was present, and Abden began to threaten him. A struggle ensued, in the course of which Abden fell backward, turning as he did so, and injured himself fatally by striking his head on the bar of the kitchen stove . . .

Fold the news cutting and slide it back into the folder. "Death by Misadventure," that's what they'd said. He'd fallen forward against the damned Aga and cracked his damned skull. Nothing peculiar about that, was there? For Christ's sake, that was the way it had happened.

Only you'd think Mother would have been put off Agas, not shoving another conveniently in her new house.

Of course it hadn't ended there. Some of the cess press, as Shona called them, had had more to say. One here: "Baronet's nephew dies in kitchen brawl." That was ingenious—brought to mind in a single headline a picture of aristocrats in a saturnalia of debauchery between the fridge and the cooker.

Pictures too. Somebody'd been around buying up old snapshots.

When I got down the sandwiches were done. I helped her bear them in and cover them with foil, flip the card table up. In spite of becoming fatter she still had wonderful legs.

She said, "You used to play bridge, David."

"Still do when I've the time."

"You were only nine when you began. Remember? With those neighbors. What was—"

"Waters. It was family bridge but a grounding. I made good use of it the last two years I was in school."

"You shouldn't have, you know. That's been the trouble all along . . ."

"I've been a write-off for you, haven't I, Mother dear. But you always used to stand up for me in the old days."

Faint beads of sweat showing through the powder on her forehead. Hair still as black as ever; quite hard to see the touching up.

I said, "Death by Misadventure. That was the verdict."

"Don't, David," she said, frowning, glancing out of the window as if someone might hear.

"After all if a man gets pissed and falls and bangs his damned head, what else can it be?"

"You've never mentioned it before?" she said. "All these years! I was hoping you'd *forgotten*. The only sane, sensible way is to forget."

"I've been reading the newspaper clippings in the trunk."

She put her hand to her mouth and drew in a breath. "Oh, I didn't *know*! I didn't know anything like that had been kept—"

"Perhaps Kenneth kept them. After all, it's a lawyer's job to hang on to all the junk. Might come in handy some day."

We listened to the tap-tap of Sandy's tail as it polished the parquet floor.

She said, "I'm *sorry*, David, I expect seeing something like that upsets you. If I'd *dreamed* there was anything like that lying about I should *never* have let you go up."

"It refreshes the memory."

"Oh dear, oh dear." She bit her knuckles. "I shall never be able to concentrate this afternoon."

"Are they good, these ladies?"

"Not by your standards."

"Is my coffee ready?"

"Oh, my God, yes! I made it and, forgot about it."

I fetched it from the kitchen and we almost bumped into each other in the door.

"David," she said indignantly.

"Yes?"

"As we have never spoken about this ever since, I just want to say, to tell you, before we stop speaking of it, that I *did* try to protect you, both that night, and in court!"

"Did I need your protection?"

She moved away from me, as if she thought I might be going to touch her again, went back into the lounge.

I said, "I suppose I've become a bit of a bogeyman, haven't I? It would be pretty grim for you if I kept turning up unexpectedly like this."

She said, "Stewart wasn't very drunk that night, you know."

"What are you trying to say?"

"Nothing, David. Except that it was a tragedy all round. I can't say *more*. And best forgotten. Best *utterly* forgotten."

I sipped the coffee. "Eleven's a middling age, isn't it. It's not quite the age of responsibility and yet it's past the age of irresponsibility."

"I don't want to talk about it any more! I won't *listen* to you, David, I won't listen! It upsets me too much even to think of that time. Dr. Meiss said we must both put it all behind us . . ."

"Old Meiss wasn't much use about that, was he? But I'll hand it to him, he straightened me out on a few points. You were very patient, all that year. It was all voluntary, wasn't it?"

"It was all voluntary. And very expensive. You don't get on with your stepfather, but if you only knew how much you owe him . . . He helped us both so much at that time."

"How?"

"I don't want to explain any more! Only to say I couldn't have done without him!"

It occurred to me to say, well, you haven't *had* to do without him; but she was breathless and flushed.

"Look," I said, "I didn't come here to cangle, as Father used to say; I came for three books; and I've got 'em. As soon as the first of your dames shows over the horizon I'll slip out of the back door. Then you won't have to introduce the gray sheep of the family."

"I never wanted you to be *that*," she said. "You had no reason to be! I do hope now that you will—will—"

"Go straight?"

"I was going to say live a happy normal life. Why don't you get *married*? Most men are married at your age. Having a wife and a family, that helps to give one stability. Do you have a girlfriend?"

"One or two."

"I suppose these days marriage is becoming unfashionable. People just live together . . . But I assure you, David, nothing is better than marriage. It makes for a stable relationship. Do you intend to stay with this perfumery firm?"

"For the time being."

"So you have settled in London?"

"More or less."

She bit her lip in vexation as if she thought I was being vague just to annoy her. "I'm only trying to think what's *best* for you."

"I'm trying to do the same thing, Mother dear." I finished the coffee and put the mug down; then picked it up again, knowing she wouldn't want it left here. "I met a cousin of mine last year. Malcolm Abden, the future baronet."

"Oh, those people! You know they never have communicated with me at all. Not even when your father died. Nor ever since. I hope you showed him what you felt about them."

"I don't go big for poseurs, but somehow he got through as rather entertaining. I could meet him again without too much pain. Anyway I was able to put the meeting to some use."

She looked at me. "Not—that sort of use?"

I said, "Oh, Mother, you do give a dog a bad name. I wonder, Sandy here, can stick it . . . Is that a car?"

It was. A Ford Escort Sport in blue was just crunching to a stop in front of the door. Not far behind was a Hillman Hunter. Her friends were spot on.

"So I'll go now," I said, gathering up the books. "You can let me out before you let them in, and then I can scuttle round the front while they're taking their coats off."

"You've no need to do that *at all*, David," she said, nevertheless leading the way for me to do it. "They'd be pleased to *meet* you! I don't think it's right for you to sneak away like a—like a—"

"A thief?" I said. "Never mind, that's just what I will do."

I kissed her on the cheek. I squeezed her arm and winked at her as she let me out, carefully not allowing Sandy to follow.

After standing admiring the chrysanthemums for a couple of minutes, I walked round to the front. I got in my car and drove away as the third car turned in at the gate.

She hadn't noticed my new car, and I hadn't given her the Shona perfumes I had brought.

III

I did a hundred and forty a good part of the way home on the M1.

It's interesting, that speed on a public highway. A pedestrian bridge in the distance arrives very quickly on your scene. The church of a bypassed village rears its spire over the hill and is gone. The contours of the land change while you watch. Decisions, like points ahead, have to be arrived at sharply. Interesting also is the fact that the cars you are overtaking in the middle lane are in fact approaching you at about seventy mph.

For a Tuesday afternoon the motorway was not busy, and I probably did the trip in good time.

CHAPTER NINE

I That night I went fencing again with Shona and Erica and the rest. Though I hadn't so much as opened the three books, I found myself doing better.

After all, fencing is an aggressive sport. It has become more so with the development of the épée and, so Erica said, under the recent influence of the Hungarians and the Russians. At school it had been pretty well controlled to the scoring of technical points by the foil; footwork, style, stroke and counterstroke, observing the rules and conventions of right of way. With épée there are no restrictions as to target: It's more like a duel than a dance.

That evening I felt aggressive enough to take anyone on, and did in fact have two bouts with men normally much better than I was, in one of which I floored my opponent with what Erica afterward sarcastically called "a right hook." The chap took it very well, but he called off the bout, saying he thought a couple of his teeth were loose. The other man beat me 9 to 7.

Afterward Shona said, "John wants you to take him to Bristol tomorrow."

"Whatever for?"

"To see TBM Ltd. Pray do not ask me to tell you what the initials mean. You have heard of them, of course."

"German, aren't they?"

"Their head office is in Hamburg. But they've been expanding in England for some time. Now they are offering us special services and discounts. Naturally it is only a way of trying to break into the market, but I do not think competition will be a bad thing, and ICI and Lawson's have been a little less than obliging sometimes. They still do not quite see us as competitors in the mass market."

"Did John ask that *I* should take him?"

"Yes."

"He doesn't like me, Shona."

"That is true."

"Of course he knows about us."

"He has learned to live with such a situation before. He has not been faultless. Usually we are civilized about such things. Perhaps if you come to know him better you will like each other more."

"Why don't you come along? It would be much easier with you there."

"Do you think so? I doubt it. Anyway, I understand they use animals for some of their tests, and, while I recognize the value of such tests, I do not wish to witness them."

I said contentiously, "Why don't you follow Yardley's practice of not employing any animal-derived scents at all?"

"It is too restricting. Maybe all right for them. Too restricting for us."

I thought to tell her of my visit to Quemby. I did not—though some day I might. It was bloody all right when you were Russian and passionately attached to your father and brother, and a sort of great welling-up of unspoken-of—unnecessary-to-be-spoken-of—affection blossomed like a lotus whenever you met. How did it operate—or did it operate at all—when your mother greeted you as if you might just possibly be a carrier of typhoid—social typhoid anyhow—and was plainly thinking "thank God for the Marines" when you thundered away in your Aston Martin out of her life for—hopefully—another seven years?

I wasn't any sort of a lover that night. I just made an excuse and drove her straight home. Then I dreamed a lot. The ghouls were queuing up all through the hours of darkness.

 The first thing John Carreros said when we were on our way was that he thought my new car was noisy.

"So it is," I said. "You don't buy Astons for silent travel."

"It is like a tractor engine."

"Wait a bit. You'll find that over seventy the engine will get progressively smoother."

"Shona warned me that you were unhinged where motorcars were concerned. Remember I am an old man and do not relish to be jolted about. Also, as you get older you will find that a shorter life expectancy makes you more, not less, careful for what is left."

Unlike the day before, I kept to a more normal speed, seldom going over ninety, at which rate the engine purred as contentedly as a stroked cat. John was looking older, I thought. Maybe it was just that on this sunny autumn day he was wrapped in a tweed overcoat, and a brown wide-brimmed trilby hat was dragged down over his heavy-weight glasses.

TBM Ltd. were five miles out of Bristol, a typical oblong box of white concrete and glass, with the serried cars in front, a bloke at the lowered barrier to screw his eyes up at your entry. The general manager was waiting for us, a Mr. Schmidt, with fair hair, a broad Teutonic face and a Yorkshire voice.

The factory had been put up for them only two years ago, so everything was of the latest. We did the boring old drag around the place, through the laboratories, where the perfumes were blended, to the manufacturing floors, where the recipes and the formulas were made up. Metal drums like beer casks ranged the shelves, while men in white coats wheeled trolleys around (which were really metal casks on wheels) and turned a tap here and a tap there, allowing the essences to run down into a funnel and into the wheeled cask. In one hand the men carried a small board with the formula pinned to it, telling them how much of each ingredient to put in; and an electronic reading on the trolley measured the stuff. Mr. Schmidt said the supplies they had available varied from an essence rare enough for them to have only a single medicine bottle of it to one so much in general use that it was kept in a 6000-liter drum.

All this was old hat to me, except that this was the most modern place I'd visited and I was interested to see by how much their new methods would be able to bring down their prices to us. Schmidt was going on to say that their parent firm in Germany, and their few large competitors, now had a hand in almost everything sold in the supermarket, except only the fresh food. Odors were added, disagreeable smells were subtracted or masked with more enticing smells; tastes were given piquancy, colors were deepened or lightened. "Name a product on the shelves that hasn't been improved by us in one way or another, from boot polish to biscuits, from washing powders to fish fingers, from gravies to cereals, from fruit pies to carpet shampoos."

"Just so long as no one gets the flavors mixed," I said.

He laughed too heartily. They always do. "We underrate the importance of first impressions. Perhaps chiefly the nose—though you gentlemen are not likely to do that, eh? Have you time to witness a little experiment?"

John Carreros grunted. "Experiment? What is this?" He might never have heard of such a thing.

"Allow me to show you."

Schmidt took us out of the factory to a small block of buildings at the other side of the square.

"As you know in England," he said, "we suppliers carry out tests on animals only when it is a matter of obvious health safety. But we sometimes experiment *with* animals, in ways which do them no harm at all. We have here some monkeys."

In the building was a cage with two monkeys. One was chewing a nut, the other was scratching his nose; but they immediately looked up and stared at us with round insolent eyes, trying to guess what business we had there.

"These animals," said Schmidt, "are healthy males of three and four years old. As you can see, they are in fine condition, well fed and well cared for. Now if you would come over here where we can observe them without them observing us . . ."

Schmidt motioned to a white-coated worker who was standing near. He pulled back a wire door and after a few moments another monkey ambled in, blinked around, hopped onto an artificial bough and yawned.

Schmidt said, "A female of the same breed, aged two and a half years, in fine condition and in heat. Watch."

We watched. Nothing happened. The first monkey went on with his nut, the second stopped scratching his nose and began to move in a bored way round the cage. The female sat on the branch.

"Where's the catch?" I asked after a bit.

"The two male monkeys have had their noses plugged. They cannot smell her so they are not interested. Now let us come back in five minutes."

We went out into the passage and he offered us cigarettes. We both said no, but a girl brought coffee, which we swallowed; then we went in again. The two male monkeys remained, one of them busy on a new nut, the second picking at the fur on his leg. The female had gone.

"The plugs have been removed," said Schmidt. "Now in a moment I am going to send in a very ugly elderly female monkey who has been sprayed with the appropriate smell."

The side of the cage was opened and the elderly female hobbled in, snarly and bloodshot-eyed. She looked as pleased as a landlady cheated of her rent. But this made no difference. The two male monkeys couldn't wait to mount her. She didn't take kindly to them at first, but presently she entered into the spirit of the thing, and fun and games went on for quite a while.

As we came out into the pale sunshine Schmidt said, "Find the erogenic odors and you have found a fortune."

I said, "All advertising is geared to that already. Cigarettes, chocolates, shampoos, vermouths. It's a question of mass hypnosis."

"Ah yes. But how much better if the subliminal suggestion is backed by fact and not fantasy."

"As it is now," exclaimed Carreros. "The musks, the lactones, the alkalines, in one way or another . . ."

"Oh, there's progress, I know. But recently we believe we've made a breakthrough. We've produced a perfume with a musk and civet base which is much stronger than any previous blend, yet has nothing offensive in the smell at all. We've discovered a synthetic which corrects the objectionable aspects and yet allows the full aphrodisiac effects to be perceived. After lunch I'll show you. It will need more work yet, but we are willing to put a team on it to produce an exclusive Shona perfume that will rock the industry."

"Is it a *new* smell?" asked John Carreros.

"To some extent."

"Because new smells are difficult and expensive to market. Sometimes it takes years for the public to accept it. Think of Chanel No. 5, L'Air du Temps, etc."

"I don't believe with the right sort of advertising one needs to *wait* for the public."

"Could hardly afford to anyway," I said. "Costs build up too quickly these days. There were forty new perfumes launched on the U.S. market last year. Only four of them are still afloat."

"Well, don't forget we are almost there, so far as the product is concerned. It will need a big launch. Naturally, if Shona had not been expanding so quickly, we should not have thought of giving you the first refusal."

III

We drove home at four.

John said, "It is all sales talk. We have heard it all before. The perfume for a woman to wear which will make her irresistible to men. The talc or the aftershave a man can put on which will draw all the women to follow him like the Pied Piper. Of course good smells help, the right smells help. This is what I have been working on for twenty years. But it can only go so far. After that it is autosuggestion."

"What about the monkeys?" I said.

He shrugged ill-temperedly. "That sort of thing has been known for centuries. We cannot completely associate ourselves with the animals. We know that human sweat, the smell of pubic hair, some other of the body odors have a sexual attraction; but as always in human beings there is the split between the purely animal and the aesthetic discrimination of a civilized creature. Perfumery is designed to elevate the senses, not degrade them."

I digested this lofty sentiment for a few minutes.

"I must say I fancied the new smell. It's heavy as yet; but I think it has a future. And anyway we need a new product to launch for 1975 or '76. Faunus is now five years old, and although it has done all right it hasn't made the impact of Dryad."

John said, "You mean the new firm you and Shona are creating needs another product because it has become so large. So one drives ever further into indebtedness in order to recoup the expenses of the new expansion. Where will it end? One cannot blow up a bubble indefinitely."

"We're not blowing up anything so that it must burst," I said. "We're learning to live with the modern world and to be among the front-runners. I don't suppose Shona and you ever *needed* to expand, because you could have sold the company for a million any day and retired to grow roses. But she didn't want to. Fundamentally you don't want to either. You just want to run along in the old groove and be content to be small-time. She didn't. She still doesn't."

He took out his pipe and began to fill it. On the rare occasions that he smoked it, he used some herbal muck. Eventually he pulled out my cigar lighter and held it to the bowl of the pipe. Stubble-burning filled the car.

He said, "I don't like you, David."

I slid past two cars and then fell to a steady seventy again. "I didn't think you did."

"Your influence on Shona has been wholly bad."

"Thanks, but you exaggerate. Shona is seldom influenced by other people."

"I know. That is why I deplore it now."

"She wanted to expand. She was looking for someone to help her to expand. She found me."

"Alas yes. Found you in more ways than one."

He was hunched like a bear in the seat.

"I'm not the only one she has ever 'found.' "

"No, but you are the only one who has ever been in the firm, and had this bad influence."

"John," I said, "get it out of your cranium that I'm pushing her to do something she doesn't want to do. You ought to know that nothing this side of nuclear fission would persuade her to do that. You might more properly say she's had an influence on me!"

He said, "I'm going to get rid of you."

It was spoken quite calmly, and for a minute I wondered if I'd taken it in right.

I said eventually, "Isn't that going to be rather difficult?"

"It might be unpleasant, but it can be done."

"How?"

"Well, you have been very stupid, haven't you. Starting this little firm of yours on the side."

So that was it. Smoke signals had been going up somewhere.

"So what?"

"It is totally unethical. If Shona knows, you will be sacked at once."

There was a freckle of rain on the screen. I flicked the wipers on, then off again. I looked at my fingers grasping the wheel.

"Been having me watched?"

"Dear me, no. That has not been necessary. I have informants in the trade."

"Same result anyway."

"Same result. You must realize that ours is a very close-knit profession."

"Well," I said, "what I've done is a perfectly straightforward exercise. Entirely legit."

"If you were not in the position you are, yes. Given your position, no."

"That's a matter of opinion. Anyway your firm is not the loser. I've made quite a little bit for Shona Ltd."

"And quite a little bit for yourself."

"Why should that matter?"

"Because of the way you've made it. The extra profit you have made for our firm is nothing compared to our loss of reputation."

"Limited Distribution System—isn't that what they call it? It's an outlook that's becoming more and more old-fashioned."

"You'll find in this respect we are still an old-fashioned company."

We drove on. I would quite have liked to stop and dump him in the reservoir we were just then passing.

He said, "But I have a better proposition for you."

"That's big of you."

"Go to Shona and resign. Say you have tired of being with her—that you are tired of *her*—that you want to start a firm of your own. Persuade her to accept your resignation. Once I am absolutely assured that you have left and cannot come back I will pay you a lump sum to help you on your way."

"How much?" I couldn't refrain from asking it.

He hesitated. "Thirty thousand pounds."

I was surprised. "You rate my nuisance value highly."

"Never mind that. It is what I am prepared to pay."

"But why?"

"Why what?"

"Why buy me off if you can see me off anyway?"

"I have the fancy."

I considered the situation while we negotiated a knot of traffic entering London.

"I think I have the idea. You are in the position of a wealthy father whose daughter has taken up with a layabout who—you think—wants to marry her for her money. He might be able to discredit the bloke by bringing up some charge against him; but the bloke would never be so completely discredited as if Father was able to say to his daughter, 'I bought him off, and he went of his own free will.' "

He fiddled with his pipe. "Think it over, David, for a day or two. You will leave anyhow, I can assure you of that. Shona has rigid ideas on such subjects as ethics. In one case you will be thrown out with nothing but your quarter's salary. In the other you will have a large sum to invest in your little firm, which I imagine is rather undercapitalized at present. Let me see, what is its name? Kilclair Ltd.?"

"You know it is."

"Just so. Well, once you have left Shona Ltd., you can pursue your little jobbing enterprises in complete legitimacy. No doubt you will do very well. You have the initiative to become a successful jobber and you would have no reason to restrict your interest to the perfumery world." John Carreros sat back on a cloud of burning hay. "Think it over, David. I give you three days."

CHAPTER TEN

I Of course I knew my little enterprise would stick in Shona's craw if she ever came to know of it, but I was pretty certain she wouldn't be as mad about it as John predicted. He was hoping she would but knowing in his heart she wouldn't: Shona wasn't stupid. Besides there was all the rest between us, and you could hardly ignore that.

All the same it fetched up in *my* craw that he had been the one to find out and would have the abounding pleasure of telling Shona.

Much better to get my word in first.

Mark it up that I hardly considered his offer of a bribe. It was a hell of a good one, and a couple of years ago I should have taken it with both hands and been off like a mechanical hare pursued by greyhounds.

But it's not natural to like being pushed around.

As it happened I hadn't set eyes on Shona since the Tuesday evening; there were minor panics I had to attend to all through Thursday and Friday, and it wasn't until the Friday evening as we were closing that I heard she was laid up with a chill. I called on her in South Audley Street and found her alone.

She let me in and then, scarlet satin kimono'd, fled back to her bedroom and the shaded lights.

"If I'd known it was you I should not have answered."

"Well, thanks a lot."

I sat down at a distance and looked at the figure in the bed.

"You should have told me. Had a doctor?"

"No. Sometimes, rarely, I get a chill—on the liver. It is disagreeable but I then take a day or two off."

"I've not noticed it."

"It is rare—I have just said—but I always keep to myself then. It is not a recommendation for a beauty firm if its head looks as thin as a toast rack and as yellow as a guinea."

"Let's put on another light and then I can advise you."

"No, David! No! *No!* I forbid you. In another forty-eight hours I shall be quite recovered."

"I'm not your public. I shan't stop buying Faunus conditioner because the woman who invented it is temporarily out of condition."

"You," she said, "are a great deal more important than the public. I do not wish you to see your mistress as an aging woman."

"Well . . . maybe that's true and maybe not. It could be that we have got too close to each other these last few years for a mere matter of appearance to rock the boat."

She breathed gently out. "Very good. Very well spoken. But do not believe it. It has never happened in my experience. Whatever good and splendid times one has shared with a person, it cannot make up for a joyless present."

"I'll remember that," I said, "when you get tired of me."

"That will be the day, as you say."

It was right out of character that she didn't ask anything about my trip to Bristol. Perhaps John had already given her his version. Yet she clearly had heard nothing else from John. He was keeping to his side of the bargain.

I found the subject I'd come to discuss rather a pig to bring up. Much easier, more appropriate, to face her across the desk of her office, tell her what was brewing and argue it out on the spot. Here in her bedroom, with shaded lights, and her obvious dislike at my being here at all, the first few sentences wouldn't quite come together. Look Shona, I'd say in a big voice, I've had a thing on the side and John's got a wild idea in his head that I'm double-crossing you. Did it sound right? Look Shona, you know you've set me up to run the firm on modern lines. Well your husband is clawing at me for running a company of my own to . . .

Instead I said, "Next week we've got to make a decision about the way we put over this polyenergizing cream. You can tell people it keeps cells alive in a test tube six times as long as any other substance. The question is, will anybody in the general public have the sense to ask, so what?"

"No," she said slowly. "It is still a good selling point. People do not think that way. But let us consider it later. My head is aching, and I can't think clearly this evening."

We chatted a bit longer. She lit a cigarette, rapidly flipping the lighter shut as soon as the tobacco caught. Then she asked me if before I went I would take a couple of checks and post them for her.

"Where's John?"

"In Richmond. He is not a good nurse and flees at the sight of the least indisposition."

"I could be a good nurse," I said.

"No. But thank you."

"You still don't trust me."

"Ah, not totally as a lover. How can I? How dare I? I am . . . almost in love with you. So I do not even trust myself. John—John means next to nothing to me anymore; so I do not have to doubt him. With him there is nothing to lose and therefore nothing to hide."

On her directions I went into the living room and fished for her checkbook in a drawer of the antique writing table. Under it I saw her passport. Well, some day I had to know, and this meant merely the flip of a page.

There it was. Born Moscow, USSR; date of birth: 12 August, 1930. The photograph stared at me accusingly. She was just forty-two. Eleven when war—their war—broke out. She could only have been about fifteen or sixteen when she left Russia, began her famous trek. Children grew up early in the climate of war. Thirty-seven when I met her. Thirteen years older than I was. That seemed about right—what I would have guessed. Forty-two was no great age, except for the standards she set herself, which were the standards of a woman of twenty. And of course, except for the fact that she was the mistress of a man still *in* his twenties.

I went in with the checkbook. She squinted at me a shade suspiciously and then put on her glasses to write the check. I thought: only ten years younger than my mother. A date made a difference. Just knowing made her seem older—though I hadn't really ever thought of her as younger than that.

Was I tiring of her? It hadn't occurred to me before. Perhaps I should take the thirty grand and run.

She said, "Did you come to see me about anything, David? Anything special, I mean?"

"Nothing that won't wait," I said. "You'll be fine by Monday."

"Yes," she agreed. "I'll be fine by Monday."

II She was not fine by Monday but she was about. And still I didn't take the pin out. And neither it seemed did John. I wondered if he was bluffing. He hadn't exactly got a full house. Maybe he thought I was still considering his bribe. And why did *I* put it off? I'd never been one to care about a row.

Shona didn't go fencing on Tuesday so I went on my own, interested to see if Mr. Crosnier's books had done me any good. With Shona absent Erica was more impudent with me than ever, and I could see she was all ready for the come-on. I think she just fancied a bit of fun and thought I'd do—it wasn't more sultry or lustful than that. I didn't take her up on the glances, but we enjoyed the evening and there was more laughter and joking all round than there were parries or feints. Yet she'd only just come back from a big tournament in Paris, and there was an international bout due in London in two weeks' time, when Miss Lease was fencing for England.

On Thursday we had our board meeting at Stevenage, and Shona seemed herself again, thrusting like the natural fencer she was at the weak points of an argument; giving everyone a chance to have their say, then suddenly, annoyingly, making up her own mind, and that was that. I'd done a report about Bristol which everybody had had, generally trying to be impartial but summing up by recommending that two of their men should come to Stevenage to bring samples and to get down to development and terms. There was a bit of general talk, and the meeting seemed to think that what I said was OK.

At this stage Shona turned to John and said, "You have not put in any report of your own, John. Can we take it you agree with David's?"

John, who had not looked at me throughout the meeting, said, "Not at all. I totally disagree with it."

"D'you mean you don't think TBM Ltd. has a proposition worth offering us?"

"Just that. I thought their product was no good at all."

There was a longish silence. Then everybody began to talk at once.

Shona, looking from one to the other of us, finally said, "Clearly we need a third opinion. Certainly samples should be sent here before we take any more positive steps."

"I should welcome that," I said, seeing she had really come down on my side.

She was looking grim today, and when the meeting ended and she asked me to stay behind I thought, well, this is it, and he's got his oar in first. But instead she took an *Evening Standard* off the table and said, "Have you seen this, David?"

I hadn't. The item was headed: "Fatal accident on M6. Heir to baronetcy dies in early morning crash."

My eyes went down the page.

"When did this happen?"

"I heard it on the one o'clock news."

I read:

Victim of an accident on the M6 near Sedbergh, was Dr. Malcolm Kilclair Abden, aged 39, son and heir of Sir Charles Abden, baronet, of Lochfiern, Ross and Cromarty. According to an eyewitness, who had just been overtaken, the car, driven by Dr. Abden, a white sports car, which was traveling at high speed, appeared to have a blowout in a front tire, and the driver lost control and turned over, plowing through to the northbound carriageway. At the time, 6:30 A.M., the motorway was quiet and no other cars were involved. Dr. Abden, who was an ex-Member of Parliament for North Banff, will be well remembered for his appearances on radio and television, where his forthright views always attracted attention. He leaves a widow and four children.

"Good grief," I said. "That's tough."

She said, "It must be in the family."

"What must?"

"Driving crazy. Your father was never happier than when he was on a racetrack or doing sixty in a built-up area."

"Who told you that?"

"You did."

"I'd forgotten." I stared at the paper. "Well, well. Too bad . . . At least he died in his bed. My father, I mean. Or as near his bed as made no matter."

"Perhaps if you have a mania for speed it is more dignified to have a blowout on a motorway."

I looked at her. If you have a mania for drink it's undignified to fall down in your own kitchen. "It's a pity about Malcolm."

"At Erica's dinner party I liked him."

"Well, it's a hard thing to say of a cousin, but in fact I didn't actually dislike him."

"John said you drove most recklessly when you took him to Bristol last week."

"So he's told you about our visit—before today, I mean."

"Oh, yes. But I wanted it aired at the meeting. Anyway I would take your opinion in preference to his. It is agreed by everyone that we need a new line, to be ready in a couple of years."

I said, "I wonder what the hell he was doing."

"Who? Oh . . . It is simple. He was driving too fast."

"The one thing I would have reckoned on from the few conversations I had with him was that he was a good driver."

"You cannot take every precaution against a blowout, as they call it."

"Hm. Good drivers don't neglect their tires."

III

So I ducked another opportunity, and it was a couple of days more before the ice cracked. I was in my office dictating a reply to a high-class Manchester store who had invited us to take a stand at a "Year of Beauty" exhibition they were getting up for the early months of the following year. They said they had assessed our contribution to the exhibition at £3000 and informed us that Rubinstein and Arden and Revlon had already agreed their larger contributions. I had got to know most of my opposite numbers in the other firms, so I rang Edward

Tolston at Rubinstein and found, as I expected, that he hadn't agreed anything yet, and I guessed none of the other firms had either. As an ex-con man I'm always quick to recognize a con when I see it. The outcome of my reply to the store would be likely to end business between us for a year or two while they got over the affront, but there were other good outlets.

Shona came in and I nodded to my secretary and she left.

Madame had certainly quite recovered her health and her austere, pallid good looks. Presumably she was off out to lunch somewhere, because the Gucci slacks and the ponytail had been put aside for a short black velvet frock with a crimson satin sash, and her hair was up and all a-glint with a recent brushing.

"David," she said quietly, "I gather you have been cheating us."

I put down the pen I had been gnawing. Ballpoints are hard things to chew and unsatisfactory; you can't get splinters off them.

"I don't think so."

"Well, you must explain to me."

"I suppose John has been telling you about this company I have floated."

"Yes."

It was low-key so far. "Kilclair Ltd."

"Who are the directors?"

"Myself, Van Morris, and that chap Derek Jones."

"With Roger Manpole in the background?"

"No. You ought to know better than that."

"So it is really you and two figureheads."

"If you like to look at it that way."

"A company created to buy our surplus products cheap and resell them at a profit."

"Resell them where they can do no harm. In the north country factory shops."

"They do every sort of harm. I had already had complaints from the big shops up there, but thought it was just a few isolated parcels which had slipped through somehow."

I went to the window and looked out. "Shona, d'you recall when we were doing the first reorganization, when we were shifting from Isleworth to Stevenage, we had a *lot* of surplus stock. At least it was a lot for those days. I saw it being loaded into three lorries and I asked Parker what was going to happen to it. He just said that one word: 'Pulped.' I couldn't believe it. Honestly. High-grade packaged lipsticks, soaps, toilet water, perfumes, the lot, all in top nick. I asked him again, hardly able to take it in. Then, just to be sure, I jumped in my car and followed the lorries. They carried them to a dump six miles away near Harlington and tipped them; then a bulldozer came along and crushed them till they literally *were* pulp. It actually happened, just like that!"

She said, "We all do it. All the most exclusive firms do it. You must know that. It is part of the Limited Distribution System."

"To keep prices outrageously high."

"To keep them at their proper level! We have research and development costs to meet! We have to build up support capital against the possible failure of new lines! As you must know, it is the exclusive perfumers who do most of the expensive pioneer work, which the big firms often exploit once a breakthrough has been achieved. That is why what you have done is so unforgivable."

I sighed patiently. "Look, so far I've sold three consignments to Kilclair Ltd. One for two thousand pounds, one for five thousand pounds, one for fifteen thousand. Shona and Co. are therefore twenty-two thousand better off than they would be if the stuff had been sent to be pulped."

"And by how much is Kilclair Ltd. better off?"

"We sold the consignments to a private firm in the north of England who specialize in supplying the factory shops. It's an ex-perfumery chap who runs it, so he understands how to deal with it discreetly."

"For *how much?*"

"How much for each package? Five thousand, eight thousand and twenty-five thousand."

"So Kilclair Ltd. is better off—*you* and your lot—are better off by some . . . let me see . . . fifteen thousand pounds. Is that correct?"

"Probably about twelve after deducting expenses."

"And for that you will throw away your position here and undermine the value of our perfumery products."

I said, "It can't affect your general price structure simply to have a few factory workers able to buy your stuff at half-price."

"It does. And we all agree." There was the old feminine whip-cord look about her now. "Let me tell you a story. Five years ago a consignment of Rubinstein products was sold at about forty percent of the wholesale price for resale in Indonesia, where Rubinstein has no outlet. But there was a double-cross somewhere and the consignment found its way on to the Swiss market. When Rubinstein heard this they immediately dispatched agents to hire people to stand in queues to buy back all their products in the Geneva and Zurich supermarkets where they were going at a reduced price. Not until the last was bought up did the queues cease."

"It would cost 'em a fortune," I said nastily, "considering the markup."

"Maybe. But I will do the same for *my* products: I understand this last consignment—the large one—has only just gone through."

"About a month ago."

"Before you leave you must tell us the name of the firm you sold to and its likely outlets."

I said, "Before I leave?"

"Before you leave. Then I will have the stuff bought back."

"There'd be more petulance in that than common sense."

"That shows your total misunderstanding of the principle involved!" She paused. "Or does it? I wonder. To someone on the outside of the trade this might seem a trivial issue." She thumped her hand on the desk. "But you *must* have known this was unforgivable behavior. You were not born yesterday! You have been in the business for *years*, first with Langtons, then with Yardley's, and now a long time with me. It cannot possibly be that you have behaved this way out of *ignorance*. Why did you not tell me what you were doing?"

"Because I knew you wouldn't like it."

"It was a deliberately underhand maneuver by which you arranged to feather your own nest at my expense!"

"I feathered *your* nest," I said, "slightly more than I did my own. You've just done your sums. Didn't you notice? Grow up, woman! Be your age! We're not living in the nineteenth century."

Her pale face flushed; I hadn't seen it do that before. I suppose I'd used the one unacceptable word. "There are certain standards of business behavior which are common to most generations, except of course to the con man and the jailbird, who naturally lives only by the ethics of Pentonville. It is really all my own fault. I should have known that once a crook always a crook . . ."

"Thanks a lot," I said quietly.

"Of course, you have been careful not to overstep the legal mark. Perhaps by your own twisted reasoning you even really *thought* you were conferring a favor on me as well as on yourself. The fact that by so doing you undermined the whole fabric of that business confidence by which we all live—"

"Business confidence!" I spat out. "Business con trick! All retail price maintenance is a con trick. My Christ, this really is a case of the pot calling the kettle black! When do you want me to leave?"

"As soon as you can clear your desk."

"That I'll do with the greatest speed—and pleasure."

"You think you're being hard done to," she snarled. "But just see for yourself! If this gets out, then—"

"As I'm sure you'll see that it does!"

"If this gets out you'll not find another high-class cosmetic firm that will *look* at you, I can assure you of that! Why don't you go and work for Roger Manpole. Perhaps a life of crime is what really suits you."

"It will suit me," I said, "just for a change, not to be a lapdog to an aging woman. That will be a happy outcome of—"

"Get out!" she said. If I had imagined beauty in her face, it wasn't there now.

I began to pull open one or two drawers, fish out a few personal possessions. The telephone rang and I snatched it up, shouted, "Not now!" and banged it down. "Perhaps you would have liked to answer it?" I queried to her taut back.

"Go to the devil!"

I said, "I wonder how you'll go along without me. Neither Marks nor Leo have the enterprise or drive to take over, and Alice Huntington will be as useful as a fileted fish."

"I shall get my own man. There are plenty about. Plenty who will jump at the job!"

"I could draft the advertisement for you," I said. "But the papers wouldn't print it."

"It's strange," she said, "that John was right about you all along. He said you were a weakling who would let me down."

I went up to her. She wouldn't face me, but I faced her.

"Have a care," I said gently. "Or I might try to disprove that. But it would be a pity to spoil your looks even more than the jaundice has."

"Get out!" she said between her teeth. "Get out, get out and *get out.*"

CHAPTER ELEVEN

I knew that was the final whistle but, for a day or so after, I hung about in my flat, not quite sure what to do next. You can't suddenly lose both a top job and a top mistress without feeling the jolt. My teeth ached, but I knew it was no dental problem. Just a psychological uppercut.

Of course I'd done the thing eyes open, knowing she might blow a fuse if she ever got to know. It had been part of the fun, so I could live with myself in this insipid profession, which at heart was based on grossly upped prices and profits, at the expense of a gullible public. As she no doubt saw, it was getting at her personally too, and this had been what she couldn't swallow. I hadn't quite expected the sort of Hiroshima fallout that had actually occurred, but if that was the way she felt, that was the way; I wasn't going to argue anymore. What I did regret, and what really got under my skin, was the thought that John had got the better of me after all. That rankled. That really rankled.

After a while, and partly to divert my thoughts, I devoted some little time and consideration to the matter of Malcolm Abden's death. This too seemed to mean a little more to me than I would have expected. The inquest had been on the Friday, and the report was headed "The Killer Tires." A Home Office forensic scientist had been called in, and had told the coroner that the tires on the sports limousine "had not been manufactured to an adequate standard." He had found a jagged nine-inch split in the tread which he was sure could not have been made by the accident. The tires had done barely five thousand miles. I looked up the type of tire in a book on new cars, and saw it was one of the new British low-profile jobs with an advanced steel-braced radial design; and it was fitted to four makes of popular luxury car. Somebody in that big tire firm would be having kittens now.

I went to see a tire man I knew. He said, "Of course they'll try to hush it up, pretend the Home Office chap and coroner are alarmists; in a week or two the motoring papers will come up with soothing syrup, you mark my words. They'll say the tire was not properly fitted or underinflated or something, so that the public will soon forget. But I'd like to bet there's ninety or a hundred thousand of those sets of tires running around England at the moment, and the firm'll either have to call 'em all in or have them examined by experts, so as to avoid anything further. A second accident would put 'em out of business—where no doubt they deserve to be, if the truth be told."

"It won't bring Malcolm Abden to life again," I said. "There should be some way of suing them."

"Maybe his wife will. Or you?"

"Me?" I said. "No. He's nothing to me. I scarcely knew him."

"It'd be a hell of a difficult case, because it boils down to proof, and that's so hard to come by if heavy damages are pending. However, if you see the widow, tell her to have a chat with her lawyers. The tire firm might cough up a small fortune to settle out of court and duck the publicity."

"I don't know the widow," I said.

"Good time to get to know her then, isn't it? By the way, what're you driving?"

"A DB6."

"Watch the tires on that."

"What d'you mean?"

"They're high-speed jobs, designed for maximum road grip but not for long life. After eight or nine thousand miles you'll find the rubber will go as soft as orange peel."

II

He's nothing to me. I scarcely knew him. Which was as true as sin. But now he was gone I was narked that he had cracked his skull in a cartwheeling car and had got himself buried too deep for me to have a chat with him again.

His stupid flamboyant arrogance had fretted me when I met him, but somehow the surface antagonism hadn't counted too much. I couldn't go so far as to say he was the first Scotsman I'd actually liked, because I wasn't sure I liked him. He was engaging, meretricious, stimulating, and worth bumping against again. That was all. But it was enough.

With more time for thought, I thought about my last visit to Quemby. Seeing my mother again in that casual way had been like jogging against an old barred window silted with dirt. Some of the muck of years had fallen off and you could peer between the bars. I wondered how much I had actually hated my father. Of course I'd been scared of him, especially when he was gassed; but a lot of the time, it seemed to me, we maybe hadn't got on too badly. I remembered him rolling down a field with me when I was about seven, all the way down to the bottom, and his bright blue eyes twinkling with enjoyment at my laughter. I remembered him telling me about motorcars and him letting me sit on his knee and hold the wheel as we drove along. I remembered him teaching me to skate, and the way he picked me up that first time I fell on my belly and winded myself. I remembered the walks we had and the talks we had. But that was all earlier in my life before the poison began to spread. Funny how you forget things and how they sometimes squirm up into your mind again.

Sometimes I get this feeling of being separated from other people, different. Not better, not worse, but living on a different plane, living another sort of life. Their problems are not my problems; my problems are not theirs. Nor are their pains. This feeling is specially strong when I'm on my own. But then again, if the truth be told, maybe I always am on my own.

It's a funny old world. You're never quite sure how much of it is real.

One day, just for the hell of it, I thought I'd see how far I could get across London without paying a fare. I walked up to Selfridge's and got on a bus going east. We were at Oxford Circus by the time the conductor came round.

I said, "Marble Arch," with a foreign accent.

"You're going the wrong way, mate. Across the street. Any bus except a 25."

"Thank you. I am so sorry."

I got off and walked toward Oxford Circus, caught a bus going down Regent Street. The conductor came when we were near Piccadilly Circus.

"Selfridge's, please," I said.

"Not on this bus you don't. Look, man, you cross over and, see that stop? Catch a 6, a 15 or a 60."

"Thank you. I am so sorry."

This way I got right across London to Hackney, never having too far to walk and earning a dirty stare from only one conductor, a Paki, who looked as if he'd seen it tried on before. In the end I got fed up with waiting at bus stops and took a taxi home.

Actually I'd had a semipurpose in going to Hackney, because I thought of calling in at Henry Gervase Ltd. to see if, now that pornography was more or less legalized, they were coming up with any new tricks. But when I got there I found they'd moved and the place was now occupied by "Best Friend Dog Foods." It did occur to me that this might be just another front, but I thought if I went in and it *was* run by Roger's nominees they might think I was looking for a job. I saw a chap coming out whom I vaguely knew—smart olive type with a thin moustache—and this tended to confirm my hunch.

During this week I caught up with my play-going. I went to something every night and three matinees as well.

I went to the zoo and watched some rather jollier monkeys than those I'd seen at TBM Ltd. On the whole I thought well of monkeys. They had a simple, unaffected approach to life, and looked a deal more intellectual than the cretins on the other side of the bars. Then I went to look at the ospreys and the eagles and wondered if my cousins in their far Highland pastures had anything as handsome to see on their lonely crags.

Odd that that relative of mine should have been done in by a defective tire, just as surely, just as effectively as by a terrorist bomb or bullet. But instead of the world—and for "world" one reads "media"—screaming their horror at another dastardly crime —from the Kennedys forever backward into the so-called dark ages—instead of that, it was all slickly passed off as a motor accident, an unfortunate mischance, a tire split that might or might not be somebody's fault, but who knows, who cares, it happened yesterday, it's past, soon over. Good-bye, Malcolm, planted in the ground.

I wondered where my father was buried. Couldn't remember a thing. I certainly hadn't been to any funeral, any cremation. I suppose I'd been then in what the shrink called "self-protective isolation." Maybe that was my normal state even now after all these years. I'd been a good sales manager for Shona & Co.; no doubt about that. But all the time—even through the whole of my fairly passionate affair with the Russian lady—had there not been this refusal to become totally committed? Wasn't this what she had always been beefing about? It all came to the same thing in the end.

On the second Tuesday, having decided to miss the first, I went to the fencing school. If Shona was there I could always duck out. She was not there, but Erica was, full of her usual spit and insolence. I found myself liking it more. The international fencing jamboree was just over and she had done well, so was feeling on a high. She had strange lines bracketing the sides of her mouth—strange in one so young, that is. They were laughter lines, chiefly. The sultry eyes were, I'd guess, not in character; she was essentially breezy, comic, full of herself, a bit superficial but ready for anything. Once again she made it clear that the anything could include me. After two weeks on my own I really didn't see any reason why it should not.

I said to her, "What comes second in your life after fencing?"

"Fencing."

"And after that?"

"Oh . . . fun. Swimming, skiing, men, sunshine, caviar, rock, dinner parties, supper parties . . ."

"Wait, wait," I said. "You've lost me. Where exactly do men come—is it eleventh or twelfth?"

"Somewhere like that. Why, are you feeling lonely?"

"You could say so."

"D'you really think you've cracked up with Shona for good?"

"Oh, yes. She made that very clear."

"And you?"

"And me."

She gave me the going-over with a long glance. "Well, I'm not above offering you solace."

"I rather fancy that."

"Just for a day or two—a week or two. Nothing serious."

"I'll probably go along with that too."

"Come to my flat to supper tomorrow evening."

"Why not to mine?"

"Because I thought of it first. But mind—nothing serious."

"Agreed," I said. "Just fun."

III

Derek had been away, but when I rang him and told him what had happened at Shona's he sounded amused.

"Well, we've made a few thou, whether or not. Shall you keep the company in being?"

"Shona suggested we might become jobbers in a big way. If she spreads the word—as she's pretty sure to—there won't be any more pickings in the perfumery industry; but there are other things. Fancy mooching round junkyards?"

"Not much. But I'll keep an eye open. Shall you keep your flat and your flash car?"

"What?"

"I suppose it's essential for a con man to have a good front, isn't it?"

"Don't worry about me," I said.

"But I do, darling—I know how irresponsible you are."

A couple of days after this I went to Bexhill and took Essie Morris out. She was an odd old girl—very ingenuous, considering that her late husband had done time for armed robbery and her son a three-year stretch for opening safes that didn't belong to him. You wondered how she had kept her illusions through it all. But she had. Men and women, in her eyes, were always better-intentioned than ordinary people gave them credit for. Even screws, she thought, were human; and the police force had some "nice boys" in it. I took her to Herstmonceux to the Observatory, and to Bodiam Castle. Another day I picked her up and drove her to a matinee of a musical at Drury Lane and then took her back.

It wasn't until then that I explained to her why I had so much time to spare. She was genuinely upset, seeing, to my annoyance, Shona's point of view as well as my own. Even more annoyingly she thought it might still be patched up.

"My dear Essie, you just don't know human nature. Or you only know your own (which is very kinky, peculiar, odd, eccentric and romantic) and judge other people by it. Shona's too hard. I'm too hard. There's simply no meeting ground anymore. I wouldn't *want* there to be. Change the subject."

"Of course, love. Anything you say. But how will it affect Arthur?"

"Not at all, I hope. I asked him last weekend if he had had any word, but no, just his pay packet as usual. So it looks as if Madame is only venting her spleen on the one who deserves it."

"I'm glad for Crack," Essie said. "But I'm scared if your influence isn't there anymore. You know what he's like, love, a little teeny bit weak. Easy led. It's risky. Especially without you."

"My dear Ma," I said, "if you can't lose any other illusions, please try to lose this one about me. The last thing I ever expect to be in anyone's life is a *good* influence! Everybody who knows me—except you—would rattle with laughter at the thought. Please laugh too, so that I can know you're not serious."

"What he needs," Essie said after a moment, "what Arthur needs is a good wife. It would make all the difference. As you do, love. Don't you think?"

IV Several times Marks and Leo rang me during the second and third week, obviously in trouble, not knowing what to do about orders and deliveries and an advertising campaign we'd been about to launch. They hadn't seen much of Shona either, and when they did see her she looked so thunderous they didn't go near. The rumor was she was advertising for my successor; but I reckoned that would take several weeks, even if she was lucky. Considering how choosy she was, it might take six months. Her best bet was to poach a top man from some rival firm. Otherwise, I wasn't flattering myself to suppose, the newly blooming expansion was likely to turn yellow.

My affair with Erica went pretty well. There was no consuming passion on either side, but often that can be a good thing. Sex on a limited-liability basis was what I'd always favored before, and it has a lot to recommend it. I was right about the sultry eyes; they didn't mean a thing, and that was a relief too. But we got along, laughing together often enough (which is rare for me) and parting and going our separate ways and coming together again without more prior notice than a telephone call. She was zesty with appetite and go, sometimes temperamental but never tired, full of fun and practical jokes. Yet under it she had a laid-back, cool, down-to-earth streak. Money she'd always had—she knew how to use it to get what she wanted in terms of enjoyment. At the moment the thing she wanted most was to be the top woman fencer in England, and that was something she couldn't buy. So she went for it level-headed and hardheaded, and that meant keeping to a rigid regime. Nothing was allowed to get in the way of that, though sometimes she had such vitality she was able to burn the candle at both ends.

In the fourth week she went off to Rome for a six-day tourney, but she said she didn't want me with her, so I stayed at home.

On the Tuesday I couldn't be bothered to go to the Sloane gymnasium, not wanting to run the risk of confronting Shona, so, at a loose end again, I drifted into the Cellini Club in St. George Street.

It was upward of three years since I'd been in the place; but I'd always held a sort of honorary membership because of the people I'd introduced there in the past. Obviously the warranty still ran because I was welcomed like an old friend. The years might never have passed; it all looked the same, and there were the same crowd there—I mean, so far as attendants went: Mario and Frederick and Kurt, and Angelina and Lucie and Maud. The men still looked as if their five o'clock shave hadn't been close enough and the girls as if they were too big for their frocks. It was a luxurious joint, full of gilt and red velvet plush. Early yet and only one of the tables was busy.

Cellini himself came out of his office to say hello.

"Ah, David, how are you? Long time no see. I observe you have your carnation still. When is it going to be green?"

The club had been going for forty years, and this Cellini, they said, came from Alexandria. Whether he had changed his name or was a son of the first owner no one knew. He was a small man with the sort of nose you used to see on pharaohs, and he always wore a crimson linen evening suit. He was fond of diamonds, and someone had once mentioned the name Liberace in his presence. That someone was not admitted again.

Yet he wasn't a bad fellow, and honest enough after his lights. Maybe sometimes his lights were not quite bright enough, but his world isn't renowned for its integrity.

"Roger is here," he said. "Playing bridge. With three Americans. This is their first visit, so I don't know how they play. We shall be starting a table of blackjack very soon."

"Thanks, Val," I said. "But I'm over twenty-one already."

The one person I really didn't want to see was Roger Manpole. Maybe, feeling like that, I should have taken off while the runway was clear. It was just that I was not in the mood to leave. Because where did I go?

Happiness, I'd said to Essie Morris once, was something I saw only through a dark window. Content—or self-forgetfulness— or a state of non-unhappiness—came sometimes, rarely, but was not in the charts just now. Even my pleasant little affair with Erica, seen from a distance, did not stir me, even though she was young, pretty, vivacious, eager, flippant, everything printed on the bottle. Why not? I didn't know. I was a new man, responsible to no one. I felt like returning to a life of crime. What could be better, given the right opportunity? I ought to be seeking out Roger, not avoiding him.

At that moment, dead on cue, he came into the room, smooth and Savile-Rowed and self-assured. Handsome house in St. John's Wood, a yacht, now a third wife mink-lined, a son at Eton. Since before the decline and fall of the Roman Empire such men have ruled the middle ground that exists between law-abiding respectability and the underworld.

With him was a tall thin chap who looked like Abraham Lincoln's younger brother.

"My dear David." We might have met only last week. "Just the man I wanted to see. Care for a rubber? My partner has to go."

"Thanks," I said. "I was just leaving myself."

"Stay an hour. It's quite a while since we've played together. Thank you, Jeff," he said to Abe Lincoln Jr., and they shook hands. "It was a great pleasure."

"My pleasure too," said the American.

"I'm far too rusty to play with you," I said to Roger.

"This will give you an opportunity to polish up. The opposition, I must say"—he lowered his voice—"is not what you would call tournament class."

He was one of those men who ask you to do something politely enough but confidently expect you to do it. They've become so used to being obeyed that the thought of anything else scarcely enters their heads.

As I hesitated he said, "I hear you've left the Shona organization."

"You hear correctly."

"Stood not upon the order of your going, eh? I always say it's a mistake to work for a woman. Fundamentally they're all unreasonable. After all, it was a very small flutter on the side that you had, wasn't it?"

I cursed Derek. Not that it mattered twopence that this man knew. Only that he made it his business to know.

"Actually," he said, "I never thought it was quite your scene, David. Petticoats and all that."

"I enjoyed it."

"But I expect you're glad it's over. She's a purposeful woman, but I've always thought her rather ghastly. What age is she—sixty?"

"Forty-two," I said.

"Go on." He laughed and patted my shoulder. "Somebody's been having you on . . . Never mind. You're well out of it, one way and another . . . By the way, it occurred to me, is she one of the Chosen Race?"

"I have no idea."

"Well, well. You're keeping your little company?"

"What company?"

"This one you floated with Derek and some other man."

"For the time being, yes."

"If it's undercapitalized, I have a friend who might be interested in putting up a bit of money."

"Thanks," I said.

"Shall we go now, then? Ben and Cliff are waiting."

I said, "I haven't dealt a card in anger for upward of two years."

We went into the card room. These Americans were two big men, both in their early fifties, well heeled you could see, a bit flushed with malt but not over the top. Until the end I never knew what they were called, except Ben and Cliff. They greeted me with hearty good-nature, and we sat down. Roger was an above-average performer but thought himself better. Come to that, you hardly ever meet a bridge player who doesn't think he's better than he really is.

"What's the ante?" I asked.

"We've been playing ten pounds a hundred," said Roger.

"Suits me."

We kicked off. I soon got our opponents on beam: honest decent players, less good than Roger, and quite happy to lose a bit if they had to in these exotic surroundings, just for the satisfaction of being here. The first three hands were very so-so. They made two no-trumps and then were two down twice on the trot. On the fourth hand I picked up nine hearts with four honors, a bare king of clubs, a singleton diamond and two small spades. It's always been a habit of mine to open high on unbalanced hands, so I bid four hearts. Cliff on my left chewed the skin round his forefinger and then said four spades. Roger said five hearts and Ben five spades. I went six hearts and Cliff went six spades. I went seven hearts and Ben doubled.

I had a feeling in my nuts it might all depend on the lead. And it did. Cliff led the ace of spades. He probably thought he might find a nasty little singleton in both our hands, but in fact Roger had none and I had two. Roger put down a doubleton queen of hearts, seven diamonds to the knave, and four clubs to the ace. Of course if Cliff had led his bare king of diamonds—as a top player probably would—I was sunk before the ship was launched. As it was, I took the ace of spades with a trump in dummy, led up to the bare king of clubs in my own hand, and then led my second spade, trumping with the queen in dummy. Then I led dummy's ace of clubs and discarded my one losing diamond. After that it was all trumps.

"Nice," said Roger, jotting down the figures. "You don't seem too rusty to me. Of course, I gave you a good hand."

It was a fair score. 1360 points in all. Or £140 if you looked at it that way.

Another couple of dull hands, both played by them. They got three spades, and were one down on a four-diamond trip. Then Roger opened with a two-club call. I had nothing, and put him up three times. He ended up in five diamonds and was four down, doubled and vulnerable. That evened things out a bit. Eleven hundred to them. Roger was just a trifle irritable. Going down gracefully was not one of his strong points.

"I had twenty-four points," he kept saying. "I don't know what got into you, partner. Three to the queen of diamonds! A couple of knaves!"

"I was pushing them," I said. "I thought they'd go one more."

After that they won an easy three-no-trump call and an even easier four spades, on which, if they had played it properly, they could have made a small slam. So they were well up on the rubber after all.

"One more?" said Ben. "Just to see how the cookie crumbles?"

"I can't resist you," I said.

The second rubber was sensational. Roger was three down on the first hand and five down on the second, both undoubled. Cliff, who had massive diamonds in the second hand (Roger's was a diamond call), said he hadn't doubled because he was afraid we'd switch suits. I explained mildly that they probably had a game call in hearts each time, and a mere four hundred points was a cheap way out. But even with the best of us it's a skinny business being five down when you're playing the hand, especially when your partner has put you up twice; and by now his systolic pressure was too high for safety.

The next hand as second bidder he opened one no-trump and all passed. We got four.

Ben said, "Missed the boat there, I'll say."

Roger said nothing, but slapped the cards down. I whistled under my breath. He didn't look at me.

It was Roger's deal. He bid one heart, and Ben passed. I had a good hand with a count of fifteen, five diamonds to the ace queen, but only a singleton heart, so I went two diamonds. Bid high, bid low, bid softly and slow. Cliff passed. Roger said three diamonds so I went six.

Cliff led the knave of clubs and Roger put down five hearts to the ace king, four diamonds to the king, a doubleton queen of clubs and two small spades. It didn't look as if I had a hope, but you never know in bridge. I covered the jack with dummy's queen, Ben put up the king and I took it with the ace. That left Cliff with the master ten—if he ever got in. I led my singleton heart and took it with the ace, then instead of playing the king and trying to discard one of my two losing clubs I led back a small heart and trumped it in my own hand and led a small trump. There was the knave out against me but Cliff didn't put it up, so I finessed the nine. It took the trick. I led another small heart and trumped in my own hand again. Only then did I lead trumps for the second time, up to the king in dummy. They broke even. So I was able to play the king of hearts from dummy, followed by the six, which was the only heart left, and discard my two losing clubs. I lost the final trick to the spade king.

"Well, honest to God!" said Ben, looking at his partner. "Lucky we didn't double!"

"That was brilliant!" said Cliff. "I have to admit it. Didn't think you had a prayer."

"Luck of the devil," said Roger. He didn't bother to say, "Thank you, partner."

"Well," I said, "the tide goes out and the tide comes in."

They bid and made four hearts on the next hand, which meant we were both vulnerable. On the following one I picked up seven clubs but only had a count of ten. I went one club. Cliff doubled. That meant either he had a void or else all the rest of the clubs. Roger went two clubs. That meant either he had all the rest of the clubs or else a void. Ben doubled, not to be outdone. I said no bid. So did Cliff. Roger went three hearts, which meant he hadn't any clubs after all and probably a strong two-suiter. Ben went three spades. I went six hearts. Ben doubled. Roger was four down.

"My God!" he exploded. "Really, you—you stupid . . . You need your head examined! What the hell did you have in your hand to put me up at *all*? Dear Jesus, you should never have opened in the first place! You're *crazy*!"

"The cookie went sour on us then," I said.

In the next hand they bid and made a small slam and took the rubber. Roger and I were in debt for £320 each.

"I hope you'll take my check," I said to Ben. "I don't carry small change."

"My dear David," said Ben, beaming. "No problem at all. Eh, Cliff? It's been a privilege playing against you two gentlemen. We've really enjoyed it. Sure have."

Roger took out his own checkbook and scribbled a check. His hands were quite steady but I could see that the lid of the kettle was ready to blow off. I'd never seen him so upset before.

Cliff said, "We're flying to Rome tomorrow, else I'd suggest a return. Very good of you both putting up with us. Anytime either of you are in Philadelphia, just give me a ring. I'll fix a game on the spot. Clifford C. Horniman. Here's my card. That's my home number. If I'm not in, Mrs. Horniman will know where I am."

"Does she now?" I asked.

"What?"

"I'm in the States quite a bit," I said. "We'll keep your invitation in mind. Eh, Roger?"

"Naturally," said Roger, smoothing back his smooth chestnut hair.

"I must fly," I said, getting up. "Thanks for the game, all of you. Thanks, partner. We'll do better next time."

"Naturally," said Roger.

CHAPTER TWELVE

I left the club and overtipped the doorman for keeping an eye on my car. It squatted there glossy and elegant in its British racing green. As I got in I took a careful squint at the front tires. The engine growled into life. Two girls walking past observed it and me with interest. Come for a joyride, I'd say; it's not far to Oxford—see if we can be there in half an hour. They'd giggle and hesitate, wondering if I was a sex maniac.

I pressed the button to lower the window, but only to shove my elbow out. I edged away from the adjoining Rolls, which looked sedate and ordinary by comparison. Then off down Maddox Street, along Grosvenor Street to Grosvenor Square; up North Audley Street.

Lucky to have this garage in Red Place. The rich cripple who had the flat below me used only taxis and an invalid chair, so he let me rent it from him. It suited me to have the car so close.

Switch the engine off, put keys in pocket, pull the sliding door down and padlock it in place. A fine night and still fairly early—about eleven. The tangerine glow of London was all around like a circus tent. Lights starred in the houses and flats, cars winked and dipped as they went past; the occasional pedestrian walked the obligatory dog. All so uppercrust; yet only on the next street corner someone had been mugged last week. Modern society prospered and festered. I thought, to hell with Malcolm, being blown up by a defective tire. What a crummy, useless way to go. Some of the Abdens seemed to have a death wish, but surely not Malcolm, already on his second wife, a clutch of children, more than a taste of Parliament, his share of notoriety, money enough at least to live a public and prominent life. I wondered how old his eldest son would be; probably purging his schoolboy fantasies running like a dingo beside the Firth of Forth.

And what of me? Talking of being useless, what of me? Clutch the rudder, David, or you'll soon be on the rocks. It was fancy talk even to consider going up to meet Malcolm's widow and suggest to her that the tire company might be taken to the cleaners. I'd never do it. I'd never go near an Abden, not from choice.

America might be a fair bet. It was a place where a good appearance—which I had—and a good accent—which I had—and good connections—which I had—were likely to pay off. Perhaps pay off too well. Yet, apart from being gullible—in a way—the Americans were also pretty hardheaded. Until now I had been there taking the bows on behalf of an esteemed perfumery firm. How would I make the grade on my own? I had a fair amount of what is vulgarly called bread, but it wouldn't last long.

As I unlocked the street door of the flats I looked up to the third floor and saw there was a light in it.

It's not the most comfortable feeling in the world to come home to an empty flat and to see a light on. Someone in there who has no business there. Once before Derek Jones had got in, but since then I'd had the lock changed. No doubt he had a talent with locks, but not that much. Crack Morris? Why should he come? If it were ordinary burglars, would they be likely to use company electricity?

I thought to go back to the garage and get a spanner but decided not. If anyone was there who had no business there, I was feeling ugly enough without a lethal instrument to hand.

I went up the stairs three at a time, noticing that in the flat below the light was also on. My door was locked. The Ingersoll key slipped in quietly enough and I let myself in. The light was on in the living room. I went in.

Shona stood there.

I said, "What are you doing here?"

"I came to return your key."

"Oh . . . I'd forgotten . . ."

"That I had one?"

"No . . . It's just that I didn't expect you."

She was standing by the window. A yellow turtleneck sweater, a close-fitting short black heavy-silk skirt, split at the side—not so much like a cheong-sam as an Apache dancer's. She looked stormy.

I said, "Been here long?"

"Just a few minutes."

I glanced down at the five cigarette ends in the ashtray.

"Well, thanks. You could have posted it."

"So I could," she said.

"Like a drink?"

"No thanks."

"Mind if I have one?"

"It is your flat."

I went across to the cabinet, gave myself a whiskey and pressed some soda in it. I poured Shona a small Glenfiddich, didn't contaminate it with water and took it across.

"I said no."

"You can always change your mind."

She took it. "Is that what you think of me?"

"That you change your mind? Not on important matters, no."

"Good. Because I don't."

"Splendid," I said. "Sit down. It won't cost any more, and you can stay five minutes."

"I have nothing to stay for," she said. "The key is on the table."

"Well, it's a pity to waste good hooch. But stand up to drink it if it tastes better that way."

She sat down. She was wearing more makeup than usual.

I said, "Considering that I've a good nose for perfume and a fair palate for wines, it's surprising that the taste of whiskey means practically nothing. One is as good as another to me." When she didn't utter I added, "For a Scot not to care enough about whiskey is as bad as for a Russian not to care enough about vodka."

She sipped her drink. I picked up a magazine and flipped through the pages. I said, "Did you go to the Sloane this week?"

"No."

"Neither did I. And Erica's away somewhere or other."

"Indeed."

I sipped my drink and put the magazine down.

"Arden's going to town on this new moisturizer."

"I know."

"Can't go into a major store without having it thrust at you. I was in Harrods yesterday. Big display."

"I'm sure."

"My spies think they won't get their outlay back."

"Your spies will be wrong."

End of conversation. After a bit I said, "How's John?"

"Fairly well."

"I expect he's happy, isn't he?"

"What about?"

"Putting the skids under me, of course."

"He tends to say, 'I told you so.' I do not enjoy hearing it."

I muttered something.

"What?" she barked.

"I was thinking aloud. Remarking to myself that you would have had no need to listen to him saying that if you'd listened to what I had to say instead."

"I am not here to listen to what you have to say!"

"Naturally not."

The next silence was good enough for the cenotaph. I brought over the Glenfiddich but she emphatically shook her head. I thought I ought to give her some excuse, some reason, even if a provocative one, to stay.

"On the assumption," I said, "that you're not here to listen to what I have to say, I'll continue—with or without your permission—to think aloud. And my present and continuing thought is that I was never built to run on a narrow-gauge track, and my employer, if she'd been as clever as she thinks she is, ought to have known that as well. Considering everything, I think I did pretty fair by her until she flew into a rage and sacked me. Nearly five years I'd been with her and hardly a finger in the till."

She said, "David, I am not here to listen to your petty excuses! That is all over—finished with. Completely. Forget it and let me go!"

"OK, I'm not stopping you; the door's unlocked. But I would really *like* to know—before you go—why you came."

"I've told you!" Lids were suddenly raised and eyes blazed. "I came to return your *key*!"

"You could have sent it round with any of your staff. Or posted it. Or slid it under the door. No . . . modest man that I am, I can't get away from the thought that you really came to see *me*."

"See *you*! I have seen far too much of you for far too long!"

"Well, I wanted to see *you*," I said. "And badly. I didn't quite know it myself until I saw you standing there—looking as if you'd spent most of the day knitting beside the guillotine."

"You stupid man! D'you suppose I—"

"Strangely enough," I interrupted, "I'm still rather stuck on you. Can I help it? Just a fact of life. All right, I can hate you, you can hate me. It doesn't remove the need. I'm hooked."

This time I was able to slop another dram into her glass. Again she tried to stop me but not with the hearty violence she could sometimes show. I tried to hold her wrist steady while I poured. It was small, delicate, iron-hard.

I said conversationally, "It's a competitive world. You know it just as well as I do. Getting more cutthroat every year. So the top firms can't *possibly* go on feeding their surplus products to the bulldozers. They'll all come to see that sooner or later. And not much later than now, I'll bet. A company like mine, like Kilclair Ltd., you may heap curses on it but it can be useful and profitable. Don't shake your head—just listen to your old friend. Kilclair can siphon off unwanted products into suitable outlets. If you say not to the factory shops of the north, then not to the factory shops of the north, but to Kenya or Fiji or Tanganyika or wherever. It's a common-sense business extension of the present setup, a natural outgrowth. It'll become that, whether you like it or not. I've been long enough in your world, and I can tell you . . . All right, I did it without your knowing, but it need not be such a disaster—"

She said, "You say you wanted to see me badly. That is just a lie. Like all the other lies you tell."

"Listen—"

She said, "An aging woman with jaundice. That was what you said! Then you were speaking the truth of your feelings—not now; now is some easy lie just to try to get your job back."

"And you didn't want to see me?"

"Never! Never!" She wrenched her wrist free and some of the whiskey spilled.

"Then why do you come tonight dressed like a—like a—"

"Go on," she said. "Pray go on."

"Like a high-grade Montparnasse tart."

She smacked my face. I thought: I rather want this woman, but not to strangle her.

"I was going to say I liked it," I said. "I mean, the way you're dressed. And they're the sort of things that will come off easily."

"As always," she said. "You have a common bourgeois mind. You're like some peasant wanting to rut in the hay. You think that's the answer to everything!"

"Well, not the answer to everything. But to some things, Shona. To some things." I rubbed my jaw. I didn't think any teeth were loose. "Look, for Christ's sake, I'm not dictating to your principles. I just want you for yourself, here and now, on the bed in the next room . . . You know what it's like between us. When it feels like this it's got to be something even more special."

"Hating and mating?" she said with a sneer.

"If you like. Anyway you like it."

She shut her eyes. "God, how you try to humiliate me!"

There was something on her cheek. It couldn't have been a tear, so it must have been perspiration.

"I will go now," she said.

"Look," I said. "Forget the goddamned job! Give it to the birds. I don't *want* it. What I want is you, now, *now*! Do you understand?"

"And you cannot have me!"

"Because it is beneath your dignity to sleep with a sacked employee?"

"No, because you have hurt and offended me so much that I cannot afford to give way to this cheap approach!"

"What is it you can't afford—your love?"

She hesitated. "Now you have seen to the depths of it! There is no more to say."

"Love is worse than pride, isn't it?" I said. "No sticking plaster available. No soothing cream. I know."

She slammed the empty glass down on the table and the stem broke. "*How* can you know? You have not grown *up*! You haven't an idea what love is! All you feel is lust!"

I began to pick up the pieces of glass, cut my finger and sucked the tip. When I found her here tonight I'd seen there was a pretty fair chance of getting her aboard again, and since then I'd been playing the line as tactfully as I knew how, to bring her in. It had been half instinctive, not reasoning so much whether I wanted it or not. But somewhere along the way the feeling had grown that I did want it, had wanted it, and wanted her. So that what I said I came to mean, instead of the other way round. Can't explain it better than that. Turn the cynic inside out and he becomes a sentimentalist.

I said, "How d'you define love, Shona? How d'you spell it out? *I* don't know . . . But if there are exams still to be taken, don't you think I could best learn them from you?"

I'd probably said the right thing in the end, because I put my hand on her cheek and she didn't hunch away or fling out another left hook. She turned and looked at me with eyes narrowed, their depths gleaming like newly cut coal.

"David, I never knew I could be so weak."

"Or strong? Isn't it a sign of weakness sometimes not to be able to give way?"

"I do not think this aging woman with jaundice can ever be in your bed and be your mistress again."

"At the moment," I said, "you're magic. Go on; be a sport. Take a chance."

III In the end Shona bought my company. It seemed to be the only way she could save her face, so I let it go. She bought it for £20,000, got rid of Derek Jones—at a handsome profit to him—and allowed me to retain 15 percent of the shares. "Van" Morris remained as a minority shareholder too. The company, she declared, was not to be operative. It was a big price for a frugal lady like her to pay for a company that was to bring no return, so I suspected in a few months she'd either suggest some use for it or allow me to suggest some use for it.

I went back, and the firm breathed a sigh of relief. Shona might be its inspiring spirit, but David was its organizer.

John took it badly. He eventually told Shona he was going to retire and wanted no part in the future of the firm. We had better find a new man to take his place. I can't say I shed any tears over him. It was a pity if he took the hump and it was a pity if this made Shona uneasy; but there was nothing I could do about it, or wanted to do about it. She and I came closer than we'd ever been before.

My thing with Erica ended as casually and as cheerfully as it had begun. She said she had a feeling in her bones that Shona and I would make it up in the end; I told her that her bones must have been sharper than mine, for I'd had no such premonition.

She and Shona were pretty close, but I don't think Erica ever let it out or that Shona ever suspected what had gone on. This was because our little affair had been a pleasure without an emotional tie-in. We betrayed nothing because there was so little to betray.

So for pretty well going on the next three years my relations with Shona were at a new high. The age gap between us didn't seem to matter at all. To be pompous about it, I suppose Mark Antony—give or take a year or two—was about as much younger than Cleopatra; and there'd been plenty of other cases. You can't explain it, except by the peculiar lure of the exceptional female. Shona didn't often pay me a compliment, but she did say once, "David, you have a way of making love which is subtle, seductive, not-resistible. I have known no other man so good."

"Am I the fifty-seventh variety?"

"What?"

"It doesn't matter."

"Oh, I see what you mean. Believe me, I am far too fastidious ever to have had fifty-seven. Less than seven. Except for several Russian soldiers on my way across Europe, and with them I had no choice . . . ."

"I sometimes wondered."

"Wonder no longer. But as for the present age, the new climate—is that not the fashionable word?—As for the present climate, it is not the amorality of permissiveness I dislike, it is the vulgarity."

"I think I see what you mean."

"But . . . if I had to try to explain what I mean about *you*, it might well insult you."

"Try."

"The best lovers—men, that is—are those with a little more that is feminine in their nature—a little more than average, I mean. Not too much—or they become effeminate. I know how you used to resent being thought a queer—"

"Still do—"

"But less so. Less so. You have changed, mellowed a little, I truly believe. You are not so combative a character, not so stark—"

"Don't bank too much on it."

"Well, it is beside the point. What I mean is that the butch man, the big he-man, the macho figure boasting his numerous conquests—what does he give to any woman? Not what you do. That is why I cling to you beyond my appropriate term. That is why I shall never now willingly give you up."

"It's a threat," I said. "By the way, when was the appropriate term?"

"Shut up."

Sure enough Shona found a new use for Kilclair Ltd. She put the idea to me one night, and, smiling to myself, I immediately said OK. It was something one or two of the other highest grade companies had been dabbling in. In spite of our much expanded market there was still surplus factory space. So we put out a cheaper product under Kilclair Ltd., called Domaine, which immediately caught on. Except that it was produced in the same factory, there was no obvious link with Shona & Co.—even the representatives were different and serviced different outlets; so that no one on the outside could have known. It didn't matter, of course, if they did, for it was a totally different product. Shona still insisted on destroying any surplus or outdated stock the main firm produced.

But it meant that we were all getting better off in the booming seventies.

We went to Paris to see Erica take part in the Women's Foil International, but she didn't win her bouts. Soon after her playful little affair with me she somehow got herself emotionally screwed up with an individual called Ted Cromer. I'd no idea what Erica's previous love life had been, but this was the first time anything had surfaced in a big way. Personally I didn't like the Cromer character, nor did Shona, so we were quite glad when it broke up. But Erica, for once in her young life, hadn't been able to wade in deep without getting her knickers splashed. She was ill for a month, and when she came back to the Sloane gymnasium the lines at the side of her mouth were not always creased in laughter. Once or twice I caught the whiff of alcohol.

I saw nothing more of Roger Manpole and didn't go to the Cellini Club again. I told Shona what had happened and she snorted her amusement.

"All the same, I am not sure it is good to alienate a man like that. I admire your resolution when you make some unpalatable decision that may be necessary" (I had just had to fire Marks for not being up to his job) "and Manpole is all you say—the unacceptable face of private enterprise. But you seem to enjoy making enemies with no good purpose."

"The purpose," I said, "was to freak him out. That's a good enough reason."

"Like your quarrel with Marini."

"No, not at all. He was just a slob who insulted me."

"All the same. You know the difficulties we have sometimes encountered in the States."

It was the first time she had linked my tow-row with Marini to the comparative lack of a big success for the Shona line in the United States. I didn't say anything in reply because there wasn't much to say. Common sense told you that such an idea was rubbish, but little hitches were still cropping up, obstacles appearing that shouldn't have. An hotel recently had denied a booking we'd made for a reception, and when we produced their letter of confirmation they said it was a mistake made by an undermanager who had since left. Things of that sort had increased since Shona separated from John. I didn't really suppose he'd cut off his nose to spite his face, but the pinpricks were there, and one got increasingly testy about them.

Toward the end of the third year we went to Vienna. We had been properly in the German market for only a couple of years, and although our representative in Vienna, a Mlle. Trudi Baumgarten, had done pretty well Shona had a hunch that things were not all they ought to be. She thought she would like to go and see for herself. A more important reason for going was that, after all this time, Mr. Schmidt and his chemists at TBM Ltd. had come up with a perfume that satisfied Shona. We had called it Charisma, but we'd decided to test-market it in Vienna and Zurich before launching it in a big way.

Test-marketing meant selective advertising in the chosen cities—or advertising in one and not in the other—and often carefully adjusted differences in price. In this case the products were going to be sold at a 50 percent markup in Vienna as against Zurich, because we were aiming at a more aristocratic clientele. The Swiss were generally much richer but more on a level with one another.

In spite of what was known and accepted about us, we never shared a bedroom or even a suite. Shona refused the first room she was offered at the Sacher—it was, she said, far too luxurious—so we occupied two smaller but still exotic rooms on the fourth floor, decorated in the gilts and crimson of the French Empire.

Such considerations however were soon elbowed aside by the arrival of our agent. I've often heard the French expression *"jolie laide,"* but have never quite seen it put across by anybody until I saw this filly. If you focused her face in repose almost everything was wrong with it, the mouth too big, the eyes too light, the nose too tilted, the cheekbones too high; but you never did see it in repose: everything moved and danced and screwed itself up and pouted and smiled until all the defects got lost in the larger picture. Shona had never met her before but knew her mother, who was Russian. She was clearly not pleased that Mlle. Trudi had not been at the airport to meet us, nor was she delighted by the fuss Trudi immediately made of me.

She didn't even seem particularly delighted when Trudi's mother showed up, a dwarfed wizened female with a rasping parrot voice who clasped Shona to what could technically be called her bosom and engaged her in voluble Russian, while Trudi gave all her time to me.

We had the usual press conference and reception and general guff which now attended the arrival of Shona in any foreign capital. It all went very well but I found it even more blindingly boring than usual. I never have taken to the phony bonhomie and the bright, brittle yap-yap and the champagne and the caviar. Shona was at her best in Vienna and spoke a broken German that seemed to enchant everyone; but these were the occasions when she least enchanted me. An imperious dame, of course, at the best of times; but it was only on public occasions like this that you'd put the words in capital letters. Maybe there was a squirt of jealousy in my sourness. I knew now I had a hold on her—as I recognized she had on me; but the phony razzmatazz of these public appearances set my teeth jarring.

When it was all over and we had a few hours to squander, Mme. Baumgarten—the elderly macaw—asked Shona to spend the evening with her to talk of old times. That left me on my own.

Trudi said, "Would you like to come with me to the Opera?"

"What is it?"

"*Tosca*."

"Do you have tickets?"

"No, I can get them. Mr. Wanninger will get them for me."

"Mr. Who?"

"The concierge. He can get you anything in Vienna."

"I'm bone ignorant about opera."

"No reason why you should not learn."

I looked into the green eyes. "No reason at all."

I knew Shona would very much dislike the idea.

I said, "Shall we eat first?"

"No, after."

"Where shall I call for you?"

"I will take a taxi here. Then we can walk over. At seven-thirty."

"At seven-thirty," I said.

IV One thing about the Europeans—or some of the Europeans—if their buildings are destroyed in war they bring all their craftsmen round to rebuild the places as near as possible to what they were before. In England they put up things that look like high-security prisons designed by the inmates. It's a matter of taste, I suppose. Or the architect's ego.

You wouldn't have known the Opera House had ever been gutted by bombs. It was all opulence and nineteenth-century glitter and was of course crammed to the last tier. But Mr. Whatever-his-name-was had come up with front-row stalls for Miss Baumgarten.

"I always ask for these seats," she said, "for if the opera is boring you can watch the orchestra."

I haven't a glimmer whether this was a good *Tosca* or not. The singing didn't grab me, but the drama and the staging were good. It even took my mind off a certain preoccupation lurking there: how I wanted the evening to end. Trudi was about my age, slim and sexy, and the expensively simple frock she wore had an immodest décolletage which showed she wasn't slim in the wrong places. It was perfectly clear which way her mind was working —if her mind could be said to come into it. Looking her over, I thought it would be fun.

The problem was Shona. In the ordinary way I would probably still not have considered her. There was nothing in holy writ between us; the fact that I had not had anyone else since Erica didn't disentitle me to step off the curb if I felt like it now. The snarl-up here was simply that Trudi was an employee of the Shona organization. If you come to Austria with your chief executive and partner in tow, it doesn't read well in the minutes if he immediately buck-jumps into bed with the lady fronting for you in Vienna. Leo Longworth, my second man, was with us, as was Alice Huntington. Unlikely Trudi would be able to disguise her satisfaction at her capture.

But it pleased me to think of kicking over a mild trace. It was what my life had been all about until I met this woman from Moscow.

CHAPTER THIRTEEN

I We flew the following morning to Zurich in a glacial silence normally reserved for climbers of the Matterhorn. In proper fashion this time we were met at the airport by Mr. Glauber and taken straight away to a press conference at the Baur au Lac. So we had very little further opportunity between us for the feast of reason and the flow of soul, had there been any desire for it on either side. It was almost dinnertime before I found my way into room 114, the large apartment on the corner of the hotel, and discovered Shona writing a letter.

"Have you a minute?"

She wrote on for a while and then took off her spectacles. "A minute, yes. No more. What is it?"

"I have the distribution estimates here and a couple of accounts for advertising that I didn't sanction. I wondered if you had."

She held out a long slim hand and looked at the papers I offered. "Yes," she said. "I sanctioned them."

"Ah . . . That takes us well over budget."

She shrugged. "So what?"

"So nothing if you feel that way . . . Are you dining?"

"Later."

"I'm dining now," I said.

"*Bon appetit.*"

I turned and went to the door. As I grasped the handle she said, "I am just writing to Miss Baumgarten. Dispensing with her services."

"A pity," I said after a moment. "I found her agreeable."

"That was obvious."

"Do we have to be represented everywhere by hags, so that you suffer no competition?"

Shona turned slowly and crossed her legs. "You flatter yourself,

David. I am ridding myself of Miss Baumgarten because her accounts are very unsatisfactory—as I rather suspected they would be. She owes us quite a lot of money, which we shall be lucky if we ever recover. It is purely on commercial grounds that I am dispensing with her services. The fact that one of my assistants happens to spend an hour or two scuffling around in her bed has not influenced my decision at all."

"As a matter of fact," I said, "she was terrific: slim, luscious, avid."

"Retain it all for your reminiscences. You will be able to sell them for some ample sum to the cess press. Now leave me."

"Actually," I said, "I was quite *exhausted* . . ."

"Oh, no doubt! No doubt!"

". . . Keeping her off."

Shona picked up her pen and turned it round. "I should not think you tried too hard, did you?"

"Just hard enough."

"Oh, come, David, you can do better than that."

"Better than what?"

"Do you suppose me to be altogether mindless?"

"Not altogether. In some degree, yes. Appearances no doubt led you astray."

"Astray! My God, me astray!" She turned back to the desk. "Oh, what does it matter? I am not interested in your squalid little affairs. Go to hell!"

"Thanks. That was what Trudi said in the end."

She jammed on her glasses and began to write. Then she crumpled the sheet of paper in her hand and threw it angrily toward the wastepaper basket.

Still by the door I said, "Trudi had her eye on me. Who am I to beef about that? Can one help being maddeningly attractive? And the temptation was there for me, like hell it was; but for some goddamned bloody witless reason I backed off. In the end, I backed off! She didn't like it. Nor in a way did I. Can I explain my reasons? Not at all. It can only have been pure nobility of character."

"Go away," she said.

"My character, I know, has always fascinated you, hasn't it? You have been puzzled by my pure natural goodness . . . So there you are, Lady Muck, you now have the answer to it all."

"If you do not go," she said, "I will ring for some member of the staff to turn you out."

Instead of going I came back from the door and stood over her. "And if you don't believe any of this, you stupid cow, I suggest you ask Leo Longworth! After Trudi and I had supper at the Sacher I parted from her, and Leo and I spent an hour afterward getting sloshed in the bar! I was not very pleased with myself at the time and I am not very pleased with myself *now*! Why shouldn't I have enjoyed myself with Trudi while you were out exchanging tearful reminiscences over the samovar with her corncrake of a mother? What the hell are you turning me into, a bloody Presbyterian monk?"

She did not speak for a few moments. Then she said, "There are no such things."

"What as?"

"As Presbyterian monks."

I used a couple of four-letter words that I knew she particularly disliked. She gave a laugh, harsh and unamused.

"Miss Baumgarten had rings under her eyes this morning."

"More than I had anyway. Unless they were rings of frustration."

"I am very sorry if you blame me for this situation—always supposing you are speaking the truth."

"D'you think I care enough to lie to you?"

She stared at me between half-closed lids. "I don't know, David. I think perhaps you do. Perhaps we both do. Perhaps it is better if I believe your lie."

Business took over for the rest of the next day. Then at dinner the following night she said, "Let us go away."

"Away? Where to? What d'you mean?"

"Away from business. Away from public relations. Away from other people. Will you take me, David?"

She was looking at me with eyes softer than I'd ever seen them before. She hadn't referred to Trudi during the day.

"Where d'you want to go?"

"Anywhere warm. Where is this place you go in the West Indies?"

"Barbados?"

"Yes. Will you take me? Just for a week or ten days."

"If you want to. What is it exactly you *want*?"

"Just to drop everything. Ever since John and I started this business it has taken priority in my life over all other things. But it has been so long. Even our—affair—even that has always been tied up, mixed up with the business of Shona and Co.—perfumery, lipsticks, night creams, the rest. Of course, it is my *life*. In a way I think it has become your life—or an important part of your life. It will always be so for me. But it has gone on too long without a break. I would like to forget it—never even mention it—for a week or two. Would your friends be in Barbados?"

"No. It's not our time of year."

"Good."

"Of course I know one or two who live there. It'll be the end of the high season now. D'you seriously think you'll enjoy it?"

"If you would be seriously willing to take me."

"It's up to you."

"No, it's up to you."

"Well . . . Why not? I'm always ready for a break."

"How could we go?"

"From here? You'd have to fly to New York. There are sure to be connecting planes."

"And from London?"

"Oh, from there you can fly direct."

She put her hand on mine. "That is the way," she said. "If we stop in New York we shall get involved again in our business affairs."

It seemed as likely to me that going back to London would involve us just as quickly in business affairs, and I thought this trip was a sudden romantic whim of hers that would tick away for a few days when we went home and then quietly die off. However, the day we returned she asked me to telephone the hotel and to book plane seats. There was a rush then, much responsibility to be delegated, sports things shoved into bags and a taxi to Heathrow, and we were off.

So there was a nine-hour flight; and a half-hour taxi ride brought us to the Pear Tree Club; adjoining cottages had been reserved for us and after a bibulous dinner we retired to them and only joined forces for breakfast on the terrace. It was warm. The sun shone fitfully among lamb's-wool clouds, there was a glisten of night's rain on the grass, and the sea thumped its occasional wave on the adjacent shore. We ate breakfast surrounded by insolent birds who tried to snatch the toast out of our hands and dug deep into the sugar bowl.

Shona seemed to be appreciative of everything, but I kept a weather eye on her, not sure how far she was really going to enjoy it, how far it was going to be a sort of self-imposed "I am Shona on holiday, this is me registering pleasure." After all, nothing could have been much further from her scene. All her life she'd been around in cities, following a profession that was all glitter and high-society commercialism and superficial noise and hard-nosed balance sheets. Here there was little to appeal to her, at least for more than a day or two, and I wondered.

We swam and walked along the sand and lay in the half-shade of the casuarina and the mahogany trees; and swam again and dozed, and drank daiquiris and lunched in the big open dining room and took an extra sleep in the afternoon, and went out for another swim to the rafts and took tea on the terrace and watched the sun sink into the sea.

I said, "Have you ever seen the green flash?"

"What is that?"

"Just as the sun does his disappearing trick, at the very moment of sinking, you can sometimes see a sudden brief green flash, or green point of light where the sun has been a moment before."

She took off her sunglasses and closely watched the sun until it was snuffed out.

"I did not see it. Did you?"

"No, not this time."

"Have you ever seen it?"

"I know people who have."

She smiled at me. "Then we will watch again tomorrow."

The clouds were congregating for the arrival of night. Still we sat there. In the afterglow the waves were an inky cobalt as they turned, against the polished bronze of the sea. The moored boats in the curved bay silhouetted themselves blackly, like cutouts in a collage.

"David," she said. "I like it here. Thank you for bringing me."

"Well," I said, "I don't know if that's the way it was, but I'm glad to take the credit."

There was no one I knew in the hotel except the proprietors; we had drinks with them the next evening, and they were deferential to Shona, as most people seemed to be since the products of her firm became known worldwide. There was a chap I wanted to ring in Bridgetown called Ronnie Baird, who was Deputy High Commissioner, but I waited until Shona was out of the way in case he couldn't do what I asked.

That evening at dinner Shona said, "Why is this called a club and not a hotel?"

"Probably something to do with the local bylaws. In a hotel you more or less have to admit anybody. If you run a club you can pick and choose."

"So that you can keep out black people?"

Hullo, I thought, here it comes.

"Possibly."

"I don't think I wish to stay in a hotel that does not admit black people."

"Simmer down. It's not just a color thing. A number of whites are probably kept out too."

"But what is the proportion of white to black in this island?"

"Oh . . . one to twenty. One to twenty-five."

"So." She breathed through her nose.

"Anyway, it's all very easygoing. Don't work up a head of steam about something you don't understand."

"Do you understand?"

"Well, if a respectable black man with money came here I don't for a moment suppose he wouldn't be admitted. Remember, this country is now run by the West Indians for themselves. If *they* objected they could soon stop it."

We were silent for a few moments while our waiter, a handsome, lightly bearded young man with the lissome walk of a fast bowler, served us our next course.

"It must be sad," said Shona.

"What?"

"For someone like him. What is his name?"

"Merton."

"It must be sad for Merton and more like him. After a hundred years or more when the white man was the master and the black man his servant, then the islands were given their freedom. But what has changed? Every diner in this room is white! Every waiter is black! So what has changed?"

I cut into my succulent little hen bird. "What can you do about it? Sugar. Rum. A few cottage industries. They couldn't maintain their standard of living on that. So it has to be tourism. And in the nature of present-day tourism ninety-eight percent of the clientele is white. Most West Indians swallow the pill. There's no way out."

"Hm." She sipped her wine. The character playing the guitar in the band had a deformed hip. He sat on a high stool with another for his feet. Oddly enough the waiters moving among the guests seemed to have no rhythmic feel for the music: They didn't walk in time or seem to be aware of the calypso beat.

I said, "Are you a Communist, Shona?"

She looked up, her eyes sparkling in the candlelight. "You ask *me* that?"

"Well . . . it could be, couldn't it? When you left Russia you were getting out from under Stalin, not necessarily from the system."

She was quiet, eating her food, until I wondered if she wasn't going to answer.

"It is possible that all good people ought to be Communists—in principle. Isn't that so? I don't know, but it is at least arguable. But no one who has lived under such a system and escaped from it would ever wish to go back to what men have made of that principle—in practice. Does that make sense to you?"

"It crossed my mind to wonder."

"There is a lot I do not like about the West, but the imperfections, in proportion, are small. As a considerable capitalist myself . . ."

"I noticed the high time you had talking to the Baumgarten woman about the good old days."

"The old days. May I correct you?" She patted my hand. "Not the good old days. But of course youth looked back on always has its rosier side."

Did it, I thought? Not mine. "She seemed to go a long way back, your chum. Once I heard her talking about the early days of Stalin's dictatorship. When would that be: 1926? 1930?"

"Oh, Ilya, she is older than she looks, and she forgets that I am not so old. She rambles on. It was enough to see her again, though most of the people we knew are dead. She lost her first husband in the first year of their marriage. Then she came to Vienna as a secretary in the Russian military command, but by the time they withdrew she had married this Austrian, Joseph Baumgarten, and she was permitted to stay."

I said, "May I trawl up the forbidden subject?"

"What is that?"

"Have you fired Trudi?"

"Would you mind?"

"I would mind if it involved me."

"Well, I did not. I have given her another chance. Does that please you?"

"It pleases me not to be involved in the decision."

"You are not. I reasoned . . ." Shona laughed deep in her throat. "I reasoned that we were far more likely to get the money she owed us if she remained in the firm than if she left."

Most days the weather was variable, with cloud and sun doing quick-change acts, and a sighing breeze. We went to sleep every night and woke each morning to the cracking of the waves on the shore. We hired a catamaran and sailed almost out of sight of land. We waterskied and scuba-dived; and I hired a yellow Moke and drove jolting round the island, up to the North Point, to Farley Hill, to the Andromeda gardens, and of course once or twice into Bridgetown. The surface of the roads was frightful. Shona said, "At least you cannot drive fast here!" She seemed to look younger every day. The invitation came I'd been angling for: The Governor General and Lady Millerton wanted us to lunch with them next Monday at twelve-thirty.

"That will be a pretty ending to the holiday," said Shona. "But this you must have arranged!"

"Ronnie Baird is in the British High Commission. I went to school with him, and he was one of the very few blokes I liked there."

"I often forget that you are so well connected."

Every night we drank too much wine, and every night we made love. Every evening at six we sat on the terrace and watched for the green flash as the sun went down.

"Nothing!" said Shona every time, and then, after a fellow guest had claimed he had seen it, "it is *subjective*! . . . But of *course*! One stares at the sun so long as it goes down that it is a delusion of the eyes . . ."

"I wouldn't think you're far out."

"But then—why isn't it *our* delusion also? Ah well . . ."

There were dances at the hotel, and once or twice we made a few circles of the floor for form's sake before retiring to our cottages. On the Saturday evening as the green flash once again failed to show up she said, "Do you know, I don't think I want to go back at all!"

I raised my eyebrows at her in the accumulating twilight.

"You're joking."

"Not joking. More than half serious. I suppose it is a wish to stop time more than anything else."

I said, "This is a dreamer's existence. Always better for being short. Another two weeks would be marvelous. But it's specially marvelous because of the contrast. That's why heaven would be such a bore."

"Perhaps this is better than heaven."

So it had worked for her. I really believed it now.

She fumbled on her lap for the book there. "You know what I have been reading? You must have seen it."

"Balzac's letters."

"I came upon this passage last night. May I read it to you?" I nodded and she put on her other spectacles, held the book up to the fading light. " 'The sudden revelation of the poetry of the senses is the powerful link which attaches young men to women older than themselves; but it is like a prisoner's chains, it leaves an ineffable imprint on the soul, implants a distaste for a fresh and innocent love.' " She lowered the book. "David, I have never pressed you for any display of your feelings in our affair. I have always been grateful when any sign of them occurs spontaneously. So I am not demanding anything extra now. But . . . does it seem to you that Balzac was right?"

I stared out over the sea. A pleasure steamer, as big as a Mississippi riverboat, was drifting across the orange glow where the sun had sunk, with fifty or sixty lights winking in the encroaching dark.

"God knows how old Balzac's mistress was; how much older than he was, I mean. Balzac was right for himself. The only other thing *I* can say is that you seem to be right for me."

She said, "When you first became my lover I was careful to keep the word love strictly out of it. I tell you that it has *never* entered into my association with any other man. *Never*. That it *has* entered this one, I have to confess—now. You must have known it for a long time. I have ceased to be the cool and calculating *boss*; I am at once dismayed and delighted at what has happened. I am at sea when jealousy and possessiveness break in. I know all the greater dangers of such an association. I ask nothing more from you than what you can give. At the very beginning I was reluctant to begin because I sensed the risks. But now I am glad. Whatever happens in the future, I am glad for here and now. This has been the most wonderful period of my life."

"So," I said. "So. It's not easy for me, Shona, to say much."

"Don't try."

"I should try," I said. "I should try."

Darkness comes quickly in the tropics.

Shona said, "Do you know, every night when we have been watching for the green flash I have been saying something to myself. I have been saying, 'If I see the green flash, David will love me till I die.' "

The band was drifting in for the evening session. The little cripple was fixing up his electronic drums.

"We've four more days," I said.

"Four more sunsets."

"Maybe," I said. "Maybe we should both see it before we go."

III The wine was good, and at dinner we drank more than usual. We didn't dance that night, but supported each other to the doors of the cottages. After some discussion we chose hers. There we did not make love but lay beside each other smoking and talking long into the small hours. In the end I told her what I had never told anyone else—about my father, and his jealousy of me and his bullying, the locking-up in the cupboard under the stairs. And then that final night when he had come home drunk and found me in the kitchen and got me in a corner, and then, when I was scared out of my wits, he had lost his balance and toppled over and cracked his skull on the iron bar of the stove. And his death, and the police and the inquest, and all the hoo-ha of that time . . .

It was a struggle talking about it. I may put it down in so many words like that, all pat and easy; but it was as hard as breaking bones.

Then later on other things came up, raked over from that last meeting with my mother, feelings that she wasn't blameless in the nasty mess-up of our lives, that in some ways she was as jealous as he was, that it had become a sort of three-way scrap for possession and dominance which had suddenly, unexpectedly blown up in her face. I told Shona things I thought I'd forgotten, maybe things that were best forgotten . . . We droned on and on.

The next morning I woke in my own bed with a thick head and couldn't believe I'd said so much—got into a state of resenting it like hell. *In vino veritas*, drunken inspiration, yak-yak my tongue had gone, spilling it all like a broken flour bag. But I recalled—or thought I recalled—that her little promptings, her sympathetic questions in the darkened room, had come at discreet intervals, inviting me to go on. Maybe she hadn't been as drunk as I was —that hard Russian head—and had baited the trail for me to follow. In future when the proper occasion turned up she'd be able to fling it back at me. Nothing I did out of step now—or what she considered out of step—would fail to be related to what I had told her last night. Like a second-rate shrink she'd have the answer for everything.

All Sunday I was in a filthy mood and her teasing good temper made it worse.

Why, she asked, did all the West Indian birds have such big feet? They all looked as if they were wearing skis. And were these little yellow birds that stole our sugar the same as those in the old song "Yellow bird, way up in banana tree"? And how did she address the Governor General's wife tomorrow—what was *her* title? And thank the merciful God for a small breakfast, for one ate altogether too much here. And if we were using our Moke today we must be careful to tip the overnight rain off the hood before we started: otherwise we'd be engulfed in a cataract. And did I mind not going to the caves? She'd always fought shy of them since she once went deep into the caves of Majorca and the lights failed.

Shona wasn't noted for her angelic temper and at the least she would normally soon have barked back at me, wanting to know what grisly bear she was living with or if overdrinking had produced too many spots on my liver. The fact that she didn't showed she cottoned on to my feelings about the talk of the night, and was "making allowances." Making allowances, for Christ's sake! Even thinking the words set my teeth grating and put me in a lousier mood than ever. We went waterskiing that morning and then after lunch had a stand-up row, raking up every subject except the one that mattered.

When it was spent we were spent, and separated, and lay and slept and smoked and fumed in our separate cottages. We met again in time not to see the green flash, and by dinner we were on speaking terms. But we ate little and drank less, and after the meal went to our cottages with isolation the only need.

Isolation was certainly *my* need. My tongue tasted like a sewer and I felt as if, because I'd given her some part of my mind, I would never want her body again.

When it came time to change for the luncheon, I went out into the garden and picked myself a bougainvillea flower for my buttonhole. When Shona saw it she made no comment and we walked to the taxi, which she insisted we take, otherwise by the time we got to Bridgetown her hair would, she said, be standing out like a punk-rock star.

She was in cool gray silk, with gray tights and black patent pumps. Her only ring, a ruby, glowed on her hard thin finger.

Government House was a handsome eighteenth-century shack, guarded by Barbadian soldiery, and we had to pull in and wait at the guardhouse while they telephoned to ask permission for us to proceed. An adjutant greeted us at the door and led us upstairs to meet Sir Anthony and Lady Millerton and half a dozen guests. We drank rum punches and made chat until lunch was dished up.

They were a fairly usual mix: the lieutenant commander of a British naval frigate that had just put in to Bridgetown; a female choreographer on holiday from Paris; two well-known television stars, the girl a sexy piece who was seated next to me; the editor of the local paper and his dame.

We ate at the smaller table, while a pianist dealt out Liszt in the adjoining salon. Conversation was fairly boring. Shona, on Sir Anthony's right, was as usual the object of special attention. I tried to be objective and compare her particular looks with those of the intelligent young critter sitting next to me. Felicity had all the puppy charm of a very pretty young woman. Shona looked hard, clear cut, spare, refined by the years, intellectual, yet never quite unattractive, always just feminine enough.

The meal was modest; afterward, over coffee and brandy, Sir Anthony Millerton came over to me. We'd had little to say to each other so far. Now he said, "I believe we have to commiserate with you—and also congratulate you. Did you know about it before you left England?"

"About what?" I said.

"About . . . But I suppose you expected it, didn't you? It was only a question of when."

"Sorry," I said. "I'm not with you."

He lifted his eyebrows and smiled. "You haven't seen Saturday's *Times*, then? No, I suppose not. Let me see, where did I put it?" He raised a finger at a servant and sent him hurrying into the next room. I was rather more keen to chat up the television star, and waited blankly and not too politely for the servant.

When he came, Sir Anthony opened up the paper and peered through a couple of pages before he found the item he wanted. Then he handed the paper to me.

The paragraph he pointed out read:

The death is announced of Sir Charles St. Clair Abden, 12th Baronet, at his home at Lochfiern House, near Ullapool, at the age of 69. Charles Abden was educated at Ampleforth College and Caius College, Cambridge, where he took a degree in Law. At the outbreak of war he was commissioned in the Argyll and Sutherland Highlanders and served in France, North Africa and Sicily, where he was awarded the Military Cross. After the war he returned to Scotland and spent much of his life managing his estate and working on behalf of his fellow Catholics both at home and abroad, particularly in Poland, which he visited twice. Sir Charles leaves a widow and two daughters, but his only son, Dr. Malcolm Abden, the onetime Conservative MP for North Banff and well-known broadcaster, was killed in a motor accident in 1972. The baronetcy passes to his nephew, Mr. David Abden, who lives in London.

CHAPTER FOURTEEN

I We flew home on the Wednesday.

"Absolute rubbish," I said. "Rubbish and hogwash." This or variations on it for about the tenth time as we boarded the plane. I had put it a thought more mildly at Government House, but Sir Anthony Millerton had looked surprised at my peevishness.

"It's just a crashing bloomer," I said. "Malcolm had at least four children; four or five. One of them will obviously inherit."

"Unless they are all girls," Lady Millerton put in.

That thought hadn't got through to me. "It's some crackpot confusion of identity. Probably Malcolm's eldest son is called David."

"But then he would not be living in London, would he," said Shona. "He could hardly be old enough."

"Would you like to telephone?" Sir Anthony asked. "It would settle the matter quickly."

I shook my head. "I wouldn't know who to phone."

"Do you not have a family solicitor?"

"*They* may have one; I don't know his name. My father was not on terms with his brother."

Sir Anthony said, "Would that explain . . . It did seem to me unusual that if you were heir to the baronetcy no one had informed you at the time of your cousin's death."

"It's obviously just a massive mistake on the part of *The Times*," I said. "Malcolm's eldest son is called David, and they've confused him with me. After all, take away the sentence 'who lives in London' and the situation explains itself."

"And the word 'nephew,' " said Lady Millerton.

"As you remark." I showed my teeth at her grimly.

"If it should be true . . ." I said to Shona on the plane.

"Yes? What is so bad about it?"

"I suppose it would be possible to throw up the title."

"Why should you?"

"I can't take anything from *them!*"

"You are not taking anything from them. You are simply accepting your ancestry."

"I don't think much of that either!"

"Ever since last Saturday," she said, "you have been in a black mood. I think you have felt so grumpy that you have not even been on speaking terms with yourself!"

"If I was cross-grained it was for other reasons."

— "Because you think you spoke too freely to me—talked too much in the night?"

"You hyped it out of me."

"Is that how you saw it? I did not see it that way. Sometimes when something is very wrong and deeply felt, speaking of it to a close friend can be a form of therapy."

"Back to Dr. Meiss, eh?"

"Who is he?"

"I told you, I went to a shrink shortly after my father's death."

"Oh, yes. But I am not in his position at all! I am someone you care for a little and who cares for you. Talking in that way, confidentially, lovingly, cannot that help to heal, to alleviate?—"

"Who said I wanted any healing?"

She kept her mouth tight while the stewardess brought us drinks. Then she said, "All right, you don't. Forget that it ever happened, forget that we ever talked at all."

"If we can."

"Very well, then."

Her skin looked overstretched in the reading light from above.

"Good health," I said, touching her glass with my own.

"Thank you. If you wish it for me."

"Dear heaven! What d'you take me for?"

"Sometimes these last few days . . ."

"I've told you to forget. You've *promised* to forget. Let's just remember our first ten days here. Eh?"

She sipped her drink. "And the green flash?"

"Which you never saw."

She looked at me. "Alas, no. Which I—which we—never saw."

| | There was a letter waiting for me from a firm of Edinburgh law merchants. It was addressed to Sir David
| II | Abden, Bt. That made the bottom fall out of the lift.
The letter said that on the decease of my uncle . . . I rang up and spoke to a Mr. Macardle and told him it was not on for me to come to Edinburgh; would he send me what information he could on this unfortunate affair. He replied that he would be in London in ten days' time and we could meet at the offices of Messrs. Taylor, Taylor and Wellington, at New Square, who were their corresponding solicitors in London. The *Glasgow Herald* telephoned me and, a day later, the *Dundee Courier* and the *Aberdeen Press*. To all of them I said no comment. Which was true. I was speechless. The only one of my friends to ring was Derek Jones, who seemed chuffed with the whole thing. I told him he could have it for himself any time he wanted, together with a pound of tea.

Mr. Andrew Macardle, WS, was a thickset elderly man in a black suit and flyaway collar. He looked just like a stage solicitor, except that one eyelid was lowered over a shrewd blue eye, giving him a squint of confidential slyness. All his clients, it seemed, must be deaf; or he was too used to speaking in court.

"The situation," he shouted, "is quite a simple one. Dr. Malcolm Abden had four daughters by his first wife, Lady Fiona, and one by his second. Sir Charles's other brother, Duncan, was killed at Arnhem and died unmarried. When Dr. Malcolm Abden met his death in that tragic road crash you became the heir presumptive."

"No one told me," I observed, remembering Millerton's comment.

"No, well, I questioned this with Sir Charles, but he thought it unnecessary. After all, he said, you were still only presumptive."

"How's that?"

"Mrs. Abden, Mrs. Alison Abden, Malcolm Abden's second wife, was four months pregnant when her husband was killed."

I looked out of the window at the scowling sky—rather a change from the ultramarine of Barbados.

"How they must have prayed for a son."

"No doubt. No doubt." Mr. Macardle raised his voice so that I could hear better. "It's human nature, isn't it," he shouted. "Sir

Charles would clearly have been happier to have had a grandson to carry on the name."

"And with only me at deep extra cover. Enough to poison any man's last hours."

"Sir Charles had a long-standing lung complaint," said Macardle severely, "resulting from a war wound."

"Ah," I said, "point taken. All the same it was a pretty come-off losing his son in that way . . . I should think the whole family is sick, isn't it, seeing the title go to a black sheep who's never had anything to do with them and never wants to."

Macardle picked up some papers from the desk and winked at them with his collusive eye.

"I think, Sir David, this is something you must discover for yourself. I believe they will fully accept the situation and help you in any way they can."

It was the first time anyone had called me that.

"Would it be possible to throw up the title?"

He drew in his breath as if the bath water were too hot for his big toe. "Nothing is impossible these days, Sir David. Peerages are renounced, so there should be no insuperable obstacle to your doing the same. But if I may say so, I think it would be a very misguided move."

"Presumably if I renounced it the baronetcy wouldn't become extinct. There'd be someone else."

"The last time I saw Sir Charles, which was about six months ago, we went into the family history." Macardle raised his voice. "The tree, you understand," he shouted. "The tree. If you were to die without issue—or indeed were to renounce the title—it would pass to a Mr. Alexander Abden, your uncle's cousin's son—or his grandson—who are farmers in British Columbia. They have been lost sight of, but of course they could be traced. Could be traced if necessary. Though I trust it will not be necessary."

I thought round this for a minute or two. "Apart from the baronetcy, do I get anything else?"

"Well . . ." Macardle flipped at the papers in his hand. "Certain heirlooms. A house. Some land . . ."

"You don't mean the house where they live? Loch Something?"

"Lochfiern House. No. That was built in the eighteenth century and is willed in the normal way. Wester Craig, about twenty miles north, is entailed with the baronetcy, and with it about five hundred acres, chiefly moorland, a stream, two crofters' cottages, that sort of thing."

"Who's there now?"

"No one except a caretaker. The tendency of the—er—family has been to concentrate their attention on Lochfiern House. Wester Craig has simply been kept."

"As a ruin?"

"Oh, no. Oh, dear no. It needs the money spending on it if one were to live there permanently; but it is perfectly habitable." Macardle could see I was stone deaf so he shouted, "Perfectly habitable."

I crossed my legs and thought about it again. "These papers you have; they're simply the bare bones, I suppose; the legalistic bones of the inheritance. I shall have to consider for a few days . . . Until then . . ."

"Clearly the first thing you must do, Sir David, is go up and look for yourself. I'm sure old Lady Abden will want to meet you at the earliest possible moment—and your other cousins. When can you go?"

I said, "I still have to make up my mind whether to take it."

III   I worked round the clock during the next month. Against my long-held principles, but the best counterirritant to hand. I also had a convenient bee in my bonnet over this new perfume Charisma, and I nagged at Shona. Seeing how it had originated, from TBM Ltd., and Mr. Schmidt and his experimental monkeys, I felt that not enough attention was being paid to the 44 percent of the human race which so far had resisted ideas of sex-related perfumes. Scent on a man was effeminate. Of course. A talc had to be given some masculine name like Old Leather or Woodbine or Big Spice. But these were really nothing more than spin-offs, just a part of the service. Even the best aftershaves were 96 percent spirit and 4 percent perfume, and if they stung like hell—as they all did—this was supposed to do your skin good.

I persuaded myself that here was an opportunity for a new approach. No man of course wanted to stink of perfume. But if the monkeys were to be believed, scent—smell—had a sex pull like a magnet on iron filings; this fact must be put to greater use. All women were sold their perfumes with that in mind; no advertiser ever made any bones about that. So why not in reverse?

Shona and Leo Longford—who was coming much more to the top since Marks was sacked and John had retired—were both doubtful.

"I like the name Semaphore," Shona said, "but previous attempts in this field have not been successful. At least two of the big companies have tried something similar in the recent past and they have fallen flat, with huge advertising bills and pyramids of unsold stock."

"It's bound to come," I said. "Sooner or later. We'd need a few subtle changes from the formula of Charisma, but Schmidt and his chemists can fix that."

Leo had been tapping his teeth.

"Would *you* use it, David?" he asked suddenly.

"What, a perfume? No, I wouldn't."

"Then why expect other men to be different?"

"Because other men *are* different. Some other men. I don't mean the gays. There are ordinary men—an awful lot of 'em—who don't do *well* with women. They're ugly—or clumsy—or just plain shy. And often the women do damn all to help. Men of this sort—if they could feel confident—would be on a new level. Just to have that confidence. They'd pay a lot."

"I think you are right, David," Shona said, "but timing is everything. We shall have to see."

In the end I decided to go back to TBM and tell them what we wanted. From then on for a bit it would be up to them.

We returned to our fencing, and Erica was the next to congratulate me on my inheritance, her eyes more than usually animated as she looked me over, as if expecting that a baronetcy might have altered my physique—which anyway she ought to know reasonably well already.

That night Shona said, "When are you going to Scotland?"

"I haven't decided to accept the thing yet."

"Well, it's a *fait accompli*, is it not? There is nothing more to do. If you wish to renounce it it will lead you into a lot of tedious legal complications. Anyway, I do not see what objection you have. For my part . . ."

"Go on."

"No, if I say that, you will take it the wrong way."

"Try me."

"I was about to say that the title will look very well on our billheads. I have often thought we might invite some person who for a small interest would lend his name . . ."

"Why didn't you ask the Marquess of Ludgrove?"

"Oh, Eddie was not the type. No, I am sorry, I can see, as I thought, that you have taken it the wrong way. You should not have pressed me to speak what was only a floating thought. Forget it. Think only of yourself."

"Do I ever do anything else?"

"Just *now* and *then*—in spite of your *best intentions*. But that proverb, not to look a gift horse in the mouth. What can you lose?"

"What have I gained? Some rickety old sixteenth-century ruin that's falling to pieces round my ears, a few acres of desert, a couple of crofters' cottages occupied by wild hairy Highlanders; and a damned title."

She patted my hand. "Go up and see. Shall I come with you?"

"I wouldn't submit you to the ordeal. It's quite clear they'll all hate my guts for stealing the title, and the dislike'll not be a one-way street."

"Your mother is pleased at the news?"

"I don't know if she knows. It's hardly likely she'll rejoice. It was her total unacceptability to them that made the break between them and my father."

Shona sighed. "As I have said, it is all quite hard for me to understand. Perhaps it is better that I should not try. In Russia I think this would be a matter for rejoicing all round."

"Yes, I can see it: Polovtsian dances, wild men leaping over bonfires, maidens throwing flowers, gypsy fiddlers with epilepsy."

"And your Highland crofters? I know they can dance! Perhaps they will all rejoice to see you."

"They won't be seeing me yet. I'm going to Bristol tomorrow to put some more of my ideas for Semaphore to Mr. Schmidt."

"Take care how you drive. It would be a pity if you held the baronetcy for too short a time."

CHAPTER FIFTEEN

I So it was late September before I finally hit the trail north. In the meantime some strain had been put on the postal system by my correspondence with Mr. Andrew Macardle, WS, and with a chap called Bruce Macintyre who called himself a factor and seemed to have been given responsibility by the Abdens for looking after my bit of property and their maleless estate. Perhaps he'd been in charge for longer than that, since Malcolm had been dead quite a while and Sir Charles had been a sick man.

I drove to Edinburgh and had a longish session with Macardle, during which most of our talk must have been heard the length of Princes Street. He said he'd ring Captain Bruce Macintyre and tell him I was on my way. I raised no objection, though privately I'd decided to come to Wester Craig when they were not expecting me. I told Macardle I'd be arriving Wednesday morning, having worked it out that I should be able to get there Tuesday afternoon.

I left his office at noon, had lunch, checked out of the hotel and pottered north to Inverness. Next morning I didn't take the direct route but followed a wayward fancy to keep to the east coast as far as Bonner Bridge and then turned west across the flat neck of the Highlands. Twenty miles out of Ullapool the scene changed: All the gentle undulation was gone and you were in a moonscape of jutting mountains and jagged cliffs and sugarloaf peaks and water, lots of water, lochs, or whatever they were called, invading the land round every corner.

I had a snack in the town and asked the way to my noble inheritance. A finger planted firmly on the map steered me in the general direction, and a bit later an old chap with a moth-eaten moustache and no teeth pointed the way from the only cottage in sight on the lonely moors. I turned the Aston up a narrow way

between fields, came to a white wooden gate, which I had to get
out to open. The land to the left fell into a valley, and the potholed
drive dipped sharply to a rattling bridge over a stream. Then up
the other side you could see the house for the first time.

I hadn't known what to expect. Sixteenth century had suggested
a turreted castle or a moated grange; but this looked just like any
other rotten old house. Two-storied with Victorian windows under inverted V-shaped roofs, the chimneys tall and ranked, the
walls done in a white stucco which wasn't bad against the firs and
larches climbing the hillside behind.

I drew up in a sort of walled garden, where the chief product
seemed to be decaying vegetables; and the entrance to the house,
if it was the main entrance, was a brass-knockered white door
inside a monstrosity of a glass porch. I put the engine to sleep and
got out; there was a metal bellpull beside the door so I gave it a
try.

Nothing happened for a while—except for a racket of dogs
barking in the distance—and then a thin, small, middle-aged man
in a shabby gray suit with a collar stud but no collar squinted
suspiciously out.

I explained my presence, and he immediately melted into a
watery welcome. His name was Coppell; he was the gardener–
caretaker and lived with his wife in the adjoining cottage. They
had been expecting me in the morn, he explained, and he had just
been cleaning up in the kitchen. Please to come ben the hoose, Sir
David, and welcome. Did I fancy some tea, or a drop of something
stronger? The cellars were not what they used to be, but there
was a jar or two he could bring up.

I wondered how many jars he had been bringing up for himself;
there was a whiff of peppermint in the air; but I said no, I'd look
over the house first.

We went through the glass porch which would have been an
excrescence on any house, and into a horrible little hall; then into
a dining room which was separated from the hall by a leather
screen. The house was just furnished but only just; the furniture
looked nineteenth century and built for dour endurance. Floors
were flagged, with a few old rugs and druggeting to hide the cracks.
A butler's pantry led off the dining room and kitchen, which was
a square stone room with pre-Jurassic fitments, and beyond that
another room with an antique boiler which, Coppell informed

me, was "where the gentlemen changed their boots and damp clothes after shooting." He had a different accent, softer voiced than most, maybe a touch of the Irish.

This part of the house was older than the first, and now he opened a heavy oak door and stood aside. "After you, sorr." And there I was being shown into a big hall with a beamed ceiling, a checkerboard floor of brown and white, and medieval windows. Between the windows, which were high up, a dozen tattered flags hung like last year's washing.

"We've come round in a half circle, sorr. It is ower aisy to lose ya sense of direction. This door, here, leads back to the dining room."

Not cold outside but bone cold in the house, particularly this hall, which smelled like a neglected church. There were two fireplaces pretty well side by side.

"I've never seen that before," I said, pointing.

"Och, it was built so that the laird and his lady might each have an equal share of the fire. Now as for these battle flags, sorr . . ."

He named names that stirred vaguely in my memory like disturbed worms. A coat of arms on the wall above and between the fireplaces had a motto underneath, but it was in Gaelic or something. The only furniture in this hall was a refectory table that looked as if it had stood years of carousing, and three tall Jacobean chairs. I wondered the Abdens hadn't pinched the battle flags as well. Perhaps they were mentioned in the entail.

We were now joined by Mrs. Coppell, who was taller than her husband but as anxious to please. Perhaps there's no trade union for gardeners and their wives. She said, would I be staying the night, and I said I was sure there was no room ready, and she said, och aye, it would be nae trouble at all, and she would get the fire going right away, and what would I fancy for supper?

A long narrow drawing room had a parquet floor and a few better chairs; its windows overlooked the valley, and you could see water. I thought it was the sea; but the sea, they said, was round the corner and over the hill. What you could see was Loch Ashe. Some portraits here, presumably ancestral portraits, on the striped walls, confirmed my view that the Abdens would have been better to keep their faces to themselves.

A staircase led up from the first hall to the upstairs bedrooms, of which there appeared to be eight. The one Mrs. Coppell showed me into was bright enough, with a four-poster bed and chintz curtains.

"Who slept here last?" I said.

Mrs. Coppell fumbled with the neck of her blouse and looked at her husband, who scratched his head.

"We've had nae one reg'lar like since Dr. Malcolm was killed, sorr. Sir Charles has nae been any too weel for lang enough. I think it must have been the American, sorr, who rented the hoose a year last August."

"Did Dr. Malcolm live here when he was alive?"

"Part of the time, sorr. He would gie stalking parties here noo and then, entertaining his London friends, like."

"Is there a grouse moor?"

"No, sorr, not on this coast. It is the deer Dr. Malcolm's guests came here for."

"What are those dogs?"

"Och, just the one or two that are left. Would ye like to see the stables while the light lasts?"

I would and did. There were two pointers and a spaniel, all very friendly and anxious to meet the new owner. There was another man and his wife too, called McVitie; a typical gillie with leggings, and a leather jacket over a once yellow sweater; scars down his left cheek as if sometime he had got in the way of the pellets. They lived in a second cottage nearby, and McVitie made a living of sorts rearing a few sheep. They got no wages but lived rent free, and in return Mrs. McVitie helped Mrs. Coppell with the household chores; when there were guests Dr. Malcolm had hired girls from the village. What village, I wondered?

The kitchen garden ran to a few flowers as well; wet michaelmas daisies and depressed dahlias shared the protective walls with cabbages and runner beans. "The winds can be a wee bit trying," said Coppell, scratching under his arm. We walked around as the sun glinted through barred clouds on the metallic sea. The bars were realistic but ran the wrong way. I wondered what Shona would have made of it all. I wondered what these people would make of Shona. Did they even know a world of perfumery existed? The answer was yes, nowadays. They'd all have their tellies.

Dinner was at eight, and Mrs. McVitie waited on. I had chicken soup, a filet of grilled cod, a grouse (what else?) and a square or two of very old cheese. Apart from the cheese it was a good meal, and the bottle of 1964 Beau Site was easy to put away. A glass of 1920 port, a cigar—slightly mildewed—and two cups of black coffee ended the meal and I went to bed.

No rattling bones or heavy breathing disturbed the night, and I knew nothing until Coppell came in at seven, pulling back the curtains with an unnecessary rattle, while Mrs. Coppell brought in the breakfast, ordered at their suggestion the night before. Shrouds of damp mist were hanging over the larches. I was about early and left the house at nine-thirty. Coppell had said Captain Bruce Macintyre intended to come at ten to be on the spot whenever I arrived that morning. I drove about three miles back toward Ullapool and parked in a narrow lane leading up the side of the mountain. After twenty minutes a fairly smart BMW went by, and I thought that was probably the car he would drive.

I started the Aston and drove fast toward Lochfiern House.

II   Lochfiern was only about a dozen miles from Ullapool, but the opposite side, and a very different kettle of fish from Wester Craig. For one thing it was in a valley, and compared to the rest of the country was wooded and fertile. For another, it was unmistakably Georgian, and no infidels had mucked about with its original exterior. A well-cut lawn with an ornamental iron seat, tall roses and michaelmas daisies in the sur-rounding shrubbery, a mass of clematis flowering over a shed. It could all as well have been in Hampshire or Sussex except for the hills and mountains never far away, and the windows of the house were not so big. As I rang the bell I saw a smaller place built of the same stone, with ecclesiastical windows, separate from the main house.

You couldn't see either the sea or loch from here, but clouds were drifting up from where the sea could be expected to be, and the sun had inhaled too much of the morning vapor and was hiding behind it. A maid came, in an untidy black frock. I asked to see

Lady Abden. She asked me what name should she say, and for the first time in my life I answered, "Sir David Abden."

She did a double take and then asked me in. A square hall with a wide, white-painted staircase and oriental rugs. The house was probably about the same size as Wester Craig, but the furniture was elegant, well kept, shining in the subdued light. I walked across to the right-hand wall where there was a cluster of miniatures, but before I could read the inscriptions underneath a footstep clicked on the polished floor.

A dark young woman in gray tweeds, hair cut short and boyish. A Sealyham scuttled at her heels but didn't yap.

"David Abden?" she said. She held out her hand. "I'm Alison Abden."

We shook hands. She went on, "We were not expecting you until tomorrow. I think Captain Macintyre had made arrangements to meet you at Wester Craig this morning. Hadn't he? Mr. Macardle rang on Monday, I thought."

This must be one of Malcolm's younger sisters. A sight more personable than the average Abden, if you could judge by the photographs and portraits.

"I've just come from Wester Craig. I expect we passed each other on the way."

Her eyes were cool, sizing up, not unfriendly but noncommittal.

"Are you? . . ." I began.

"I'm Malcolm's widow."

"Oh . . . I see." The Ayrshire heiress. Who, it seemed, had brought good looks as well as siller. "I thought you might have been one of his sisters."

On cue another female showed. Shorter and older than the first, a thick black jersey over a shabby black woollen frock. We were introduced. This was Lucie, Malcolm's sister, sallow-faced, and her lips tight and plump like a closed fist. She looked as if she'd missed her man by saying too many Hail Marys.

"Do come in," said Alison at last, and led the way into the drawing room. "Can I get you coffee? Or something stronger?"

"Coffee would be fine."

We talked, Lucie sitting by the window staring out and joining in with a few dry crumbs when she felt like it. I reckoned she must have been Malcolm's elder sister; maybe most of the troubles of the family weighed on her.

Alison rang the bell for coffee and the same little maid came in, glancing at me askance before she left. The Sealyham wobbled across and sniffed at my shoes, probably scenting the gun dogs. He thumped his tail and whimpered.

"You'll be wanting to see Mother," said Lucie abruptly.

"If she's to be seen," I said. "Not that it matters if she's not."

"I don't think she will wish to talk business," said Lucie, as if there was a disagreeable smell about it. "That is all left for Mr. Macintyre."

"I didn't come to talk business."

"I'll see if she'll see you, then." She got up and left.

When I sat down again I said, "I'm a bit hazy as to the number of Abdens in this house. Or even in the district. I never met one until I met Malcolm a few years ago."

A very still young female, this: Her head might have been one of the cameos in the hall.

"Malcolm's four daughters are away at school. My own . . . she is out with her nurse. Apart from Lucie and myself there is Lady Abden and—er—Mary."

"Mary?"

"Malcolm's other sister. She is not well and tends to keep to her room."

"Do you live here yourself all the time?"

"Most of the time. Should I not?"

"I wondered whether you spent part of the year with your own family in Ayrshire."

"Kirkcudbright," she corrected.

"Sorry," I said, "or is ignorance no excuse?"

She half smiled; very delicate lips, choosy, fastidious. You wondered if Malcolm's extravagant, extrovert style mightn't have jarred on this contained young female.

She said, "We spent one summer at Wester Craig. Then after Malcolm's death I was waiting for the birth of my daughter. Then Sir Charles took ill. I have felt it my place to be here . . ."

Coffee came. The little maid looked so goggle-eyed at me as she served it that I was tempted to pinch her bottom. Just in time she moved out of reach.

"And you," said Alison Abden when we were again alone. "Shall you make your home here?"

I thought to cough up what I felt about the place, but restraints were growing on me with increasing age. "Depends what I've inherited."

"I thought Mr. Macardle would have explained . . ."

"A little. Anyway, I've a profession in London . . ."

She stirred her coffee. "I know. It was you who made a present to Malcolm of perfumes and things—four years ago, was it? More? Yes, well, I've used Faunus ever since."

"Bread upon the waters," I said. "As a matter of fact, I had noticed it."

She did not raise her eyes, which were long and pale-lidded and brown when you saw them.

"Do you know this part of Scotland?" she asked.

"I've never been to Scotland before."

"I thought you went to the same school as Malcolm."

"I don't count schooldays."

The faint smile again. "Don't you like your family?"

"They haven't given me much cause to." Then I added, "As a Lowlander, you may also have found their exclusiveness hard to bear."

"Not at all."

"Not at all?" I echoed.

She looked at me then. "But you seem such a typical Abden, if I may say so. Not in looks perhaps, but something in your manner. Forgive me if that seems impertinent. But is it possible that the exclusiveness was not all on one side?"

I stared back at her and laughed. She flushed and seemed about to join me, when the door came open and Lucie was on view again. She looked disapprovingly at us both and said,

"Mother will see you now."

III Lady Abden was a small woman, well upholstered with cushions in a big black chair. She'd been quite a looker; her face broad over the bridge of the nose, which had probably grown more noticeable with age, arched brows still dark over stony-blue eyes, very fine-textured wavy hair which was now curled over her forehead; you could see how jolly that had been. She looked older than her late husband's sixty-nine.

Did one kiss one's aunt? (One wouldn't have minded kissing one's cousin-in-law downstairs.) Lady Abden came up with the answer by putting out a wrinkled hand on which a couple of diamond rings looked out of place. (The trouble with diamonds is that they're ageless.)

"So you are Stewart's son?"

"Yes."

"Pray sit down." Her voice had just a trace of Scottish accent.

I took a hard seat. Lucie squatted by the window and looked out, just as she had downstairs.

"So you have come to claim your inheritance."

"Some people achieve greatness," I said, "some have it thrust upon them."

Big ears for a woman. She shouldn't have worn the pearl drop earrings because it drew your attention to them.

"Your name is David, is it not? David Kilclair?"

"It is." She'd scored 100 so far.

"Are you a Catholic?"

"No."

She put out her bottom lip and breathed deeply. "Your father was."

"He was brought up a Catholic but let it lapse; I don't know when; before I was born."

"When he married. That's when he lapsed."

"Could be."

"Is your mother still alive?"

"Oh, yes. Not old yet. Remarried, of course."

"Of course." You didn't know whether this meant she ought to have known, or that she would expect nothing else of such a woman. "You were the only child by the marriage?"

"Yes, Aunt. Fortunately."

Lady Abden frowned. "My brother-in-law died in unhappy circumstances."

"Yes," I said, "he was drunk."

Lucie stirred. "I don't think my mother wishes to hear all the—" She stopped as Lady Abden raised a hand.

"You come of a very old and staunchly Catholic family, as you

194

must know. In this area in particular we are rather—an enclave. I hope you may in due course consider returning to the Faith again, for the sake of the family, for the sake of your ancestors and your descendants."

I checked my first reply. "I doubt it, Lady Abden."

"I could arrange—we could arrange . . ." She looked across at Lucie. "We have an excellent priest here, Father Donald; you would not find him without an intellectual basis for his beliefs. You might consider that you owe it to your family to arrange one or two meetings . . ."

I said, "It's just not on." I couldn't ask her what the hell she thought I owed her or her family, which had shrunk in horror because one of its sons had married a Jewess.

Silence for a bit. The color in her cheeks didn't look artificial. But there was no warmth in her eyes.

"The baronetcy carries little with it. As I expect you know."

"That was my impression."

"You may wonder at the—er—division of the Abden family into two properties some thirty miles distant. But perhaps Mr. Macardle will have explained this."

"I don't think so."

"Wester Craig has been the family house of the Abdens since the sixteenth century, but over the years the land we inherited or acquired came to be around the shores of Loch Fiern, so in the late eighteenth century we built this house and moved, keeping the other as a hunting lodge. Then the family fell on hard times, most of the land round Wester Craig was sold and the house was allowed to fall into ruin. Some fifty years later, when our fortunes had taken an upturn, Wester Craig was rebuilt and made habitable again, and that is how it has remained."

"A family home," I said, "unused by the family."

"Oh, indeed not! The eldest son when he married has always lived there—that is, until he inherited."

"I see. I see."

She put her bottom lip out again. "There is, of course, a degree of money and property in the family itself. This house, for instance. And we have eight thousand acres, and some other possessions. Had Malcolm succeeded he would have inherited all of it—or most of it, with of course adequate provision for my daughters. So it is very sad for me to see the baronetcy and all that it has meant to us through the generations going to a—forgive the expression—to an outsider."

I said, "I understand how you feel, Lady Abden. You've had two tough breaks. Malcolm could father nothing but girls; and a famous manufacturer's rotten tires saw to the rest. Without that you'd never have had to meet me, let alone see me slip undeservedly into the ermine, or whatever one does slip into on these great occasions. But as for being an outsider . . ."

She waited. "Yes?"

"Well—not to split hairs—I am just as much an Abden as Malcolm was . . . And more so than you, since you married into the family—"

Lucie was on her feet. "Will you please leave! I will not have Mother spoken to in such an insulting fashion!"

"No," said Lady Abden. "Let us hear him out. I do not suppose you will come here again, Sir David, so you may say what you will while you *are* here."

An odd moment to think of Shona, but I did. It was suddenly as if she was beside me saying once again, "Behave yourself, you stupid man!"

I was swallowing thirty-odd years of spleen but couldn't keep it all down.

I said, "My dear Aunt, I am not here to insult you, but to *meet* you. I came up—was nagged into coming up here by Macardle —for the first time yesterday. I don't much like Scotland or the people in it; I have my own life in London, so whether *I* shall ever come here again remains to be seen. I shall certainly not trouble you more than I can help—you or your daughters or your daughter-in-law or anyone else. But it's my name too. I came by it honestly in the marriage bed. This title frolic is nothing I ever wanted or ever should want. But presumably we've got to live with it. Don't you agree?"

There was a pause while Lady Abden fingered her pearls.

"I understand you are with a perfumery firm." She said it as if I was trading in French letters.

"Yes."

"Are you married?"

"No."

"Living with a woman?"

"Yes."

Lady Abden wrinkled her nose. "That's all the rage nowadays, I believe."

"It was when I left London."

She glanced at me coldly. "We have—we try to keep to—more traditional forms of behavior in the Highlands."

"I've no doubt there's plenty of fornication goes on."

She sighed. "I think you are rather a disagreeable young man."

"Quite a lot of people think so," I agreed. "Perhaps it was a bad mixture, the Scot and the Jew."

"You have said it, not I."

"I had no choice in the matter. You do understand that, don't you?"

She sighed again. "At least the mixture did not produce a nonentity. Perhaps it is better to dislike a person than to ignore him."

"At last, Aunt," I said, "we have agreed on something."

CHAPTER SIXTEEN

I "I'm *sorry*," I said to Shona. "I know you warned me, but practically every conversation went downhill."

"How unnecessary. Life is so short. Why should one have to quarrel with one's relatives? A blood relationship should not be a blood-poison relationship."

"After I left Auntie," I said, "I met the other daughter, Mary. She was on the landing outside, in a blowsy dressing gown, complaining to the maid. She was as drunk as a tick."

"Dear, dear. What time would this be?"

"About midday. I must admit she was the only one to greet me with any real warmth. Possibly drink runs in the family."

"A lot of things seem to run in the family! Did you see your factor in the end?"

"He caught up with me when I was at breakfast yesterday."

"Why try to avoid him? You had to see him sometime."

"I wanted to take people on the hop. Not be cushioned by some smooth gent who had arranged it all in advance."

"And was he a smooth gent?"

"Well, very tweedy. And rather well bred in that way that never quite carries conviction. But all right. He's agreed to continue to look after Wester Craig for me."

"What is it you have actually inherited?"

"Well, this house, Victorian of the worst period but with a Tudor core, sizable but rickety, needing money spent on it; two cottages; about five hundred acres of scrub."

"Not a grouse moor?"

"Not a grouse moor. Grassy sort of shallow-soil land with boulders and a stream running into the nearby loch. Some trout or a salmon or two, no doubt. Sheep."

"And beyond?"

"One way the sea and the loch; behind the house moorland going up to mountains. Stags up there and a few grouse, I suppose; but that's all owned by the Countess of Something-or-other. Abden land is pretty extensive at the further side. Not mine, though."

"Will it pay its way?"

"What, the property? Oh, *no.* Nothing like. Maintenance and repairs, caretaker, no shooting or fishing to rent out."

"But the house might let?"

"It might. But there's obviously not much demand for such a godforsaken place."

"You could live there yourself."

"Do me a favor."

"You can't sell it?"

"Yes. I asked Macardle, who looked very pained but eventually admitted that I could apply to bar the entail. I think that's what he called it. Then it can be sold."

"And shall you do that?"

"What else?"

"It seems a pity. And the title."

"I shall keep that."

"What has made up your mind?"

"They have. The other Abdens."

She laughed her broken laugh. "Can you not think of some less cross-grained reason?"

"D'you know what Alison said? That's Malcolm's widow. She thought I was very much like an Abden—not in looks but in character."

"Well," Shona said, looking at me. "I think I know what she means. But it need not be something to be ashamed of."

"She was probably pulling my leg."

"I suppose it has never occurred to you to consider taking your aunt's advice?"

"As to what?"

"Becoming a Catholic to please the family. To preserve a tradition."

"Shona, you're joking."

"Yes, I am. I suppose."

"Well, either you are or you're not!"

She yawned behind her hand. "My mother was Russian Orthodox—though she had dropped it all by the time I was born. I am brought up pagan, though I suppose a few of the old habits survived in my mother's behavior. By the time I am twelve I am the complete atheist. Communism did its work well, and I have not had occasion to change that since."

"Very laudable."

"Is it? Yes, I suppose. We stand on our own feet. That is so good. You are the same."

"I am the same."

"But sometimes I read history and wonder what the answer really is. It is not only Russia that has lost its religion, it is the West too. I think so. Perhaps I am stupid. Sometimes I think the human race suffers today not merely from a lack of religion but a lack of superstition."

"Is there much difference?"

"Oh, I know all the horrors and cruelties that have been perpetrated in the name of religion and superstition down through the centuries."

"So what are you trying to say?"

She patted my hand. "I sometimes wonder if the existence of superstition does not have its good side; the sensation of there being something more powerful than oneself, more powerful than—or at least independent of—the state; this is surely a salutary feeling. No? The need to look over one's shoulder, which may be necessary in the Communist states for other and wrong reasons, does not exist in the West for other and perhaps right ones. But it's good to have a sanction outside oneself. We have all become orphans."

I grunted. "Maybe yes, maybe no."

"*Yes*, because there is no father figure, no day of judgment, no retribution, no expectation or fear of ultimate justice left. We run about like children, don't we, doing what we like, building what we like, smashing what we like, indulging as we like. There is no one even to rebel against. There is no one to call us to bed."

"You surprise me," I said. "You always surprise me, Shona."

"That is good."

She looked older than I remembered her a week ago. It took me a few days to get used to her again. Perhaps it was Alison Abden with her boyish haircut and her long brown eyes and her elegant legs.

The usual working day also took a bit of getting into after my trip to Ross and Cromarty—more so than after the break in the West Indies. Then we had plunged in together, Shona and I, reluctant to be back but willing to get stuck in. This was not a holiday, this trip to Scotland, it was a glimpse of a different world, a barren world, a boring world, an irritating world; but after it what I was doing to make a living seemed once again awfully tinsel-smart.

For instance, arguing with the advertising agency about the position of one of our adverts in some of the magazines—Shona always insisted that our full-page advertisements should be printed opposite the astrology page; she said that was the one page every woman read. For instance, considering again the use of royal jelly, and the claims made for it, and the advantage of the name from a psychological angle.

Soon after this a minor crisis blew up in the firm. Charisma had come out in the British market with two hundred thousand spent on publicity, and it had gone well. One of the allied products was a foundation cream called Charisma Bio-cream E, and before I left we had had one or two complaints about it. An isolated customer here and there claimed it caused skin allergies, but I didn't think the number or the style of grievance important enough to do anything about. Then, at one of the weekly meetings at Stevenage, John Carreros unexpectedly showed, looking raddled and old, and attacked me for passing up these complaints.

I said quietly enough, "Oh, come. With almost everything we put out there's the occasional gripe. Isn't there? I can quote you chapter and verse."

"With a new product it is different," said John. "I think the reaction has been bad."

"What is the proportion?" Shona asked. She was sitting beside me, her hair in a casual knot. Frock of heavy cream silk, short, with a daffodil scarf, cinnamon-colored tights, white sandals. She had known about the reports but for once had allowed me to influence her.

Parker said, "The complaints are about two in a thousand."

"What is the unacceptable proportion?" Leo Longford asked.

"Two in a thousand I would argue, with a new product," said John.

"There's a spate of orders coming in from the shops," I said, "Many of these complaints are entirely phony, as you well know.

Some young biddy has spent too much; her husband raises hell, so she brings back the cream to the shop complaining that it doesn't suit her. It's a good way to get your money back."

"These cannot all be such cases," said John.

"Well, half the girls who buy this stuff really need treatment for acne, not a skin food."

"That is a risk in our business. But I do not think this is a risk we can take."

We all waited. In spite of the growth of the firm, the expansion of its board of managers, Shona still had the last say.

Presently she gave voice. "I'm sorry, David, I agree with John. The whole consignment must be retested. It can be done in a few weeks."

"By which time," I said, "the effect of the TV advertising will be entirely lost."

She nodded. "It is a difficult decision, I know."

"Why not let what has been issued go through, while tests are made on the rest of the consignment?"

"I'd agree with that," said Leo. "It seems a reasonable compromise."

Again we waited. "*No,*" said Shona. "It must be withdrawn. I think it is a matter of principle. We have set ourselves the highest standard and we must adhere to it."

The meeting went on for another hour before we broke for lunch. I was feeling fairly peevish because the countermanding of my orders made me look a ninny. There was a nearby pub which catered very well, but I made an excuse and didn't join the others. I went out to get into my car and saw that John was also not joining the party.

He said, "Are you going in to London, David?"

"Yes."

"May I thumb a lift, as the saying is? I have business at the Hanover Club before I return to Richmond."

I opened the passenger door for him without comment.

As we started off he said, "I have not had an opportunity to congratulate you on your title."

"I didn't notice."

What I did notice was that his hair had gone white these last two years, and that his hands shook.

"Yes," he said, noticing I'd noticed. "Parkinson's disease."

"Oh," I said. "Sorry. Shona didn't tell me."

"Shona does not know. It would make little difference if she did know. She no longer cares for me at all."

"I certainly wouldn't say that."

"Wouldn't you? Anyway, it is relatively unimportant. This is not a killer disease, you know. It only makes life difficult and renders you more prone to other complaints."

"Too bad."

"Yes. For the young and healthy, 'too bad' is a convenient phrase to cover most of the diseases of the old. Although I am not *very* old by modern standards. I am sixty-six."

"Oh?" I said politely, and drove on.

After that there was silence for a while. I had fixed to go fencing with Shona tonight and she was to come back to my place after. Now I felt like cutting out the scene just for a day or two. Maybe I'd go along to the Cellini Club and see if I could get a rubber of bridge with Roger Manpole.

But did this rather silly argument this morning, in which I had been bested by John Carreros, really amount to anything? It was too petty to put on a big Achilles scene all for the sake of a few thousand pounds' worth of foundation cream.

"I did not know," John said, "in fact had no idea, that you were likely to inherit a title."

"Neither did I."

"I suppose it will make a considerable difference to your way of life. I have no doubt we shall be losing you."

"From Shona's? I don't think so."

"Of course it will be an asset now to have your name on our letterhead. But I should think you will have far too many obligations to continue to play your present active part."

"Perhaps I should make one thing clear, John. The title brings no money; so I'm not likely to be among your pampered rich."

"Come, come," said John, trembling fingers filling his pipe with the usual hay. "You will soon make a good marriage. You must be among London's most eligible bachelors now. It is a foregone conclusion."

"Foregone by whom?" I asked politely.

He shut up then, and we drove on into London. We droned up Park Lane and waited for the lights at Brook Gate. Then he said suddenly, "I don't think Shona looks well, do you?"

"I thought she looked extremely well."

"She works too hard. All the extra responsibility of the enlarged company has been a great weight on her shoulders."

"Which Leo and I and others have helped her to bear. She doesn't delegate readily, but she's learning to do so more and more."

The lights went green but it was a long line of traffic.

He said, "You know, she is only ten years younger than I am."

I stopped when the lights turned yellow, and a taxi behind gave an impatient toot.

"I don't think I can wear that story. She's forty-six—"

"No. Fifty-six."

I shook my head. "Forty-six. Don't come that on me. I've seen her passport."

"On which a false age is stated."

"Rubbish. You can't do that. She was born in 1930."

"1920. I ought to know."

We were off again down Upper Brook Street, and were stopped at the next lights, by Claridge's.

"Drop me at the Hanover, will you?" John said. "I fancy a rubber or two of bridge. Thursday is their day. Would you care to come in?"

"No, thanks."

"I didn't ask you again after that first time. I fancied you thought you were a little too good for us."

"Also you hated my guts."

"Not in so many words. I found you a little too brash and smart for my friends in the club."

"Some of them," I said, "were only just alive."

"Well, that is probably true. To a young man, anything over fifty is dead meat. Shona is dead meat, David. Mark my words. She pretends—oh, she puts a splendid face on it—but you can't convert old flesh into young, however hard you try. She's dead meat to you, David, mark my words."

"I'll let you know when I feel that. It's very warmhearted of you to point all this out to me."

John shrugged. "Perhaps I should have told you when you first became infatuated with her. Perhaps I was not so bitchy then."

We drew up at the Hanover Club.

"Incidentally," I said, "if what you say has any truth in it, Shona takes a risk every time she comes in or out of the country."

"Oh, the passport is quite genuine. Indeed it has been renewed since then. It was the naturalization papers that were forged. It cost her five thousand pounds, which was a lot of money in those days."

"Pull the handle toward you," I said.

"And so unnecessary, don't you think? What is the good of lying about one's age?—life always catches up with one in the end. Thanks for the lift."

"Don't mention it."

<table>
<tr><td>II</td></tr>
</table>

II

I said to myself, it makes not a blind bit of difference. If you are a woman's lover—and more than half *in* love with her—what sort of odds does it or should it make if she is twenty-three years older than you instead of thirteen? The woman is still there watching you with those cool, fondly assessing eyes. (Annoying at times but unchanged.) Nor has her face or her body changed. Shona was ageless—a bit like She in the Rider Haggard books (which incidentally I'd never read). Ayesha, the ageless.

Of course she'd done me up brown on this. But it was not specially me. It was a con she had thought up years ago (while I was still at school) to put over on the world at large. She had deceived her other lovers in the same way. But *we* had been so close; particularly in Barbados. Why could she not then have said . . .

But, the deed having been done, what woman *would* have said, David, my real age is fifty-six, breaking all the eggs in the basket? Probably she more than half believed her passport by now. Living with a man of thirty-three, even forty-six was a bit to confess to. To have admitted her real age would have put the years on her like a sack of coal. Psychologically and physically overnight. Her whole life, her whole mental balancing trick was geared to the age she had given herself. John was a prime bastard ever to have let it out.

I rang her and said I couldn't meet her at fencing because I was starting a cold.

"You never have a cold," she said.

"Well, it's a sore throat. Same sort of thing."

After a pause she said, "David. Are you still there? I'm *sorry* about this morning. I was sorry to side with John, and I understand your frustration."

"Oh," I said, "it's sweet nothing. I'd forgotten it." Which I had.

"*Really?* Are you serious?"

"Quite serious. A vote was taken and that was that."

Another pause. "Nothing else has come up?"

"Nothing."

"So I shall not see you tonight after the fencing?"

"Not tonight. I expect I'll be in in the morning."

"Take a day off if you do not feel well."

"Thanks."

After I had put down the telephone I dialed Derek. He sounded pleased.

"His Lordship in person! Wow! Are you thinking of offering a line in chastity belts for the belted earls?"

"It just occurred to me—I've nothing to do this evening and wondered if we could meet somewhere for a drink?"

His voice quietened again. "Fine. The Cellini?"

"More prosaic. Such as the local pub."

"My pub's the Lamb and Flag. They put on a fair line in snacks. How about eight o'clock?"

"Right."

"Mind if I bring Donald?"

"Who's Donald?"

"A friend. A ballet dancer."

"What ballet is he in?"

"Resting at the moment. You know how precarious that life can be."

"Derek," I said, "could we do without Donald?"

"He won't be pleased."

"Displease him."

"Oh, very well. I'll tell him it's a Royal Command."

We met at the Lamb and Flag. He was usually so well dressed that I thought him down at heel tonight. He was always making money one way or another, but spent it fast. He was also probably supporting Donald during his time of rest. There was always this

attraction–repulsion thing going in my feelings for Derek. He was
a good companion and his flippancies were welcome tonight as I
told him of my visit to Scotland. We had a good enough meal
together and, apart from the fact that I had to withdraw my hand
when he tried to pat it, all went well.

Late on he said, "What made you ring me tonight, matey?"

"Hadn't seen you for a long time."

"I was thinking of you yesterday. Donald is too fond of garlic."

"That's nice. When your friend hovers around you with bad
breath it reminds you of me."

"Well, you know how thoughts fly."

"No, I don't."

"Seriously, matey, I sometimes wonder, if you hadn't taken up
with this Shona woman, we wouldn't have made a go of it together, you and I. Those were—"

"Seriously, matey," I said, "you know darned well we never
would have made a go of it together in the way you mean. As a
relationship it wasn't on. And, if you recall, I fled the nest before
I took up with this Shona woman."

"Ah, but not before you *met* her. It was just after you met her
that you broke up our happy home."

"Never mind," I said, "we've remained 'good friends.' "

He grunted and finished his beer.

"Aren't you sick of her yet?"

"Nor that."

"I suppose you'll be leaving anyway now. That may make a
difference in your affair with her?"

"I don't know why everyone supposes I shall be leaving. I've
inherited a title and a shabby rundown house with a few acres of
rock and moorland. What am I supposed to live on—peat?"

"Does that mean you'll need *more* money, to keep it up, not
less, eh?"

"Correct."

He was thoughtful. "Another beer? It's my round."

"I'll get it," I said, and did so.

When I came back he said, "I wouldn't say money was the root
of all evil but it's the root of a lot of good ideas, and one or two
ideas have been floating around recently whereby money could be
made out of the perfumery industry."

"A lot of money is being made *in* the perfumery industry."

"Ah, but that's different. This would be a way—might be a way—of making a nice something out of one or two of the giants. Only this wouldn't be chicken feed like the little operation we ran together before your old woman latched on. This might be high flying enough to interest the big boys."

"Like Roger Manpole?"

"Like Roger Manpole."

"How is the big phony?"

"Bigger than ever. He's gone into horse racing in a sizable way."

"Well, that's as good a way as any to lose money."

"It's as good a way as any to get in with the best people."

I sipped at my new beer, which I realized now I didn't want. Nor did I want the sweat and the noise of the people around me.

"What is this splendid game you're dreaming up?"

"Oh, it's all very embryo at the moment. Matter of fact, it was our little flutter that gave me the idea—disposal of surplus stock."

"It's been done."

"There's always a new angle to an old trick. An insider like you can be a help."

"I've heard that somewhere before."

"Well, matey, do give me warning if you're thinking of leaving Shona's. I'd like that."

"I'm giving you warning I'm thinking of leaving the Lamb and Flag," I said. "It's nearly ten and the smog in here is overdone. So be a good lad and finish your beer."

"You not having yours?"

"My father was a soak," I said. "And I met another of my family in the same way in Scotland."

III I said to myself again, what difference does ten years *make*? She's still the *same* person, exactly the *same* person, as she was before. If she was attractive to me last week—as she certainly was—she must be attractive *this* week. Jesus Christ, I said, she's barely a year younger than my mother.

I got home and almost wished I'd asked Derek back. But I knew if I had that he'd have taken it the wrong way. I snorted a little laughter at myself. I needed *company*. Not company in bed, just company. David the loner, the man who has learned to rely only on himself, needs a friend to chat to. Even a friend to talk about *this* to.

Of course I could go out and pick up a tart, a *young* tart, go to her pad, tell her there'd been a misunderstanding at home. She'd never guess what. Only I didn't really want sex, especially bought sex; it was a bore. And anyway they all used such cheap scent.

CHAPTER SEVENTEEN

I In the egalitarian society in which we were supposed
to be living, being a "sir" should have made no difference at all. Instead, you noticed how people's eyes
changed. Not all, of course, but too many. No difficulty about
credit in shops. The cocktail party, the business meeting, even
people in the firm, even Mr. Schmidt of TBM Ltd., even my
neighbors on the floors below; the garage. (I was negotiating to sell
the DB6 and buy one of the new Jaguar XJSs, with its twelve-
cylinder fuel-injection engine.) I was also receiving a lot of appeals,
the confident assumption being that I was now worth half a million
and anxious to give most of it away. And a number of invitations
from Scotland: Would I open this or present that or be a guest
speaker at a dinner to commemorate the other. I used my secretary
at Shona's to do the paperwork. After a while it would settle down
and die away.

Things were no longer right between Shona and me, but we
got along. In fact it was just the sexual act that went missing; I
was in her company a lot, and often privately too; I made excuses
about the other and she accepted them with only the occasional
questing comment.

Once she said very directly, "Did something happen in Scotland, David?"

"Something?"

"Did you meet another woman whom you fancied more
than me?"

"I did not. And you can stand on that, as the boxers say."

"Yet this—all this—cannot have grown out of a quarrel over
the withdrawal of a foundation cream."

"I don't know what 'all this' is. But I can tell you *nothing* has grown out of the foundation-cream fiasco that adds up to a bag of beans. Except a few more complaints from a few more spotty girls."

She stared at me narrowly, the skin taut on her smooth high cheekbones. God, it was still such good skin! There must be *something* in her preparations.

"So then you are just tired of me?"

"Not except when you ask crummy questions."

"It is not crummy to be concerned when something so good has been between us and suddenly it vanishes like a puff of smoke."

"Like the green flash," I said.

She made a move of distaste. "That we shall perhaps not see now."

I put my hand on her arm, feeling its steely firmness under mine. A little lick of desire moved again. "Maybe you have a right to be concerned, Shona. Maybe you should have an answer. But, search me, I haven't got it. And if I don't know the answer, how can you?"

I *could* of course have answered her. I could have said, "Yes, you stupid bitch, you lied to me and this is the result. I don't want to lay an old woman of fifty-six." But first I couldn't quite muster the viciousness to say it, and second, that wasn't really the issue. The question I had to answer was *why*—since nothing in effect had changed except in my thoughts—did this mean such a lot to me? *Why* did I feel so strongly about it?

I thought, so let it drift around in my mind for a few weeks. The knowledge of her age will either get the better of my need for her, or my need for her will get the better of my knowledge of her age.

II   It was Christmas before I went to Scotland again. Shona's father was ill, and she said she must spend the break in Paris. I stayed in London and then at the last minute decided to whistle up to Wester Craig and look at it again. There was a certain masochism in the notion, because the place would be as cold as an icebox, with no central heating, and lucky if I cut my way through the drifting snow. But I'd just taken delivery of this sleek white Jaguar and felt like trying it out.

The engine was sensational, whispering power with none of the traction-engine noise of the Aston. Just to look at it, cramming the enormous bonnet, gave me an aesthetic lift. It answered the slightest call like a dream.

On the other hand at anything over ninety the Aston would tuck in its tail and lie solid on the road with some sort of centripetal adhesion; at over a hundred and twenty the Jaguar began to feel lighter and a bit less secure.

Wester Craig wasn't three feet deep in snow but pickled in a sort of perpetual autumn, with the cold old sun gleaming heatless in the sky and all the pines and things clubbing together to maintain a pretence of false verdancy. I had rung them up this morning so they knew I was on my way. Fires blazed in the dining room, the drawing room and my bedroom. Dusk fell smartly as soon as I arrived (I had left London well before dawn) and a tinsel moon fell on the loch and the spiky trees. Mrs. Coppell—who was always smiling and cheerful; maybe it was her *nature*—gave me smoked trout with roast duck to follow and apple tart. I drank a Charmes Chambertin 1961 and thought well of old Malcolm. I slept late and solidly. Coppell, raking out the ashes and setting a light to a new fire, woke me as the sun peered over the shoulder of the hill.

It was another fine, dry day; the house biting cold in a way new to me since schooldays. There were three semicircles of heat, deriving from the three fires; everything outside those orbits was like a morgue, like a fashionable New York restaurant in the summer. You latched on to the Scottish cult for tweeds; did they ever take baths? To strip off one's clothes and stand under a shower was an exercise in masochism.

24 December. Coppell said, would I like to go shooting? Shooting what? I asked. Well, he said, there wasn't much, unless, he added with a peculiar look, I fancied an eagle. They were a dire pest in the district, seizing McVitie's young lambs. To get rid of one or two of them would be a public benefit.

Christmas Eve. While I was not full of the milk of human

kindness or a wish to make my fellow men rejoice, I didn't really feel I wanted to down an eagle just for the fun of it. Had I known that it was against the law to shoot them I might have thought again. Fortunately maybe, Coppell didn't understand my peculiar nature.

I said I'd walk to the sea.

"To the loch, sorr?"

"No, the sea."

"It is further away than it looks, sorr. Upward of four miles. Will I saddle Chieftain? He's a good sober animal to ride."

The last time I had ridden a good sober animal was when I was nineteen, and then not with any great success, so I said no to this too and went off in the direction he pointed.

It was certainly rough old land, the path this way not much more than a sheep track—which, I gathered from the droppings, it was mainly used for. As you got nearer the sea, sharper and larger rocks began to jut out and there was a steep sheer mountain on the left. Where I came off my own meager acres I don't know. There was only one cottage to be seen all the way. As I slithered down to the foreshore large gulls chattered overhead, and I crunched across to the edge, to where the waves crimped and hissed and played crap with the pebbles. I skimmed a few stones on the sea. At least you couldn't complain about the air. One way to pass Christmas Eve.

A more roundabout way back, making a semicircle to come past the cottage. This was a bit more of a road, with a few cart tracks and tire marks on it where the ground was soft.

As I got near the cottage I saw a large orange-colored mound in the roadway, as if a forklift truck had dropped a load of cloth or skins or brick rubble in the path. It was about three feet high and about eight feet long. I came up with it and it raised its shaggy head and observed me bloodshot through a curtain of hair. A very large Highland bull.

I stopped and looked at the bull, then at the cottage, which was deserted. The tremble of smoke seen earlier had ceased. The fire had gone out. No doubt whoever owned the cottage was hacking away in some distant field. The bull looked at me without much favor. I took a few casual steps, sideways. His tail whisked once. I saw a gate just behind me to the right. I climbed casually over it. The bull didn't stir. I was now in a moorland field with a low wall of crumbling stones by way of slight protection. A stupid sheep baaed noisily, drawing attention to me. I walked along by the wall, not looking at the bull. Presently I was past and tried not to quicken my step. Then I was above and behind him. At a broken gap in the wall I rejoined the road. I looked back. His head had gone down; his horns just showed through the tangled hair like curved periscopes in a ginger sea.

I worked up a fine sweat climbing the hill to Wester Craig. At the door, just behind my Jaguar, was a yellow Mini.

Alison Abden colored at the sight of me as she came down the steps. "I didn't know you were here. Why didn't you tell us you were coming?"

"Impulse," I said. "But I did ring. Didn't Coppell let you know?"

"No, he said he thought we would know."

She stood on the bottom step, the breeze barely stirring her urchin cut. A Harris tweed costume with flecks of green in it, a yellow polo-necked fine woollen blouse, lisle stockings and brogues, but she still seemed to look slim and well shaped with it all.

"Why don't you come in?" I said. "Or have you been in?"

"Yes. I still come up here sometimes to see the Coppells and the McVities. After all, this was my home on and off for nearly two years."

"Ah, yes. Well, take a sherry with me. That's always supposing there is such a thing."

"I would think so."

"I'm indebted to Malcolm, by the way," I said, as she led the way in, "it wasn't a big cellar he left but it's first-rate stuff."

"I doubt it was not all his doing. His father would buy wine from time to time, and it's a better storage cellar here than we have at Lochfiern."

"Perhaps I should buy it from you."

"You must ask Lady Abden."

"Surprising that the wine wasn't transferred to Lochfiern before I came."

"I think," she said, "you underestimate the shock of having two male deaths in the family within so short a time."

"Ah, yes."

There was a brief silence.

She said, "Is it true you are breaking the entail and selling the property?"

"Yes."

"Isn't it—a bit precipitate?"

"What, to get rid of it? I don't think so. The place is costing me money that I can't afford."

"Pity."

"Someone else said that."

"Who?"

"Oh, a friend."

We were now in the drawing room. I said, "I don't know where Coppell is."

"Do you know where the *cellar* is?"

I'd been down but I let her show me. The best I could find was a medium amontillado, and I carried it up, admiring her legs on the cellar steps ahead of me.

We had to go through the medieval hall, and I stopped there. Even on this shiny day the room was somber, the low sun squinting through the windows.

"What's the motto?" I said. "I can't read Gaelic."

"I believe Malcolm told me once but I've forgotten."

"Could he speak Gaelic?"

"No. For all his roots, he was very Anglicized."

"These banners could do with a wash. Is there a laundromat in Ullapool?"

She looked at me to see if I was serious. "Don't you—*feel* anything, coming up here?"

"Feel anything?"

"Any interest, any pride?"

"None at all."

As she moved, a shaft of sun fell on her head like a klieg light. "Perhaps it's too soon yet."

"D'you think if I gave myself time I might go native—start eating the haggis?"

"No . . . but I think it would be strange if you gave yourself time, as you say, if you felt *no* pull, *no* sense of ancestry, no stirring of the blood."

"I'll let you know when it happens."

She flushed. "Pray don't bother."

215

In the drawing room I found a corkscrew and soon we were sipping sherry. Feeling I was probably overplaying the unfeeling Sassenach, I told her of my encounter with the bull. She laughed.

"Oh, that would be Dornoch. He's an old dear really, but he can cut up rough sometimes."

"That seemed to be a public road he was occupying."

"Oh, yes, it is, but people don't mind. It's part of the Highland scene."

"It isn't part of my scene. Next time I go down there I shall go in a jeep."

"I see you have a new car."

"Yes, that's an Abden failing."

"One of many," she said.

I raised my eyebrows but she didn't provide a list. We made small talk.

She said, "Will you come to lunch with us tomorrow, Christmas Day?"

"No, thank you."

"As you possibly know, we don't make so much of Christmas in Scotland, but it would be unsociable if we left you here alone. And Malcolm's four daughters will be there. I'm sure they'd like to meet you. Why won't you come?"

I hesitated.

"I'll come when my mother is invited."

"Is she here?"

"Of course not."

"Well, isn't that rather an academic point, then?"

"Not to me, it isn't."

She bit her lip thoughtfully, eyes slanting toward the windows. "I understand how you must feel. But isn't it rather out of date, all in the distant past? Christmas is a season of good will or it's nothing. One can even, I would have thought, sit down to a meal with people one doesn't much like."

"Ah," I said, "would that not be hypocritical?"

She sighed and finished her sherry. "If you say so."

"I'd point out," I said, "that the part of the family I don't much like does not include you."

She shook her head as if I had offered her more sherry. "Roundabout compliment? I am spared from anathema."

She got up. "Are you very fond of your mother, David?"

It was a nasty question. "No, I don't think so. No, I'm afraid not."

"So it's really a matter of pride, not sentiment, that makes you see only one side in this?"

Was it? "I expect so. But don't forget the Abdens rejected my mother because she was of the wrong blood. I am her son and must have at least half the wrong blood myself. The fact that I'm called Abden and have come in for their place is beside the point."

"All this happened thirty-five *years* ago. Don't you think attitudes have changed since then?"

"Has theirs?"

"A little, I would think. Besides . . ."

"Besides what?"

"I don't want to interfere—intervene in what is not my quarrel—but you do know, I suppose, that your father was difficult as a young man long before he married your mother."

"Difficult in what way?"

"Well, I only know what I'm told, but there seems no reason why they should wish to deceive me. There would be no purpose, would there?" She waited, but I didn't answer. "Only that he often ran himself into debt. His father bailed him out more than once. Then they made him an allowance. But after that, some time after that, they had to help in a bigger way because it was a matter of the law. I believe he had been passing bad checks. They saved him from prosecution but told him it was the end . . . It wasn't until after that—after all that—that he married your mother. I don't think the break was originally to do with your mother, if you see what I mean . . ."

"This is the gospel, as you remarked, according to the Abdens."

"Of course. But you have to try to see their side."

"I'll try."

She stood up. "But I didn't come here to argue. I'm sorry if I have said too much."

"I hope you'll come again. I'm sure there are topics we won't argue on."

She smiled. "Are you fond of many people, David?"

"Not many. One or two. I tend to fight shy of getting involved."

"Why?"

"Why? Saves the risk of being let down."

"Yes," she agreed. "There's something to be said for that. But it wastes a lot too."

I went with her to her car, admired her legs again as she swung them in.

"Anyway . . . Happy Christmas," she said.

"And you too. I shall be leaving on the twenty-seventh. Do come for another sherry if you can."

She nodded noncommittally and drove off. I watched the yellow Mini until it disappeared. Clouds were creeping up to ambush the sun.

III

That night a storm came on, and it blew and rained all through Christmas Day. It blew and rained like the devil; the windows rattled, and some of the slates; the doors were ill fitting and the drafts were like a hi-fi gone wrong; the fires spat at water dripping down the chimneys.

Before I was up, Coppell had put three buckets in the old hall, and the splash, splash could be heard above the wail of the wind.

"Och," said Coppell, "it has been like this for aye, sorr. It gives nae trouble in the fine weather."

"Well, it wouldn't, would it? Has anyone ever been up to see?"

"Och aye. Dr. Malcolm had it all looked at in about 1961, soon after he was wed to the fairst Mrs. Malcolm—Lady Fiona. They said it was the lead."

"And it was repaired then?"

"Well, it was never vairy satisfactory."

I spent most of the day in the drawing room—which was the only decent room in the house. There was no television except in the Coppells' cottage, so I made do with my own company and a few magazines. Somehow they had found a young goose for lunch, and I opened a bottle of 1966 Gevrey Chambertin. This was a flop—even the great Burgundies can go off sometimes; it tasted of rubber tires—and a bottle of Santenay that we got up later was too cold to enjoy. But there was a plum pudding and mince pies, and by the time I'd finished the lot I was ready to doze off before the fire.

It was an uneasy doze, the sort when you can't draw a line between thinking and dreaming. I half supposed I was a kid again when I was devoted to this rocking horse—used to ride it like mad and imagine I was a knight in armor attacking a bandit's castle. One day while I was out my mother gave it away to a bring and buy sale. She said I was too old for it, and anyway it was a mistake to get too attached to a toy like that. I was brokenhearted and started kicking the furniture until she took an umbrella to me. I'd forgotten this—totally. Where had it come from, this memory? Out of some primeval sludge? Yet I'd loved her through it all.

Then there was the episode of the pen. The boy sitting next to me at school, Alec, had a fountain pen, and lost it and said I'd stolen it. It was found in my bag. There was a stink about that. I swore I'd never touched it. Someone had planted it there. Melodrama. To be falsely accused when you're eight years old is a traumatic experience. Hell. I never afterward felt quite the same about people and things. Sitting there dozing in front of the fire, a man in early middle age, I fought all the old battles, the old resentments, over again. Sometimes I wondered, *did* I take it? I *couldn't* have. You could never feel that bitterness, that searing desolation, unless you were *falsely* accused. Was that the start of a bent career or the *cause* of a bent career? Ask the shrinks. But odd to have resurrected it all now, like a nightmare, like a promise.

I woke as the last light was ebbing out of the room. Without encouragement, the fire had been spitting dangerously from rain down the chimney, and bits of ash were smouldering up to the edge of the stone surround. I shoved them in with my shoe, and wondered idly whether it would be worth burning the house down for the sake of the insurance. Solve a few problems. I'd pocket maybe a hundred thousand, and would incur few future costs in maintaining a burned-out shell. In many ways it would be a very suitable solution—ridding myself of an unwanted burden and thumbing my nose at the clan.

On the other hand the Coppells and the McVities would be sure to be bonny firefighters, and I would have to convince the insurance company that it was not a planned affair. Surest way of doing that, of course, was to be in the house and to get incinerated at the same time. A very distinguished Scotsman I knew had recently inherited an estate from his cousin who had gone to sleep over his whiskey and done just that; but in spite of my general displeasure with life I'd no fancy to end things that way. It would be uncomfortable.

I chucked on a couple more logs, which instantly spat back at me. Then I walked through into the old hall to see how the buckets were filling. They had recently been emptied, for the water gave hollow plops as it fell.

Bone cold in here, and almost dark. The gale still ranted outside, and I wondered how many centuries of winter storms this beaten-up old room had weathered. What had Alison said? "I think it will be strange if sooner or later you don't feel some pull, some sense of ancestry, some stirring of the blood." Fat chance of that. I'd never known my grandfather, Nicholas Abden, who had died the year I was born. I wondered if they had ever sat together in here, Nicholas (1880–1943) and Joanna (1886–1956); one chair in front of each fireplace, talking, making plans that a world war would knock over. Or was that habit and this hall abandoned long before then?

There were names here and there, engraved in the stonework. I switched on the lights, which flickered uncertainly and dismally from two hanging candelabra. *Fraser Abden, Bannockburn. Grant Abden, Culloden. Malcolm Abden, Glenfinnan. Charles Abden, Homildon. Douglas Abden, Sauchieburn.* The names were clumsily cut, and not all by the same hand; but they didn't look very old, probably not more than half a century. We'd been a bloody lot—though there was nothing to show whether these were the names of men who had fallen or merely of men who had fought.

I peered at the coat of arms between the two fireplaces. It looked like a unicorn and a heart and a shield. Underneath was written: *Creag mo chroidhe-se a chreag ghuanach.*

I wandered about the room and saw some more scratchings: these much older, looking contemporary with the dates. *Bruce Abden, beheaded, January 1572. Malcolm Abden, died on rack, November 1583.*

Lovely. There was another coat of arms here, more primitive in style, with something like a lynx or a leopard snarling. *Algionnach no nadur fhein.* Someone much more recently had been obliging enough this time to write underneath what I took to be a translation. *The beast itself both bright and bold.*

A shiver went down my back, caused by the tomb-chill of this hall. I'd think myself in a haunted house soon. Where was the old woman dragging her son's head along the floor or the man screaming as his bones were stretched from their sockets? The beast itself both bright and bold.

I supposed I must come of a family of Jacobites. Whom else could they have followed but that born loser, Bonnie Prince Charlie? Yet somehow they'd hung on, in their arrogant, single-minded, obstinate way. They'd hung on to the house and the name and the faith, through all the plots and counterplots and uprisings and conspiracies, the beheadings, the rackings, the sequestrations, the oppressions, the denials of right and privilege. And later on there were these other names on the walls: Lucknow, Salamanca, Waterloo, Sebastopol, Omdurman, Loos, Tripoli, Arnhem. At some stage they'd thrown in their lot with the English, helped their old enemies in their quest for Empire.

And the end of it all was me, a sales manager in a perfumery firm. No wonder my old aunt was wetting herself with disappointment.

Yet what had her own son Malcolm been? A failed Member of Parliament, a raconteur, a minor television personality, a poseur, a womanizer. Was that much better? It was the strain that was deteriorating, wearing out, trickling like a spent river into the sands.

And who would follow me? Some Canadian farmer or Canadian farmer's son, with even less concern than I—if that were possible—for his long and peculiar and narrowly proud ancestry.

Unless I married and had a son. It was at least a laughable possibility.

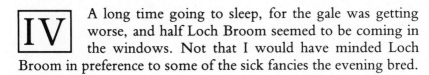

A long time going to sleep, for the gale was getting worse, and half Loch Broom seemed to be coming in the windows. Not that I would have minded Loch Broom in preference to some of the sick fancies the evening bred.

That thing on the second crest was neither a lynx nor a leopard but some man-invented nightmare animal, half real and half imagined, half alive and half dead, smelling like a skunk and a charnel house, snarling a spittle slime over all it could reach. The beast itself both bright and bold.

When I did go to sleep I dreamed I *had* a son; I don't know who the mother was but the fat nurse was bringing it in her arms away from the labor ward and smiling at me as she came up. "Be prepared for a shock, Sir David," she said with rubbery lips. "It will be a little shock at first, Sir David, but I'm sure you'll be able to adjust. Your wife is adjusting nicely, Sir David." She opened the blanket, and there in her arms dribbling slime was the Beast, fangs bared in a lecherous snarl, little blind bloodshot sockets where the eyes should have been, fat arms outstretched waiting for me to take him . . .

I woke with a grunt. Christ, if this wasn't worse than dreaming of prison or a drunken father and a leather strap! I got up and dragged on my trousers and heavy overcoat and went downstairs, switching on lights on the way, avoiding the old hall with its phantoms and its incubi, made the kitchen and snapped on the kettle. If it was colder than this at the North Pole I didn't want to go.

With coffee I stepped into the drawing room and kicked some embers of the fire together, blew on them with the bellows until the glow broke into flame, then erupted all the rest of the wood out of the woodbox and watched it catch.

I sat there for about an hour while the fire blazed and warmed the front two inches of me and the cobwebs of nightmare blew away. Then I went to bed.

I decided this was the last time my ramshackle inheritance would see me. The quicker I sold the place the better. It was curtains for Wester Craig.

CHAPTER EIGHTEEN

I When I got back to London a big fencing thing was on, and I went along with Shona to watch Erica. In the morning there were eliminating bouts in which all the competitors had a go. If you got through these, then there were quarter finals in the afternoon, and ultimately in the evening the last eight contestants fought it out in Seymour Hall before an audience, many of whom were the eliminated fencers.

The French women were particularly good, and the Italians and West Germans not far behind. By the afternoon every English-woman except Erica had gone, and she was beaten by a French-woman in the first contest of the evening. She joined us to watch the final bouts, a pink flush of fatigue hollowing her skin. I thought she looked high generally.

"For Pete's sake," I said, "this is an endurance test!"

"Oh, it's OK. It's the same for everyone."

"How many bouts have you had today?"

"Seven."

"And if you'd got through to the end it would have been nine. You can't be expected to have the same stamina as that kangaroo from Marseilles."

"They're going to run it over two days next year." She looked at me with her sultry eyes and laughed. "It can't be that you're feeling sympathetic, David! Shona, something has happened. David is becoming a ladies' man!"

"He always was," said Shona. "Did you not know?"

I suppose Shona had decided to play it cool, see how things went, not press or nag. Presumably she still hadn't a clue as to what had gone amiss between us, no doubt had come to all the wrong conclusions. I ought to tell her. Some day I ought to tell her, in fairness to myself. Because if it did begin again, even in only the most desultory way, how long could it last?

Knowing made me notice more, or hypnotized me into imagining more. Skin of her face showed puckerings in certain lights, not so much round the eyes as round the mouth and chin. Used spectacles more. Veins of hands becoming prominent. Had she ever had a face-lift? Certainly not in my time . . .

Not that there was any sign of slackening off on her part. She still moved only a little slower than sound, driving me and others to ever greater effort, chairing our monthly meetings with all her old fire and passion, making public appearances, attending her health farm, fencing on Tuesdays—maybe, who knew, having it off with some new fancy man Mondays and Fridays. (Wouldn't have liked that if I'd thought she did. Dog in the manger, etc.)

Semaphore was launched at last and, true to Shona's road sense, didn't make it big. To my way of thinking the advertising wasn't explicit enough. What it really should have said was, "If you want to lay a bird, this will help you as nothing else does." Leo Longford summed up the general feeling: "You're still before your time, David. It has to come, but we're still among the pioneers. Other people will score later on."

It was notable among the Shona products for making the biggest loss. This didn't help to sweeten relations between us.

I did an extended tour of the U.S., coming again up against a few more prickly obstacles but generally getting the feeling that we were inching our way into the big time. If all went well, in another year or two . . . But we needed to spend more money, and Shona wouldn't.

A couple of weeks after getting back I was best man at Van Morris's wedding.

I wasn't mad about the lady Arthur had finally decided to make an honest woman of. Coral was a pretty little thing with a willful twist of hair on her forehead and ingrowing blue eyes that were cool with the knowledge of her own importance. Her parents had a tobacconist's shop in Dulwich and clearly thought themselves a cut above my old friend Essie and her two sisters, who turned up in three-tier-gateau-and-sultana-almond hats. However, my presence, I'm ashamed to say, corrected the social balance.

Unexpectedly at the wedding was Derek Jones—though they'd

got to know each other pretty well during the Kilclair affair. Over the Sparkling Anjou I asked him about Donald and was told they'd broken up. "He was altogether too demanding, too argumentative. We used to get awfully stroppy with each other, and then one day he just walked out on me. We were in a pub and he went for a pee—never came back; just pissed off, as you might say."

"When did you suffer this bereavement?"

"Oh, weeks ago. I'm on my own at the moment—though there *is* a young man I met on Sunday; we'll have to see."

"And Roger?"

"Roger Manpole? I hardly see him, my dear."

I looked over the top of my glass. "I think you really must be fond of me."

"Of course, darling, you know. But why so suddenly convinced of it?"

"You lie to me so badly."

His blue eyes flickered, and it was as if a hint of malice had crept in by the back door. "Of course you don't *like* Roger."

"That isn't an overstatement."

"I can't see what's wrong with him."

"Only that he's alive."

"Anyway, you could safely come back to the Cellini; he's *never* there. Very much involved in the City these days, you know. In with the nobs now. Royal Enclosure. Garden parties, the rest of the old carnival. You got rid of your place in the Far North yet?"

"Not yet. Want to buy it?"

"I'll think of it, old dear. But how about offering it to Roger? I know one thing."

"What?"

"He'd give his eyeteeth for your title."

In fact I went to Scotland twice more that year, in spite of other intentions. The first was to a garden party at Holyroodhouse. Curiosity and a sense of profound irony pushed me to accept this invite. Also the old con man surveying a new scene. It does no harm to meet the best people, whether you're trying to raise credit for some dubious enterprise or to persuade the public that you have a night cream that induces cellular rejuvenation.

But as soon as I got there I wished I hadn't come, because who should be strolling by but Tom Martin of Greenock, in the company of a plump rosy girl in a picture hat; and of course the usual busybody introduced us. Obviously Tom's first impulse was to turn his back on me and walk away, but he was too much on his best behavior in the not-too-distant presence of the Queen. Expressions crossed his face like a television weather map.

Then his Adam's apple wobbled in his tight wing collar and I found myself being introduced to his wife. "David Abden," he muttered. "I suppose it's Sir David Abden now, is it?"

I smiled at the girl. "Tom and I were at school together; but the last time we met was at the Old Bailey."

"Oh?" she said, looking from one to the other. "In London, you mean?"

"Yes. Puzzling case, wasn't it, Tom?"

"Very puzzling." He glared at me.

"How long have you been married?" I asked the girl.

"Oh, just two years. Are you married, Sir—Sir David?"

"No. I'm still looking for the ideal," I said. "Glad Tom found his."

She blushed. She didn't look top-drawer but she looked all right. Probably monied. The thought of Tom fumbling his way about her was a disagreeable one. Martin had had some crude and dirty ways when he was at school.

"What is your name?" I asked.

"My name? Susan."

"Well, it's good to meet you, Susan. Any time you and Tom are in the Highlands, please give me a ring. I don't have a card but my number is Ullapool 41515. Come to lunch."

"*Thank* you," she said warmly. "We'd love to, wouldn't we, Martin?"

"Oh?" he said, still glowering. "Well, yes."

We went our ways, but not before I'd done my best to win her over. I could see she was taken and would react unpredictably to Tom's story of my criminal tendencies. I'd given them the wrong telephone number, the number of Lochfiern House, where I imagined they wouldn't get the warmest of welcomes. Not that I supposed for a moment that Tom would go near the place. He'd want no further truck with his swindler, and in any case would be afraid if he took his wife I would seduce her behind the woodshed, and she a willing victim.

II The second time I went north was in the autumn. Nothing in law can be hurried. According to Mr. Mac-ardle you had to apply—though not necessarily at the top of your voice—to the Court of Session for authority to execute an instrument of disentail in a form provided for by the Entailment Act of 1848. The "instrument of disentail" then had to be recorded in the Register of Entails; once that was done, you were at perfect liberty to try to sell your probably unsaleable property.

The man Macintyre had recommended some estate agents, McSwaine, Heeney and Garvice of Inverness, and, in anticipation of the great event when I came into free possession of the property, they had been up to look at it. They were generally and jointly of the opinion that Wester Craig's iron-age kitchen would be enough to put most prospective buyers off, and certainly would discourage Americans or others from renting it for the summer months. The cost of rejigging the kitchen was likely to be high, but I didn't realize how high until the estimates came through; then I told them to forget the whole thing. Lots of telephone buzz followed, in the course of which Macintyre dug out a firm that offered a full replan and refit for 40 percent less than the first; but he thought I should see and approve what they aimed to do.

So did I. I said to Shona, "Would you like to come?"

"If you would wish me to." I could tell by the way she breathed through her nose that she was pleased.

We went and met Macintyre and the builders and the plumbers and finally agreed the deal. Shona was useful because, aside from being a woman, she had this razor-sharp business instinct which saw through builders' waffle and plumbers' moonshine. But as still happened even now I found myself edgy about the way she took over.

"It is not beautiful, I agree. It is on the verge of being ugly. But I do not mind the contrast of styles, the asymmetry, the lack of taste; they are all part of an ancient house, are they not, a house which has grown with the years. In Russia we have houses like this—or had—because they have become a part of the family that has lived there. I do not think you should sell it, David."

"You observe the board."

"Oh, yes, but it can be taken down. Is there *nothing* you can turn to account, nothing you can sell off or rent instead?"

"Turn it into a trailer park? A motel?"

"Heaven forbid. There must be fishing rights. Does none of Loch Ashe belong to you?"

"One bit. The landing stage. And where the stream comes out."

"You shall go into it with Mr. Macintyre. You will not wish to live here, of course, but I would have thought somehow the property could be made to pay for itself. You should not cut yourself off so quickly from your own inheritance. Look, the sky is clearing. Let us go for a walk."

We went as far as the loch, which under the sheepish sun had white water with black rocks reflected in it and two toy boats each propping up a single fisherman. Overhead a few birds circled.

"It is so *quiet*," said Shona.

She'd had her hair cut differently for this trip. Shorter at the back, with the front hair dyed and graded a lighter brown, and a wispy fringe. It suited her, made her almost pretty, and outrageously young.

Next morning it was pouring with rain again, but I drove her up north, further than I'd been before, past Loch Assynt and Loch Glencoul. The traffic didn't exist, the road was wide enough only for a single car, with passing places; one loch after another, no end to them; you could hardly have seen better in Norway.

Shona said, "This is a deserted land! Why is there no one about? And all these fences! I do not understand."

We crossed a loch by a ferry big enough to take only two cars. Twenty miles further on we stopped and picnicked in the car off things Mrs. Coppell had made up for us, the rain fairly drumming on the roof. After lunch we decided it was far enough, the weather being what it was, and turned back, whereupon the clouds split their sides with laughing and the sun came out.

She was quiet beside me on the way home, watching the land and the lochs being brought out in discreet Technicolor. Water was spouting from the hillsides like burst water mains; mountains were the color of a soldier's camouflage tunic, reeds in the shallower lochs grew out of ink-blue water. I could see she was liking it. As I suppose I was too.

She insisted on going to Lochfiern House—or insisted as near as she could without actually getting out the thumbscrew. When we arrived Alison was out.

So a long talk with Lady Abden, and to my surprise the women got on. Shona's reputation and her elegance and personality made her a woman to be reckoned with, and I guess Aunt Helen recognized a kindred and formidable spirit. I wondered how the family would have reacted if my father had wanted to marry a Russian.

One thing I handed to Shona: However much she liked to be boss, she never by so much as a whisker showed any proprietorial attitude toward me. In the early days when we'd been trying to hide it from John she had hit on a style which implied we were simply business colleagues and that still went. But I expect my aunt with her cold clear eyes perceived the cloven hoof.

After a while Shona said, "Yesterday we went north, almost as far north as we could go. Why is there no one about? Why is it such a deserted country?"

We were in the upstairs sitting room again, with the inevitable Lucie squatting like a broody hen by the window; but present today also was Cousin Mary, raffishly dressed in stained tartan but less lubricated than when I'd last seen her.

Lady Abden said, "The land has always been deserted, ever since the clearances."

"What are those? I do not understand."

"At the beginning of the last century it was decided it would be profitable to raise sheep in the Highlands. At first they were put on the hills, but when it was found that they could not stand the winter, the glens were cleared to accommodate them and the people driven out."

"Driven where to?"

"To the coast, where they lived in hamlets on the edge of the sea, to the slums of Glasgow and Edinburgh, or to emigrate. All the Highlands were depopulated and have remained so ever since."

"And who did this?"

"Oh, it is a long story. The English. Perhaps more the Scots. It all goes back to Culloden."

"Whist now," said Mary. "It was Sutherland who started it, and it was all done in the name of progress and reform." She hiccuped. "Since then the deer forests have followed. But the crofters were a shiftless lot, living in squalor, hard to get on with. Unwilling to be helped."

"Helped indeed!" said Lucie. "You do not help a family by burning the roofs over their heads."

I said, "And what was our part in all this?"

My aunt said, "Sir Charles Abden risked ruin to keep his crofters housed and fed. There were others, Protestants as well as Catholics, who did the same. But it did not stop the march of progress, as my daughter calls it. Who was it said: 'Four shepherds and three thousand sheep now occupy the land that once supported five hamlets'?" She rubbed a bony hand across her face. "I forget."

"And so many fences," said Shona. "They are to keep people out?"

"To keep animals *in*," said Mary. "That's natural enough, ain't it?" She put her hand to her mouth. "Pardon. But, Mother, the clearances are way back in the past, so far as to have no relevance *anymore*. The land is empty because it can support so few—not up to any modern standards. If the clearances had never happened the Highlands would have depopulated themselves!"

The same little maid whose bottom I had once thought of pinching brought us coffee. Shona had said no to sherry because she thought it bad for her touchy liver. I thought, I wonder which baronet Sir Charles was, sixth or seventh? I was thirteenth. That's me, unlucky number, maybe I shall be the last, and good riddance; but you can't kill the damned thing off unless there are no male heirs anywhere. Fourteenth baronet, Hiram K. Abden from Oregon or Nova Scotia.

"What is the motto under the crest?" Shona asked. "That in the hall. Under the larger crest."

It was Lucie who answered. " '*Creag mo chroidhe-se a chreag ghuanach.*' It means: 'Rock of my heart, the secure rock.' "

"You speak Gaelic?" I said.

"A little."

"We all speak a little," said my aunt. "Not as much as we should."

"There are many languages in Russia," said Shona. "Too many,

I sometimes think. It makes for lack of communication and understanding."

"That is what many Scotsmen have felt," my aunt said sourly. "They have become so anglicized that you can scarcely detect a hint of their native tones. They live in their big houses in Edinburgh and in London and ape the people who conquered them."

"Ah, now," said Mary. "Did we not agree before that it is all too long ago? One hundred years, two hundred years, it is all so far past. Why, nearly half the prime ministers of England this century have been Scottish!"

"You miss my meaning, Mary. They should have been prime ministers of Scotland!"

"Did Margaret no' bring anything in to *drink*? David, I'm sure, would like a dram."

"We should be going," I said. "By the way, that other motto in the hall; whose is that?"

"What motto?"

"On the wall away from the window. There's another coat of arms and another inscription which someone has translated underneath. 'The beast itself both bright and bold.' That ours too?"

Lucie coughed and stared out of the window. Lady Abden said, "It is the insignia of the Fiernes of Loch Fierne. At the end of the eighteenth century the families were joined. Duncan Abden married the only surviving Fierne daughter, who brought this property with her; though for some time after that, until this new house was built, they continued to live at Wester Craig."

"Not quite the motto for a Christmas cracker," I said.

"What? Oh, such things were chosen long ago and times change."

"They were a mad lot," said Mary with relish. "Made their own laws, more or less. Wish we could."

"As always, you exaggerate, Mary," said Sister from the window.

"Well, the Highlands have always been a wee bit wild. A lot of folk still have the mind that civilization ends at the Grampians."

It looked as if Shona had made a hit with my aunt, and I had a hunch that when they were a few minutes alone Shona had promised to send up some sample night creams to combat "a dry skin," a not unknown ploy of hers. There was even a lack of hostility—can't claim more than that—in Aunt Helen's cold eyes as I took her hand. It was so shrunken and thin the rings almost rattled. If Shona had offered her something for a dry skin she was dead right.

Mary, whom I began to think would quite likely become my favorite Abden, followed us out and weaved a way down the stairs to the front door.

"A mad lot," she said, "the Fiernes. Definitely weak in the crumpet, if you follow me. Their motto fits 'em fine." She glanced behind to see if Lucie was following. "Stop and have a dram wi' me. Take the flavor of the coffee away."

I glanced at Shona, who smiled and shook her head.

"Tell me more, Cousin," I said.

"Ha, well the Fiernes were here before us, and that's saying something. Time of Robert the Bruce they looked on themselves as little kings. Didn't change much through the years neither. When they stopped murdering their neighbors they would sail off to Ireland and do the same there. A standing feud with the Abdens, of course, whom they looked on as upstarts. And they were neighbors, more or less. Neighbors always quarrel, don't they?" She pushed back her hair, which immediately fell forward again. "Then one day it all blew up into a bitter fight—when Fierne of Loch Fierne and both his sons were killed. That did not stop Duncan Abden—who was desperate short of siller at the time—from paying court to the one remaining daughter, Cathy Fierne, who was queer as a bat, and marrying her. She gave him three children and then was locked away under a keeper."

I opened the front door. A thick fine mist had come up unnoticed, blotting out the sun and dulling the day.

"It's the haars," said Mary, twisting a button on her shabby jumper. "Got to expect it; time of the year. D'ye know, I never go out. Why should I? Far better indoors with a dram."

"Maybe you're right," I said.

Mary put her knuckles to her mouth. "Pardon again. One feels empty at this time of day. Do you know . . ." She stopped.

"Know what?"

"The three bairns Cathy Fierne bore. One was normal, one took to drink, one went to the madhouse." She chuckled. "They say it has been in the Abden family ever since. Getting born into our family you have a one in three chance . . . I know which straw I drew."

CHAPTER NINETEEN

I As we were about to drive away a yellow Mini zoomed up. I had to do the introductions. They summed each other up in pretty smart time, and I didn't suppose an offer of samples of night cream would create sudden spiritual affinity. Alison was at her stillest and coolest and most composed, and Shona in her fur hat and short sable coat looked like the tsarina out slumming. When we finally pushed off, screenwipers working overtime, she made no reference to Alison, or even to the others; we talked of the kitchen alterations and what chance Bruce Macintyre had of making a few summer rentals to meet some of the cost.

"One trouble with con men," I said, "is that they sometimes con themselves. I can't do that here. Unless I sell it there's no way of seeing the house as an economic proposition."

"I can give you more money."

"I know. I'm worth it. But I don't want an increase just to tip it away on something I don't value."

"Don't you? I think you should."

"Didn't know you were such a romantic."

"I think you should go into it more carefully with Captain Macintyre and Mr. Macardle—and even with Coppell and McVitie—to see if something cannot be worked out. For you may not be *able* to sell it."

"That thought," I said, "had certainly occurred to me."

"Tomorrow morning we will inspect your property thoroughly, see if there is any profitable prospect."

"But we're leaving for London first thing. It's no short hop as you observed coming up. Near on six hundred miles."

"Tomorrow morning," Shona said, "we will inspect your property."

The sea mist stayed thick all afternoon, partly clearing now and then and pulling the bedclothes back from the sickly sun, but then rolling down again from the moorland ridges that surrounded the house. Next morning it had all gone, but Shona, keeping to her resolutions, said we could leave late and spend the night in Edinburgh: She wanted to call on two shops, and if we were back in London by Friday it would do.

So we went off, part of the way accompanied by Coppell, who knew exactly where my land began and ended. She strode along beside us with the vigor of a youngster.

There was no real height behind the house—but once you'd climbed it you seemed on top of the world. It was primeval land; most of the moor probably hadn't been turned over since the wild Duncan courted his dotty wife. Heather and stunted birch and rabbit tracks and small rocks and clumps of Scots pine; and the stream tinkling among the rocks and forming pebbly pools here and there, one at least of which might have been rated as a small loch with an island in the middle covered with spruce and fir.

I said to Coppell, "Why no grouse?"

"Och, there are some, sorr. But all this season I only got a dozen brace."

"Why so few?"

"It is not quite the country. And there has been disease among 'em. More gamekeepers are needed. And there are ower many poachers aboot."

"Would it ever be profitable to raise them in sufficient numbers to let off the shooting?"

"I doubt it would pay. Neither Dr. Malcolm nor Sir Charles ever tried."

When Coppell had loped off she said, "That hillside over there, with the young trees all growing in rows. It is like a knitted pullover drawn across the shoulder of the mountain."

I picked up a flat stone and skimmed it over the water of the small loch. It hopped a half-dozen times, and some birds rose and flapped away into the next coppice. Cold standing there, not so much the air as the wind, which gimleted its way through.

"Yesterday," she said, "when we were in Ullapool and you left me in the car to buy that magazine, I heard two men passing by talking Russian. I was so startled that I jumped out and spoke to them. They are here buying herring from the local fishermen to take back to Leningrad. It makes the world suddenly so much smaller!"

"I thought you looked excited. Did they know you were a lapsed Communist?"

"We did not speak as political people—only as Russians."

"You still love Russia?"

"Of *course*."

"So you expect me to feel the same about Scotland, eh?"

"Not the same, for you never lived here; but, well, yes, I do not think you will be able altogether to resist the pull of your ancestry."

"That's what Alison said."

Unspoken name. "Did she."

"She's wrong. So are you." I scratched my head. "Trying to remember some poem I was forced to learn at school. 'Breathes there the man with soul so dead who never to himself hath said, This is my own my native land. Whose heart hath ne'er within him burned as home his footsteps he hath turned from wandering on some foreign strand.' After that curses are heaped on the poor bastard if he doesn't fairly drool at the thought of porridge and haggis."

Shona said, "I am glad something was beaten into you. No one has ever succeeded in impressing you since."

"Except for you, it might be true."

"Thank you, dear David."

"Incidentally," I said, "it was news to me yesterday that there was insanity in the family. Though, God knows, I should certainly have had a fair inkling."

"Oh, look into anyone's ancestry and you will somewhere sooner or later see the gibbering madman behind the barred window. It is most fortunate when people don't *know* what their ancestors have been."

"Well, the drink problem still recurs. I wonder if I had a child whether it would take to the bottle."

"The feeding bottle, I am sure."

I threw another stone. "For a Russian you're optimistic."

"You have been reading Dostoevsky."

"Since I was never beaten to do so I've never opened a book of his in my life."

"David, I weep for your education."

"Never mind that. Never forget I know a lot about perfume and a lot about cars, and maybe a fair amount about women."

Shona was staring sternly at some birds high in the sky.

"Talking of women, perhaps you should marry money."

I looked at her. "That's a little off the beaten track, coming from you."

"Well," she said, "you could always marry me."

There was a longer silence.

"This is so sudden," I said.

"Well, you could. As you know, you would certainly be marrying money. We should not need to sell the house. We could renovate it—spend a good deal on it. Remove some of those tasteless additions. Rebuild the entrance so that it is suitable to match the old hall. Thin out those plants—they are rhododendrons, aren't they? Your aunt says some of them are fine ones; the Gulf Stream—is it?—makes them possible. We could do good things with the property, together." Her voice stopped as if suddenly cut off.

"And John?"

"We haven't lived together for two years. It should not be at all difficult to get a divorce."

"Are you serious?"

"Of course. Never more so."

I hitched the shoulders of my coat. "Those birds you're glowering at—what are they?"

"Birds? I do not know. Birds of prey."

"Hawks or buzzards, I expect. Odd sound they make. Like cats. Mewing."

"No doubt they are after the rabbits."

"And the grouse—if any."

We turned and began to walk back. The wind was coming off the sea and it was hard going even downhill. The Gulf Stream didn't seem to be working too successfully just then.

"One thing I'd never know if I married you," I said.

"What is that?"

"Whether my child would have turned out to be a drunkard or a lunatic."

She was silent, walking beside me. We were striding over soft damp moss and it deadened even the sound of our feet. The birds had been blown away and we were quite alone.

I said, "Joke over."

"What? No matter. It is blunt. What you have said. And it is the truth. Would it be important to you, having an heir?"

"No."

"I think it would be important to you," she said, "having an heir."

II Next morning Mrs. Linda McNeill, the buyer of Stovolds of Edinburgh, had something private to say. While Shona was making a royal progress toward the general manager's office she drew me aside.

"Pardon me, Sir David, but we have had a complaint from a customer about a bottle of your Faunus perfume. I have no wish to bother Madame with it if ye could attend to this yourself."

I followed the stout little body into her office, where she unlocked a drawer and took out a bottle of the perfume. It had been opened and about a quarter used. It was the one-half fluid ounce size which sold for £26. She took the stopper out and handed me the bottle. I sniffed, and made a face.

"Where did this come from?"

"It was bought from us, most unfortunately, by the sister of the Lord Provost. It seems last week that they were dining out and after dinner Mrs. Grant and another lady had occasion to discuss perfumes. They were, as it happened, both using Faunus, but when they compared the scents there were differences. The other lady had bought her perfume from McLeish's, and Mrs. Grant from us. They both agreed that Mrs. Grant's perfume was inferior in quality, and she brought it back yesterday."

"How did you come by this bottle?"

"It was—hm—part of a consignment from Hilliers. You know them, I'm sure. They're usually vairy reliable."

Hilliers was one of the smaller wholesalers. We never, of course, dealt with wholesalers ourselves, otherwise we could not control our distribution.

Mrs. McNeill said, "Do you think there has been some error in the manufacture?"

"No, I don't."

"Then what has gone wrong?"

"Why did you get our stuff from Hilliers?"

She coughed. "This was a special offer."

"At a discount?"

"Er—yes. It was—surplus stock. We bought it in really for the January sale but decided to put it in right away."

"Where did the stock come from?"

"I've no idea, Sir David. It was quite a small consignment and Hilliers have always played fair with us before."

"Have you more of it?"

"Yes. I *think* we've kept it separate. We gave Mrs. Grant a new box, naturally. She opened it in the shop and seemed quite satisfied."

"Can I try another?"

She sent for a couple more of the elegant silver-faced boxes. She opened one and smelled it. "I—I think *that*'s all right, isn't it?"

I took it from her and sniffed it. "No. It's a much better copy than the one Mrs. Grant returned. But it's still a copy."

"Copy? D'you mean . . . But the boxes . . ."

"I suppose you realize this could make a nasty scandal if it were brought out into the open."

Mrs. McNeill's fat little face colored up. "This was all done in the greatest good faith, Sir David! Otherwise clearly we should not have drawn your attention to it!"

"I only hope Mrs. Grant got a genuine box this time . . ."

"Of course, of course, of course."

She said it so often I wondered if she was certain.

I didn't say any of this to Shona on the way home. The Scottish visit was petering out on a sour note. However civilized and sophisticated she might be, the fact stood out like a sore thumb that she'd suggested marriage to me and had been turned down flat. And it was a flat that left no doubts as to the cause: She was too long in the tooth. Her lover thought she was too old. So it happened to be true: Did that help? Why should it? If her fancy boy had been even halfway in love with her—as he'd once thought he was—his bird brain would have contrived to smooth over a few rough corners before he loosed off his reply. Instead he had simply come out with the facts of life.

All right, it was done, and as she was honest she would know it was the truth. More than ever if she remembered her phony passport. But that didn't make it easier going, and I was sorry.

I took the bottles of perfume to Stevenage and called in Phil Parker and we put them under the gas chromatograph along with some of our own Faunus. The "fingerprints" were quite different. Fingerprints are a series of block charts rather like the things you see showing world population changes. The copy perfume had been made on the cheap to a formula that closely resembled ours, without the costly items. In all perfume you need an expensive fixative. If you don't have a good fixative the perfume loses its "note" very quickly. That's why Mrs. Grant's first bottle smelled much less right than the equally phony one just opened by Mrs. McNeill. But there were many other economies as well. One of the main ingredients of Faunus was Bulgarian rose absolute—rose petals gathered by the thousand at dawn in Bulgarian fields and costing £2000 a kilo. This thing had got some synthetic substance in it that had never been near a rose bush in its life and probably cost £2 a kilo.

"What do we do now?" asked Parker.

"Find out who supplied Hilliers who supplied Stovolds. I'd like to bet . . ."

"What?"

"That it'll be a paper firm with a good address and nobody there when you call."

So it was. A company called Moth and Benny Exports, specializing in the buying-up of bankrupt stock, had supplied Hilliers; their address was in Leighton Buzzard, and when I sent Van Morris up to make a few enquiries he found nothing but an accommodation address and bank accounts that had been transferred elsewhere.

I know I should have told Shona at this stage, but our meetings were now very brief and the opportunity didn't come up. As there were no more cases it seemed to me that this was a one-off affair: Some crook had got hold of a consignment of our boxes either from a contact in the printing works which produced them or by some other nefarious means. Stovolds were to blame—or rather Mrs. McNeill—for trying to get our stuff on the cheap (because the device upped her commission), and I sent an acid letter to her warning her that if anything like it happened again we'd cut off supplies. There the matter ended—or seemed to.

The winter went by, and things went on much the same. Some wag offered £40,000 for Wester Craig and said he wanted to turn it into a hotel. I told Macintyre to advise him to go and jump in Loch Broom.

Then Shona's father was ill again and she had to go and see him. When she came home we had a drink together. Her father was losing strength but the doctor said he had such a tenacious hold on life that he might last for years yet.

All the aggro between us seemed by now to have worn off, and we talked in the old companionable way. We went back to her flat and she played Brubeck and Scott Joplin and we had a last drink together and then went to bed. I suppose I should have known better, but I thought it would be all right.

Later, around eleven, she said, "Are you sleeping with someone else?"

"No, Madame."

"It would not be surprising, as it is a year now since anything was right between us."

"Well, the answer's still no."

"If you have found no one else, is it just that you are very tired of me?"

"I'm not *tired* of you, Shona. These things come and go." Why so weasel-mouthed, why not come out with it?

"And now between us they have gone, eh?"

"I don't know. Who knows?"

She got up, shrugged into her black silk Dior dressing gown, stood erect beside me but not looking at me. "After all, who am I to complain? I went into this with my eyes wide open, well aware of the risks. We have had some splendid years. The danger always existed that I should become too fond of you. I have become too fond of you. You must know this well, for in these last years I have confessed it to you often enough—"

"And do you think I'm still not fond of you?"

"—It is not the same thing. I do not believe it to be the same thing. I am getting too old for you and it is becoming obvious.

You want a fresh young girl. Perhaps, in spite of what you say, you have one such in view."

"No, Madame."

"Don't keep saying that . . . But I think in your heart you hanker for some new person, eh? Your mistress is a little *passé*: Turn on the light and you may count the wrinkles."

"Shona," I said, "you've done a lot for me. I've learned quite a bit since this wagon started rolling—rubbing shoulders with you and—"

"Shoulders is it, now?"

"But things change. It's not the way love affairs last—to put on an act, to claim a smash hit when the customers have gone away. OK, things have changed, but I've no wish to *end* anything. It's just a different game we may have to play from now on."

She stroked her straight nose with a long thin forefinger. "You want to marry—isn't that it?"

"I don't want to do *anything*. I am trying to explain, to rationalize what may be going on between us. You say yourself—"

"All right. All right," she interrupted. "This—this inevitable thing is happening. Do you wish to leave the firm?"

"Why should I? Unless you'd rather."

"Naturally not. For years with my firm I stood on my own— John did not count in that way—but now, these last few years, you have stood close beside me. I depend on you for many things. The last thing I wish is that I should lose you in both ways."

I said, "The tragic scene isn't called for. You haven't lost me in any way yet. Ten years from now we may still be tagging along together. By the way, I don't consider my pension scheme is very generous."

She laughed. "It will be brought up at the next board meeting. Seriously, David . . ."

"Haven't we been serious till now?"

"Seriously, I have a deep, deep affection for you. My primitive nature says, fight for him, do not let him go, you cannot *afford* to let him go, he belongs to you as no one else ever has done; stick in your claws and hold fast! You know, one grows . . . barbaric in love."

I waited, saying nothing.

She went on, "But my intellectual nature says there is no such thing as lasting love, as lasting fidelity; you have enjoyed what you have had and, by God, it has been good at times—especially in Barbados. D'you remember the Green Flash?"

"Of course."

"And what I said about it?"

"Yes."

"I was talking about it to someone in Paris not long ago, and he said it was an accepted natural phenomenon, not an optical illusion or a subjective fantasy."

"Like love," I said.

"Like love." She sighed. "That is the way of it . . . so I must withdraw my claws and let you go."

"My dear," I said, "in the first place, no claws would hold me if I wanted to go. In the second place, I don't want to go anywhere. Unless right at this moment it's somewhere to eat."

"We're too late for the Dorchester," she said, looking at her watch.

Food at the Cellini went on until one-thirty and was very good, but I always fought shy of taking her there.

"Got any eggs?" I said. "I'll make you an omelette *fines herbes.* You know I'm a kingpin at that."

"I brought some foie gras back from Paris," she said. "And there's some Gewürztraminer in the cupboard. You will know if it will go."

"It will exactly go."

We ate hungrily and companionably. There was still no conflict between us. She told me her father refused all her persuasions that he should come to England. He was determined to die in Paris. He said he couldn't possibly allow it that there should be sea between him and Russia. John her husband was also ailing and was something of a drag on her conscience.

Toward the end of the meal, while we were still nibbling at the Brie and sipping the last of the wine, she said, "Why don't you marry Erica?"

CHAPTER TWENTY

I Among a large number of useless things I picked up
—or was pushed into—at Loretto was a smattering of
Latin, and I remember a tag which ran: *"Quem Deus
vult perdere, prius dementat."* "Whom God wishes to ruin, he first
drives mad." It was used as a bit of a joke in the lower fifth.

Well, personally, I don't believe God or anyone else was interested enough in me to plot my ruin, but probably I was a little
mad already, so the job was done without His help. But what
about Erica, I wondered? Was she demented too?

Of course it wasn't quite as manic as all that. (Nobody gets the
benefit of hindsight until it's too late.) And of course I didn't take
the directive from my former mistress and hurry over to Knightsbridge with a formal proposal of marriage sealed with red tape.
All I suppose Shona's suggestion did was to nudge along something that had been in the back of my mind for quite a while.

I knew Erica well; I'd slept with her during the interregnum, and
that part was all right; she had plenty of money and was free with
it; and for her part she would be marrying a title. In back of that
was a much subtler and maybe deeper reason for the whole thing.
I still didn't go big on personal relationships. (Shona had become an
exception but I didn't want any more.) I'd come to tolerate people
better these last few years but still preferred them one step away.
This, it may be thought, was a pretty lousy recipe for getting hooked
up to anyone; and it was this maybe more than anything else that
had kept me from contemplating the holy state before. But Erica, I
thought, was very much of the same cast of mind. In her nervous,
tensed-up, vital way she was always hard to get near to; body and
mind would tend to wriggle from under the affectionate approach;
she didn't like to be pinned down; she was independent; wanted
her arms free of the bedclothes; a bit of a solitary. Yet she had feelings

enough, had high spirits, and a what-the-hell, happy-go-lucky attitude to life that I thought would fit with my own.

I asked Shona once why she'd made the suggestion.

She shrugged. "I knew I had lost you anyhow."

"I'll think that remark over."

She gave me a quick glance. "Why?"

"It sounds disingenuous."

"What a big word for such a simple statement."

"Well, it's not true, is it? You've told me you don't want to chuck out your sales manager. Nor do I want to sponge on Erica. So we shall see a lot of each other still."

"Ah," she said, "but after working hours not at all." Her eyes were heavy on me, clear and warm and glistening like the eyes of a young woman. "I have lost you for a long time now, David. I do not know why it happened, but you have told me it was *not* some other woman . . . Is it—can it be—anything to do with your coming into the title?"

"What *are* you talking about?"

"Well, it happened about then."

"Nothing is to do with *anything!*" I said, getting angry, which was unusual now.

"Well then, peace be on us. I do not know why it happened and you do not know or forbear to tell me. So it has come about and I have to give you up. This I now do. Fully and freely—and regretfully."

"Fully and freely," I said, kissing her. Her lips were harder but warmer than Erica's. "And regretfully."

Even at the time it seemed a bit too good and too civilized to be true.

 One thing Erica had said when I first dropped the idea in her lap, "Should we wait a year?"

"For some reason?"

"The Olympics. A year next July."

"I'm willing to come along and shout in Russian."

"I'm sure. You'll have had plenty of practice in that. But it is not just the games themselves, it is the long preparation, even to be picked."

"I'll train you."

"Be sensible, boy." She hopped about a little, squinting at me comically. "If I want this I really have to *work*—no half measures. Have you any idea what that really *means*? Fencing at these levels, you've to build up a system of points over four years—since the last Olympics, in fact—and if you want to stand a chance you need a whole lot even to qualify. I'm doing all right at the moment, but at least twenty-five percent of the points have to be scored in the last year, so there couldn't be any slacking off just because of a mere marriage. I've got to be . . . mind-free."

"Is there anything else in your book against having a husband?"

"Nothing at all."

"But you'd like to wait a year—more than a year?"

She hesitated, her eyes kindling. "Not for any other reason. Obviously."

"Then let's risk it."

Still, we took our time. I went to Reading to meet her parents. He was a big wavery clumsy man; she was small and petite like Erica but never had been pretty. I asked Erica to excuse me from taking her to meet my mother. We decided to live in her flat in Knightsbridge, which was big enough for about four families. She had a two-seater convertible Mercedes, so we decided to keep both cars. She seemed to enjoy my style of driving, but I was less easy with hers; she drove like a cat on a hot tin roof.

So it was marriage at Caxton Hall—with the minimum cast—and off to Hungary for our honeymoon. This had a double target; Erica was taking part in a foil contest there, and Budapest was one of the few capital cities I hadn't visited with Shona. The choice wasn't a howling success, as she gained fewer points than she thought she was going to, and the weather, for the last week in April, was grim—chief memory is of damp snow falling across the Danube. And there had been an influenza epidemic raging, so that everyone's larynx reminded you of hinges that needed oiling. Maybe it was the enervating effects of the flu bug, maybe it was the regime; but everything moved at a crawl; people were in shabby clothes, with unkempt buildings and unrepaired streets. No wonder all the cleverest Hungarians had emigrated.

Four days in Paris on the way home. Different hotel, different *arrondissement*; it all helped to break the Shona pattern; but one afternoon while Erica was visiting her fencing chums I went to see Shona's father, old Pantelevich. I knew I'd never be able to make him hear, but relied on the middle-aged niece to translate. He was in bed, troubled with his breathing and circulatory problems. He remembered me and we exchanged sentences at a high level of perceived noise decibels. The niece reminded me of Cousin Lucie. They'd both grown gray-faced caring for other people, but instead of a life of self-sacrifice making them benign and gentle it had turned them sour.

Back to London to begin a new life as Sir David and Lady Abden, 24 Knightsbridge House, SW3 and some other postal hieroglyphs. I hadn't yet taken her north.

I stayed on as sales manager of a highly successful, still privately owned perfumery firm with branches now—or outlets—in most of the civilized world. About this time Shona fairly dived into a new round of publicity and benefit capers; I saw less of her as she went out more into the social world and left the day to day running of the business in my hands and Leo Longford's. Of John Carreros there was no sign at all.

The fact that Erica was hitched to a husband with a fair knowledge of her amateur profession couldn't, she thought, be wasted; so whenever we were at home and there was half an hour to be filled we'd have a sparring match. We had this enormous kitchen; God knows what it had been in the original house, but it was ideal for the job in hand. Usually we fenced with the épée, which is a heavier weapon than the foil—foil being the only class for women in the Olympics—but Erica said she preferred the épée. It's a different technique too: With the foil you have a very restricted target; in épée the whole body is the target; it's much nearer to old-fashioned dueling, rather like the stuff you see in corny historical films. Erica said it strengthened her arm and made her reactions quicker when she went back to the foil.

All this was extra to the hour she spent with her fencing master five nights out of seven, and all the other exercises she did: running in the park, heel-toeing to music to develop footwork and rhythm; and reaction training—that is, catching things rolling off shelves at unexpected angles, and the like.

Can't say this regime altogether grabbed me, but I'd been duly warned and I went along with it. What she hadn't told me was the amount of traveling she'd have on her plate, going all over Europe for these joustings. Sometimes I went with her but more often not. Fencing, it seemed to me, was OK for recreation, but at this level it became a bore. But I kept these opinions under careful wraps, and doing these practices with her certainly improved my own fencing, for what that was worth. With my extra reach she began to find me quite a hard nut to crack—or maybe I should say pin down. In our kitchen it was all distinctly haphazard, because although we always used the protective gear there was of course no mechanism for recording hits and we had to make do with yells and counteryells. I thought once in a feverish moment she was going to suggest having electric wiring put in so that we should know the exact score.

Although she still fenced under her own name, there was one element of our wedlock that Erica certainly found OK. She took to being Lady Abden like a cat to cream, and when her other occupations allowed she threw large dinner parties and invited all the distinguished bodies she could scrape together. Caterers came in and did it all, so it was no work for her; but twice she gave extravagant parties in a private room at the Dorchester.

When I grumbled she said, "But we *do* get something out of it, boy. It helps in all sorts of ways. Maybe we don't need social advancement, but we get good conversation, friends in all walks of life, and *fun*. That's the most important thing of all!"

A bit later I realized what she meant by "all sorts of ways," when she was invited to give a half-page interview to *The Times* in which details of our marriage and her determination to carry on with her sport squared away most of the column inches.

Now and then she'd pull off a practical joke on one of her friends; and she seemed rather overfond of gays. There were always more men at her dinner parties than women, and while I didn't mind a few I felt a few was enough. She said, "It simply doesn't occur to me. You're old-fashioned even to notice. I simply ask people who are witty and talkative and help to make the party go."

I said, "What *about* Scotland? We ought to go sometime."

"Yes, well, I'd like to. I want to. But it can't be next week because of—sorry, sorry—university fencing matches. And the week after that I have to be in Barcelona; and on the Saturday it's Lady Brotherton's dinner party . . . What about the—let's see, it would be the second week in June?"

"That's our sales conference. Third week?"

"Isn't that Ascot? I really must go this year with my new and titled husband. Then there's a week—I shall be in Vienna for part of it. After that comes Henley."

"Hallelujah, what a prospect!"

"Can't we leave it until late summer, when the social frenzy has died down?"

I went to the window. "It's stopped raining. I think I'll go for a walk. Coming?"

"Not another little bout?"

"Not another little bout."

"OK. If it's not far." She stretched her long legs and smiled sweetly at me. "Where shall we go?"

"As far as the Prince Consort," I said.

III

So it was August when we finally made it, and in the end the visit wasn't exactly a ten-strike. For one thing, the wide open spaces I'd come to appreciate were full of trippers, and for another, Erica, who had a very fair and fine skin, was nearly driven off her nut by the midges. Even I couldn't stay out of doors in the afternoons.

But anyway for the next year nothing was really going to be of lasting interest to my girl-wife except her blasted foil. The only thing that might have lit her up would have been a fencing contest in Inverness. Needless to say we'd brought weapons with us, so that she need not miss the whole of her routine.

She was bright and cheerful and interested, and looked very young with her fresh face and blond ponytail; but her interest was shallow. The new kitchen was finished and Mrs. Coppell was delighted with it, except that she was was afraid to use some of the gadgets in case they jumped out and bit her like bigger midges. Two more prospective clients had been shown round but no offers made. Nor any rental this August. A minimum of £20,000 was needed, Macintyre said, to bring the house into a state of good repair. Most of this would be spent on the roof. When he had gone Erica offered me £20,000 and said she would write me a check as soon as we got home. I said, "Thanks. Thanks, love. Thanks a lot." But when it came to the point I found it quite hard to go along with the idea of her shelling out all that to pay for my toy. It had been part of the implicit deal, maybe—"we like each other and you've got money and I've got a title"—but and but and but.

It would have been easier if she'd shown the sort of interest that Shona had shown, especially in the old hall and its odd inscriptions. She didn't. Nor was she as excited as Madame had been about the countryside—which was very explainable considering the drawbacks the Highlands were then suffering from.

When Alison knew we were "in residence" she invited us to lunch. It was not something high on my agenda of goodies, but it was hard to say a flat no again, so we accepted. When we got there there were eight other guests and this helped to dilute the Abden women. Lady Abden herself came down to meet the new Lady Abden and was fairly gracious, considering. There was the local doctor and a Mr. Hamish Fraser, a laird from near Inverewe, and a Mr. and Mrs. Dalgleish who owned a lot of property in Ullapool; a Mr. Lovat Donald, younger brother of the head of the clan; a couple of others whose names I heard and instantly forgot; and Captain Bruce Macintyre, being more gentlemanly than the gentlemen.

Alison and Erica were a shade sniffy to begin, but later seemed to get on; there was nothing like the feline enmity there'd been when Shona and Alison met. Over lunch I was at the other end of the table from Erica, and not for the first time perceived my young wife to be a bit too socially conscious. What would bring her back to Wester Craig—once Moscow had been worked out of her system—would be if the society here was sufficiently grade A. After all, the wife of a Scottish laird with an old title might rate more in the Highlands than she did in London. But if this was the society she could expect to meet—monied and landed though it was—then she'd be likely to stay in London.

On the whole this attitude suited me. Wester Craig had little or no appeal, and I would be glad to be rid of it. But that wasn't the whole picture. In squash you have a wall to hit your ball against. Could be that I would have liked Erica to be that wall.

When we got back to London Shona's father had died and I didn't see much of her for a while. Though things were going well between Erica and me, I would have had to confess if you twisted my arm that I missed those quiet evenings in Shona's flat, her piano playing, her intimate company. Our love affair had had too many agreeable accretions for you to be able to throw it away like last year's credit card.

By ordinary standards we had our moments, Erica and I, but for the most part we stayed at the three-foot paddler's end. But I did seem to have something going for me in her eyes. In between the endless athletics and other sporting operations she could be amorous enough. She was still young; and as unpredictable as only pretty women can be. I reflected that another five years of fencing and the high life and it was not impossible she'd turn right round and perversely want a family life far more than I ever should.

Shona and I stayed on fair terms; but once there's been this powerful thing between you and it's gone—especially if it has only gone on one side—the look changes, the way of tackling a thing together. It becomes a sort of friendly cooperation with an undertone of hostility.

Big changes were taking place in the perfumery game at this time. The old system of strict agencies, whereby Mr. B the chemist was granted the sole agency for Elizabeth Arden perfume—provided he took and stocked a number of her less popular items—was going. General traders were muscling in, often undercutting. Writs and summonses were flying through the air like autumn leaves on a windy day. But there seemed to be the beginnings of a recession, and in its cold draft they couldn't be stopped. The big stores began to buy less and to be more choosy what they took. *People* were buying less. No use marketing some brand-spanking new perfume with ballyhoo in the press and on TV and scoring a bull's eye so far as the wholesalers were concerned, and then finding that the first orders weren't followed up. *Women* were buying less, not because they were less interested but because they hadn't so much money to spend.

The infant mortality in 1979 of brilliant, original, seductive and irresistible new perfumes reached record heights. Even Shona and Co. had some extra warehouse shelves built.

For my part, if I'd had the power and not been just a paid slave, I would have done something to try to break out of the vicious circle of price and production costs. Old John Carreros's rough arithmetic all those years ago was still valid—inflation hadn't altered it. A woman buying perfume still got about five pennyworth of content for every pound she paid in the shop. Yet the whole perfumery lark was so contradictory that no one could come up with easy answers. On the one hand it was a con trick; on the other hand women accepted—demanded—this sort of sales psychology and would take no other. They wanted their perfumery dear; they wanted it in elegant boxes; they wanted to feel that what they were using was the most expensive they could afford. It did them good to feel that way. Put some Charisma in a medicine bottle and offer it at a quarter the price and sales would drop like the stick of a rocket. It was all very odd and very hard to work out in simple economic terms.

Anyway events in my job took quite a lot of my attention just then, almost as much as Erica gave to her fencing, and there were weeks when we were only nodding acquaintances. At Christmas I suggested we might try Scotland again just for the devil of it, but she had a training camp at Penzance, so we went there instead.

It was in March that a report came in from a rep covering the Midlands that he had had a complaint from a customer, who had a sole agency, that a shop in the same high street was selling Shona products, particularly Faunus and Charisma, and at a lower rate. When the rep went along, he found them selling what appeared to be the right stuff. He had brought two boxes back with him.

They were taken to Stevenage and analyzed. The Faunus forgery was exactly the same as the one at Stovold's, the Charisma better. Of course this was aired at the next meeting, and I told the company about the Stovold forgery last year and what I had done. The general feeling was that I hadn't done enough.

Afterward Shona said, "You must have known there would be a repetition."

"A clumsy forgery like that? I thought someone was making use of a few dozen of our boxes to cash in."

"You did not think the boxes might have been copied also?"

"Not at the time, no."

"Stovolds were greatly at fault. Did you tell them so?"

"I did."

"But you did not choose to inform me."

"Just at that time we were not on the best of terms."

She said austerely, "It is a grave error, David, to confuse business with pleasure."

I grunted. "As I told you at the meeting, I sent Morris to make inquiries and he drew a blank. What else could *you* have done?"

"What we shall do now—alert all our representatives to examine the stock in the shops to see if any more of it is forged."

"And how will that help to catch our little forger friends?"

"We shall see . . . I would like you to take charge of this, David."

I looked at her ironically. "Set a thief to catch a thief, eh?"

"You are talking nonsense. But I believe you will have the best ideas how to go about it."

The following day I picked up Van Morris and drove to the Midlands. Van with his square shoulders and hard, chiselled face would be an asset, I thought. After all, if de Luxembourg could do some Mafia work in the old days, a vaguely threatening approach might help us along now.

The character who ran this shop was called Callender and he didn't want conversation with us at all. But we pressured him to talk and he gave us an address in Manchester from which he said a firm called Matthew Smith and Co. had supplied the goods. In Manchester—it was almost in Salford—we found the usual accommodation address: a cornershop tobacconist who ran postboxes as a sideline and described the man who came in to pick up the letters as driving a big Jaguar—"though not so big as yours, I fancy"—and as being middle-aged, with a moustache.

"Hasn't been near for a month or more now. Don't suppose I shall ever see him again."

Back to Callender's shop again, which by courtesy of the motorways we reached just before closing time. Callender was ill tempered, angry at being disturbed again, unhelpful as a pig. I asked him how he came to meet this Matthew Smith.

"I never did. His rep came round one day. Seemed all right to me. We're working men up here, Mr. Abdy . . . Sir Donald. We trade in and out; we have a mixed business; I'm a busy man; margins are getting narrower, what with the recession and all the small traders muscling in. I'm busy ordering and trading and selling all day long. Can't weigh up every offer that comes along, make certain it's simon-pure. Bankrupt stock, he said; how was

I to know different? People do go bankrupt, especially in the Midlands and the North; different world up here from your soft South, y'know."

I said, "What was he like, this rep?"

"Oh . . . middle-sized, thirty-five or forty, more dark than fair; only saw him for five minutes."

"Clean-shaven?"

Callender blinked a couple of times under his eyeshade. "Well . . . he had a moustache—thin moustache—bit Frenchie-looking."

"How were the goods delivered?"

"Delivered? *I* don't know. By van, I suppose. Maybe my stockman would know, but he's gone home an hour ago."

I insisted on seeing his storeroom and after more angry choplogic he let us through. In the end we turned up a carton which held twenty-four boxes of Charisma eau de toilette. The carton itself was marked "Wellington's Baby Foods."

"That'll help you a lot, won't it?" sneered Callender, apparently not aware that I'd taken a great dislike to his face.

Then we came on a similar carton with three dozen boxes of half-ounce Charisma perfume. They were good copies of the original boxes. I took a couple of samples.

"OK," I said. "That'll do. Make sure you destroy these."

Callender grunted. "Maybe yes."

"I'll send someone round next week. If they're not gone we'll get in touch with the police."

In the car going home Van said, "You looked in a bit of a pucker then, guv. What was you thinking of doing, belting 'im?"

"Of course not!"

"He was asking for it, wasn't 'e. But if we'd knuckled him it'd have been *him* sending for the fuzz, not us."

"It was just a whim I had. Don't know how you guessed."

"Remember that whim you had in stir? I just held you back, else you'd have lost your remission.

There was silence for a bit, then Van said, "Do it make you feel queasy, like, being on the side of the law?"

"It hadn't occurred to me."

"Jees, it does me. Even after all these years can't see a fuzz car without coming out in a rash . . . Know what I'd do if I was Callender?"

"What?"

"Steam the labels off and sell the bottles as fire-damaged stock or some such. We couldn't touch 'im neither."

"D'you know the addresses of any carton traders, Van?"

"What traders?"

"Those were new cartons, not old ones picked up at a supermarket."

Most of the big business trading in what used to be called household names overproduce their boxes and their cartons from time to time; the shape is wrong for the latest products, or different delivery vans pack different ways; then they flog off the old stock to carton traders, who get rid of them to small dealers who can put them to good use. I thought Van must know this but he didn't seem as well informed as I was.

"There's four or five of them in London," I said. "A couple in the Midlands and the North. One at least in Scotland. We'll have a go at some of them tomorrow."

"I'm not with you, guv."

"Somebody must have sold the cartons to Matthew Smith. It's a long shot but we can try. Doesn't it strike you as all being a bit of a one-man band?"

"Because the rep and the man picking up the letters was the same bloke?"

"Yes. And it only seems to have been an isolated incident again."

"Dunno, guv. I've a hunch it's bigger than that."

CHAPTER TWENTY-ONE

I

A woman of many moods, my wife. As many moods as she had hairstyles. For fencing or other athletic occasions the ingenuous ponytail was spot on; but for supper parties she began to fancy it brushed straight down at the side of her face, where it made a shiny blond curtain that fell forward all the time and had to be forked back; or it was extravagantly backcombed and worn high; or it was looped at the sides with her ears showing through like a Jane Austen girl. Each coiffure called up a different persona: dignity, elegance, girlishness, sophistication. She even spoke a bit differently and was cross when I twitted her about it. I told her marriage hadn't gone to her head, it had gone to her hair.

One day the following month she said to me, "David, I think I've found you a new job."

"What as: coach-in-chief to the Women's Foil Champion?"

"Don't be funny. Have you heard of Globe Differentials?"

"I should have. I've had them in at least two of my cars."

"Well, did you know they've just been bought up—by the Japanese?"

"Who told you this?"

"Daddy, at the weekend. Nihon Kuni is buying into the English market and Globe is one of their first purchases. They want to manufacture most of their car engines and gearboxes here: It's some deal they have with Austin Rover."

"They're buying into England to get into the Common Market," I said.

"Maybe. Anyway they're going to expand Globe by opening two new factories in the first year. One in Wales, one in Lancashire. But that's only a beginning. And what they're looking for is a new man to take over the whole operation in England for them."

"And where do I come in?"

"Where d'you think?"

I smiled at her. "This one of your practical jokes?"

"Certainly not!"

"Then there's more to it than meets the eye."

"Well, Daddy knows Mr. Matsuko, who is over here at present, and you could call and see him."

I said, "The sales manager of a *perfumery* firm? With no special know-how of the kind he's looking for?"

"You've a terrific knowledge of cars—and interest in them. You're titled . . . all right, all right, it shouldn't count but you know damned well it does. And you've got abilities far beyond selling Charisma. It's organizing skill he's looking for, not narrow technical knowledge."

"Did Daddy tell you all this?"

"I sometimes wonder—you must have a pansy streak! You can be bitchy enough!"

I patted her arm, which she withdrew out of my reach. "You have it all planned. Go on."

"I've nothing planned, David. But it seems to me a wonderful opportunity. And you'd get much better paid."

I was pretty sure Erica was jealous of the fact that I still saw Shona; this would be a way of ending it as a business thing. All the same, you couldn't just throw the idea out of the window because of that. I was now her husband, she was pitching for me, just as I was hanging in with her on the Moscow job. We were husband and wife; I still sometimes had to remind myself of that.

In the end I said all right, if Mr. Matsuko wanted to see me I'd go along and listen. It wasn't quite the right attitude for some bright-eyed, white-cuffed, youngish executive eager as a squirrel to better himself, but that was the best I could muster.

A week or two before all this Shona had complained of me being irritable. "I've not known you so—irascible before. I hope you are not still thinking of the failure of Semaphore."

"I've not given Semaphore a thought. In fact I'm not thinking of anything in particular."

"That was my impression."

"Are you suggesting I'm not doing my job?"

"Far from it. But tell me what else you can do about the forgeries."

My impression was I'd done pretty well all I could do, even though it hadn't come to much in the end. I'd traced the particular carton firm to a place in Tottenham. The manager was a fat little Pakistani. I told him the truth, that we were on the track of some forgeries, that the forgeries had been delivered in Wellington's Baby Food cartons which had probably been supplied by his firm, said could he help us by giving us the name of the firms he had supplied with these particular cartons.

Pakis are usually law-abiding because they're ingenious and industrious enough to make money legally; and he played ball at once. Only four names. The second one was Matthew Smith and Co., Webster Park Road, Ealing. We went.

"This is the same as what happened to me last time," said Van, who had a trying habit of establishing a telling sentence and then repeating it.

The Matthew Smith shop was empty. It had been taken on a short lease, the owner said; the lease had still a month to run but the firm had moved. No forwarding address.

I said to Shona, "They'll slip up sooner or later. They'll get careless, or somebody will talk."

"In the meantime . . ."

"Oh, yes, I know. But the boxes are such good copies that it's hard for the reps to see any difference without opening the bottles and sniffing."

"You still think this is a small operation," she said. "I have a feeling it is large. Rochas, Lancôme, Chanel have all been complaining."

Erica being hock-deep in her fencing left me at a loose end most evenings, so I began to drift over to the Cellini Club. This was really an excuse because it was the early evening when she fenced and the late evening when I gambled; but in fact marriage had put my habits out of joint. I hadn't seen Derek for months, and twice recently I'd rung him but no reply, so I thought I might catch up with him at the Cellini. I didn't for a moment suppose him to be linked with the forgeries, but in his funny airy way he knew a lot of shady things about a lot of shady people, and I thought he might help to point my nose in the right direction.

This, I told myself, was why I was going to the Cellini, but the reasons were fairly complex. Waiting for him to turn up, I began playing poker and lost £2500 in no time at all. I switched to bridge and began to recoup.

In the second week he was there. He said, "No help from me, darling. I've never passed a bad *check* in my life, let alone a bad bottle of stink. I've figured the angles and it doesn't pay."

"Know anybody who might see it differently?"

"What? D'you mean do that sort of caper? Pass off copies as the real thing? Search me."

"D'you see much of Roger now?"

"I *see* him. He's more than ever busy these days, become rather a drone, collecting honey for the Queen Bee. His new mistress, Lady Beatrice Something-or-other. She's leading him a fine dance and spending his money like *water*. *And* his last wife's threatening divorce. I often think how lucky I am not to have to live a life with *tedious* legal complications. How's yours, by the way?"

"My legal complication? We'll be happier when the Olympics are over."

"I *adore* Erica, you know. But sometimes I wonder if she really is the girl for you."

"I'm sure you sometimes wonder if any girl is the girl for me."

"Too true, matey. Too true."

We talked and drank for a few minutes and then he said, "Roger's very thick with this Laval fellow these days."

"What, Maurice Laval? The ex-de Luxembourg man?"

"Yes, I suppose that's him. It would be."

Laval had been managing director of de Luxembourg in England until he had lost his job a couple of years ago. He was the most brilliant innovator of his time, but had got thrown out on his ear and no one in the perfumery business had offered him a job since. When I'd been sacked in those early days and Shona had been looking round for a replacement, she had probably had her beady eye on him more than anyone else.

"I haven't seen him for a couple of years. What's he doing now?"

"Something with Roger, obviously."

"And you?"

"Me?" he grinned. "Oh, I get along. Been into one or two little things with Vince and Gerry."

"Who are they?"

"Gerry Baker? Vince Bickmaster? You must know them. They're both members here. Look, David . . ."

"What?"

"Mind, it's none of my business; I keep on the right side of the law as you know. But what's pushing you, what's pressuring you to do the bloodhound act? All the difference in the world between keeping clear of the rozzers and doing the rozzers' work for 'em. Is it Madame?"

"Not specially."

"Because now you've married money you don't need to let Shona trample on you any more."

"She never did."

"No, well, you know best about that. But if you start snooping along the lines you've told me, who knows what hornets' nest you may stick your nose in."

"Such as?"

"Darling boy, I'm generalizing. Maybe it's all a thousand miles from here. But characters indulging in a forgery lark could take it amiss to see a bright young chap like you digging up the dirt about them."

"Never thought of it that way," I said without blinking. "Why should I do any bloodhounding? You're quite right. Let somebody else do it."

II   I'd seen Laval only two or three times in my life—at trade shows and the like—but I hung around the Cellini for a few nights in the hope of seeing him again. I wanted to check certain recollections of what he looked like. Derek told me he was a compulsive gambler, and that fit with my memory of how he'd come to leave de Luxembourg; there'd been some trouble over the accounts—money was missing.

I'd no intention whatever, of course, of taking Derek's well-meant advice. Can't think why; I've never suffered from moral righteousness, and what did it really matter if some rich firms had their overpriced products forged? Maybe it was the hunt for the hunt's sake.

I never did see Laval but I met Derek's two new friends, Gerry and Vince. I remembered Vince now; he'd been around in the club once or twice when I'd been leading on one of my Scottish friends. A big hefty chap, running to fat even in his middle thirties, a squash fanatic, did something in the City, Derek said. But here was a compulsive gambler if ever there was one, never mind Laval.

Being a sucker myself for some things, it interested me watching other suckers get their little fly feet caught in the sticky webs. Roulette is fun if you've £500 to spare and you don't so much mind whether it flies away or comes home with more. It's no fun if it gets tied up with greed and ego and avarice and the urgency to win and the terror of running out of chips. Still less is it a joyride if you fancy yourself as a mathematical whizkid who by following your own system and watching the drop of the little ball can beat the bank and make a fortune. Vince Bickmaster was one such. He kept careful notes and had odd bits of paper and scribbled on them, and chewed the skin round his left thumb every time the wheel set off. Sometimes he won but more often he lost, but this didn't at all shake his conviction. It all had to come right in the end.

After playing bridge most of the evening I'd spend twenty minutes losing my winnings at roulette; but I always got up then and called it a day. Sometimes I'd stand behind and overlook the others. Rosy-minded idealists who argue that human nature is really rather sweet if given a chance would do well to watch roulette players. Almost all the seven deadly sins, except perhaps lust, are on view at the table—every night and all.

One night by mischance I almost bumped into Roger Manpole. It was the nearest to physical contact we'd ever made, and he brushed the sleeve of his jacket distastefully. He had a tall black-haired girl with him who was a stunning looker but had an expression as if she didn't care for the natives.

"Well, David, what a stranger! I thought perhaps you'd left England."

He was fatter, no other change. No attempt to introduce me to the girl.

"No," I said.

"It occurred to me you might have wanted to emigrate after that last disaster."

"What disaster was that?"

"Well—are there so many you lose count? I mean the total flop of Semaphore."

"It'll come again," I said.

"I wonder. Shona must have lost a hundred thousand, didn't she? *She* wouldn't like that."

"Charisma is making up for it."

"I wonder at that too. I hear it's going to be dropped from your American line."

"You hear a-wrong."

"Coming, darling," he said over his shoulder to the girl, who'd wandered on. "You know, old chap, men just won't wear scent. It gives the wrong impression."

"You ought to know," I said.

"Ah." He laughed. "I have unimpeachable references. It's knowing where one belongs in the sexual world . . . Talking of such things, how is the old lady now you've thrown her out? Or was it the other way round?"

"Run after your girl, Roger," I said. "Otherwise you might get into trouble."

"From Lady Beatrice? Hardly. She eats out of my hand. By the way, I hear old John Carreros is very sick. Did you know? Got the big C."

He moved on before I could speak again. Resisting a temptation to spit, I turned back into the roulette room, stared unseeing at the wheel for a bit, then moved behind Vince Bickmaster out of curiosity to know what possible calculations he could be putting down. When he felt someone was actually trying to see them, he reacted like a snail that comes upon a foreign body. Nothing was to be seen but the shell of his clenched fists.

I didn't mind. I didn't suppose his system was going to solve the riddle of the universe. What I did see—though, Lord knows, with Roger's jibes in my mind I'd hardly been looking or caring—was that he had been scribbling his sums on the front of an envelope. It was an unused window envelope. And in the left-hand top corner was the printed name: MOTH AND BENNY EXPORTS.

III I went to see Mr. Matsuko in his suite at the Savoy. Either he was among the higher aristocracy or it was a Japanese custom, for all his subordinates bowed low every time they came into the room and left.

He was very civilized, very grave, scrupulously polite, but discreet conversation brought out the fact that Erica had rather jumped the gun. It was true that Nihon Kuni and Co. had bought Globe Differentials, but it was not true that they had made any firm decision about new factories in Wales and Lancashire. They were considering it. They were in negotiation with Austin Rover, with the government, with several town councils. It was all rather airy-fairy, well meant, sincerely intentioned, soberly considered. If or when this full expansion took place they would want a new man to oversee it. They were not at all averse to considering me as an immediate possibility to represent their present interests in England. But whether the position offered real scope—and really big money—depended on decisions yet to be made.

When I told Erica this, she was furious that I'd not grabbed the half-chance that had offered itself. She had heard, her father had heard, it was only a matter of time, perhaps only a few months, before the big deals went through. Then there would be others with far wider experience clamoring for the job. This was the time to take it, at the outset, before anyone else was in the running.

I said I'd keep it very much in mind. Just what I'd told Mr. Matsuko. For a while she wouldn't speak to me.

But just at the moment Erica was on teeters about everything as the Olympics drew nearer. She'd collected the necessary number of points; there were five or six others who had, but she was second in total, so selection was pretty much of a sure thing. But that was only the first step before Moscow. She hadn't, she said, a hope of a gold or a silver—there were two outstanding women who'd fight it out between them—but she fancied herself for a bronze. There was a very good Rumanian she'd never seen, and a West German she knew well and was sure she could beat. It was a matter of luck and fitness on the day.

From now on, she told me one night, she was going to remain a virgin.

"I thought it might be a relaxation," I said. "All work and no play makes Jill . . ."

"You think sex only tires a man? Think again."

"I've never been husband to a female athlete before. I wonder how tennis players do. Hardly worth marrying, I'd think. Or do they say, 'I've only got old So-and-so to play tomorrow: It's all right tonight, John'?"

As it happened the withdrawal of sleeping facilities didn't upset me too much. Things hadn't been too happy between us for several weeks. It was as if I was losing the taste—or this particular taste. No doubt it would come back, because she was an attractive girl.

I told Shona what I had learned and seen in the Cellini, and she at once wanted to bring in the Serious Crimes Squad from Scotland Yard; but I said no, give me a week or two more. There wasn't much to go on yet but it was more than we'd had before. I consulted Van Morris and we found there was only one Vince Bickmaster in the book and he lived in Maida Vale.

No idea of his personal life at all, and I couldn't ask Derek for fear of rousing suspicion. Van went up to watch. It seemed, he reported after a few nights, that Vince lived by himself, second-floor flat, no buzzer device on the door and the lock would be a doddle.

I hesitated at this moment, wondering whether to involve Van Morris further. For some years he'd been following the fount whence honor springs, beating out a modest living and married to a respectable girl. What would old Essie think if we got copped for something and I'd let him into it—even with the best of intentions? What was worse, he was clearly enjoying it.

The fourth night I went up with him in an old Austin he owned—this being a lot less conspicuous than my big thing—and we parked a few cars down from Vince's flat on the other side of the road. We chatted and listened to the cricket close-of-play scores, and Van told me some of the problems of his married life. Coral was a queen, ace-high and the rest, kept everything nice and tidy, careful with money, always there to welcome him home; only trouble was she couldn't stand his mother. If he went to see Mum there was always a row when he got home. Jealous as fire. Couldn't understand it: He never objected to her going to see *her* mum. Women are peculiar that way—

"Here he comes," I said.

Vince Bickmaster walked down the steps and got into a flashy Mitsubishi parked nearby.

We watched him drive away. We sat in silence. Van lit the stub end of a cigarette and smoked it till there was nothing but a few flakes and a bit of rice paper sticking to his lip.

"How about it, guv?"

"What would Coral say?"

"Won't know, will she?"

"Not if we're quick, I suppose."

"Then let's be quick."

We went in and up the stairs to the second floor. Van'd been up before and knew the way. The lock took him, I suppose, ninety seconds. Then we were in.

What neither of us expected was a yapping dog.

It was a long-haired dachshund. But these furry things can nip. It came toward us in an ecstasy of annoyance and hostility yet half ready to be servile. Not a guard dog in the proper sense of the word, but the racket sounded like a burglar alarm. Did the neighbors underneath complain?

Taking a chance, Van stretched down a hand, and the object rolled over on its back expecting to be tickled.

To the accompaniment of dog noise urging us on, we began to go through the flat. Four rooms, all sizable, set out in art-deco style. I did the living room while Van tried the bedroom, rooting for scraps of paper, old letters, notebooks, visiting cards which might be in his suits.

I went over to the desk and began to go through the drawers. You'd think a damned dog would get a sore throat, but this one didn't. There was no guarantee how long the owner would be away from the flat.

Van came in with a wad of £20 notes he'd found in an envelope under the mattress.

"Nothing else," he said. "Keeps all his pockets nice and clean."

"Put them back," I said.

"Seems a pity, guv."

"It's black money somehow and he'd never dare to complain; but I don't want him to know anybody has been here." I was staring at a little Beretta automatic pistol in one of the drawers. Not quite the City gent picture. Just as well maybe if he came back unexpectedly that he wouldn't be carrying this.

Van was looking through the curtains, watching a car parking nearby.

"For God's sake can you do something to that dog?" I said. "Anything short of strangling it!"

I pulled out another drawer. Under the file were some girlie magazines, under the magazines more letters. One, without address, but dated April, said:

Dear Vince,

Now the stuff has all come in I'm more or less a free lance again, so shall be trying out one or two of your new ideas. When I saw Roger last he was cagey about getting tied in to it all personally. I rang you a couple of times at the old address in EC, but the telephone people said the number had been disconnected. Hope you get this.

Yours,
Maurice

There are many Maurices in the world but it isn't the most common of Christian names. Under the letter were half a dozen pieces of printed paper with the Moth and Benny Exports heading, an address in East Croydon. Apart from that not much. Nothing new. I wanted something to lead on, not lead back. The dog had stopped barking. The sudden silence scared me. Van, as I knew, did have strong hands.

Another drawer and a file. Bills of lading, receipts, check stubs, letters. Would take a week even to skim this lot.

Van was back. "I'll have a mouse around the bathroom. Some folk keep odd things in bathrooms."

"What have you done to the hound?"

"Given him something to eat, guv. Seemed the best thing!"

As he loped off I looked at my watch. We'd been in twenty minutes. Half an hour ought to be the maximum. Unlikely Bickmaster would take his car if he was intending to be back sooner than that.

The living room didn't have any other drawers apart from this desk, and precious few pieces of furniture that looked likely to give me any information to help. Try the kitchen.

No windows in the kitchen, so I put on the light. Dachshund was in a corner slurping up some sort of food Van had found. Must remember to clear it up when we left.

The supply cupboard: usual tins of coffee, packets of tea, jars of jam and marmalade, spices, etc. Pans in a lower cupboard; must say it was all pretty orderly, more so than my pad before I married money and had a slave to do it for me.

Van again. "There's some of this in his medicine chest. Looks like skag. Want to catch him out for possession?"

"No. Put it back. It's time we went. There's nothing else?"

"Nothink I can latch on to."

"OK. By the way, was this dish on the floor?"

"No, on the side. By the square box. Greedy little bastard, aren't you; I give him a fair dollop."

Hound had finished and looked as if he wanted more. As I picked up the dish he began to yap again.

I rinsed the dish under the tap and dried it, put it beside the box which was called LITTLE WOLF: "Finest food for all dogs. Gives his teeth lots of vital crunching. An enriched, meaty, compound food nutritionally balanced to contain all the proteins, vitamins and calcium your dog needs to get the most out of a happy life."

It was packed by Best Friend Dog Foods of Hackney.

"You look as if you've found something," said Van, reappearing round the door.

"I don't know for sure."

IV After all, dogs have to be fed, and how better than by a product which promised so much and must be in every other supermarket? And yet and yet. An odd coincidence.

Years ago when I'd had that first big row with Shona over my little side venture and she had dispensed with my valuable services, I had fooled around one day and made my way across London without paying my bus fare to see what Henry Gervase Ltd. were doing now that all but the hardest porn magazines were freely available at the local station bookstands. I had found that Henry Gervase were no longer there; the premises were occupied by Best Friend Dog Foods. Roger Manpole had been the controlling shareholder in Henry Gervase. Was it not likely that he was behind the new firm? Clearly they produced dog foods. What else?

On that day I had not gone in, not wanting to come up against anyone who might think I was looking for a job; but, as I passed, a man came out whom I thought I'd seen before somewhere. I realized now that I hadn't properly recognized him because I hadn't ever seen him wearing a hat before. At certain perfumery exhibitions I'd observed him at the de Luxembourg stand.

My mind also ticked off the fact that Maurice Laval was slim, dark, early middle-aged, and wore a thin moustache.

CHAPTER TWENTY-TWO

I was home about ten, not displeased with the evening's work. It might still be all guesswork but the threads were sporing other threads. In another week with luck I might have something to put together. I thought maybe I ought to have been a cop. There was more to tracking down this bit of dirty work than the boring old routines of everyday.

A light in the flat; in fact, lights; nearly all were on. I whistled but no reply. I hoped to God I hadn't forgotten some affair Erica had arranged: too awful if there were a dinner party and the host didn't turn up till the coffee was served. Or maybe the two maids were here scouring the house or polishing silver for a future event. Both of them had daytime jobs.

I went down the hall and into the living room. Having not so far described the furnishings of this room I won't bother now, except to say that it was all very elegant and expensive. And the lady who had spared no expense was at present standing at the bay window, the curtains undrawn, hands on elbows, stiff as buckram, gazing out over the lights of Hyde Park.

"Hullo," I said. "OK?"

She didn't speak or move.

"Hope you didn't wait supper," I said. "Fact I've had none myself, so a bite or two wouldn't come amiss."

No answer.

"Erica," I said. "Remember me? There's nothing wrong, is there?"

She turned slowly then. Hair in ponytail this evening. Cream silk jumper, heavy cream slacks. I had a good opportunity to admire the down-curve of her mouth; the brackets around it said the weather was stormy.

"So the conquering hero returns. What have you been doing, having it off with Derek at the Cellini?"

I picked up the evening paper, looked at the headlines. "The Cellini has a lot of facilities but none of that sort, at least as far as I know. What's the matter, pet? Been waiting in for me?"

"You could call it that. I've been trying to telephone you since four. They said you'd already left the scent shop . . . After a couple of hours I even lowered myself to ring Shona asking if you were with her. Apparently not, if she was telling the truth."

"So probably you tried the Cellini too, did you?"

"Naturally, since you seem to spend all your spare time there nowadays. They pretended you hadn't been in."

I turned to the back page. "I was out at Stevenage. Then I picked up Van Morris and we've been on this forgery lark I told you about. Just that. Nothing fancy. Doing a bit of tec work that I think will pay off. What's wrong? I thought you were fencing tonight."

"Not tonight."

"So what? What's bugging you?"

"Oh," she said, "I've just heard that I've not been picked for Moscow."

I folded the paper, put it down, stared at her. She stared back.

"You're fooling . . . No, you can't be. *Erica*, how could that happen? I don't believe it!"

"Don't you? There's the letter on the table beside you."

I picked up and straightened out the piece of paper. It was from her coach. "Dear Erica, I very much regret to have to tell you that . . ."

I scanned through it and dropped it back on the table. "It's scandalous! It's outrageous!"

"I'd be more moved by your sympathy if you sounded as if you meant it."

"*Meant* it? Why *shouldn't* I mean it? It's what we've been working for for the last twelve months!"

"*We've* been working for it? *I've* been working for it, and you've been paying lip service, playing along with the little woman, pandering to her fancies, hoping she'll grow out of them in the end!"

There was just the little poison drop of truth in this that made the distortion all the harder to swallow.

I said, "What d'you expect of me? You've been exercising, practicing, prancing around, getting coached all day long. The parties you've had, the parties you've been to, have all been of *your* own choice, not mine. I've never objected for a minute to any lark you wanted to get up to. I've even practiced with you myself day after day, night after night, in the bloody kitchen!"

I went over to pour myself a drink and saw one of her foils on the floor. The blade was broken.

"Did you do this?"

"No," she said, "it came to pieces in my hands."

I picked the bits up and laid them on a bookcase. "How did it happen, this Olympic choice? You must know more than you say. Who chooses? Isn't there some way you can appeal against the selection?"

She shrugged and sighed. "Well, it's the Joint Weapons Sub-committee that recommends the selection and this is approved by the Amateur Fencing Association. Then it all goes to the Fédération International d'Escrime, who usually just approve the domestic choice without question. So in the main it simply comes back to the selection of the Weapons Subcommittee, who are the serious foil fencers and the like."

"Most of whom you know."

"Of course I know them!"

"There's no reason given in this letter! Your scores were good. Surely you're entitled to some explanation!"

"Why should I be? If you pick an English rugby team you don't have to send letters of explanation to those who've just missed it! In fact, of course, I did ring Francis Norbury as soon as I got his letter."

I waited but, provoking me, she didn't speak. Eventually I said, "So he told you to mind your own business?"

She squinted at me in pure dislike. "He said it was the view of the committee that I wasn't strong enough yet. I said, what rubbish, and he absolutely agreed, but he said the others felt I wasn't psychologically ready; nerves weren't sufficiently under control, etc. He instanced various things . . ."

"Such as?"

"Such as that I lost my temper at the bad decision in Madrid in April. Such as that I was very well-to-do and tended to use my money extravagantly. *Parties*, I suppose. Such as that I was recently married and might not feel sufficiently single-minded about the Olympics. Such as . . . well, that'll do, won't it?"

I got as far as the Scotch this time. "Drink?"

"I've had one."

"So it all comes down to me, does it?"

"Not all. Just a little here and there."

"Sufficient to tip the scale?"

"Who knows?"

I squirted two fingers of soda. "Anything to do even yet? Can you appeal? Appeal to the Amateur Fencing Association."

"You don't know what you're talking about."

"Thanks. Perhaps you're right. So where do we go from here?" She turned to the window.

I said, "Am I to take this broken foil as symbolic?"

"You can take it as you sodding please."

"It's as *you* please, Erica. It's your ambition that's come un-gummed. If I can help you, let me know."

"You can help me by getting out of my sight."

"Right," I said. "I'll go and cut myself a sandwich."

II

I said to Van, "Would you like to do a bit of private tec work on your own? Nothing dramatic. Scout round Hackney, see if you can smell anything out about the Best Friend boys? I was coming myself but I can't get away for a few evenings—a spot of trouble in the home—and I think it will be evenings when anything suspicious will show."

"Right, guv. The wife's out tonight so I'll be free, but no car. Use the firm's van?"

"Of course. I've forgotten the name of the street where the warehouse is, but it's off Victoria Park Road. South Hackney. A 6 bus goes somewhere near."

"I know all round there. Used to deliver round there before Armstrong took over."

"Well, *don't* put your head in where it won't be appreciated. Remember that, won't you? If it comes to more lock-picking I'd like to be with you."

"OK. Leave it to me."

So I left it to him. During the next few days I got home in time to spend each evening in the flat with Erica. It wasn't much more than that. We ate in—she said she wasn't going to any damned restaurant—but most of the time in silence. She read a book at the table and was usually asleep, or pretending to be, when I turned in. She was drinking too much. If there's one thing irritates me it's a woman who drinks too much. But I said nothing, reckoning it would all blow away in time.

I'd not seen anybody quite so down or quite so bloody-minded as Erica just at this time. I suppose you had to face the fact that life had spoiled her up to now. She was very pretty, she was intelligent, she was a fine athlete, and her father allowed her more money than she could use. All her life she'd had nearly everything she'd wanted—including, presumably, me (or my title)—but something she'd set her heart and mind on, fencing for Britain at the Olympic Games, had been taken away from her by a stupid committee that didn't recognize her worth. Because it was all nonsense about her not being psychologically geared to take the strain. I was coming rather to take against my little pettish wife, but I'd no illusions about her fencing abilities. She was—at least in England—the tops.

On the second day I went round to see Norbury and asked him what we could do about it. He said there was nothing. The decision had been made, the four fencers and the one reserve chosen, and short of one of them being taken ill, there wasn't a hope. I tried to get him to admit that some unfair favoritism had been shown toward one or more of the girls now chosen, but he gave nothing. I reckon he agreed but he wouldn't say.

In the meantime I was saddled with a wife who was almost impossible to live with. Funny if you think of it. I'd always been the one with the chip—or the tailored hair shirt, or what you will—now I was on the receiving end. Gentle hubby taking the insults, the fretful silences, the sarcastic innuendoes, soaking it all up, never hitting back. It wasn't my part. I'd walked into the wrong play.

And after all, for crying out loud, it was only a *game*. She was not struck down with polio or muscular dystrophy; nor had she lost all her money; nor had her father gone off his rocker; nor had I been hopping from bed to bed and avoiding hers.

But if I showed any impatience with her it only proved to Erica that her original estimate of my attitude toward the whole fencing thing was correct.

I decided I'd been a prime fool to marry anyone. Whether you liked it or not, you got attached, involved with someone else's life, dragged in, tied in; you couldn't go home at night and wash your hands and say that's it till we meet next Friday. I'd got nothing out of this marriage except a few perks such as a greater luxury of living. I'd spent none of her money yet on Wester Craig—though to give Erica her due she'd reminded me a couple more times of her offer to cough up the cost for the repairs. If in the darkest depths of my seamy subconscious I had had it in mind that some day one might have a child, there were certainly no signs as yet. As a result of getting hitched up I was more in personal debt to the bank than before. And I was stuck with a temperamental blonde who used all her considerable talent for spite on the nearest person she could see. And guess who that was.

I didn't say anything of this to Shona, but as soon as she heard about Erica's failure she went round to see her. My little wife was putting on a pretty good act to people at the Sloane gymnasium, but with so old a friend as Shona it would be unlikely that some of the bitterness wouldn't show through, like a bony elbow through a coat that was wearing thin. Also her view that her marriage with its diversionary effects had likely just tilted the scales against her selection. Anyway, Shona tactfully didn't press me to talk about it, and work proceeded to plan. She was going to Vienna again in a couple of weeks' time but she didn't invite me to go with her, either because she thought it tactless or because she didn't want to expose me again to the charms of Trudi Baumgarten.

A few days after the fencing disaster a letter came from Messrs. McSwaine, Heeney and Garvice saying they had a client who had seen Wester Craig and had made an offer of £60,000 for it. If they could get him up to £70,000 would I agree? To distract Erica from her gloom I showed her the letter.

She read it. "Why not?"

"It's peanuts. Even a ramshackle place like that, and even if the five hundred acres are rock and scrub. It must be worth more."

"What are you asking?"

"A hundred and fifty thousand."

She tossed the letter back indifferently. "Please yourself."

"Even without the repairs it will still stand for another half century. I would just shut it up and forget it. Give the Coppells notice."

"Why don't you?"

I looked at my watch. "It's time I was off. What are you going to do today?"

"Do you care?"

I finished my coffee. "I like to know."

"I did tell you, didn't I, that I'm going down to Reading at the weekend."

"You didn't actually. I take it I'm not included."

"I'd rather see my parents alone."

"It's up to you." I pushed back my chair. "Have you decided anything yet about what you'll do now? Are you going to give up fencing altogether?"

"Don't know. I feel like it. Francis, of course, urges me not to. He would, wouldn't he? He tells me there's plenty still in the kitty to win apart from gold medals."

"Well, it's a thought . . . I suppose you wouldn't still like to go to Moscow, see it all happen this time round?"

"No, I don't think so. Thanks for the idea."

"Thanks for the thanks," I said.

She stared at me as if winter was just round the corner. "I could kill somebody for this, you know; for what's happened."

"You've looked as if you could."

"Our marriage has been a flop, hasn't it?"

"Has it? I suppose you could say that."

"What time will you be back tonight?"

"About five."

"I'll probably be here. Maybe behind the door with a knife."

"Well," I said, "thanks for the warning."

III It was a fine sunny morning, and I decided to walk to work. Exercise for the sake of keeping fit has never been my strong point, but once in a while London doesn't look bad, especially the parks. On the way I thought about life in general and mine in particular. It seemed to me that human beings occasionally make decisions of their own, but for the rest they get in the swim of some tidal pull and are carried along. Kick out, keep your head above water, breathe steady, pretend you're in control; but in fact you're being influenced and shoved along by forces stronger than yourself and your own pathetic strength. A branch in a stream, a straw in the wind; that was what my life had amounted to so far: Who could change it? Not I. And yet and yet, who talked this stuff about free will? Divorce was almost as easy as marriage. Once you'd plunged in, this was the lifeline, the rope dangled from the bridge. Did I want that? I wasn't sure. And in spite of all the abuse she was throwing around like a human muck-spreader, was Erica even sure? There had to be at least another month before anything was clear at all. Perhaps she would talk it all out with her father and mother next weekend.

I walked into the Bond Street shop, noting that a smart new designer I'd engaged had rejigged the whole of the layout in a much more modern and enticing way. This centerpiece of our business, in spite of its importance, carried minimal weight compared to the huge outlets we had, along with all the competing firms, at Selfridges, Harrods, Barkers and the rest of the great stores. Perfumers such as ourselves engaged and paid for the assistants there, and for all the promotions and giveaways, and sometimes even for some of the furnishings. It was debatable how important a fashionable shop and office such as this was, or Rubinstein's in Grafton Street, once one reached a sufficient size and eminence. It was a prestige expense more than an essential one.

Going up the stairs I met Leo Longford.

"Oh," he said, "Shona won't be in today. She's gone to Paris to see her brother—something to do with her father's death. Oh, and did you hear about your chap? What's his name, Morris?"

"What about him?"

"He's written off one of the firm's delivery vans. Must have been joyriding in it, because apparently it was after hours."

"What happened? Is he all right?"

"No, he's in Hackney Hospital. I think he's got concussion and bruises. Shona will be furious. It's a bit thick when employees start using the firm's delivery vehicles for their own fun and games. Fortunately his wife wasn't with him. Maybe he was after some new bird."

"I'll go and see him right away."

"Well, there are one or two things I want to see you about first. This chap you engaged to redo the shop has put in a claim for—"

"I'll go and see him right away," I said.

IV "Accident?" said Van from under his bandages. "Jees, I don't know, he must've been hopped up or loony. It's still daylight, see, and I'm off on this nice little trip into Essex. Tell you about that in a jiff, guv. This bloke, this lorry, come at me on the wrong side of the road. Couldn't believe me winkers. Not much traffic. Big bloody van, it was, not a little lady van like ours. Near as big as one of them continental juggers. What was I to do? Hit 'im head on—that's curtains for me as sure as sure, and little Mrs. Morris a widow and old Mrs. Morris losing her one and only? I went into the postbox, spoiled somebody's pools. I reckon. When I come to I was in here."

"What do the doctors say about you?"

Van moved a few inches and screwed up his face. "Says I'm lucky. Says he reckons me head's OK, but it'll be three days before they let me out, just in case, like. Crikey, it's the bruises that hurts!"

I looked round, but the nurse had not yet come back. She'd said ten minutes at the outside.

"D'you think it was laid on, Van?"

"What, for me, that? Nah. Feller in the jugger was risking *his* life—won't get 'em to do that. Nah, I reckon it was just a screwball weaving his way 'ome. Regardless, as you might say. Put a man like *him* in jug! He's *really* antisocial!"

"Has Coral been?"

"Oh, yes. Trouble an' strife. Still it just shows . . . When she thinks she might've lost me she's all lovey-dovey. Human nature? You can't beat it."

I said, "I told you not to go in anywhere without telling me. I hope you haven't—"

"Nah. Not on your Nellie. But it's been interesting. Looked

up Best Friend, found 'em where you said. All very proper, like. Coming and going. Closed at five-thirty. All quiet. I just go up, snoop around, can't get in. Alarms on the wall. Safeguard, Lifeguard, or some such. Too many just for dog food, eh? I give up. Came back next day. Nothing. Then Monday, six-thirty, full daylight, look, no hands, three lorries pack up, load, leave, skive off. I follow, see. We take a little drive."

The nurse said, "Mr. Abden, I think he's had long enough."

"Of course. But please just give me three more minutes."

"Well . . ."

"Go on, Nursie," said Van, smiling his haggard smile. "Give us a break. He's my boss, see? Have to keep on the right side of him."

She went reluctantly away. Van said, "Not far from Dagenham. Much bigger place. High wire fencing all round. Barred gates. In they go, all three of 'em. Waited a while but they didn't come out. Couldn't see what they was about. Got out of van and strolled past. Guard at gates. Back to van. Felt I could do with a wet and a bite to eat, so drove home. Next night the same."

"You went the *next* night?"

"Yes, just out of curiosity, like. Haven't I *told* you. It was following 'em the second night I met this jugger. Tuesday it was. Yesterday. Cripes, you get lost for time when you take a slug on the head!"

"So they could have recognized you from Monday—or hanging around Friday?"

"Don't think so, guv. I wasn't born yesterday."

"The van is distinctive."

"Yeah. But Thursday and Friday I went in me own car."

"Did it have a name on it, this factory?"

"Just a plate on the gate. 'BF Imports and Exports.' Nothing showy. You had to go up to it to read it."

"And where is it exactly?"

"A mile or so past Dagenham Dock. I couldn't thumb it on a map but I could take you there."

I grunted and got up. "I'll explain to Mme. Shona about the van, say you were acting on my orders. There isn't any charge pending, I suppose? Careless driving or the like?"

"What, for *me*? Not's I know of! I didn't hit nobody. It'll be just the insurance claim on the van, I suppose."

"And the postbox," I said.

"And the postbox. And guv."

"Yes?"

"Wait till I'm up and about before you go looking for it."

"Why? I thought you said this collision was an accident."

"So it was. Bet you on that. But when it comes to putting a finger in a pie, two's better than one."

CHAPTER TWENTY-THREE

I Could probably have done it by telephone but I went personally to the London Search Room of the Registrar of Limited Companies in City Road. Fly-by-night circuses like Moth and Benny traded without a genuine corporation, however much they might like to put Ltd. on their notepaper to make it read good. But the Best Friend people, having a permanent place to maintain, would probably find it safer to be in the registry. So, as I thought, Best Friend Dog Foods was in. The directors—those whose names figured on the notepaper—read like nominees, but the shareholders were more interesting. Matthew Charles (a man I knew slightly, who'd been on the fringe of the perfumery business for some years and who at one time had worked for Roger Manpole), Frederick Maurice Laval, Surya Sitram Smith, Arthur Vincent Bickmaster. I looked up BF Imports and Exports Ltd. Charles, Laval and Bickmaster were among the six shareholders. No actual mention of Roger Manpole. The address of PG Imports and Exports was there, and while Erica was off for her weekend in Reading I drove round to look over the land.

A fairly grubby piece of England, not far from the Thames, commercial and gray. The warehouse matched the countryside for color, was about the size of a small plane hangar, with a few outbuildings, all surrounded by this high fence that Van had described. Being a weekend, there was no activity, but I saw a guard come out and walk round the perimeter.

Nothing, of course, specially sinister in any of this. Large and small factories are easy meat for villains to raid, and have to have their own protection. There are firms in various parts of the country who make up perfumes to the orders of the big companies—the parent companies supplying the partly prepared ingredients—and these firms, which may make up an order for

Arden one week and Revlon the next, are prime game for land pirates if they can break in. There's nothing easier to flog on the black market than expensive perfumes; not many people in a pub can resist the temptation to take a box of Mme. Rochas home to the wife, at a quarter the normal price.

Not much, except in my suspicious soul, to tie in BF Imports and Exports Ltd. to the forgery of our goods and chattels. I sat in the car in Dagenham and tried to work it out. It went like this:

Stovolds—Hilliers—Moth and Benny Exports. Full stop.

Callenders—Matthew Smith and Co.—Wellington's Baby Food—Matthew Smith and Co. Full stop.

Derek Jones's chum Vince Bickmaster, once a director of the now presumably defunct Moth and Benny Exports, is a director of Best Friend Dog Foods, and a director of BF Imports and Exports Ltd. Best Friend under special suspicion from me because operating in warehouse once used by Henry Gervase Ltd. to turn out porn magazines, with Roger Manpole as a sort of sleeping Managing Director. Also I had seen Maurice Laval come out of Best Friend warehouse, and he was a director of both companies. Two years ago he had lost his job with de Luxembourg. He was a perfumery expert.

Van Morris, following lorries from Hackney, had had a nasty accident and was lucky to be alive.

Did this add up to anything? To me, a lot. But supposing I went to the Essex police and told them all I knew, would they have enough to apply for a search warrant? Fat chance. The Henry Gervase operation had been specially clever at hiding everything away in ninety seconds flat if someone unwelcome should tap on the door. If Van had in fact been seen and his Shona vehicle noticed, wasn't it likely that the warehouse in Hackney would have been cleared of anything likely to merit the attention of the gendarmerie?

This place in Dagenham looked too big for that sort of thing; but supposing only a very small part of the whole operation was illegal? It could well be. Anybody can put out a copy of a well-known perfume for the Arab market so long as it is clearly marked as a copy. They could be manufacturing that *and* dog foods *and* God knows what else all in a normal legal way of business.

I went home.

Erica arrived back on Sunday evening looking as snagged as a piece of silk caught on a thorn bush.

She said, "I had a long talk with Francis on Friday before I left. And I've talked it over at home. I'm going on fencing but dropping activities by about half for a year or so. Francis says there's always the Los Angeles Olympics to look forward to in 1984."

"Christ!" I said.

"I don't think fencing was invented in his day. Let's try a bout, shall we?"

"What, *now!*"

"Yes, *now.*"

I was a fool to humor her, but I went into the kitchen and put on the protective gear and we did fifteen minutes of épée. It was mildly satisfactory to see when she took her mask off that her face had some color again.

She said, "How's the forgery frolic?"

So she could remember that far back! Recovery must be stirring. "All right," I said. "And all wrong." I told her.

She said, "So what are you going to do, if anything?"

"Sit on it for a week or so. If there's been an alarm in the enemy camp, give it time to simmer down."

"And then?"

"And then I don't know."

"Is Derek involved in any of this, d'you think?"

"In the forgeries? On the whole I'd think not."

"Otherwise you might not pursue it with such vigor?"

"Wrong again. So there."

"I just wondered."

"It's up to him to look after himself . . . Let's go out somewhere. I'm hungry."

We went out and ate mainly in a silence which was not really companionable yet.

She said, "I forgot to tell you. He rang on Friday."

"Who?"

"Derek."

"What did he want?"

"Didn't say. Presumably to make some amorous appointment with you."

"I don't make amorous appointments with Derek."

"What, have you fallen out?"

"I never fell in."

"Oh, go on, you lived with him for a time."

"I was on my beam ends. He offered me a pad. End of story."

She considered me. "You're not the most famous lover, are you?"

"Am I not?"

"Well . . . sometimes brilliant. Sometimes poor."

"It's quite difficult to be on top form when your other half assumes a chastity belt to further her chances for the Olympics."

"But before that. Well before that."

"Life blows hot, blows cold," I said. "You're not always the most engaging person yourself."

"Thanks. At least we haven't any illusions about each other."

"You must have some about me if you think I'm turning my eyes on Derek."

There was a look in her eyes that was challenging, ready to have a go; but it faded.

She said, "Have you written to Mr. Matsuko?"

"No."

"Daddy was wondering."

"Tell Daddy no."

"Does that mean you're not going to apply?"

I considered the restaurant with its sham Chinese decorations. And I considered my own emotions, in which there was also an element of sham.

"Until this forgery thing is out of the way I'm not ready to commit myself."

"Does Shona know?"

"About the forgery? . . . Oh, about Mr. Matsuko. No. There's no point."

"I thought you might have asked her advice."

The claws were showing again.

"Her advice, I'm sure, would be to try to better myself. But, Erica, you have to know sooner or later that you are married to a man who hasn't much interest in bettering himself. I like doing what I like doing, and I'm not sure that I really want to change a Russian master for a Japanese."

"Russian mistress, you mean."

"Well, at one time yes, as we all know. But can't we swap the subject to something fractionally more pleasant?"

"Such as?"

"I'm thinking of changing my car."

"What for?"

"A Ferrari 400, five liter."

"Did I see you in one the other day?"

"They came and I had a test drive."

"I had a boyfriend once who had a Ferrari, and he said he always kept a spare set of plugs cooking in the oven to change when the weather was damp, otherwise it wouldn't start."

"This is newer and better."

"And faster?"

"Probably. Though I think there's a limit to what a production car can do on modern roads."

"I'm interested to hear it." She looked at me slant-eyed. "I sometimes think you don't care about living, do you?"

"Oh, yes. On the whole. Yes, I just drive fast, not rashly. Speed kills sometimes, I know, but incompetence more often."

"It might be a pity if I became a widow before *all* the shine had worn off."

"You were threatening me with a knife not long ago."

"Metaphorical one."

"They can wound."

She said, "You'll never take that job, will you? You know that."

"What job?"

She sipped her wine. "You're a born loser, David . . . No, that's not it. You're a loser from choice. That's about the truth."

"I won you," I said.

 We sat in Van's little Morris.

I said, "You've seen the place. Now we've seen it together. Could you get in?"

"Course. A piece of cake."

"How?"

"Cut the wire. Or over the top with a rope ladder."

"There are lights."

"Not all round. You can see where they don't reach."

"And the building?"

"One way or another. Windows break easy and quiet. But I'd like a go at the door. That's more my line. Can't see what sort of lock it is even with the binocs. But I doubt if they'd have it on a chain."

"Any sign of alarms?"

"Nothink I can spot."

"Or dogs?"

"Nah. Wouldn't want to be too conspicuous, would they?"

I said, "We've got to keep it in our tiny minds that this is not a break-in in search of plunder. All we want is information and maybe a sample or two of what we've found."

"I get."

"Does Coral know what you're up to?"

"She knows I'm helping you."

"I suppose you realize it wouldn't look too good if a couple of old lags like you and me were caught breaking and entering."

"I'd lay a fiver you'd talk your way out of it."

"Don't rely on that. You've been on the narrow for a good many years now, and it would be a pity to spoil the record, wouldn't it?"

"Same applies to you, guv."

"I know. But it's different for me."

"How?"

"Can't explain." I thought of Erica's challenge to me. Was I a born loser? Was I a loser from choice? Or a sham? Did I care about my own life? Intermittently, yes. I said, "Look, it may be enough to shine a light through the windows, if we can spot something incriminating. That would suit me best because we might even do the job then without letting anyone know we've been in."

"Not with me and the wire clippers, guv."

"Then let's go over the top."

"OK."

I thought for a minute. "In any event they may suppose we're just land pirates looking for a quick touch and scared off before taking much. Sure the fence isn't wired up?"

"Not sure, but fairly sure. I'd a good look when I bent to tie me shoelace at the gates."

"Well, we'll have to take the chance. Are you all right now? Head all right?"

"Gawd yes. Right as I'll ever be."

"It was a full moon last week. By Thursday there'll be nothing but a sliver rising late. It should be as good a time as any."
"Suits me."

III Thursday Shona was not yet back from Vienna. It had been a busy day because the firm had gone in for extensive advertising over a free gift of a beauty pochette with every two or more Shona purchases, the pochette to contain Satin lipstick, handbag mirror, and Bio-E cream, "especially created to feed dehydrated skins." Some of the big stores in the provinces were moaning that the advertising had been too successful and they were running dry of the Special Offer. It would only have meant more emergency supplies being ferried around by our reps except for the fact that the handbag mirrors hadn't all come in, so there might be a shortfall for a couple of days. Anyway we did our best and I was still able to get home early, carrying a bag with a black sweater in it and a skullcap and a black silk stocking. These and a pair of old evening trousers and fencing shoes would make a reasonable fancy dress.

Erica was in a mood again. She had been reading about the departure of the various teams for the Moscow Olympics. I knew well that for the next month there'd be practically nothing else to read in the papers.

She didn't ask what was in the bag, but when I came back from the spare room she said, "There's a letter for you. Came by this afternoon's post."

The postmark was Ross and Cromarty. It was from, of all people, my aunt:

Dear David,

You will perhaps be surprised to receive a letter from me, for we have not seen eye to eye on the majority of important subjects since we met. But now that you are married and have a charming wife and will no doubt soon have children, I felt I should bring up the subject of the family medals. There are, as I expect you may appreciate, since we have taken part in many wars over the last four centuries, quite a number of these—including one VC—and of course not only medals but battle souvenirs of many kinds. They make an impressive and historic array which I think cannot fail to move anyone with any pride of family in their blood.

When first Malcolm died and then your uncle, who willed no other disposition of them, I had thought of leaving these souvenirs to one of the museums in Edinburgh. When I first met you, you made it plain you were not interested in the family as such; but it could be that you would eventually like them—when I die—to hand on to your son. The unfortunate circumstances of the quarrel in our family will not concern him, and he might come to treasure them for all the history and the bravery and the sacrifice that they bring to mind.

If you are at Wester Craig sometime, you and Erica might call to see them and then let me know. There is, I imagine, no hurry.

Yours sincerely,
Helen Abden

Erica was helping herself to another vodka and tonic, but I put the letter on the table and she read it while sipping her drink.

She said, "What have you done about that offer for Wester Craig?"

"Turned it down."

"You don't really want to sell the place, do you?"

"Not to give it away, no."

"You can still have the money for the repairs if you want it."

"Thanks. You're very generous about that."

She put the drink away in record time. "What you can't have, you know, my pet, is an heir."

"Who said I wanted one?"

"I got the feeling that you were thinking, now the little woman has been cheated out of her fancy sport she can settle down into a comfortable *Hausfrau*, breeding and feeding children and spreading her hips and smelling of milk and nappies. It's what the chauvinist man wants, isn't it?"

"I'll make a note of it in my diary."

She said, "Come and fence for a bit, get the cobwebs out of your hair."

"Not with you in that mood. You'd prick your bottom sitting on the point."

"You think I'm drunk?"

"Not really. But over the breathalyzer limit."

"Rubbish." She stared at me for a long moment. "How's Shona?"

"She's in Vienna."

"Didn't take you this time?"

"Didn't take me."

"You don't care for me at all now, do you."

It was half joke, half serious, the way people in their cups can get, even slender pretty girls with clean limbs and fine features. You don't know which of two people you're talking to.

In the end I said, "I like you better off the booze."

"I meant what I said, you know."

"About what?"

"Not giving you an heir. First, I don't want children. Who'd want to bring children into this lousy world? Having babies these days is a form of pollution . . . Anyway from your latest performances I doubt if you could produce one . . . But second you couldn't ever produce one on me."

"What's that supposed to mean?"

"I had a steamy affair with a layabout called Edward Cromer. Remember? Well, I became pregnant. Horror of horrors, just when I was building up my fencing points. So I decided to lose it. I lost it. Something went wrong. With the op, you know. Result: I can't have any more. It doesn't worry me, of course. But I just thought I'd tell you in case you were having the same thoughts as Auntie."

I took the vodka bottle out of her hand. "Scout's honor?"

"Scout's honor. If you want the dreary details ask Shona. She knows all about it."

 It was a drafty night, with a cold wind blowing up the Thames and an occasional spat of rain. After the hot weather of last week it didn't feel like summer.
But maybe better for nefarious purposes. If you want to break into a seedy warehouse you don't need a nightingale singing over the Dagenham mudflats. As it happened, in my checkered career as a public enemy, this and the little foray we'd made into Bick-

master's flat were the only times I'd ever done any breaking and entering. I was stepping out of my league. Con men don't climb fences.

Which is what we were preparing to do now. Wire clippers might be easier; but I knew the whole foray would be a much greater success if no one knew we'd been in. Although there was no sign of any wired alarms, there might be some sort of signal relayed to the warehouse if the fence circuit was broken. My own bet was that they were wary of alarms because alarms go off in error sometime or another and they didn't at all want packs of flatfoots arriving in patrol cars. You try to read the mind of the enemy, and that was the way I read it.

So we'd brought rope ladders.

Van had done a good bit of looking around in the last two nights, and he said that there were two guards who spent most of their time in the warehouse in a room at the back, and who came out as regular as clockwork every hour on the hour and paced the perimeter. So just after three o'clock would do nicely. I'd never worn a stocking mask before, but Van advised it.

Three days ago I'd bought a small but expensive Japanese flash camera and had annoyed Erica by trying it out around the house. It bulged now in the back pocket of my evening trousers.

The fence was about ten feet high and bent outward at the top. Van had chosen a place near the corner of the perimeter where a black shadow from the arc lights was cast by a tree. He threw the first ladder up a couple of times and it soon caught. With the other ladder under one arm and carrying his small professional bag, he clambered wobbling to the top and threw the end of the other ladder into the compound. He went down. I followed him and pulled the first ladder up to the top, rolled it up there and propped it against a stay where it would unfurl easily when we needed it to return.

Stocking masks are stuffy things. We went up to the tree. From there it was about fifty feet to the door of the building. We crossed the semidarkness and came to the door.

There had been no way of knowing beforehand what the lock was going to be. Van peered at it and grunted and fiddled a bit.

"Five minutes," he said.

"I'll look in at one or two of the windows," I said.

"Watch your torch."

I slid round the building, peered in, flicked the torch a couple of times. "Ask Shona," she said, "if you want the dreary details. She knows all about it." You could see boxes in here, some open, but it all looked more like machinery than perfume. "She knows all about it. Scout's honor." Another window. Workbench studded with bottles, but too big for our stuff. More the size of lung tonic, hair restorer, etc. "Scout's honor." You're telling me.

A couple of cars droned past, and I flattened against the wall. I tried a third window but this had Venetian blinds and they were down. Back to Van.

"Progress?"

"Yeah. Take a bit longer than I was reckoning."

Three-fifteen. Plenty of time if the guards kept to routine. Stand against the wall and think of your wife. Think of an elegant blond girl, tense, excitable, full of fun and full of spite. Jolly, vital, jokey, tongue barbed like an adder. Think of the Russian bitch, planning everything, influencing, suggesting, knowing the ultimate end of the *mésalliance*, the darkness and the frustration. Think of your broken-down inheritance and of the general nastiness of human nature.

"These locks get ever so fancy," said Van. "Thank Christ there's no chain."

Stand against a knobby wall, its bumps pressing into your back, dressed like a bank robber, like a clown, like a gatecrasher at a fancy-dress party. What are you doing it for? Not for anybody you could name. Certainly not for the Russian bitch. Maybe you're not here, it's just an illusion, like those dreams of locked cupboards and drunken men with straps. Are you growing out of that—or growing into something worse?

"OK," said Van, and we were in.

Corridor, doors, divisions. This was machinery all right, nothing to do with Shona or Chanel. Might have come out of a car —or be going into one. Gears, time switches, air valves; you could hazard a guess. The cases in here looked well traveled—as if they'd contained the machinery, not that they were going to contain it.

"Where are the guards?"

"First floor back."

I took out the camera; four snaps of the machinery.

"Flashes'll show through the windows," said Van.

We went into a longer room, probably used in the daytime for making up stuff. This was more like it. Benches, pulleys, labels, cartons, a printing press in a corner. Labels all blank but I found some unattached ones marked Lancôme. *Click, click.* Were Lancôme a group that ever farmed out its products?

Next room half empty. Cases of whisky in a corner. Proprietary brands: White Horse, Haig, Teacher. My father's dream room. In the corridor outside, stacks of Best Friend Dog Foods.

Stairs.

"Look around down here," I said to Van. "If there's anything you can pocket easily, grab it. I'm going to see what's up here."

"The guards for one thing," said Van.

On the first floor were the offices. From under one door a light showed. I crept across and listened. Silence for a bit and then a snore. Comforting. Let sleeping dogs . . . Then someone coughed and struck a match. No doubt they took it in turns, one dozing while the other sat up. It was nearly half an hour before they would take their next promenade. We ought to be out of here in fifteen minutes.

Another room, empty except for some broken boxes. Then a room with what looked like word processors. A couple of snaps recording the brand names. It might still all be perfectly legal.

Out of this room and across the corridor, into a largish room that reminded me of the old Shona workshop in Isleworth. On a slab on the far wall two or three score of boxes of the familiar silver-faced pattern of Faunus and another lot of Charisma. I didn't need to see any more or even to take photographs. These perfumes had no business here. No one had farmed anything of ours out to this company.

Of course the workforce who came in every day would continue filling the bottles and sealing the boxes, unaware anything was wrong. They'd probably been doing Rubinstein last week—maybe quite legitimately. How would they know or care?

Camera back in hip pocket, take a sample box of Faunus and one of Charisma, stuff them into my other pockets. The lights came on.

A big square-shouldered ugly type. Sweater and slacks. Belted. In one hand the sort of truncheon that used to be laughingly known as a life preserver. The biggest surprise was I knew him from Pentonville.

He'd been in the same time as me. Charley Something. Charley Elton or Ellis. A right bastard.

Going straight. Or a different sort of crooked.

"Ah," he said. "Got you, me little buddy boy."

I crouched and said in a whining voice, "I was only looking round."

"You'll come and look around in my office," he said. "What are you, a little nancy boy? Wait while I get the bulls."

I've never been a hard man; my joustings with the law had never included streetcorner thuggery; I'd done more fighting at Loretto than all the rest of my life; but things hadn't been sweet with me recently.

I went for him. I went head down and fists up. The truncheon thumped on my raised forearm; my weight took him back against the wall with a slam. I hit him with the torch, breaking it to splinters over his head. He collapsed but grabbed me round the waist; we rolled across the room and I came upward, got him by the throat, bashed him again and again with the remnant of the torch. Blood on his head. Both hands now to his throat. I was losing the use of the left arm. His life preserver was rolling on the floor, his eyes turning up in his head. He tried to knee me; I kicked back. His struggling began to stop.

A hand on my shoulder. "Hey, guv! Creeping Jesus, that's *enough*! You'll croak the son of a bitch!"

Lights began to return to normal. Van pulled and pulled until my hands came away; helped me to my feet. Charley Ellis rolled over moaning but didn't try to cause any more annoyance.

"I was 'alfway up when I heard the racket. Out of here double-quick!"

As we turned to the door the other guard showed up.

He was a shorter, fatter character than the first. He looked at us, both tall and masked, then at his partner rolling on the floor; he turned about very sharp and made off at speed down the corridor to his office. Van ran after him but the door slammed and the key turned just in time.

Van put his ear to the door. "Telephoning for 'elp. Les go."

We went. My arm was numb now from shoulder to wrist, and

Van had to steady me down the stairs. There was blood on my gloves but it wasn't mine. The camera must be broken, the way we'd rolled over on it, but the film should be all right.

"It all depends, don't it, guv," said Van as we got to the outside door.

"What on?"

"Whether they ring the roz or whether they've got more pals of their own nearby."

I stumbled a couple of times on the way to the fence, but I realized from the way he was breathing that Van was the more afraid.

CHAPTER TWENTY-FOUR

I I took Van home and had coffee there and bathed my arm and did a few other running repairs—all, thank God, without waking Coral, who was "a light sleeper"; then I put my feet up on a chair and tried to rest my arm for an hour before going back to Dagenham. Van wanted to come with me, but for all his reformed life he still looked such an ex-lag to an expert eye that he'd have been a dead liability in any contact with the police.

Old antipathies don't die easy, and it was an effort even for me to push open the door of the station and ask for the officer in charge. But I wanted things done and done at the double.

Detective Inspector Chalmers had just come on duty, and he saw me right off. Immense help to be a baronet!—suddenly you *realize*—it's as good as money in the bank. I was Sir David Abden, manager of the distinguished firm of Shona and Co., not some dissolute ex-public-school boy frequenting a shady nightclub. And I'd come to provide evidence of a large-scale forgery business being carried on in their patch. Tactfully explain the provocations the firm had been suffering for months; as a result, two of my employees had taken the law into their own hands last night and broken into a warehouse nearby. This was unknown to me—clearly I wouldn't have sanctioned it—but the outcome had been a bull's eye. Exhibits: roll of film, two boxes of forged perfume, a Lancôme label and some consignment notes mentioning a number of other proprietary goods which it seemed unlikely this firm would be dealing in on a valid basis.

Chalmers was a stout chap, a bit short of breath—and likely short of temper if the need arose—but he cottoned on quickly. The roll of film was whisked away while I completed a statement and signed it. He did some telephoning and offered me more coffee, and the film came back developed and printed, and we looked at the results together.

He said, "Of course you know, Sir David, what we'd like to do now is keep the warehouse under observation for a few days."

I said, "If they know the place has been broken into they'll rupture their guts trying to hide the evidence."

The inspector's eyes flickered to what must have looked like a flowering anemone on my cheekbone. "Did you—did your men have to make the break-in evident? You were not able to cover your tracks?"

"Afraid not. The alarm was given as they left."

"Too bad. By going in right away we stand much less chance of catching the principals."

"I see that."

"Also one other thing, sir. You do appreciate that yours is . . . well, call it a luxury trade, in which prices are somewhat artificially maintained by the top companies such as yourselves. We have to look on this not just from the point of view of stopping an alleged forgery but of bringing the forgers to book. Are you, for instance, absolutely certain that these boxes you brought out are forgeries and not copies? A different wording, a different spelling of a name and the magistrates would dismiss the charge out of hand. There's no crime in making fair copies. We would get rapped over the knuckles ourselves if we raided some firm which was doing a legitimate business."

I said, "These are the same boxes we've found up and down the country during the last few months. The boxes are pretty exact copies, the perfume is a forgery." He was going to say something but I went on. "But apart from that, look at these photographs. This one is a bit blurred, but I can tell you those are brake linings of some sort—probably from Taiwan. This case you can see here is full of consumer jeans—famous names—maybe made in Korea. And these—I wouldn't swear to it but they look to me like helicopter rotor hub bearings. It's *much* more a mixed bag than I ever dreamed. You may say it'd be hard to get rid of all this with the police watching, but I do know one man—I suspect he's got a hand in this somewhere—and he has a Houdini gift for spiriting things away when the police walk in."

Chalmers pondered a moment more, rubbing his cheek. "All

right, sir. I get your point. We'll obtain a search warrant right away. Where can we find you?"

He had the firm's address on the card, so I gave him my own address in Knightsbridge.

"And the name of your two employees who collected the evidence?"

"I don't want to give you that if you can get along without it. They were two young men who just looked on it as their duty."

We stared at each other. I hadn't been so close to a cop for more than ten years, and it still didn't feel right. It's not a smell, it's an aura. Your skin prickles. I wondered if he had any reactions to me. If he had he didn't show them. "You've laid the information yourself, sir. We can leave it at that for the time being."

"I'd like my name kept out of it too."

"Any particular reason?"

"I think I know some of the men concerned. They're members of a club I belong to in central London."

He raised his eyebrows. "Like that, eh? Well, I'll use my discretion. At this stage it's hard to promise anything for certain. It greatly depends on what we find, doesn't it?"

"And what you find depends on how quickly you go to find it."

"Could you give me the names of these friends of yours?"

"They're not friends of mine, but I know them."

I gave him the names. Fortunately it was my left arm and shoulder that were hurting and stiffening, and I hadn't had to use either during the interview.

| II |

Shona was back. She looked slim and dark and handsome, and I could have wrung her neck. She wanted to talk to me about an expansion she was planning for the Italian market, but I cut her short by telling her what had been going on.

"But, David, that is wonderful! You have succeeded beyond

my best hopes! But you took a risk. You have a bruise on your cheek! What will happen next?"

"The police should be in the place by now."

She waited. "And then?"

"Then, unless the BF people are witch doctors, they won't have been able to hide everything."

"When shall we know?"

"I've got Chalmers's private number to ring him about five."

"This is wonderful, David! Are you not pleased?"

"I'm glad it's over."

"You have not injured yourself in some way?"

"Nothing that won't heal in time."

She came up to me. Her skin was still so clear and fine. "I have something in my medicine chest: a little unguent. Not one of our products but excellent to reduce bruising."

"Leave me alone," I said.

She looked hard at me. "Have I done something wrong?"

"Good God," I said ironically. "What could *you* do wrong?"

"In this, nothing, I think. Do you wish to go home to rest?"

"Yes."

"Does Erica know you have been on this mission? Is all well between you?"

"Blissful," I said. "Thanks for the recommend."

"What recommend? . . . Oh." She stared at me again, then went over to her desk. "You have to be patient with her, David. This month—once this month is over—it will all be better again. You do realize how obsessed she was with the idea of going to Moscow?"

"That came through to me in time."

She sighed. "I am sorry you are not in a good mood after so splendid a success. I have to thank you for all the trouble you have taken."

"Van Morris needs a rise," I said. "A substantial rise. Be sure he gets it."

I didn't go home but drove to the big garage near the South Kensington tube and saw the manager. I said I was willing to trade in the Jaguar for the Ferrari if the transaction could be put through in three days. He didn't hesitate to say yes.

When I finally returned to the nest my little lovebird was not there so I cooked myself bacon and eggs and made a fair job of one-handed eating. I was chewing the last piece of toast when she came in. The ponytail again today, with a green décolleté blouse and green Pucci pants.

"Where the hell have you been?" she said. "You've been out all night!"

"I didn't think you'd notice."

She put her Fortnum bag on the dresser. "Not from anything you do while you're here, I agree. But since we cohabit . . ."

"AWOL," I said. "I know. I'm just finishing breakfast."

"It's after midday! Didn't she feed you? Or was it a he again?"

"A he," I said. "We finished up rolling on the floor and I damned near strangled him."

After a minute or so she said, "You've got a hell of a swelling on your face. Did you walk into a wall?"

"That sort of thing."

She took down the foil from where the pair were hanging and flexed it a few times.

"Well, we didn't get anything."

"What d'you mean?"

"In Moscow. Eliminated even before the semifinals!"

"Good."

"Yes." She dropped the paper on the table folded at the appropriate page. "Perverse and peevish satisfaction." A few edgy feints and jabs in my general direction but I took no notice. "Question is whether I would have done any better."

"You do yourself an injustice."

"Irony kills me, boy. Careful how you use it: This point is sharp."

I got up slowly and began to put the dirty things in the sink. "I'm going to turn in for a bit. I've a few telephone calls to make at five, so I'll be on my way."

"Out again tonight?"

"No."

"I suppose you're telling me the truth and it all ended in a terrible quarrel. Poofters fight like cats; I've seen 'em."

At the door I said, "Oh, I've bought that car."

"What, the Ferrari? Going to buy a loud blazer and a cap to match?"

"When it comes I'm going to take off for a bit—rid you of my presence. It'll be a few days yet, this is just prior notice."

She went on with her feints and ripostes.

"Don't hurry back," she said.

|III| Inspector Chalmers was careful not to sound too pleased, but satisfaction kept breaking through. Shona, de Luxembourg, Chanel, three others. Packages, boxes, empty bottles. In the basement were large vats with hundreds of gallons of fake perfume.

This was good, but though Chalmers was willing and anxious to sort out the perfumery forgeries, he was more interested in the other stuff. My guesses had been spot on. God knows what had come out of the Far East destined to be sold as genuine, but word processors, brake linings and helicopter parts were among them. He explained patiently that legally he was on much firmer ground with these when it all came up in court. Warrants for the arrest of the six directors of BF Ltd. had been issued, and in the morning early they were going to visit Best Friend Dog Foods in Hackney. I wished him luck and told him not to overlook the house next door.

On the Monday the car came. It wasn't so quiet or so good-mannered as the Jaguar, nor so well finished as the Aston Martin, but the engine and the handling were matchless, and the throaty exhaust noise stiffened the back hairs on your neck every time you started up. Erica wouldn't go in it. Not that I pressed her hard. Monday evening Shona rang to see if I was ill, as I'd not been near the firm since Friday. I said I was well enough.

She said, "Take a couple of weeks if you are out of sorts. You did not look well *pleased* on Friday morning—that seemed strange after your remarkable success . . . for which not only this firm but many others will thank you. Is there something else wrong?"

"Life's funny," I said, "but sometimes the jokes get a bit dirty."

"You will have to be a little more explicit than that, David."

"Perhaps I will, before I leave."

"Leave? Is Erica going with you?"

"No."

"I shall be home every evening."

On Wednesday about five as I was turning in toward the flats I met Derek coming away.

"Oh," he said, smiling his bookmaker smile. "I just called. The little wife seemed to be out, and you still at the sweat shop. I was about to give it all up and slink away."

"No need. Come in."

"That yours, that monster by the curb?"

"Yes. New this week."

"Wow-ee. What d'you feed it on?"

"Four star. Care for a spin?"

"Well, not actually. I came really to pick your brains on one or two little happenings . . ."

"Jump in," I said.

We took the M40 and went as far as High Wycombe.

"It's lovely, darling," he said, "but I'd enjoy it more if my stomach could catch up."

On the way home we did seventy, the engine coughing now and then in protest; I'd seen a police car three or four cars back in the rear mirror.

"He's gone," said Derek, blowing out a breath as we turned into Hyde Park. "I felt sure he was going to waylay us."

"Talking of the fuzz," he went on as we got in the lift to go up. "Have you been seeing anything of them lately?"

I unlocked the door. "Who? The fuzz? Why should I have?"

"Because they've been to see me."

My arm was still not right. Better to wait a couple of days more before leaving. Shifting gears seemed to make the muscle stiffen.

"What have you been up to?"

"I?" he said. "Nothing, darling. Cross my heart and spit. But you know Vince, don't you?"

"Vince who?"

"Bickmaster. You met him quite *recently* at the Cellini."

"Oh, him, yes," I agreed quickly. "What about him?"

"He's been arrested and charged."

"Whatever with?"

"They came to see me because we've done a few teensy jobs together and they found my name in his flat. Thank God I'm not *in* this, whatever it is. But them coming like that! Two great flatfeet! I mean! It put me in rather a *whirl!*"

Derek wasn't looking his best. But I was glad he was in the clear—if he was. He pretended to be too simon-pure these days. (Never passed a bad check indeed! It could only have been for lack of opportunity.) But well and good, if he wasn't involved. For personal reasons—though not for the sort of personal reasons Erica pretended to think existed—I should have been sorry to shop him.

"That machine," he said. "*Infernal*, isn't it? Positively. But it fair turns you on. What speed were we doing on the way out?"

I began to tidy up some magazines that Erica had left sprawling.

"What's Bickmaster been up to anyway?"

"Dunno, mate. He's charged with some quite horrendous crime—conspiracy to defraud, I think they call it. Remember Gervase Ltd. in your golden youth?"

"That lot that turned out the porn magazines?"

"Yes. They were raided too."

I picked my way carefully over the rocks. "Who else was raided?"

"Oh, some factory in Essex. So the fuzz said, but you never know whether to believe 'em. Have you been to see the Gervase setup lately?"

"Not since the year I got out of the nick. Why?"

"I was wondering . . ."

"What are they doing now? Shouldn't think the girlie magazine trade was quite so brisk."

"Oh, you'd be surprised. Videos are the in things, of course. They've changed their name, by the way."

"Who have?"

"Gervase. You won't find them in the book any longer. Forget what the new name is."

I yawned. "I've been out of it all for the last few years. Don't say you haven't noticed?"

"Yes, I suppose . . . I put you on the transfer list soon after you joined La Shona."

"Have a drink," I said.

"Thanks."

We chatted about Erica and the Olympics. I could see he wanted to get back to the object of his visit, but I kept heading him off.

In the end he said, "There're other jolly comrades struggling in the mire, David. There was a piece in the *Telegraph*. Didn't you see it, dear?"

"No. When was that?"

"Monday. D'you remember asking me about Maurice Laval?"

"Who? Oh, the de Luxembourg chap. Ex. What about him?"

"You asked me about him more than once. You can't have forgotten."

"Did I? Oh, yes." It wouldn't do to be too innocent. "Has he got another job?"

"No, he's been copped too. All the shareholders of Best Friend."

"What's that?"

"Didn't I tell you? That's the new name. It just escaped me—"

I helped him to a second drink.

"I wondered," he said. "It seemed to me . . ."

"What?"

"Well, you remember you asked me all those questions when we met at the Cellini?"

"About? . . . Oh, yes."

"Well, you said you'd take my advice and leave it all alone. You remember I said it wouldn't be popular with some of the characters if you pressed on regardless."

I stared. "I remember. But I *gave* it up. That's what you told me to do, wasn't it?"

"Yes. Oh, yes. Glad to know it. Very glad indeed to know it. So . . . this is nothing at all to do with you?"

"I don't know what *this* is. If it's to do with forgery, the answer's no." Might as well be hung for a big sheep as a small.

He rubbed his knees, a sure sign he was uncomfortable. "I thought maybe if the fuzz had been to see you and grilled you as they grilled me, some incautious words might have slipped out."

"You can't let slip what you haven't got," I said. "I know no more than you. If your pals have become involved in nefarious doings and are in trouble it's their worry, not mine."

He looked at me curiously, and I wondered if I'd washed my hands too obviously. If I knew nothing about it, wouldn't I be more keen to hear the details?

However, at that moment Erica arrived with two young men called Houseman and Crary. As Steve and Tony they ran an interior-decorating establishment in Beauchamp Place, and were of course of Derek's persuasion. But while I liked Derek, these two got in my hair, and I suspect Erica knew it. Anyway she was in the overmerry mood she seemed to favor these days. It was usually the product of four vodka tonics.

We had a noisy session for about half an hour before they all left to go out to dinner, Derek included. I was saved the effort of refusing by not being asked. It occurred to me after they left that my efforts to put Derek (and presumably his friends) off the track could very well be wasted, since Erica knew I hadn't given up the forgery inquiries; it only needed a remark from her and the cat was out.

It occurred to me that I didn't care.

I went to see Shona.

IV I spoke into the box and the buzzer went. But she was a while opening the door of her flat; I suppose she spent a couple of minutes on a hasty refit; she was in a short-ish yellow frock with dark stockings and yellow mules; her hair had been disciplined.

"Ah, David. This is good. Please make yourself at home. Have you eaten?"

"No. But I'm not here for food."

"A drink?" I shook my head. "You are still not yourself, eh? We have missed you this week, but no matter. Leo has been rallying round. When are you going away?"

"Soon."

"And where are you going? To Scotland?"

"Maybe. I shall spend a few days there anyhow."

"Things are not well between you and Erica?"

"Things are not well between myself and mostly everybody."

"Including me?"

"Including you."

"What have I done?"

"What have you done? Nothing, I suppose. Nothing that a fair-minded man could complain of."

"Well, tell me. You spoke like this over the telephone."

"First of all, I'm leaving Erica."

She drew in a slow breath. "I am sorry. It has not worked out? Is it to be permanent?"

"I think so. Second, I'm leaving you."

Her mouth tightened. "So? Do you mean the firm?"

"What else?"

"Indeed," she said bitterly. "What else? . . . But why? You are on top of your work. We are a financially prosperous and distinguished company. You have just pulled off a noted coup, for which Chanel, I know, and other companies wish to thank you personally. You have never been in a better position, and your salary comes up for review next month. You should be very proud of yourself."

"I'm very sick," I said, "of the company I keep."

There was a pause. She took out a canary-colored handkerchief and dabbed her lips.

"Well, thank you, David. Once again I must say that I do not know what has made you feel this. Of course, always, you have tended to despise the profession—"

"D'you remember," I said, "it was you who first suggested I should marry Erica?"

"Yes, of course. And now you blame me—"

"D'you remember when we were in Scotland you suggested we should marry, you and I, and I said with more truth than tact that you could never give me a son?"

"Of course I remember. I was a stupid woman, forgetting my age. I thought we might have been happy, using your strange inheritance as a place to get away to, from the artificialities of our London world." She shrugged. "Perhaps a little like Barbados . . . You were—abrupt. It would have been more comfortable to my conceit to have come to realize your feelings more gradually. But there it was."

"Any man," I said, "who accepts his rejected mistress's recommendation whom he shall marry must rate high among the feeble-minded invertebrates of this world, so I take most of the flak as self-inflicted. I decided to marry Erica and she agreed. But why the recommendation in the first place?"

She hesitated. "I thought you might suit each other."

"So did I. We don't. But that's beside the point. The point is that, having been turned down yourself because you couldn't give me a child, was there not a certain satisfaction in commending me to a girl who couldn't have children either?" It was crude but it simply had to come out that way.

She blinked at me a couple of times with her fine Russian eyes. "What are you saying?"

"Erica tells me that in her affair with Edward Cromer she got pregnant."

"Of course. I knew about it. Before you came between us, Erica and I were very close."

"And she had an abortion."

"Yes. It was not quite legal but it was easy to arrange. She was very upset at the time, being much attached to the Cromer man, who let her down."

"And then?"

"And then what?"

"It went wrong, I gather. So she tells me. She couldn't have children now even if she wanted them."

Shona went across to the windows, drew the curtains. "She told you this?"

"Who else?"

"She never told me."

"D'you expect me to believe that?"

She turned. "What evil worm is *working* in you, David? My *God*, what is *wrong* with you? This is poison that you are thinking."

"It's not poison that I put there."

"Who, then?"

"Erica said, ask Shona, she knows all about it."

She came back, lit a cigarette, puffed away furiously. Her face looked suddenly small and bitter.

"David, knowing me so long as you have done, do you suppose I would do this to you?"

"Erica said, ask Shona, she knows all about it."

"Perhaps she was drunk. Perhaps she was jealous. Women say strange things when they are jealous."

"And do them."

That stopped her. She gasped and screwed out the cigarette. "All right! When I suggested that you marry Erica I have one other thought in my mind. You are—for some years you have belonged to *me*. To *me*! I have made you what you are! That is a claim you may resent; but in fairness it is the *truth*. You are a different man, more responsible, more normal. We have become a part of each other's lives and I do not know how I shall survive without you! More important, how will you survive without me? Even if the sexual thing is lost, there is still much more between us—understanding, trust. Yes, trust, David, when at one time it seemed the last quality one could apply to you."

"Thanks a million."

"Do not be flippant. I am telling you the plain truth. But now . . . I was going to lose you, to another woman. I find it hard to bear. My life is poisoned by the thought . . . I am going to lose you. But if you marry Erica I think I do not altogether lose you. You will stay with the firm. And Erica is—not deep; she will not perhaps altogether satisfy you; sometimes, now and then maybe, you will come back. If not just for love, at least for companionship. Perhaps that was not a noble thought, but it was *there*! And after my visit to Scotland I know that if you do not marry Erica or someone like her, in London, where contact can still exist, then you will marry that woman up there and be lost to me altogether!"

I stared. "Up there? . . . You mean—Alison? Malcolm's wife? *Rubbish* . . ."

"Not rubbish at all. But *that* was my reason for suggesting Erica, no other! Why should I have any other—except a motive of petty revenge? And if I cared for you—as I do care for you—do you suppose I would stoop to *that*? You must think meanly of me, David, even to entertain such a thought!"

She had her back to me, but I could see her hands were trembling.

She said, "Did Erica tell you this *herself*, about her abortion, about it going wrong? I do not *believe* it!"

"She ought to know."

"I think she was lying." Shona turned angrily. "This was no back-street operation! You know Erica, with all the money in the world; it was done, I know for a fact, at the *best* clinic then in England, by the *best* surgeon. Do you suppose anything would go wrong with *that*?"

"She ought to know," I said again.

"I think she was lying. Do you know she is in love with you, you fool?"

"That joke's gone a bit sour."

She came across and took me by the shoulders as if to shake

them. "She is saying these things, doing these things, to try to get a *response* from you! She said to me two months ago she cannot *reach* you! You are behind a glass screen, untouchable; there is no feeling, no emotion there. You are partly there, partly in the room with her, partly absent. I know how it is with you, I know how it was between us in those first years! Only later was there contact, fusion, communication; then I knew you cared, were feeling things as a human being should do. It did not last, of course. Three years—was it as much as that?—and then it slipped away . . . But I know how Erica must feel, barred away, kept at a distance. If she cares for you she will try anything to break the barrier down!"

I grabbed her hands off my shoulders, held her wrists for a few seconds, let them go.

"Erica's talent for communication is not of the highest either," I said. "Except when she wants to communicate some personal insult. So conceive of it that this splendid glass screen you've imagined existing between us may act both ways."

"Yes, but don't you realize what it is like for a woman? Not being able to get through, asking for responses, getting nothing in return; wanting even to quarrel if that is the way to break through. Demanding a meeting, an emotional exchange where perhaps each one of you can lay your feelings bare, and then begin all over again afterward on a new footing of understanding and caring and comradeship?"

I said, "You tell me Erica is shallow. I think so myself. It was what I wanted. Now she complains because I won't give her what she never had herself!"

She stood brooding beside me, then shrugged and turned away. "Well . . . what has gone wrong between you and Erica is between you and Erica. I am very sad if it has come to this pass, and I am to blame if in any way I encouraged you to marry her—"

"Don't bother," I interrupted, "it was my own choice—"

"But what goes wrong between *you* and *me* is another matter and we must get it brought out into the open at once. Yes? If she told you that she cannot have children, that is your affair. If she told you that *I knew* she couldn't have children, then that is mine!" She went to the telephone and dialed a number.

"What now?" I said.

"Either she must come over here or we are going over there. At once. At least *this* can be cleared up!"

At the window and peer through the curtains. Raining now. Not the best night for a long drive. But I was going tonight. The hell with my arm.

She slammed the receiver down. "There is no reply."

"She's out on the town with Derek Jones and those two creeps from Beauchamp Place."

"Steve and Tony? I'll ring them."

"They weren't going home. They were off to some restaurant for dinner."

"Then it must be first thing in the morning. What time will you be up?"

"I'm leaving for Scotland tonight."

"Why tonight? With this unresolved? You can stay another day! I want to know if Erica was lying about herself and I want to know how she came to lie about me!"

My sharp rage had blunted itself on Shona's angry response. I neither believed her nor disbelieved her. All I knew now was the sickness and the frustration and the need to get away.

"Look, Shona." I stopped.

"Yes? What do you want to say?"

"Work it out with Erica tomorrow. Just now I've only one real need in the world and that is to drop my wife and to drop my job. I'd like it to be a clean break—but maybe you can't have clean breaks in matrimony even these days. So if you'll accept my resignation from the firm—"

"I will *not!*" she said.

I made a savage gesture, and then tried not to wince at the pain in my arm.

She said, "Take leave of absence. Take four weeks. If at the end of four weeks you still feel the same I'll not quarrel further. Until then, let it be temporary."

I shrugged. "Play it how you want so long as I'm free."

"What time are you going?"

"What? . . . To Scotland?" I looked at my watch. "It'll take me half an hour to throw a few things in a bag. About ten, I suppose."

"Have you time to eat first?"

"I'm not *hungry!*"

"Then I'll make you a few sandwiches. And a flask of coffee. It's a long way."

I didn't want the food, I didn't want her stupid attentions. After all we'd said, it was ridiculous. I wanted just to get away. You can't suddenly turn from the cutthroat to the domestic. It was anticlimax.

But maybe to end with a whimper is the best way to end all scenes.

"Yes," I said, "it's a long way."

CHAPTER TWENTY-FIVE

I needn't have worried about my arm. Once out of London the traffic was thin, and I could hare along most of the time in fifth gear. Then after a stop for an hour near Doncaster, when I began to use the car more as it was designed to be used, I found the shoulder wasn't too painful.

You think a lot on the way. Driving a car at night you don't have nightmares, only fleeting visions of what you are and what you hope to be and what you pretend you're not.

I began to think about Malcolm's title, which he should have inherited and instead had thrown away. It didn't belong to me. It never would belong to me. It had been bad enough sometimes believing in myself as David Abden. The "Sir" in front of it seemed to make a rubbish of my existence. There's a belief somewhere, isn't there, that if you don't have a name you don't exist. And the "Sir" in front of my name seemed to have dug under the foundations and left only an empty house ready to fall in.

I thought of a book I'd read once by John Steinbeck in which he says that practically all the creative sweat men put into life is an attempt to prove that point: that they're *here*, that they've *been* here, that they've left their *mark*. Unfortunately very few of us can be Shakespeares or Michelangelos or Christopher Wrens. Not many can even be Shonas, building a fancy pile of bricks, a little reputation that'll stick around for a few years.

As for me, the sum of my activities wouldn't fill a thimble, hardly raise a drift of dust. It could be that even those narrow, conceited, bigoted Abdens, for whose original home I was now heading and who had died for this or that useless cause, leaving only a name scratched on a granite wall, were one step up.

But their causes were *useless*, weren't they? Indeed what cause in the long run was not useless? Was there any purpose in life that was not better served by an early death? Maybe the faulty tire wasn't such a bad way out.

I drove very fast but still very steadily, the car fairly snorting its pleasure at the long run. As the night went on my head grew heavy and my legs light. This was only a continuing process based on the way I'd been feeling all last week. I might have thought I was coming down with flu, if I hadn't known a whole lot better. All my adult life I'd hardly ailed a thing physically, never been to a croaker, never taken a pill. How about it if I stopped now in Edinburgh and went to see a quack and moaned, "Oh, doctor, I'm ill, help, help!" He'd say in his stupid Scottish brogue, "What seems to be the matter?" and I'd reply, "I can't make up my mind." Big deal. "One of these, four times a day, and you won't have any mind left to make up."

Dawn rose over the Grampians. I thought about the last few days. Deceit, deception, disgust. At least it looked as if Chalmers and his boys were going to make a tidy sweep of the counterfeiters. I wondered if it really would touch Roger in his Hampstead fastnesses. Very unlikely; he would have covered his tracks too well.

As the day, a fine day, settled on northern Scotland it occurred to me, not without a certain sensation of alarm, that there had been one moment in the last weeks that I had really enjoyed. That had been the almost successful attempt to throttle Charley Ellis. And it wasn't the repayment of an old grudge I had enjoyed so much as the actual violence.

II

The roof repairs were nearly finished. They'd pretty well had to strip the whole roof off the old hall, but apart from that had been able to patch up the rest. They were still working on a steep slanted roof over two of the end backrooms, but as these were never used it wasn't much inconvenience except for the scaffolding and the track up to the house, which was more rutted and muddy than ever.

Of course they weren't expecting me at all this time—they were hardly up—and there was the usual panic while they made breakfast. Mrs. Coppell fussed and pattered about the largely unused but now highly efficient kitchen; Coppell led the way up ladders and showed me what had been done. While I was eating eggs and bacon the roofers arrived for the day's work.

After I'd parked my new car safely out of reach of spattering stones or turning lorries I went to bed and, undisturbed by hammerings, slept for five hours. It was then almost time to eat again. I ate again. My life was in a scintillating mess but the juices were not deterred. Maybe the long drive up here had helped.

It had certainly helped in one way. The unclean spirits of the night had had a good airing; now for a time they were gone—not far away, but I didn't *think* of them. I thought of practically nothing but went up on the roof, watching the men, talking to them and trying to help. Maybe I should have been a builder—of walls or houses or ships or cars: something to get my hands on; the old creative impulse again.

But it wasn't much of a creative impulse I felt on the Saturday. The workmen weren't there to divert attention; a walk in the morning, with one of the dogs, a terrier called Drago who seemed to have taken a fancy to me. He looked like a cross between a Scottie and a Bedlington; I threw sticks for him and he thought that fun. When I got back I looked up at the house and thought: It's still as ugly as sin and the ugliest thing about it is that porch. What misbegotten, snotty-nosed, bare-legged ancestor had ever allowed it to be put up, let alone maintained with paint and polish all these years? The front door behind was a bit church-going in shape but the oak was good and the stonework OK. I disturbed McVitie at his gardening to ask if he had a pickaxe or a mallet. He had both.

Ten minutes later Mrs. Coppell appeared at the front door. "Holy Mary, mother of God! 'Tis you yerself, sir! I heard the banging before; but then the clatter of glass! . . . Are ye knocking doon the whole hoose, sir?"

"No. Just this piece that I don't admire."

"Would ye allow me to move the pot plants, sir? I can take them to our cottage if they don't pleasure ye."

I worked all Saturday afternoon and all Sunday. By that time the porch as a porch was not. There was a tidy muck of broken glass, another of brick and a third of wood and plaster, ready to be taken away by the workmen when they came with their lorry on Monday morning. The house looked better without the excrescence, but there were too many signs of its having been there. Some of the exposed stonework needed pointing and a cement wash would have to be used to cover the scars. I told the foreman this, and he scratched the nape of his neck and reluctantly agreed. Then I went into Ullapool to shop. Then I went on to Lochfiern House.

I saw my aunt. She said Alison and her little daughter were away for a month visiting her parents in Castle Douglas. I thanked her for her letter that I'd not replied to and said I'd be glad to inspect the military relics sometime, but as my wife was a champion fencer and unlikely to have children at least for some years, it might be better to delay making speculative gifts. She was right in supposing that I was not a safe repository for so much of the family history and I advised her to leave all the medals, etc., to a suitable war museum.

She heard me out gravely.

Then she said, "Perhaps you might just like to see this one." She went to a cupboard and laboriously produced a bronze cross with a red ribbon. The cross had a crown and a lion and *For Valor* underneath. "The only one we have in our family," she said, hands trembling as she held it. "But it is something we specially prize. It was won by Colonel Cameron Abden of the Scots Guards, at Loos in 1915. He was with the 9th Division in their attack on the Hohenzollern Redoubt. The piper leading the company was killed almost at once, but Cameron Abden at once picked up the pipes and led his company to capture the enemy positions, playing on through it all, though himself severely wounded. He died a year later on the Somme."

She wanted me to hold it so I held it, wondering if she thought it would convert me to right thinking. It didn't, but I handed it back politely enough and helped her to put it away. To say that there was a growing accord between us would be piling on the lush, but at least we weren't actually sharpening dirks.

She said, "I believe your wife has money."

"Yes."

"That will be a help to you in maintaining Wester Craig."

"Yes."

"Perhaps even in making a decision not to sell the property."

"I don't think it will affect that."

"Your wife is not in Moscow?"

"No. She wasn't chosen."

"Oh. That would be a disappointment . . . I understand the repairs to Wester Craig are almost complete."

"So far as they are going, yes."

"You are staying here awhile?"

"Oh, a week or so."

III   I stayed a week or so. There were other things to do besides massacring a porch. By a rickety old jetty at the edge of Loch Ashe was a boat. It was in poor shape but apparently belonged to me. The frame was fairly sound but it needed a repaint and new oars. I set about that and with Coppell's help worked on it all week.

I thought once or twice about Cameron Abden and wondered who was the dafter: him playing his pipes while the bullets whistled or me half strangling an ex-convict with a stocking-mask over my face.

On the second Monday a letter from Shona:

> I do not know if you have heard from Erica but I have confronted her with her statement and she says she does not say *I* knew about the problems she might face if having another child. She says that she meant that I knew all about the abortion. In any case the specialist does *not* say she could have no more children, only that she was so constituted that childbearing shall be difficult and perhaps dangerous.
>
> John died last Monday. In later years we were not so close but he was my husband and colleague and kind companion so long that I have lost a piece of my early life. He will be missed in so many ways. And coming so close after the death of my father leaves a gap in my existence it is hard to fill.
>
> As you know, John was strongly opposed to the idea of our becoming a public limited-liability company. Now I shall go into this with my lawyers and accountants, and if or when you shall come back I would wish you to participate in these talks. There is

much to be said for the idea. As from next month we are also increasing your salary by £10,000 a year. I could not make this sort of increase in John's lifetime without offending him more than ever. This brings your salary to a higher level than the comparable position in much larger companies like Rubinstein, de Luxembourg, or Arden.

Now I have to tell you that six men have been charged with conspiracy to defraud, and remanded in custody. To my astonishment one of them is Maurice Laval who was so prominent in our trade not so long ago. His namesake, when prime minister of France, was called a turnvest—as indeed he was—because you could read his name backward or forward the same. An Inspector Chalmers rang for you yesterday but I said you were on leave. I gave him your telephone number in Scotland, where I presume you still are.

The newspaper says further arrests can be expected.

I trust you are enjoying your holiday. It has been very stuffy in London, and sultry.

Shona

The following day Alison turned up.

I'd forgotten how composed she was, how smooth her hair and her voice and her manner. Yet smooth didn't mean slick, it meant unruffled. I wondered what it would be like to ruffle her.

She had a little girl with her. "This is Trina. This is Uncle David. You are a sort of uncle, aren't you, by marriage?"

"Second cousin probably. Ask Aunt Helen, she'll be sure to know. Hullo." We shook hands. "Trina? Is that short for something?"

"Catriona."

"Romantic."

"Stevenson didn't invent it," said Alison shortly. "You have a new car?"

"Yes, I'll take you for a run in it sometime."

"Oh, super!" said the little girl. "How fast does it go?"

I made a face at Alison. "Fairly fast. But the engine sings lovely noises: That's what I like most about it."

Trina ran across and stared at the low red thing. I said to her mother, "Sorry. Wrong instincts to encourage."

"Oh, she has them already. She always wants me to drive fast in the Mini."

"I thought you were away for a month."

314

"I have been. We came back on Saturday."

We looked at each other with a degree of interest you couldn't disguise. Wind blew my hair more than it did hers. She broke the moment by turning to glance up at the house. "You've had the porch taken off."

"I did it myself the first weekend. The builders were supposed to be repairing the marks I'd left—said they'd do it this week."

"That means six weeks. But the house looks better anyway. I never thought of having it taken off."

"It didn't offend you?"

"Not a bit." She laughed coolly. "I have no architectural taste . . . But I suppose you know what will happen? The winter gales and rain will beat directly on the front door and seep into the hall. The porch also acted as a valuable dam for the wind. You could close one door before opening the other."

"Ah. Whereas now carpets will flap all the way through the house. We'll have to hang a curtain inside. You lose one eyesore and put up another."

"We?" she said. "Your wife is not here, though?"

"She may come again."

"Of course. She gave me the impression that Scotland was not really her scene."

"At the moment she has other things on her mind."

Later I took them for a ride in the car, driving pretty steady on the busy roads, but showing off its enormous acceleration. Trina shrieked with delight.

"You are ruining her character," said Alison.

"And yours?" I asked.

"Oh, mine is already set in its own peculiar directions."

"Which don't include an unstable cousin-in-law?"

"There could be dangers in that."

"What sort of dangers?"

"Physical, of course." She added quickly, "*In this car*. What else?"

"I thought your Catholic soul might feel imperiled."

"Mine is not a Catholic soul. I was born a Protestant, but changed to please Malcolm."

"Did that worry you?"

"Not particularly. My convictions are not of the strongest."

"It doesn't give you an extra feeling of guilt?"

"No. There's no guilt one can't be absolved from."

"Happy thought." I stopped to allow some sheep to drift across the road. "Tell me, what did you mean—or someone mean, was it you?—speaking of the Abdens as being a Catholic enclave here? As if—"

"As if the whole of this area were strictly Protestant? Well, it is. Nobody cares so much now, but they used to care. There are Catholic families dotted about Scotland, but relatively few in Ross and Cromarty."

We drove home. Alison refused to come in; they had to be getting back.

"Come again," I said.

"Thanks." Trina climbed into the driver's side of the Mini and was persuaded to move reluctantly into the passenger's seat. Alison got in and swung in her legs, pulled down the seat belt.

"Saturday," I said, "would be a good day. Come after lunch and we'll go for another drive. Or a walk if it grabs you."

"Trina has a French lesson on Saturday afternoons from Father Donald."

"Well, come on your own, then."

"Aw," said Trina. "That's not fair!"

"Come to lunch with us next Monday, then," said Alison. "Trina can have a ride with you after."

"And Saturday?" I said.

Alison looked speculatively at the gathering clouds. "What *about* Saturday?"

"Come without Trina. We'll still probably find something to talk about—even if it's only old ghosts."

"All right," she said, her eyes not higher than the steering wheel. "See you about three."

CHAPTER TWENTY-SIX

I One advantage of breaking the entail on the house is that you can then raise a mortgage on it, and this was the way I'd paid for the roof repairs without calling on Erica's bounty. The cost of the new Ferrari, even with a generous trade-in price for the Jaguar, was ghastly, but this was to be paid for monthly by banker's order. All very fine so long as I stuck it as now highly paid sales manager of Shona and Co., still easier if I became, as I was likely to become, managing director of Shona and Co. Ltd. It was there for the taking but I wasn't in the mood to take it.

All very fine too if I stayed married to the daughter of Lease's Cream Crackers. But if we were getting unhitched the picture wasn't so jolly. What shall we do for the rent? as Sickert said.

I sweated away at the boat. No great fisherman me, but I thought when it was done I'd have a go at enticing the trout and the salmon.

The jetty was groggy too and wood had been ordered for a rebuild. As usual everything took forever to come, but a pile of stuff arrived on the Friday afternoon and we got it sorted out to begin. When Alison came on the Saturday I took her down to see it.

She said, "I didn't know you were so ready with your hands."

"Don't remind me of it."

"What does that mean?"

"Sorry. Sick joke." I lifted a plank and pushed it in with the rest. "Seriously, this just shows what frustration will do."

"Frustration?"

"So much of the property is falling around my ears. And I took a course in fretwork once."

She didn't smile. "Pity you can't stay longer."

"Who says how long I'm staying?"

"Nobody. I presume this is only a holiday?"

"Not with definite limits."

"Mme. Shona is very understanding."

"She can be. What are we going to do this afternoon—drive or walk?"

"Let's walk."

"It looks like rain."

"Are you afraid of getting wet?"

"Not if you're not."

She was wearing a polo-necked sweater of fine green wool with one of those shortish tweed skirts fastened at the side with an ornamental safety pin. Hefty brogues.

"Is that the Abden tartan?"

"As a matter of fact, no. It's my own family."

"Got a mack?"

"In the car. I'll fetch it."

We started off up the hill, rather the way I'd gone that morning with Shona, but we went further, walking into the low clouds, but no rain yet.

She said, "Up here at one time the whole place was full of briar roses. It must have been a picture in the spring. That was before the sheep came and ate them all."

"Who told you that?"

"Coppell."

"Must have been a long time ago."

"Well, his father was here, and his grandfather before him. Do you never talk to Douglas Coppell? He's a mine of information."

"Are they Catholics?"

"Yes. They go in their old car every Saturday to mass and confession."

"It never occurred to me until I knocked down the porch and Mrs. C. started exclaiming about Holy Mary!"

"Coppell's grandfather was Irish," she said. And then, "D'you know those fine pines behind the house—the six big ones. Well, Malcolm's great-great-grandfather planted those and put briar roses in at the same time so that the cattle wouldn't push the saplings over rubbing their hides against them."

We voyaged in silence for a bit, then she stopped and nicked a strand of hair out of her eyes, looked back. We hadn't gone much higher but the land was stone-barren, just rock and peat, the odd patch of heather. We couldn't see much because of the mist.

"Know your way back?" I said. "Because I don't."

"Och aye. I've been this way afore, afore."

"With Malcolm?"

"Not often. He was not fond of walking."

"Tell me about him," I said.

The exercise had dabbed a touch of color in her face, which was normally pearl-pale.

"You met him."

"Well, yes, but."

"Well, what did *you* think of him?"

"Interesting. A few unlikable characteristics—least they seemed so to a misanthrope like me—but stimulating. Quality in him. Larger than life, and maybe that's a plus in a gray society."

"He was certainly stimulating."

"You'll miss him a lot, I suppose."

"Yes," she said, "like a high temperature."

I stared at her still face. She was really a looker, but you wouldn't lay any odds on what she was thinking.

"Feverish?"

She glanced at me, summing me up before returning to take a view of the unviewable horizon. "You could say that."

"Up and down, in fact?"

"Oh, down and up, certainly. Of course there were moments."

"Only moments?"

"Let's go on," she said. "There's a cairn up here. That usually marks the limits."

"Who owns the land?"

"The Earl of Schofield. But he lives too far away and his keepers, such as there are, know me."

We reached the pile of stones, and as we did so rain began to infiltrate in the breeze.

She said, "Tell me about *yourself* for a change."

"You must have my history at your fingertips."

"Personal accounts differ, don't they?"

I muttered a few things, which she listened to with her usual care and stillness. As the rain got thicker I took a cap out of my raincoat pocket, and she put on a mackintosh hood. We began to walk back. It was thick, clinging, dense rain, not the sort my tailor had been dreaming about when he fitted me with this coat. Doubtful whether she was going to be much better; the mackintosh was only the length of her skirt and in the fashion of those garments the rain ran straight off them on to the legs of the wearer.

On the way down she asked me about Shona, and I gave her an edited version. She appeared to have cottoned on to our former goings-on. She didn't seem to have much to ask about Erica; only Shona, as if she were the real rival. Rival for what, I asked myself? Jumping Jerusalem, let's not take anything for granted.

By the time the house came in sight we were both more than a little wet. In spite of the hood the rain was glistening on her eyelashes.

"This is Scotland. People here are used to getting damp; they take no notice of it."

"Any more than the sheep?"

"Well, if you like to say so."

As we reached the door of the house she said, "I always carry a spare skirt and pair of shoes in the car. I'll get them."

I waited for her and then we went in and I put a match to the drawing-room fire. "Help yourself to anything you want. You know the house better than I do. The new kitchen provides hot water everywhere, so take a bath or a shower if you feel like it."

"I'll just change these things."

While she was upstairs I made tea and brought it in. The fire was leaping for joy but spitting resin all over the place. My own jacket and trousers were soaking, and when she came down I went up and changed.

She was pouring tea.

"Thanks," I said. "Sorry to tell you it's the Coppells' day off."

"I know. It's always been Saturdays."

"Ah." I put my hand on her shoulder. "This is damp."

"It's *nothing*."

"I'll stoke the fire," I said. "Pull up your chair."

So we sat and sipped for a few minutes. She clearly hadn't brought a change of stockings and her legs were the same color as her face—pearl-pale—and of the most seductive shape. I thought, if Erica finds me a shade unsatisfactory at present I'm damned sure Alison wouldn't.

"Did you do this often with Malcolm?" I asked.

"Do what?" she asked, sounding startled.

"Sip tea together in this room in companionable silence."

"Oh . . . No, not often. In fact I don't remember a time. He was a very restless man."

"Yes, I could see that." I thought of his big eyes, restless indeed, when I introduced him to Rona Anderson at Claridge's.

"He was always looking for something *new*. Always trying to impress someone. Always concerned about his public image."

I realized it could have been a bad idea to grasp her shoulder, though so lightly. It turned the attention.

"Also," she said, "he was a terrible liar."

"Oh," I said, looking her over. "Pity."

"Are *you*, David?"

"What, a liar? Was at one time. No longer, I think." Quite surprised to say so, never having asked myself the question. Except to Derek, which perhaps didn't count.

"Ordinary things of course he didn't lie about, but anything to do with his ambition, his presentation of himself. I suppose you never saw his entry in *Who's Who?*"

"No."

"Wrong age; too many accomplishments; laying claim to some distant barony of Kilclair, so that he could be known as Abden of Kilclair while his father was still alive."

"Was he ever a Doctor of Philosophy?"

"No. He spent a year on it, then threw it up. Yet he was really very *clever*."

"Malcolm?"

"*Yes*. If he'd taken politics seriously, or anything seriously enough. He'd such a good brain. But it was always clouded with conceit."

"Perhaps that's an Abden failing," I said. "More tea?"

"Thanks, no. I ought to go."

"Why?"

She looked at me. "No reason at all."

"I'm glad of that."

"Tell me," she said, "why did you say you were misanthropic?"

"Because I am. People on the whole I find hard to take."

"Is that why you are not getting on with Erica?"

"Who said I was not?"

"It's a little obvious. What's the matter? Are you shopping around?"

"No."

"Nor going back to your old love?"

"Shona? No."

"Is Erica off with other men?"

"No. Her favorite company at the moment is the gay boys."

"How strange. I can't stand them. So what are you going to do?"

"About Erica? I don't know. Just at the moment I don't much care."

"Why not?"

I smiled at her. "I'm shortsighted, I don't believe in looking beyond the next hour."

She was very still again, hands clasped around one bare knee, her hair dank; she might have been listening.

"Was Malcolm often unfaithful?"

"Constantly. But he always came back."

"And made up for it?"

"You don't really 'make up' for infidelity. It becomes a way of life."

"Was Malcolm a good lover?"

Her long brown eyes slanted up at me, little points of reflected fire sparking in them. "Yes. Why d'you ask?"

"So that made up for a lot."

"Not everything."

"What did it not make up for?"

She sighed. "Probably for the fact that I never really loved him."

"That's a pity, isn't it?"

"Maybe."

"Can you explain more?"

"I'd rather not."

"If that's your decision I have to abide by it."

"Yes, you do, don't you?"

There was a long pause, with no sound except the crackle of the fire.

"In fact," she said, "he made love to me once in this room. It was early on, six weeks or so after we were married. There *are* locks on both doors."

"So I've noticed."

"The window curtains were heavy."

"*Are* heavy."

"Yes. The fire was roaring—rather like this. There were plenty of rugs."

"*Are* plenty."

"He put out the lights and I took off my clothes and knelt down. Then he stroked my breasts by the firelight."

I bent to put another log on. "What a splendid idea . . . Would it seem rather *déjà vu*? . . ."

"What?"

"To suggest that we might do exactly the same thing now?"

There was an even longer pause. Then she rose and stretched like a pale beautiful cat.

"Not at all. In fact, David, dear David, I'd twenty times rather it was you than ever Malcolm."

CHAPTER TWENTY-SEVEN

I She left at nine before the Coppells got back. She came on Sunday with Trina, and Mrs. Coppell took Trina for a walk; we had almost an hour. I went to Lochfiern House for lunch on Monday and couldn't get out of being shown some more of the military relics: letters, ancient maps with threadbare joints, captured spears, dented helmets. In the afternoon I took Trina for a ride in the Ferrari on her own. That night, just before midnight, Alison arrived at Wester Craig and didn't leave till four A.M. Somehow we missed only one day in that first week. We drank each other dry and came back for more.

People were bound to know. I said to Alison, "What does it matter? Come and stay here."

"With Trina?"

"Ah. Leave her with Mary, who's mad about her."

"Maybe we can expect our relatives to turn a blind eye, David. I hope so, anyway. But that would smack of connivance and encouragement."

We talked; but not that much. Alison brought Trina with her most afternoons and we went for walks together. It was a way of being with me, said Alison, if nothing more. Usually somehow it became something more. Mornings I labored on the jetty and the boat.

Perhaps the forbidden—or if not forbidden, then something done by stealth—adds an extra zest. And there was never time to indulge to the point of satiety. Every fresh meeting was a new adventure, a new thrill.

We walked down to the mouth of the loch and Alison pointed out the sea pipits and the Arctic terns. We got expert at talking to each other while pretending to talk to Trina. Innuendoes flew over the infant's head like arrows in a Robin Hood film.

I had another letter from Shona telling me of the plans at present being put together by her accountants and her lawyers for a company flotation. She would like me to be back not later than the week after next, if only to attend one or two of these meetings; whether I remained in London after that was my own affair. She proposed I should receive a substantial slice of the equity, whether I remained with the firm or not. "This expansion has been so much your work that that seems only fair." Not only fair, but *generous*. Yes, Shona being generous with money! Was age softening her up? I did a few sums on the back of an envelope and realized, if my figures were approximately right, that I should never again lack for a crust. I had to write to her, and soon. I'd never written about John's death. Hard to say much about a man I'd never got on with and who so plainly disliked me.

I wrote to Shona saying what I could that was nice about him and telling her I'd probably be in London the week beginning the 15th. I thanked her for the proffered gift and said I'd be glad to accept it. I had a feeling she was banking on my better nature.

Then Chalmers rang. He'd tried a couple of times before, he said. The arrested men were still in Brixton but were due shortly to come up in the Magistrates' Court to be committed for trial. Sometimes, Chalmers explained, the defense admitted there was a case and reserved their ammunition for the Crown Court. Then the committal proceedings were a formality. But the defense in this case was proposing to contest the committal, and the hearing might take a couple of days. It would be very useful if I could attend, at least for part of the time, to give evidence if required, possibly with our technical director as well. There were people coming from Chanel, Lancôme, etc., and it would be of assistance to the police.

I said: Where and when? He said, Barking Magistrates' Court, about Tuesday, the sixteenth. I hadn't wanted to show my hand as freely as this, but probably by now one way or another the crooks would have come round to the idea that I had had a finger in their pie. So I said, yes, I'd come.

In the second week I paid two visits to Lochfiern House after lights-out. The throaty exhaust of the Ferrari meant parking a distance away; then a burglarious approach to the stone-porched side door where the bolt had been slipped back; tiptoeing up the creaky stairs and along a square, carpeted landing to a door which had been oiled that morning so it wouldn't groan. Then by the light of a tiny night-light the long sensuous eyes of Mrs. Malcolm Abden peering over the sheet, watching me undress and knowing she was naked herself.

But after two nights we decided reluctantly that it had to be a home fixture at Wester Craig; it was not nice thinking of her driving back at three in the morning, but there were too many people in her own house, including Trina, who woke on the second night and came tapping at the locked door. But the passion went on just the same; she was a ravishing woman and had been a widow too long.

You could hardly say I'd been a bachelor too long but there it was; I couldn't have enough of her.

Came time almost for me to go. The roof was finished, the boat was finished, the jetty was repaired and would last groggily another year or so. The marks of the porch hadn't been made good but they promised it before I returned.

Returned? Well, yes, it looked like it. Within a week? Probably. I still wasn't all that taken with Scotland but Alison was here, which brought the scales down with a thump. The simple life and high sex went well together.

She made no demands on me when I said I'd to go to London. The stillness and steadiness of her showed up plain enough then. After I'd made love to her a few times I cottoned on that the poise and balance was mental, not physical; unlike me, she was steady as a rock; she knew exactly what she wanted, and when possible took it.

She said she'd thought of going back to live with her parents, since there was nothing specific to keep her with the Abdens; but the very first time I called she'd changed her mind.

"Like that?" I said.

"Like that." She trailed her hand in the water. We were out in the boat near the mouth of the loch fishing—fishing for sillocks; I'd never heard of the damned things but that's what she said they were called. "I knew you'd come back."

"Even with the old shoulder chip, eh?"

"You must tell me about that sometime."

"Haven't you heard enough?"

"That your mother was Jewish? That your father was a bit of a wastrel? Doesn't explain a thing."

"All the Abdens are bad news—more or less—aren't they? It's what Mary never tires of saying."

"She's got a thing about it. Malcolm was not all that difficult —if you try to be detached about it. Neither are you. Stop playing at being a bad boy."

I laughed. Trina said, "I think this poor little fish is dead, Mummy."

"Well, you wouldn't throw it back," said Alison. "Let me see . . . Yes, I think it is. Pity. It's a tiny baby plaice."

"How d'you know that?" I asked.

"My parents had a house on Skye when we were young. Used to spend our summer holidays there. Often went fishing with my brothers." She turned to Catriona. "This is a very baby plaice, Trina. D'you see, it has eyes on both sides of its head. It swims like this." She held her hand vertically. "But when it gets older both eyes come almost together and it swims on its side." Hand held flat. "Like that. It always swims on its left side, right side up. But a turbot does the opposite, swims on its right side, left side up."

"I don't *believe* you!" I said, laughing again. "It's a fairy story, isn't it, Trina?"

"Nothing of the sort!"

"Yes, yes, yes!" said Trina, clapping her hands excitedly. "It's a fairy story! Mummy, can I go for another ride in Uncle David's car?"

"Certainly you cannot if you don't believe my true stories!"

"But Uncle David doesn't."

"Uncle David," said Alison, "is a foolish man. Not yet quite grown up."

"My God!" I said. "Many a true word." Then I looked her over, carefully and particularly and possessively, from her cropped hair to her fawny eyes, to her open blouse, to her worn blue slacks, to her clean, bare, naked feet. "Yes, I'll take you out, Trina, when we get back, on one condition: that you first have an hour's walk with Mrs. Coppell over the moors."

In my pocket I had a letter I didn't tell Alison about, a letter from Erica:

Dear David,

Surprise, surprise, a note from little me! I depend for news of your movements on your Russian friend, who tells me you have spent all these weeks in the bonny Highlands acquiring a Gaelic tan; but are shortly returning to London, at least for a visit. Does this mean I should air your pajamas and put the electric blanket on? We are still officially husband and wife and cohabit according to the law, so I rather assume you'll make use of Knightsbridge House, No. 24, at least as a *pied à terre*. Don't let my presence disturb you; as you know, it's a large flat with plenty of living space and no need to conjoin unless we feel like it.

The Muscovites are of course long since back, and general opinion is that the selection committee boobed frightfully by not including me. Consolation? Not much. Except that we could hardly have done worse. Francis wants me to go into strict training again. I'm hanging fire. Maybe we've got to get our own lives straightened out a bit first. We can't just go on living forever in Dead Pan Alley. Perhaps a jolt or two would get the works moving again. Who knows what a little polite confrontation might do?

It may not have occurred to you—why should it?—that I was born twenty-six years ago next Tuesday and to celebrate an event which certainly has some importance in my life, I'm throwing a dinner party at the Dorchester. Only about eighteen. All our closest friends. Actually seventeen without you. Black tie; but a sweater with your face above it would pass. Time eight. No flowers by request.

Love (or what you will),
Erica

P.S. I will call you Sunday night for yea or nay.

On the way back to London I stopped in Inverness and Edinburgh to see the estate agents and old Macardle. I told Heeney to withdraw Wester Craig temporarily from the market. (I didn't want it suddenly whisked away in the present stage of my affairs.) This all took longer than expected and as it was blowing a gale and pelting with rain and the motorways were sure to be gurgling and splashing with traffic on a late Monday afternoon, I decided to get an early night, being sleepy after last night's long final hours with Alison. I left Edinburgh on Tuesday as dawn was breaking, but it was still a messy journey and I didn't break any records. I spent some of the driving time chewing over in my mind about the women in my life.

Shona was probably right in saying my marriage with Erica hadn't ever had a fair field. Her preoccupation with her fencing and my unwillingness to get drawn into another female web had strangled the thing in infancy. Was there any point in trying to revive it? Surely not. If I got a slice of the equity from the flotation of Shona & Co., I wouldn't need Erica's money; and Erica was sure of her title whatever happened in the divorce court. Seemed unlikely she'd raise many difficulties.

Yet Shona's rousing words to me, accusing me of not being willing to give anything to my marriage, scored at least a double ten on the dartboard. I hadn't given much, I knew I hadn't given much—I'd relaxed far more with Alison in a few weeks than with Erica in a year; not knowing why; it wasn't love; they were different women. Alison offered more, was warmer, more sexual, more demanding. Erica lived by the throwaway line. Yet maybe she cared when her throwaway lines were not picked up. Shona had said so, very pointedly, very angrily.

I didn't think I wanted to stay hitched to Erica, in any event. Her prospects, or lack of them, for producing another sprig of the Abden line was not the most important thing. She was light, easy company, cynical, amusing; perhaps as good a person as anyone to choose to spend the rest of one's life with? But not for me, I thought, not for me.

On the telephone her voice had sounded like a stranger's: deeper, the flippant words not matching, like a movie out of sync. Had she really tried to make a go of it, was now facing two failures? After the fencing flop she'd needed all the support she could get, and I'd hardly given it her. But could I be blamed since she'd turned on me like a rattlesnake?

Anyway I'd said I'd go to the party. She sounded a bit coy about the people she'd asked, and I wondered whether her closest friends were going to be mine. As an incurable climber, she was likely to have asked all the titles in her address book. But, I said to myself, put a good face on it and play the old homecoming through with a minimum of fuss and a maximum of good will. For a while I'd see how things went before dropping the word divorce into our connubial bucket: It would probably hardly create a splash; if it did, if she objected for some unexpected reason, then we could just separate for a time. There was no hurry, and my aunt could wait another decade before I presented her with a suitable heir.

The Ferrari was playing up on the way back, needed a retune after all the taxiing it had done in Scotland, and I thought if there was time I'd try to take it round to the garage for a service, and get a taxi or something out to Barking. But there wasn't time. I went direct to the court and even then was half an hour late for the kickoff.

I sat next to Parker and Leo Longford but wasn't called. The culprits were duly arraigned in the dock: Vince Bickmaster, Sitram Smith (wearing a turban), Maurice Laval, Matthew Charles and two others. They looked at me and I looked at them. You could pick out a few of their friends both in the court proper and in the public gallery. There was a man in sunglasses at the back of the court who wasn't unlike Charley Ellis but I couldn't be sure. Derek was noticeably not there.

When the day was ended Chalmers thanked me for putting in an appearance and said that, the way things had gone, there would be no need for me to turn up on the second day. But he wondered if as a last favor I'd mind coming back to the Yard with him. I had mentioned a man called Roger Manpole once, hadn't I? There were one or two photographs he would like me to see and comment on.

III The glass and concrete beehive. The one thing modern architects can certainly do is design anonymous buildings. You could have found twenty like it in Tokyo or Hamburg or Chicago and been puzzled to know what the people did who worked there. You might have guessed a hospital or a TV studio before thinking it a police headquarters. Perhaps it had to be a bit of all three these days.

I'd thought Chalmers, though still polite enough, was a shade less respectful of me than when we first met, and after we talked a bit and I'd picked out one or two photos and I told him what I knew about the subjects, I said bluntly, "Maybe you wonder how I know so many of these characters, even by sight and reputation. Or I expect you've already had it all printed out, have you?"

He straightened up from the photographs. "I imagine you know most of them from the Cellini, don't you? It's a well-run gambling club; it's never stepped out of line by breaking any of the fairly strict regulations governing such places; but it's known to be a meeting place for a number of the criminal classes. Not the big names perhaps: We look elsewhere for them; but the borderline people, the fringe people who occasionally break out and cause us trouble. I expect a moralist would say that wherever you get high-stake gambling you inevitably attract such people. How long have you been a member, Sir David?"

"Oh . . . Sixteen, seventeen years. But what I meant was that I expect by now you've run my name through your computer and found that I've a record of a sort. One of the fringe people, in fact. In my jolly youth I spent four months in Pentonville."

He pulled his trousers up over his stomach and went to the window.

"As a matter of fact, we never did put you through the computer, Sir David."

"But you knew?"

"It was pointed out to us about a month ago."

"Who took the trouble to point?"

"That I'm not at liberty to say. But I have to tell you that it doesn't carry any weight with us."

"You surprise me."

The telephone rang and he briefly answered it and hung up.

"Don't get me wrong, sir. Of course our work is all about people with records. The average man who breaks the law more often than not has done it before, often in the same or a similar way, often in his youth; so inevitably we bear this in mind when looking at particular types of crimes and particular types of criminal. But we would be exceeding our brief if we allowed prejudice and suspicion to cloud our judgment in any way. Let me see, when were you—er—in prison?"

"1966."

"Fourteen years ago. Well, after ten years it is a breach of the Rehabilitation of Offenders Act to cite or speak of or publish details of any crimes committed by a person before that time."

"Or even to bear them in mind?"

"That may be too much to ask. But I assure you you're quite in the clear, Sir David, so far as we are concerned."

"And you would not have mentioned it if I hadn't mentioned it."

"Of course not."

I took out my car keys and weighed them in my hand. "But I take it it was no friend of mine who brought this little incident to your notice."

"I'm really not at liberty to say."

I listened to the rumble of the traffic. Going to be late for Erica's dinner. "D'you think I could ask your secretary to ring my wife, tell her I'm on my way."

"Of course. And thank you again for your help."

I stood up, stretching, suddenly feeling the long night, the short day.

"A pity we can't pin something on Roger Manpole."

"I haven't given up hope," said Chalmers.

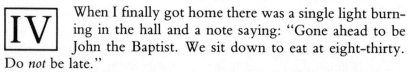 When I finally got home there was a single light burning in the hall and a note saying: "Gone ahead to be John the Baptist. We sit down to eat at eight-thirty. Do *not* be late."

It was eight o'clock then and I was tired and sweaty. I took a quick shower and while not yet dry pulled out a dinner jacket and black tie, found shoes; no socks (red socks, they would do); began dressing. I'd left the car at Owen's with instructions for it to be serviced, and reckoning anyway that it was easier to get a taxi from here. I could thumb a lift home with Erica at the end of the function. But when I went out all the taxis were busy. Eventually I found one and bundled in, clutching the thing I'd bought Erica in Edinburgh. It's all hell buying a present for a rich wife; she has everything except what you can't afford; in the end I'd found her a French bracelet with a few diamonds and sapphires. I knew she specially liked sapphires, but for £600 these obviously couldn't be top class. All the same it was pretty and was a gesture of good will and she couldn't throw it out as a trinket.

Park Lane was full of slow-moving stuff, and I reckoned I could have made it quicker jogging across the park. As I went up the steps of the hotel it was twenty minutes to nine. "Lady Abden's

party? Oh, yes, sir, in the Belvedere Room on the seventh floor."
"Thank you, I know my way."

Up in the lift, silently along the plush corridors; a waiter almost indistinguishable from the guests let me in. Laughter, talk, a bit high-pitched, they were already at supper, gilt mirrors reflecting endlessly the black coats and the sleek heads. Erica at the head in a brilliant sapphire-blue, off-the-shoulder dress, blue gloves to above the elbow, £20,000 diamond brooch at her breast; fine earrings too. Hair drawn up in the high, backcombed style showing elegant neck and shoulders.

They were laughing as the waiter brought me in, and she was the first to see me.

"Hi, David, come in, come in; we're only just through the caviar." To the waiter, "Bring some for my husband, while we pause for breath."

I was being offered a seat at the other end of the table. I sat down. My next-door neighbor was Derek Jones. On my left was a chap called Palmer who was a successful theatrical agent, good-looking but gaunt. Caviar and toast. Taittinger 1970. I picked up a knife and held it a few seconds unused.

This was a *male* gathering. Not a woman in sight except my own young wife at the other end. We reflected and multiplied through many mirrors, but still there wasn't a female to be seen.

I said to myself: Am I mad or is it true? This is the Belvedere Room on the seventh floor of the Dorchester Hotel, London, West One, on Tuesday the 16 September 1980. It is happening. It will be recorded in the books of the hotel that on that evening Lady Abden gave a party for eighteen people; the menu was . . . the wines served were . . . the cost was . . . A check in settlement was received the following week. Nobody will ever record, no one will ever remember that, except for the hostess—and just possibly the host—the entire party consisted of pansies.

As I began to eat I looked down the table and recognized many of them, men I'd met here and there, at parties, at dinner parties, at Erica's dinners. But never together before. Never all in one great bunch. Separately you'd hardly have noticed, but together they made strange sibilant sounds, whispers and titters and sighs. On either side of Erica were Steve and Tony, the two who got up my nose. Next to them was Lord Alfred Dugan (popularly known as Lord Alfred Douglas), with his latest boyfriend. Opposite him an elderly distinguished actor with his young Yugoslav companion. A top ballet dancer; the owner of a big restaurant; a couple of youngish "hons" recently out of the Guards. Some of these chaps I actually liked in isolation. Together they were a fist of talons shaken in my face.

"Take it easy, dear," said Derek, patting my arm. "Relax the old blood pressure. It'll all come out in the wash."

At the other end of the table Erica was in passionate conversation with Tony; catching my look she smiled politely and flapped four fingers in salutation.

My plate was taken away and another course was served: some sort of chicken; never knew what.

Wafts of talk up and down the table.

"I told the silly little cow she wasn't to touch it. But she got a dreadful thing about it, thought it was going to *explode* or something . . ."

"Well, it wasn't exactly a rosy rapture, my dear. But, you know, his hand resting casually on my thigh . . ."

"The bathroom didn't really suit us at all until Denis suggested a dash of surprise pink to take the cold out of the walls . . ."

"Well, you know what it's like when someone wants to play the Tragedy Queen at every opportunity . . ."

Everything was terribly *black*. Sixteen black coats like sixteen black crows all hissing and whispering on their branches in their desperate jargon, and all multiplied by trick mirrors. This was a dream, it couldn't be *true*.

The chap Palmer was trying to interest me in an account of some play he'd just got put on at the Royal Court, about a man who raped his daughter and the resultant child had spina bifida.

In between times Derek asked me about Scotland.

I said, "I could murder that woman."

"Hush, dear, don't holler so. It's just her little joke . . . By the by, I suppose you know both Vince and Gerry are still in the clink. Police have opposed bail all along. Same with Laval. Quite a holocaust."

"So you're not in it."

"Would you suppose it! Nanny always insisted I should keep my nose clean and my feet dry."

"The point is," Palmer was saying, "the daughter, Marietta, comes to dominate over her father, and the child over *both*. It's a three-tier drama with very poignant symbolism. *Do* make an effort to see it while you can. Kevin Smithson is quite superb as the child. First night there was hardly a dry eye."

I don't know if time passed or whether it happened next, but sometime a bit later the clown Tony got up and began to make a speech.

The words washed over me. "Well, dear hearts, we are here to wish our dear little scrub a happy, happy birthday. In this gay mad world there really aren't many like her. Unique, my dears. Erica the unique. She sits among us but metaphorically she is atop a pedestal, and not one of us would dare to stretch out a finger to bring her down to the level of us unfortunate *males*." (Laughter, as they say.) "David down there is *married* to her—yes, married to her, would you *believe*—lucky sweep! No wonder he looks like a cat that's been at the cream." (More laughter. Or perhaps I should say titters.)

This went on for a bit. I didn't even know if I was smiling at him or scowling, as if the cream had turned sour. Then he turned to Erica, drips of excited champagne spilling from his glass. "It's your very own birthday, darling, and we wish you just everything a girl could wish for: health, wealth, wine, song, and connubial bliss, all gift wrapped for the rest of your natural . . ."

We were standing on our feet, drinking champagne. We were sitting down. Erica had got up, to high-pitched squeals of applause.

She said—or I think she said, "Tony and all. Thank you for the presents you brought. I won't say you shouldn't have bothered, because you *should*." (Titters.) "All these divine things. Even though my husband—that dark man glowering at the end of the table, who's not even wished me a happy birthday yet—even though he works—intermittently—for a perfumery firm, he keeps me very short on home products; so I shall have the *loveliest* time bathing in all these *delicious* essences you've given me from all the rival establishments." (Titters.)

This also went on for a bit. The champagne was working in her, and she was being quite bright and witty. She always had been witty, from the moment I first met her. Her father was a dull man, her mother a dull woman. But somehow the genes had blended to produce this razor-sharp—rapier-sharp—female with the lightness of foot and quickness of intellect to be one of our champion fencers and, when she felt like it, one of our champion bitches. What *was* this in aid of? Was it all calculated as a great slap in the face for me? Or had she already invited this scrum before she even knew I was going to be here? Trying to provoke a reaction? She'd certainly done that! I wanted to strangle someone.

She was ending. "This modest little get-together of some of my oldest—and dare I say oddest?—friends . . ." (Another titter) ". . . is just to celebrate my first quarter-century plus one. Drink your drinks and finish your cheeses and then maybe we'll have a dance. Eh?" She looked directly down the table at me, eyes glittering. "Eh? Let's clear the table and have a dance. Perhaps not the Gay Gordons. That would be too rowdy. A more delicate, intricate dance, which we might call—which we might call—the Gay Abdens!"

A laugh, but this time it was a halfhearted one. Beady eyes were on me from all down the table. Crow's eyes. Weasel's eyes. Cobra's eyes. Assessing. Wondering. This really *was* something to gossip about at the Jacuzzi tomorrow. Poor, dear David. One *wondered*. Hadn't he really been up to it? There were rumors, of course. *And* he'd been with Derek at one time.

I got up. "Thank you, dear," I said. "Message received." I dropped my champagne glass on the floor. "Oh, sorry. Look what I've done. Careless, careless." I picked up another and dropped that too. "You'll notice. Not even house-trained." A waiter made a movement but I stopped him. "That's all. Just a little frolic. Happy birthday, dear. After all, a quarter of a century plus one is rather a long time to be alive. Many happy returns."

I put my hand on Derek's shoulder as he began to get up. "Sit down. It is all over. Uncle David is going to bed. All by himself. It makes a welcome change."

I went out. A waiter anxiously followed me. "Did you leave a coat, sir?" I shook my head. "No, and I'm not going to *steal* any. Go back and see to your *guests*."

CHAPTER TWENTY-EIGHT

I The lift was a long time coming. Some damned fool seemed to be working his way up and down. Outside it was a fine night but cool after that overheated room. I walked down Park Lane and then crossed into the park. I sat on a seat for a bit; there were a couple of people at the other end smoking pot; the smell drifted across. I went on. I got back to the flat. No idea of the time. Maybe I looked at the clocks without taking in what was on them. Coffee seemed a good idea to break the fumes of the champagne. But something much stronger was really needed. Not alcoholic; a barbiturate or maybe an old-fashioned leech to drain off some of the overheated blood. The bad blood.

I kept taking deep breaths. That was supposed to steady you. Only, if you took too many, you passed out. That wouldn't do yet awhile. Not until I had got right away from here. I went into my bedroom. The case I'd brought from Scotland was still packed. That would do. I pulled a second case out of the wardrobe and began to stuff a few personal things in it.

The telephone rang. I went into the living room and picked up several books that belonged to me, went to a drawer and fished out some papers. Really, most of the things were hers; I'd no interest in them. Even in Red Place my own personal possessions had been minimal. The telephone stopped.

The kettle was boiling and I made strong coffee. Into her bedroom and to her medicine cupboard, swallow a couple of aspirin, the hot coffee scalding. At the nightmare party I'd just left a fair amount of champagne had gone down. I am not by choice a champagne drinker, claret and burgundy being preferred. Erica had always been the one for champagne.

The suitcase was nearly full and I would have to take a second one. (Third, counting the one that had come back from Scotland.) Not worth getting the car out again tonight. A taxi would take me to Claridge's, where they'd probably try to squeeze me in.

The telephone rang again. Francis wanting to talk to Erica about her lessons? One of Erica's female friends ringing up for a chat? Mrs. Whatsit who came in tomorrow couldn't come because her little girl was off school with a chill? *Burr-burr, burr-burr.* Some people wouldn't take no for an answer. Or Chalmers had some last-minute question he'd forgotten to ask me? There's nothing so tyrannical as a telephone. *Yak-yak, yak-yak.* I went in and snatched the thing off its hook.

"Yes?"

"David? This is Shona. I thought you were returning today. Have I caught you at an inconvenient moment?"

"Yes."

"Well, I am sorry to bother you on your first night home. But there is a meeting tomorrow at Moorgate. Our stockbrokers, with accountants and two men from Morgan Greenfell. I have had to make a number of decisions about the stock issue without your help."

"Ah," I said.

"David, I am sure this is not the proper moment to discuss what your future with the firm will be; but I should value your advice on matters of detail. The notice will be in the papers next week. I am told the shares will be heavily oversubscribed, but the wording of the announcement does not please me. It is something we have to decide tomorrow. That and other things we need to talk of. Can you come?"

"When?"

"Tomorrow morning at ten-thirty. 91 Moorgate. I have ordered a car for myself, so if you came to my flat by nine forty-five we could go together."

"Ah," I said.

She waited. "Well, do you think you could come?"

I said, "I don't know."

"Are you all right, David?"

"Why shouldn't I be?"

"You sound strained."

"I am strained."

"Is Erica with you?"

"She's giving a party at the Dorchester."

"Why are you not there?"

"I just left."

I was waiting to thump down the receiver.

She said, "Perhaps I could ring you in the morning. About eight. Would that do?"

"I shan't be here."

"Where will you be, then?"

"Some hotel."

"What has happened? Have you quarreled with Erica again?"

"You could say that."

"What has she done this time?"

"It's too boring to tell you. But I'm getting out once again."

"Of the flat?"

"Of her life."

"David, she has not been happy while you have been away. She has been very strange. You need to have patience."

"Long past time, Shona," I said. "The ship's on the rocks. Running repairs are out of date."

I banged down the telephone. Shona bored me. Erica bored me. Maybe all women bored me. Careful! Not Alison too! That certainly can't be true. I was tired and fed up. Just tired and fed up with *life*.

The second case had a defective clasp. Too pathetic that a potentially well-to-do baronet with a rich wife should have to pack his things in a tatty old case with a broken clasp. (In fact it wasn't tatty or old, having been bought in New York and of fine white pigskin; but what the hell was the use of a handsome case with a broken catch? Who the hell ever repaired broken catches these days? Once a small thing broke on a suitcase you might as well stuff it in the dustbin.)

Better take my extra things from the bathroom: spare razor, toothpaste, a few other odds and ends. In the living room books on fencing. Crosnier. Unlikely I'd ever use *these* again. Never mind, they were mine, I grabbed them up.

Some of the clothes I could send for; no point in arriving at Claridge's or wherever looking like a refugee from a fire. I suddenly saw myself in the mirror in black tie and dinner suit. Must be pretty crazy; these I could leave behind.

As I changed trousers, flung them over a chair, I heard the front door bang. I pulled off my shirt, tearing the armhole, put on a gray striped one, tucked it into the waistband of a pair of slacks, found a gray tie.

Footstep. Door open. Erica there.

She was wearing a white mink coat over her blue dress. Her face was hard, the smile lines turned down.

"Where are you off now?" she said.

I began to knot my tie.

"Going home to Mother?" she asked.

"You're back soon," I said. "Did your friends need their beauty sleep?"

She watched me. The tie had got stuck, and I carefully took it off, knotted it again. I hung my dinner suit in the wardrobe, put on a tweed jacket.

"As a matter of fact," she said, "I thought it was a good joke. Everybody did except you."

"Ah," I said, "you know what it is: Scottish lack of humor."

"Lack of something. Could it be conviction?"

I began to transfer my wallet and other things from one jacket to the other. "Conviction of what?"

"You tell me."

"No," I said, turning to stare her down. "You tell *me!*"

She smiled a bit crookedly. "Everyone else in that room knew where they stood. So they saw the joke. You didn't. *Quod erat,* as they used to say at school."

"This is the last time we ever need meet," I said, "so finish what you want to say."

"Why? Why slink out? What are you afraid of, David?"

"Strangling you," I said.

She laughed. "Take me to bed. Prove what you can prove. My neck's waiting for you."

A sudden lurch of desire came on me for this woman. But there was so much anger in it I drew back.

"Erica," I said wearily. "It's finished. Go away. Let me leave in peace."

She said, "To think I stood them up to come back and see you. Well, well . . . God, I need a drink!"

It was the last thing she needed in my opinion, but anything to get her away from the door. She went out, and as I finished my packing, I heard the kitchen table being moved and thought, what's she up to now?

I glowered around the room. Find a permanent place, then send someone over for what's left. *Leave* the case with the broken clasp: You can't go migrating round London at this time of night with more suitcases than you can carry. For that matter Erica can burn the lot.

Two ways out of my bedroom: one through hers and one through my bathroom, which had a second door leading into the kitchen. Not sure which way the cat would be likely to jump, so chose the kitchen.

She was there.

There in the opposite doorway. Quick as light, she'd got out of her evening clothes and into her fencing array. Black mask, tight trousers, white padded tunic, gym shoes, the one fighting hand gloved. In her hand was her sword. When I stopped in the doorway she pointed her sword at the table. On it were my fencing clothes and my weapon.

"On guard," she said.

Bags in hand, I took a deep breath and looked at her.

I said, "Go and jump in the Serpentine. It will cool you off."

"Your kit's there," she said. "Put it on. Spare a spar for an old scrub."

"Take your jokes elsewhere."

"No joke, boy. I'll pin you to that wall."

She came forward a yard or so and made a lunge in my direction. She was deliberately short, but the point seemed not too far from my face. It continued to flicker in the bright neon light, in and out, up and down. I noticed her footwork was good; champagne hadn't impeded that.

I said, "I'll send round for the rest of my stuff tomorrow."

"Scared to try me?" she said. "I'll bet you a hundred pounds I score ten hits to your one."

I took another step forward and she gave me a prick on the arm.

"Old times' sake," she said. "Fight me and we'll go to bed together."

"You fool!" I shouted. "Take *no* for an answer!"

She pricked me on the neck. "You can't *dérober*. It's too late."

I put the cases down. "What are you trying to *do*, Erica, patch up a broken bottle? There's nothing *left*!"

She jabbed me in the other arm. In temper I swung round and picked up my sword from the table, made a fierce hacking sweep at her with the blade. She danced easily out of reach. I pointed my épée at her and the two swords clashed.

"Put your things on," she said, "otherwise I might hurt you."

I said, "Get out of the way!"

The swords clashed again. I made a lunge at her and she took the point on hers; sidestepping and executing the perfect parry.

"Aah!" she shouted, as her point made a small rip in my coat.

I was almost at the door but she counterattacked swiftly, and I had to stop in my tracks and back away from a series of sharp probing jabs that came near to my sword arm.

"First blood!" she said. "Put your things on! I can't fight you like this!"

There was a trickle of something coming down to my wrist. She was laughing.

"Armistice!" she declared, lowering her weapon. "I give you two minutes to put your things on."

I grabbed one suitcase, but instantly she was in fencing position again. I flung the bag aside, grabbed my mask and put it on. We squared up again.

"You're still at risk!" she said, and *"Aah!"* as her blade found my shoulder. "Two up and eight to go. Hundred pounds if you score more than one to my ten! Come on, husband, be a man, if you can be. Otherwise I shall go back to my fancy boys!"

Thereafter we fought in earnest. She scored twice more almost at once, pricks made with enormous ease and skill. Anger gripping my bowels, I tried the flèche, which I can only describe as a swift run forward, point directly at an opponent, depending for its success largely on surprise. It was fatal against someone as good as Erica. She stop-hit it with ease and cut at my gloved hand as I recovered my position.

"Aah!" she shouted again. "Five."

We sparred around and I kicked my other bag out of the way. She scored again, a nasty little nick below the ribs—my own damned fault, of course; the padded jacket lay on the table. But pride and anger were too stiff.

For a change she decided to attack, and for her that was equally a mistake. A normal skillful opponent will riposte or parry and give ground in a normal way. I wasn't a normal opponent. I knew what it was like to fight a man with a torch and a pair of fists and knock him down and bash him about the head: I knew the pleasure of it, I knew the thrill of it; and there was blood on my wrist and blood on my neck.

She came at me. God knows what she was attempting: I imagine a lunge followed by a *redoublement*, which is more or less a renewal of the preliminary lunge if the opponent fails to parry or riposte. I refused to do any such thing. I held my sword stiffly at her as she came forward, and her sword jarred and slid off my mask. Mine sank in.

"Aah! she cried it seemed in triumph, but as it faded it changed into a gurgle.

I tried to withdraw my épée. It came, but Erica came with it. Then the sword came free and was a crimson color. Erica stood upright, probably staring at me, but I couldn't tell for the mask. I half raised my weapon again expecting some new attack on her part. Instead there was a terrible retching sound. She staggered and dropped her own sword, went down on one knee, then got up again, clinging to the table. She was coughing. Blood was dripping from the mask. She walked round the table like a blind woman looking for a way out.

"Erica!" I said. "What the *hell*! . . ."

She tried to get the mask off. It might have been glued to her face. I dropped my sword and went to help her. As I took the mask off, her face and head drooped slowly away from it toward the floor. There was a sound like sawing wood as she tried to breathe.

 I don't know what I said to the Dial 999 girl or what she said to me but it seemed to take longer than it should.

When I'd banged the telephone down, I stumbled back into the kitchen. I'd fetched a pillow and tried to unbutton and unlace her jacket. She was lying quite still, her eyes half open—you could see their blueness—I'd pressed a flannel against the wound in her neck. There'd been a lot of blood to begin but now not so much. I spoke to her a couple of times but she didn't answer. I tried to feel her pulse and thought it was there, very faint, or that I was imagining it. I wiped the blood off my own wrist as the front-door bell rang.

Well, they've been quick. Or maybe time, more time has passed than I think. I get to my feet—should have left the door ajar. Out into the passage and to the front door. Not the fire brigade, not the ambulance, not the police. Shona.

"I'm sorry David. I thought—My God, what is the matter? . . ."

I say, "I think I've just killed Erica."

She comes in. Her face goes gray and patched. She takes me by the arm and pulls me round again. "*What* are you saying, David? What is this you are *talking* about?"

"In the kitchen," I say. "She's there in the kitchen. Just go and see."

She hesitates, looking into my face, then goes off. When I get to the kitchen door she is kneeling beside my wife, lifting the flannel gently, putting practiced fingers to her heart. In old Mother Russia, of course, she learned first aid. Like she'd shown that time at the motor accident.

"Get a doctor!"

"An ambulance. I dialed. I thought you were it. Is she . . . ?"

"I do not know. Oh, my God, what has happened?"

"We were fencing."

"Fencing? In heaven's name, man! You told me she was at the Dorchester and you were leaving her! You sounded so upset I thought I would come round."

I was feeling very sick. "She came back, didn't want me to leave—challenged me to fence. I told her, go to the devil. She wouldn't let me get out. So I fenced with her."

"Was she wearing her mask?"

"Of course."

"Oh my God, oh my God, oh my God! What a thing! My poor Erica! My poor David!"

I begin to talk, suddenly the words spill out as if they're blood from a punctured vein. I say, "This has all happened before, hasn't it? I killed my father, much this way, half accident, half purpose; he didn't fall, bang his head on the stove, you know; I hit him with the iron bar; it was all hushed up; my mother and her boyfriend, Kenneth Kingsley, they made up this story to deceive the police. I was eleven. Now I'm thirty-seven. History has this habit of repeating itself. Criminal tendencies will out, that's how the police work and—"

Shona has got up and taken me by the shoulders. "Listen to me, David, listen. Are you *listening*? Can you attend to what I say?"

"What? I tell you he didn't bang his head—"

"David, whatever you *think* happened to your father, *this* could only have been an accident! This gear, this mask, this protective jacket should be proof against *anything*! Don't you understand? Even if you'd *wanted* to wound her you shouldn't have been *able* to. It was the purest accident. Don't tell me people do not rush at each other on the fencing *piste*! Sometimes they are like wild beasts, charging: You have seen enough to know the truth of that! So this was an accident. Understand, an *accident*. Do not be a fool and say you stabbed your wife deliberately or it will be misunderstood. *You should not have been able to do so. Can you hear me?*"

"They're at the door now," I say. "Let them in."

III I don't remember much about the next half hour. I vomited for a while and was then in shock, as they call it. I suppose I was entitled to be a bit off center, taking everything into account. A man, even one like me, doesn't knock off his wife every day of the week.

I was told afterward the police came first in a Panda car. A detective constable and a police woman. They went right in and the policewoman tried mouth-to-mouth resuscitation and then the policeman came out and a couple of minutes later the ambulance and a doctor arrived.

I was in the living room by this time but I just couldn't concentrate to answer questions. It's a funny feeling, this policeman has come out of the kitchen and asks you something and your tongue bulks up and you as near as hell keel over again. You'd have thought good old David was better on his mental pins than that.

What's slightly worse is that you can quite clearly hear Shona talking. She's in a gray worsted frock, I remember, and a yellow scarf and her hair has grown longer again and she doesn't look well, and you wonder if she's been ill while you've been having it off with the beautiful Alison in Ullapool. But what she's saying is outrageous. *Outrageous.*

While people are walking in and out and a stretcher comes in and, after a bit, goes out again, she's saying to this detective constable and the policewoman that she has been *here all the time.* She's saying that she called to see the Abdens about ten, as Sir David has been away for some weeks and there is a company stock issue looming in which Sir David is to play a central part. And she's saying she arrived just after Sir David returned from a dinner at the Dorchester and was followed by Lady Abden a few minutes later. And she's saying that Lady Abden—who is of course a distinguished international fencer—suggested that they should spar for a few minutes in the kitchen, which has been their habit and custom every evening since they married eighteen months ago. And Sir David was reluctant and wished to talk business with Mme. Shona, but Lady Abden pressed him to take a turn with her as a joke.

And she is saying—the bitch Shona is saying—that she was a witness to the whole contest, which, like many others she has seen, was conducted in perfect propriety, with masks and protective clothing, and the accident, which is quite inexplicable to her, occurred in the course of this normal, conventional and totally orthodox bout. And she is saying that she thinks the point of the sword must have broken.

You bitch, I feel like shouting, you're covering up for me, just the way my bitch of a mother covered up for me once before. My husband seemed to overbalance and turned as he did so, catching his head on the rail of the Aga as he fell. Not true. I hit him across the head with the heavy iron handle that you use to empty an Aga stove and the blood gushed down his face and he fell over backward, clutching the rail of the stove as he fell. But he wasn't dead; he crawled across the kitchen like a half-crushed beetle and my mother rushed to help him up. But he never got up; he just got half up and pulled a chair over with him, and half got up again, twitching while he did so, and clutched at my mother, and slowly sank down and twitched a good bit more before he died in her arms. It was almost as good as Mercutio.

Did I want to kill him? Who knows? I wanted to hit him and stop him and punish him, just as I wanted to hit and stop and punish Erica. Bloody murder, that's what it is; don't try to make excuses, you Russian bitch. I did it, I did it, I did it, I did it, I did it, I did it.

And the policeman is on one knee beside me, because I've got my head in my hands, and he's saying, "Your wife has been taken to hospital, Sir David. I'm sure they'll do everything they can. If you and this lady would like to follow, we can give you a lift in our car." And Shona is thanking them and saying we'll go; and then at the last there's a few minutes' wait until two more policemen turn up to take charge of the flat. One of them is an inspector who has to be told part of it over again. And the detective constable has already taken notes of what I've said and what Shona has said, and his little notebook is back again buttoned up in his breast pocket, all proper as pie.

Of course I know it's no use going to the hospital: They have to try all the latest drugs to reactivate a dying person; but when someone has a hole in the jugular modern science doesn't have much of a remedy.

CHAPTER TWENTY-NINE

I Shona has taken charge. She's taken charge. She's been helpful in her own way. I sleep in the spare bedroom in her flat for the first two days, clutching at pillows and wrestling and turning; but then I go back to Knightsbridge and see it through on my own. The maids come as usual, and then her mother and father come. They stay at the Hyde Park Hotel, thank God, but they see me and I try to tell them what has happened—he lumbering and dazed with grief, she looking at me with Erica's eyes, damp with crying and puzzled, seeking something from me that I can't give. She was their only one, on whom they'd lavished everything. Too much. They gave her too much too soon. But what have I given her? A sword jab in the throat. That's it, isn't it?

But lying by omission already—the first time in this affair. You can't say outright to them, yes, I meant to kill off your daughter because she was a spoiled slut who irritated me beyond endurance and I wanted her out of the way. Because it's not true. She drove me wild but I never meant to do that. Or did I? Not consciously. But in a split second does the subconscious take over? Like other times. There were too many other times.

Shona had muttered in my ear so often and so much, talking to me, willing me, driving me—even saying that if I denied her story she'd be prosecuted for perjury. But in the end you don't deliberately take on the role of stunned husband—it falls on you like a winter overcoat. It wouldn't last. How could it last through the inquest?

Edmond Gale walked with a polio limp, had big eyes and a careful manner. Shona had taken me unwillingly to see him. Well-known barrister. He would attend the inquest to look after my interests. I muttered that my interests were plain: I'd killed my wife in unfair fight and should be prepared to take the consequences.

"In what way was the fight unfair?" he asked.

"Man against a woman."

"Even if the man was a novice and the woman one of the leading exponents in the country?"

"Brute force," I said.

Gale coughed into his fist. "I think, Sir David, this is a matter for the experts rather than for ourselves. Force on the point of a rapier is largely a matter of timing, and timing is a matter of high technique. With such technique I should suppose a woman is as capable of a lethal thrust as a man. You were practicing, with her choice of weapons and at her request. You should leave it to the coroner—or his jury—to decide whether there was any measure of unfairness in the contest."

"Will there be a jury?" asked Shona.

"I don't think so. But—er—there has been a slight complication. I believe the police have received one or two letters informing them of threats you made earlier that evening, at some party, as the result of some quarrel you had with Lady Abden . . ."

"Yes."

He waited but I said no more. I sat and said nothing. All you had to do was wheel Dr. Meiss on. Eventually Gale said, "It will be a matter of whether the coroner, in consultation with the police, decides to call a jury. He may well think that these are merely unsavory rumors which often occur when there is a sudden death. Or he may take the view that a jury's verdict will be more likely to clear the air."

"Who is to be the coroner? Do you know?" Shona asked.

"Reginald Summit. He practiced at the Bar for a time, chiefly trade union law. A hard man but fair, I think."

"I just want it over," I said.

On the Sunday Derek Jones rang. He said, "Really, David, what a tragedy! My heart bleeds. It was utterly an accident, of course?"

"What the hell d'you mean?"

"Well, after that row you had at the party. D'you know I think Erica was having us *all* on that night. Poor Erica! Never tell with the little girl, could you? Oh, it *was* all planned as a special surprise for you. She was very down in the mouth when she thought you were not going to turn up. *Hamlet* without the Prince, she said. Or do I mean Princess? You know what she was like, couldn't resist the quip."

I said, "Derek, I don't want to talk."

"Sorry. I'm sure you don't. I just wanted to say—"

"Forget it."

"I just wanted to say it was so *unfortunate* you made that remark. 'I could kill that woman.' And Reg Palmer overheard it. I wanted you to know that if anything comes up about it at the inquest I'm not the one responsible."

"OK."

"You know, matey, I hate to be thought true-blue or anything of that sort, but I don't split on friends."

"Glad to know it." My head was aching and drink wasn't going to do any good. Two of those pills the medic had given me might save me from the worst nightmares.

"By the way," he said, "maybe you know, the lads were committed for trial."

"What lads?"

"Bickmaster and the rest. It all happened at same magistrates' court. On Wednesday. The day after this happened." When I didn't speak he went on, "So they'll be languishing in durance vile for a couple of months before the trial comes on."

"Derek, I'm going to hang up now."

"Right, old dear. I'll not be there on Monday cheering or anything. But when it's over, *if* it's over, you'd do well to go away for a bit."

"Why?"

"Oh, *you* know, dear. Some of the lads stick together."

I hung up, and when the line was clear I took the receiver off again and left it off.

II Memory is a funny old joker. It pretends not to recall something, though you know if you were challenged you'd have to admit it's somewhere just under the crust. Then something fairly basic—such as killing your wife— makes a little nick in the crust and out everything pops as dark and as clear-cut as a witch's profile.

All that hour was back with me; I could even remember the smells of the kitchen. There'd been something boiling on the Aga and it had boiled over and begun to hiss and spit before someone took it off, and there was the smell of burned potatoes. And the mat had twisted up in the struggle, and lay away from the stove almost like another body. And my father's overcoat was on the chair where he'd thrown it when he first came in: green-brown Harris tweed, belted, a bit shabby, with a handkerchief half out of the pocket; he'd been too cronked to hang it up. And my mother's shoe had fallen off, and the metal handle was cold in my hand before I let it drop, and I kept wiping my sleeve across my nose trying to stop it running; the tears seemed to be coming out of the wrong place.

The inquest—this inquest—was at Horseferry Road, and they'd decided not to have a jury. Reginald Summit wore a black tie and a wing collar and looked like an undertaker. Very bald, with a voice that sounded as if it was coming out of a microphone troubled with static. Mr. and Mrs. Lease were nearby; they'd taken it well, considering; if I'd been in their shoes I'd have been applying for a hunting license.

The detective constable was first in the box and gave his evidence out of that nice neat little buttoned-down notebook. On the night of Tuesday last, etc. . . . Called to flat No. 24 on a 999 emergency, went in and found the deceased lying in the kitchen suffering from a severe throat wound. Very considerable bleeding . . . Police-woman Mary Wallace attempted to do what she could . . . Could feel no pulse . . . after the arrival of the ambulance, returned to the sitting room where deceased's husband appeared in a state of shock . . .

"Yes, yes," said the coroner, "a little more slowly, Constable. The husband, you say, appeared to be in a state of shock. How did he appear so? What brought you to that conclusion?"

"Well, sir, he had his head in his hands and seemed hardly to take any notice of what I was asking him. Just sat there, muttering to himself."

"Could you hear what he was muttering?"

"Well, some of it, sir. He kept saying, 'I've killed her, I've killed her.' Over and over again."

"Nothing more than that? Just 'I've killed her'? He didn't enlarge on it—try to tell you how it had happened?"

"No, sir. The other lady, Mrs. Carreros, she explained what she had seen."

"Never mind that. We shall be able to call her, shan't we."

Stupid to hear her called Mrs. Carreros. Brought her down to earth. Should have been Mme. Shona. Why hadn't she insisted on it? This had all happened in another kitchen, hadn't it, for Christ's sake? Did one's life run in repeating ruts? But such a different kitchen. This one was big enough for a squash court. The other, that other, had been too small for fun and games; we'd just fallen over each other in it, in a complicated dance of drunkenness, envy, jealousy, love and death. And in the middle of it a boy with a heavy iron handle . . .

Mr. Gale asked the detective one or two questions, but I couldn't remember what, and then the doctor took the stand. Cause of death was severance of the carotid artery by the broken end of an épée or fencing sword. The sword was of Russian manufacture, a type much favored by the Amateur Fencing Association, and had broken off about three inches from the tip. The sharp point had penetrated the gap between the fencer's jacket and her protective mask and bib. The blade had pierced the throat and Lady Abden had almost certainly been dead when he arrived. However, he had thought it proper to inject a heart stimulant and to have her taken immediately to hospital. By the time they reached the hospital life was certainly extinct.

Extinct. Odd word. It meant nothingness, it meant what was left after a wild panic blow to the head or a fierce jabbing thrust. They weren't there any longer. Flies swatted away. Nobody knew where they were. They'd absented themselves permanently from the scene, just a decaying body in a casket left behind.

Mr. Gale had nothing to ask the doctor, but some other type got up, who, it seemed, represented the makers of the protective clothing. Did the witness think? . . . Could he agree that if? . . . I tried not to yawn. I knew it would be looked on as callous and insensitive to yawn. I remembered old Meiss once all those years ago asking me, just when I was yawning at him, if I had ever had any impulses to kill him, because if so it was not just him I was thinking of killing but the whole of my past, schooldays, family memories, associations. I must learn, he said, to live surrounded by my past but not fixed to unalterable emotional patterns. Had he *really* said that, to a boy of eleven, or had I dreamed it up in some sort of folk memory since?

Shona was in the box. Never saw her move but she was there. *Wham.* She looked slim, proud, Russian, but elderly. Everything she wore built up the picture. Yes, she was Mme. Shona, the perfumer. Yes, she had known the deceased for many years. Yes, Sir David was the manager of her perfumery firm and was shortly to become a director. Yes, she had arrived that night and witnessed the practice fencing. Sir David had in fact been very reluctant to engage in this practice, because he wanted to discuss with her the flotation of the company. Lady Abden had insisted on challenging him, and eventually, to satisfy her, Sir David had picked up his weapon, put on his mask and fenced with her. So far as she, Mme. Shona, could see—and she was an experienced fencer herself—there was nothing out of the ordinary in the bout, and she had been calling the hits as they were made, when Lady Abden made a sudden running attack at her husband; he had partly sidestepped, and the blade in his hand had gone under her protective mask. What a liar, I thought. Shall I stand up and shout at everybody in court what a blinding, dyed-in-the-wool, up-to-the-crop, stark, unmitigated liar she is? But the chance'll come yet. They're going to call me.

Francis Norbury came next. He described himself as a "master coach" and Lady Abden's teacher. Both Sir David and Lady Abden were members of the Sloane Gymnasium Amateur Fencing Association, and had in fact first met in the fencing hall. Sir David was a fair, adequate performer but not with a sufficient technique for any real excellence; but Miss Lease, as she then was, was one of the outstanding young women fencers of the day, and had only just missed being picked for the Olympics. Then there was a lot of stuff about the strength of the protective mask, the four layers of cloth for the jacket, the 5 mm thick bit of reinforced plastic foam and canvas. There had apparently been two other fatalities in modern fencing, one in Hungary two years ago, when again a blade had snapped and the end had slipped through the gap between the safety mesh and the jacket; an earlier one, nine years ago, in England, when a young man had been struck in the head by a blade. Since her death the safety equipment worn by Lady Abden had been examined and had seemed satisfactory in every way except perhaps that the bib had a tendency to curl upward, thus very slightly accentuating the existence of a gap between the bib and the collar of the jacket. Norbury said he was convinced the accident could only have occurred as a freak, and pointed to the tremendous safety record the sport had, seeing that some five thousand people fenced every week of the year.

Summit then asked if it wasn't unusual for men and women to fence against each other. In competition, Norbury said, it was never done. But in practice quite often, though usually when one was the teacher and the other the pupil.

Norbury drifted away and Summit held up proceedings for a couple of minutes while he finished his autobiography. Then he said, "I have no wish to add to any disagreeable publicity which has attached itself to this case; but it appears that shortly before the tragedy a dinner party took place at a well-known London hotel, given by Sir David and Lady Abden, and the police have been approached by two guests at the party who wish to give evidence. This seems the most appropriate moment to call them."

I hadn't seen Palmer in the court, but there he was picking his way toward the witness box, stooping and theatrical and gaunt. To look at him you'd never have thought his fancy was teenage boys.

He had, he said, been a guest at a party given by Sir David and Lady Abden to celebrate her twenty-sixth birthday. There were about a score of guests. Sir David had arrived very late and had looked angry and disheveled. He did not greet his wife, but sat down at the other end of the table, next to him, Palmer, and carried on little or no conversation with anyone. Lady Abden's attempts to bring him into the generally jolly mood of the party fell completely flat. He ate little and drank only champagne in considerable amounts. In the course of the dinner one of the few remarks he made which was audible to most of the table was, "I'm going to murder that woman." A few minutes later he smashed two champagne glasses on the floor and left.

Mr. Gale got up awkwardly on his peg leg and bowed slightly to the coroner, who cleared his throat of static and nodded.

Mr. Gale said, "Is it your opinion that Sir David was intoxicated?"

Palmer licked his lips. "He seemed to have had a lot to drink."

"With the coroner's permission I will recall Mrs. Carreros to the stand, but I understood her to say that was not her impression. Have you known Sir David long?"

"About eighteen months."

"Since his marriage, in fact? Did you know Lady Abden before that?"

"Oh, yes. About seven or eight years."

"Are *you* married?"

"No."

"But you must know many married people who in a moment of frustration will say of their wives, 'I could murder that woman,' or, if it is the other way round, 'I could murder that man.' "

"This seemed to me more than just frustration."

"It seemed to you. But it must surely be a matter of opinion in what tone it was spoken."

"I have given you my opinion."

"Just so . . ." Mr. Gale hitched himself on to his other leg. "Now, Mr. Palmer, you are, I understand, a theatrical agent who at times helps to put packages together in the West End for the production of experimental plays."

"Not only in the West End. And not only experimental."

"Is it true that Lady Abden sometimes helped you with the financing of such ventures?"

Palmer smiled. "We call them angels. There are quite a number of such people who like to help in this way."

"Is it true that Lady Abden has not helped you since her marriage?"

"As it happens, yes. But we were still on the best of terms."

"With her husband as well?"

"Er—yes, I think so."

"Is it true that you made a special effort to interest her in the play you have recently put on at the Royal Court Theatre and that, in refusing to help you, she said that her husband had advised against it?"

Now where in hell, I thought, has he got such an idea? It was news to me; Erica would never have consulted me on such a thing.

Palmer said curtly, "I am not giving this testimony today out of enmity for Sir David Abden."

"Thank you, Mr. Palmer."

The coroner had got a cold: that was all that was wrong with his voice. After he'd tuned in again he said, "Was it your impression that Sir David Abden and his wife were usually on good terms with each other—that this could well have been just a lovers' quarrel?"

"I saw too little of them to say. I can only assure you, sir, of the genuineness of this quarrel."

Genuine enough, I thought. All my quarrels are genuine; they boil up in a moment, whether it's shaking a Mafia boss till he drops his drink or stabbing my wife. If only my ego would get out of the way—was that it?—something to stop me doing these things; if only I were paralyzed all over. But this ganging up against me by people who pretended they were quite impartial . . .

Steve Houseman was saying he had been at the dinner party and that he had witnessed the quarrel, heard me threaten my wife, and she had expressed her anxiety about going home, yet feeling she must do so, with her husband being in such a violent mood. My arrival, he said, had cast a complete blight on the birthday party, and the other guests had gone home soon afterward.

Then little Edmond Gale was on his feet again. Witness had spoken of Sir David being violent. What evidence did he have that Sir David was a violent man?

I could provide plenty. Steve said, "Well, throwing those two glasses like that. I'd call that violent, I really would, wouldn't you?"

"The previous witness has spoken of Sir David *dropping* two glasses. Do you insist that he threw them? And if so, what at?"

"Well, on the floor—he threw them on the floor. I thought, *what a frightful temper!*"

"This was a large dinner party, Mr. Houseman? Eighteen, I believe. I suppose it was like any other party, was it, people eating and drinking and talking, waiters moving about?"

"Well, naturally."

"Where were you sitting?"

"On the right of my hostess."

"Yet you were quite able to hear what Sir David said about his wife, separated as you were from him by about eight people?"

"Yes, of course I was."

"You were very friendly with Lady Abden?"

"Well, I've known her for simply ages."

"And Sir David? A newer friend?"

Steve tossed his head. "Oh, I've nothing against him."

The coroner was looking at the clock. He compared it with his own watch, then nodded to the clerk.

"Sir David Abden."

Someone gave me a nudge on the shoulder, otherwise I probably wouldn't have recognized the call. I got up and made a wandering way to the box. Scruffy old book. How many tearful hands had grabbed it, how many lies spilled over it? Were mine going to make it worse?

Close to, the coroner was an older man than I thought. One eye was bloodshot. Summer colds are the devil. It couldn't be a help to his temper. He was inviting me to tell it in my own words. Whose other words would I use?

". . . then when I got back from the dinner party I decided—"

"No," said Summit. "Earlier than that. Just summarize what you were doing earlier in the day."

I swallowed a piece of tonsil and stared across the courtroom. Lot of people. Curiosity and the news hounds. I wondered if Chalmers or one of his men had come to watch. Mrs. Lease was dabbing her nose with her handkerchief. *Hers* wasn't a summer cold. Poor dear. Oh, Christ, what had I done to *her*?

"Tuesday morning I was up about four, drove from Edinburgh to London—actually to Barking Magistrates' Court." Summit looked puzzled so I explained wearily what I'd been there for. "After the—d'you call 'em committal proceedings?—Inspector Chalmers asked me to stay behind because he thought I might help them with their further inquiries." I stopped. You couldn't have put that bloody worse if you'd sat up all night thinking how to give the wrong impression. "Someone I once knew," I said tonelessly. "I helped to provide a background . . . Then my car gave trouble and I took it to the garage for servicing. So I was late arriving at the party. Must have been just before nine . . . I had a light meal there and then left again. I walked back across the park to our flat and began packing—"

"Packing?" said Summit.

I gave him a stony stare. "I'd decided that things weren't ever going to work out between myself and my wife and it was time to opt out."

"I see . . . And then?"

"Well, my wife returned from the dinner party earlier than I expected and challenged me to a bout."

Summit said, "Just like that?"

"Well . . . There was conversation first."

"But you agreed?"

"Reluctantly. She seemed overexcited."

"In your view, was she drunk?"

"Not at all. She'd *had* drink. As I had. But I don't think there was drunkenness on either side."

"May I ask what caused this sudden quarrel between you? You must have been at odds before?"

"Oh, yes."

"Then there was nothing special about this evening?"

"Oh, yes . . ."

"Could you explain to me what it was?"

I saw Shona had got Alice Huntington with her. That old Fairy Queen. Did she need that sort of moral support?

"I didn't like some of the guests at the party. They were people whose—habits I don't care for. It seemed to me that my wife had invited them specially to get back at me . . . to show her contempt for me," I explained.

"Ah." He wrote down a few words. It was like the Recording Angel doing his stuff on Judgment Day. "So, being insulted, you threatened to kill your wife; broke two glasses and left."

I met his eyes again. I came to the sour conclusion that he had come to a sour conclusion about me.

When I didn't speak he said, "I'm asking you a question, Sir David. Two of your guests have apparently testified to this effect. They may have given me the wrong impression. You are now in a position to correct it."

I thought, what is there to say in a court like this about a personal relationship? Was a personal relationship between me and Erica ever *possible*? Can a man begin to explain his own violence and, by spilling it out, be able to draw away from it, detach himself, say, "Look, that wasn't really me"? Yet so far, I'd played the innocent. Was that what I'd been *intending* to do?

"There's nothing to correct," I said.

After a pause Summit cleared his throat and said, "I see." He sighed. "Well, let us leave it at that, then. Now in the matter of the fencing bout, do you say that you often had such practice tourneys with your wife in your own home?"

"Usually once a day. Sometimes twice, when she was training for the Olympics."

"Did you ever injure each other before?"

"No."

"Why did you choose the épée for this bout? I understand it is the heaviest of the fencing weapons."

"I didn't choose it. She did."

"Did you usually use the épée for such practice bouts?"

"Always. My wife felt the extra weight and power made foil fencing easier when she returned to it."

"Was it not extremely unwise to enter into such a bout on an evening when there was such ill feeling between you?"

"Yes."

Summit looked over his glasses toward Edmond Gale. "Do you wish to ask Sir David anything?"

"If you please."

Distance from Gale, you saw that his stumpy figure and gentle voice didn't seem to matter: He came over well; no risk of him not being noticed.

"Sir David, is it true that your wife made a special point of asking you to return from Scotland in time for this party, and that you made an extra effort to do so?"

"Yes."

"So that when you arrived at the party to find it a party entirely of men—and of men, shall we say, to say the least, you did not like—it could not have been unexpected to her that you should show some annoyance?"

"I think it was meant as a gesture. A rude gesture, if you like."

"And did you threaten to murder your wife?"

"I said, 'I could murder that woman.' "

"In a loud voice?"

"No. It was in an aside to the man I was sitting next to. Derek Jones."

"Could the two witnesses have heard what you said?"

"Palmer probably did."

"Was your remark meant as a threat?"

"Of course not." That was *true*, wasn't it? You couldn't lie to *lose* your skin.

"And you threw the glasses? Dropped them?"

"Dropped them. Bad temper. I just wanted my wife to get the message that it was the end between us."

"And when she followed you home? You were preparing to leave. She tried to stop you?"

"Yes."

"Did you want to fence with her?"

"It was the last thing."

"Why did you finally agree?"

"Not much choice. She had her weapon out and blocked the doorway."

"Sir David, did you at *any* time have *any* intention of harming your wife?"

Probably the hesitation was only split second. "No," I said. Pilate saith unto him: What is truth?

Gale had gone away. The coroner was writing again. I thought, now he's going to ask, where was Mrs. Carreros in all this? Because if he does I'm going to have to say, she wasn't there. David, the practiced old liar, isn't prepared to tell that sort of lie. But Summit just wasn't thinking along those lines. Shona, it seemed, had put her evidence over with such precision and authority that in this husband and wife squabble she'd inserted herself as the witness standing in the kitchen watching the contest from beginning to end. Bitch. All women were bitches.

"Very well, Sir David, you may stand down."

Almost before I got back to base the coroner was on his way.

"This," he was saying, "has been a very tragic event, which could and should have been avoided. Two talented and distinguished people engage in a routine fencing exercise, but in a situation charged with a degree of dislike which may have made the exchanges more robust, more hostile, than they would normally have been or should ever have been. We have two witnesses who have come forward, voluntarily, to testify that this hostility had been newly fueled at a dinner party, at which Sir David had either issued a threat against his wife or muttered a casual aside. There is a conflict of opinion on this point. We have, however, a further witness who says she witnessed the fencing practice and saw nothing unusual or remarkable in the bout until the fatal blow was struck. Both contestants had been drinking, but again this witness confirms Sir David's own statement that they were not drunk. It was not a drunken brawl. Fencing conventions were observed. It was no different in appearance from any other practice bout—until the fatal blow was struck."

Summit turned over his notes as if he was cooking them on a slow fire.

"Those as I see them are the facts. In arriving at a verdict I must ask myself one or two questions. It is fully admitted that Sir David stabbed his wife in the throat with his sword. Now, whenever any person does an act which without ordinary precautions is or may be dangerous to human life he is bound to employ reasonable precautions in doing it. If he does not, and if death results from his criminal misconduct in failing to take these ordinary precautions, then he is guilty of manslaughter. Did Sir David so behave?"

Summit had problems clearing his voice. Then he said, "Now we have evidence that, irrespective of any good or ill will which existed between the contestants, both wore the fencing masks and protective clothing which are the standard equipment of the Amateur Fencing Association. In the thrust and counterthrust of such a contest neither good will nor ill will should have made any difference." He paused and then said in a hurry as if anxious to get away, "The fatal blow was struck in a proper manner, and in accordance with the rules of the sport. In my view, no criminal misconduct took place. I record a verdict of Death by Misadventure."

Shona put out a hand as if to touch me, and then withdrew it.

"I should add," said Mr. Summit grimly, "a rider that fencing safety equipment should be carefully overhauled, and if necessary the protective clothing strengthened. This may be only the second fatal accident to occur in England, in a sport with an excellent safety record, but someone died from a similar accident on the Continent two years ago, and I would like to feel that this tragedy may serve some purpose if it alerts the authorities to the dangers that can exist."

III When I left the court I was too punch-drunk to think clearly about anything; but later it occurred to me to remember that I had gone to the inquest intent on saying everything that was on my mind—to come out with it all, so far as that was possible; but then these two men stalking into the witness box and trying to frame me with their exaggerations and distortions had brought out a combative instinct that I guess is not solely the property of awkward types like me. If anything was ever counterproductive I suppose it was the evidence of Messrs. Palmer and Houseman.

CHAPTER THIRTY

I
It's odd how sounds can make you listen to the silences. And it's odd how many telltale sounds there are in a silent flat. Worse than Wester Craig in a thunderstorm. Because here there are no ancestors to curse you or haunt you but only the curses and ghosts you've created for yourself. Some men are only half made; they've got this underlying conviction that nature has slipped up in their manufacture, and because they're like that their only real purpose is breaking whatever their hand touches. I was such a type. The history of my life was a history of disaster. Wherever I'd gone I'd left a trail behind me like a poisonous snail. No one who knew me was the better for knowing me; in fact everyone notably worse. Even Shona you could hardly say had benefited. The firm had certainly prospered, but she had broken with her husband and they had been estranged when he died. She was looking unwell now and rather lost. Not quite the imperious, austere, beautiful, mysterious Russian dame I'd first set my sights on at the Rowtons' cocktail party. The change wasn't all my doing; Father Time had chipped in with a heavy hand; but I wasn't blameless.

Good-bye to the Leases; we'd not had much to say to each other all along; nothing to *be* said. But just at the last minute Mrs. Lease murmured, "She loved you dearly, David, you know that, I'm sure." Bit of a stab that, under your guard; you think you've got all your protective clothing on and the sword slips through the gap between the bib and the collar, right into the jugular.

Later a stout elderly chap turned up who said he was Lady Abden's lawyer and told me that Erica had not made a new will since her marriage, so legally it was as if she had died intestate. This meant that I was the main legatee, but—he hurried on—it was unlikely that Miss Lease, Lady Abden, had left a great amount of money of her own, living as she had almost entirely on the very large monthly allowance made her by her father, and living, by all accounts, up to the full limits of that allowance. There would be some money, of course, and the jewelry and personal effects.

"I want none of it," I said harshly. "Make what arrangements you can, and if you'll see what she wanted done with her money in her will—"

"The one she made when she was twenty-one—"

"Whenever. See that it's disposed of in that way. If you need me to sign things, let me know as soon as you can."

"Very well, Sir David." He looked a bit surprised. Had he thought I'd bumped my wife off for the sake of the cash?

I thought off and on about Alison up in her northwest fastnesses but made no attempt to get in contact with her. "What was there to say? I asked the exchange to disconnect the number of the Knightsbridge flat. The stock issue of Shona Ltd. could go ahead without the benefit of my invaluable advice. Most of the time I didn't answer the doorbell, knowing it would only be some weasel-faced reporter, pretending to sympathize but trying to cash in on the fact that I might still have a retrospective and scurrilous news value. I'd pushed several out already.

But inevitably Shona came and inevitably she got me to let her in.

Not a woman given to hesitation in the ordinary way, but hesitant now.

She said, "Well, David, it is over."

"Over?"

"Yes. In so far as it can be."

"You did your bit, didn't you," I said harshly.

"I lied so that the truth would be more evident."

"What particular truth is that?"

"That it was accidental, that it *was* death from misadventure, that you had no intention *whatsoever* of injuring her."

"Why are you so sure?"

"Because I know you too well."

"That's the oldest cry in the world, isn't it? 'I know him, so I know he didn't do it.' Ask Hitler's mother."

She came into the room and untied her scarf, drooped it on a chair. "Are you telling me that you intended to kill her?"

"*No* . . . Well, I don't *know* . . . there was a moment of sheer bloody rage when I wouldn't give way."

"You have moments of anger—not rage, anger. I have seen them before. How many have you had in your whole life—half a dozen?"

"Many more than that."

"So it could be said, if you wished to argue that way, that two have proved fatal. One when you were a terrified child, one when protective clothing proved faulty. In both cases you were being goaded, had your back to a wall. It is something to be lived with—outgrown."

"What's the point?"

"Because there is so much in you that is too good to lose."

"Don't make me cry."

She shrugged. "Why should you not believe it? Because you have got into this mental habit of self-criticism, of self-blame."

I laughed harshly again. "Self-blame? Brother, that'll be the day!"

"Well, is it not so? Of course it is! You grew up with frozen emotions. In these last years they have become partly thawed out. Circulation is very painful when it returns, even to frozen fingers. As a child I knew it often! How much more so when it is to a whole personality."

I poured myself a stiff whisky and then put it down untouched. "Not long ago you were accusing me of not responding to Erica!"

"And you did not. But you respond to me!"

"As I do to Alison," I said. It was a bitchy remark, but I felt turned inside out, wishing I could vomit my life away.

"So . . . May I have a drink?"

"Why not?"

She busied with bottles and stoppers and siphons.

"So you will marry her?"

I didn't answer. My voice had gone.

"The flotation is well under way now, David. We had to go ahead without your participation and advice. The final date for subscribing will be Friday week. If you never enter our house again you will be a rich man."

"Thanks."

"So there is nothing to stop you entering into your inheritance in Scotland with enough money to maintain it in reasonable style."

"Thanks."

"And marrying Alison or some other fecund young woman who can give you all the heirs you require."

"D'you suppose—" I stopped and she waited—and waited. I knew she wasn't going to let me get away with a half-finished sentence, so in the end I went on. "D'you suppose I'm tumbling over myself to perpetuate the Abden line? Drunkards, liars, cheats, killers . . . ?"

"I think you stand as fair a chance as anyone of producing a normal child. There are drunkards, liars, cheats and killers everywhere. Do not be so conceited for your family: The Abdens do not have a monopoly! I doubt if they even have a higher proportion in your family than anyone else."

No response to that. She stood erect in the middle of the room, left hand holding the elbow that held her glass. I prowled around the room, a prisoner wanting to get out.

"You don't look well," I said. "What's wrong with you?"

"With me?" She blinked. "Nothing. I have had these liver attacks all my life. As you know. In the old days I used to hide away until they were past; I hated people seeing me at less than my best. Now . . . I don't so much care."

"There are plenty of other lovers in the world besides me."

"Oh, that I *well* know . . . But you happen to be the one that matters."

"Pity."

"Yes," she agreed. "A pity . . . Of course the firm will go on now without you—without even me, I suspect, though there is then the risk of its being taken over by infidels. For a few years yet I think it is safe."

I said, "It would have been better if you'd not picked me up out of my particular gutter, and let the firm run on in the old way, as John always wanted."

"Better? Who for? I do not regret it. Why should one fret about past choices? Life is too short for looking back. Besides . . . what we had together was so *rich* while it lasted. I do not regret having loved you: It gave my life a deeper channel. You cannot say it had no effect upon you!"

"It went too deep for my petrified emotional life."

"If that is a joke then let it stay as a joke . . . Will you promise me one thing?"

"What?"

"Let this tragedy distance itself from you for a few months before you make any rash decision or wanton move. You have always hated yourself. Now you hate yourself more than ever. But it will pass—some of it will pass. I want you to promise to do nothing—irrevocable before you have given yourself time."

"Can't promise," I said. "I'll do my best."

"Well," she said after a moment, "keep to that if you can. Perhaps for us this is good-bye."

I put my hand on her steady shoulder but did not speak.

She blinked and shook her head. "Now I must learn to live without you. Perhaps the hardest part is already past. Still it is difficult. Still I will try."

II Darkest hour before the dawn? It's a load of old rubbish. But the next hour certainly was in competition for the proud title. Couldn't settle, couldn't rest. Couldn't eat or drink.

Oddly enough, suicide—which Shona was hinting her fears of—had never been a front-runner. Perhaps the Abdens have some sort of stamina which enables them to endure the various hells they make for themselves. Perhaps it's egoism, if you boil it down to the barest truth. Egoism is a built-in survival kit; without it you're apt to perish and die. With it you just *wish* you were dead.

I thought of a lot of boring old things. What to do from now on? Go to the U.S. for a bit, as I'd thought of doing once before? Try Vienna and look up Trudi Baumgarten? Go and be a navvy somewhere, working on a building site, sweat the evil humors out of my system? Return to Scotland and Alison?

The one thing I disliked most of all was my own company, yet there was no one else's company I could see myself keeping. I lifted the telephone up and found it was still gently purring. In the old days you were cut off even without asking. I rang Derek and suggested we should meet somewhere. He sounded hesitant and a bit startled.

"Shall I come round?" he said.

"God, no. Anything to get out of this place. What about the pub we went to once near your flat?"

"The Lamb and Flag? Yes, if you must."

"What d'you mean, if I must?"

"Well it's—er—it's a trifle noisy, isn't it, dear?"

"Suggest somewhere else."

There was a longish pause. "No," he said, "that'll do, I suppose. The food is fairish, I remember."

"O.K. See you at eight."

I picked up the Ferrari at five, its splendid throttle roar completely restored, parked near the flats until seven-thirty and then drove across London to the Lamb and Flag.

Derek was waiting for me at the door of the saloon bar. He looked seedy and shifty, and I wondered why I'd come. No one went more quickly up and down in his circumstances than Derek. When he had money it went through his fingers like sand. I wondered what his love life was at present and hoped I'd not have to hear.

We went in and ordered steaks and talked about Erica. And then I realized why I'd come; it was for just that reason. There was no one else. I couldn't discuss her with Shona in the same way; and with her parents not at all. Derek was my oldest friend; we'd kept in a sort of contact for fifteen years.

I'm usually tight about the mouth, but I suppose it had to open sometime. You don't realize till you start talking that you are just going to go on and on. Often over the same ground, asking myself questions as well as asking him, half answering them before he did. I got near to bringing Alison into it, but just held my tongue on that. Otherwise it was the history of my life for the last twelve months in seven reels with barely a commercial break. I suppose it did me good like nothing else since Erica's death. Now and again the old headshrinker and his couch are useful. Or Aunt Helen's Catholic priest. Or even a tall thin elegant ramshackle pansy with his bookmaker's smile and his sham-innocent faded blue eyes that have become shifty over the years.

When for the second time we got to the inquest I suddenly remembered I'd never asked Edmond Gale where he'd dreamed up those peculiar questions about the dinner party: He seemed to know as much about it as if he'd been there himself.

"I rang him, dear," said Derek. "Told him all I could. I couldn't *come*. Scared out of my pants about the whole thing. Still am, if the truth be told. I wouldn't take the stand and say things *against* you. But I didn't *dare* be my noble self—they wouldn't have liked that!—so I thought, give Mr. Whatsit all the info I could."

"Did you make some of it up? Erica would never have consulted me about backing Palmer's play."

"It was the cold truth, matey. She said to me she couldn't bear this latest offering that Palmer was foisting on the public so she'd made the excuse to him that *you* wouldn't let her."

"Ah . . . well . . . thanks for the help."

Derek lifted his empty beer glass. "I've a further little item of news to tell you . . . But first let me tot you another one out."

"Thanks." I pushed my glass toward him and saw him hesitate. He half got up and then sat down again. His color changed. I said, "Something wrong?"

He looked at me. "Sorry, old matey, I think there may be. I'll get the two wets."

He was gone a couple of minutes, came back with heavy pint glasses, spilled the beer as well as the froth putting them down. Then he said, "I think you've been rumbled."

"Meaning what?"

"Don't look round. There's a couple of blokes at the bar. I think they know you're here."

I took a long draft. "So if they do?"

"It won't be nice . . . Oh, Christ, I think it may be my fault! . . ."

"Stop wailing. What's it all about?"

"I'm living with a little boy called Leonard. He knew you'd rung, he knew where I was going. He's as jealous as jaundice. If he's given you away I'll wring his sleazy little neck."

I glanced around, not knowing what I might be looking for. The pub was not more than half full. A fair scattering of women. In spite of everything your heart begins to beat a bit quicker.

"I was going to tell you," Derek said desperately, "this item of news. But I held it up as a surprise till later . . . I was going to tell you, knowing you'd be pleased. Now I've got to spit it out like a deathbed confession . . . Roger's scarpered."

I stared at him. "What? Roger Manpole?"

"Yes."

"What d'you mean, scarpered?"

"What I say. Done a bunk. Flown the coop. Got the hell out of it. And from what I hear, with the police not far behind. The result of those raids in Dagenham and Hackney. One of the blokes is turning Queen's Evidence. I guess Roger's just made it in time. He dropped everything: wife, family, luxury home, racing stables, the lot."

"For the first time something is reaching me," I said. "And making me feel good."

"It would maybe if you were not in the birdlime yourself now. I expect they're acting on Roger's say-so."

"Nobody can disrupt a pub," I said. "Not unless you're IRA with a hand grenade."

"No, but they can wait outside. It's only half an hour to closing time."

"Then we've got half an hour," I said, "to gloat on Roger's fall."

Derek rubbed his knees angrily. "I don't know if you realize, old dear, that these men are *nasty*. And—and as for me, I'd never *rat* on you in a court of law or an inquest, *never*; but I'm not the stuff heroes are made of. If it comes to a roughhouse I tend to be among the missing persons."

"Don't worry," I said angrily. "It's my party."

We sat there sipping the beer. My mouth was dry and the beer didn't go to the spot.

"Where's your car?" Derek said.

"About five cars down on this side of the road."

"They're bound to have seen that. You can't mistake it, can you. Look, old chum, I've an idea. Why don't you leave your beer half drunk and go as if you were going to the loo and never come back."

"The way Donald did?"

"All right, all right. Joke over. If I remember rightly there's a side door leading directly out from the Gents. If you can make that, then beat it like hell and pick up a taxi. There's a rank actually just beyond the cinema on the next corner."

"And my car?"

"Forget it, for the time being. Even if you're on a yellow line it won't cost you the earth. Come back tomorrow in a taxi, keep the taxi ticking, pick up your car and drive it out of town."

"Thanks, I'll consider it."

"Consider it fast. They'll be calling last orders soon."

"These gorillas might mash up the car."

"Well, so what? You're insured, aren't you? Some things you can't insure for."

I brooded a few moments rancorously, watching him dab at the sweat on his forehead. It seemed to me that if Roger really went I would at least have done something in my life I wouldn't ever regret. You can't put psychological things on scales, but this news, if it was true, brought some weight off the debit side in my mind. Maybe it just shows the total lack of proportion in everything I do—how to equate the calamity of Knightsbridge with putting the skids under a big but essentially petty criminal? —but I can only say it was like a spark of light in a black room.

"Tell me about him," I said.

"Who?"

"Roger, of course. Is it really the end of him?"

"Seems so. He was only tipped off half an hour before the police called."

"Why didn't he bluff it out? With expert criminal lawyers he could surely have got out of anything. He's usually been so clever at covering his tracks."

"Don't ask me. I suppose he knew Laval had grassed on him. He and Laval have been pretty close these last two years. He must have weighed the odds and thought himself safer on the Costa Blanca."

"Is that where he's gone?"

"Christ, how do I know? I only know he's gone and left it all, and no doubt he blames it on you."

"I'd *like* to think so." I took a long drink. "Well, here's to Roger. Of course Laval is the man he should beat up."

"Laval's in jail in Brixton, chum, and you're not."

"Who are these heavies? Point them out to me."

"Be your age. I'd no more lift a finger in their direction than I would in yours."

"Sure you're not mistaken? They could be here for a casual drink."

Derek blew his nose expressively. "Darling, if you're mad enough not to do a bunk while you can, I'm in no position to help you. Only I warn you, I'm going soon and leaving you here on your teeny-weeny own."

I thought it over again. Maybe I wasn't so brave as I thought. Brave? No, that wasn't the word. Angry. Viciously angry. And not caring what happened to me. But I'd only recently been contemplating and rejecting suicide. The old Abden ego. So why accept, if you could avoid it, a nasty encounter with bully boys?

"OK," I said. "I'll go. Thanks for the supper, Derek. And the warning. See you sometime."

"So long, pal. And good luck."

I got up, hitched my trousers, left the half-glass of beer, nodded at Derek and made for the lavatory.

It was a poor light in there and there was one man relieving himself. I didn't, but turned back and saw the door Derek had spoken of. By the door were some beer bottles, so I picked one up and weighed it in my hand. Better than nothing: if not so good as an Aga handle or an épée sword.

Push open the door, into the street, flatten yourself against the wall. The pub was on a side street; the main road a hundred yards away. Parked cars; a few people walking. All quiet on the western front.

At the double now for a taxi? Hundred yards' sprint. What was the record? Somebody in Moscow this year had done it in about ten seconds. Or was that the hundred meters? Yards, meters, what the hell. When I got to the main road there'd be far too many people about for any rough stuff, assuming they were not the shooting sort.

I put my hand in my pocket and felt the keys of the car. If I got away they'd probably vent their irritation on the Ferrari. Kick the headlamps in, slash the tires, smash the windows, break the instrument panel. Unfortunately the car was just past the entrance to the pub and facing this way. But if two of the gorillas were inside the pub, there probably wouldn't be more than one more outside—I wasn't that important. Coming from an unexpected quarter, I could be off in the ten seconds it would take me to reach the main road. And once in the car, a fat hope they had of catching me then.

Shoulders hunched, one hand in pocket, the other clutching the beer bottle under my jacket, I turned and slouched past the entrance to the pub. As I got to the door four people came out, but they were ordinary lads laughing and larking.

The car. The bright red Ferrari. This was the moment when

any watcher would recognize me. Out with the keys, got the right one in the keyhole like a dream. Open the door, swinging wide, slamming after me. Key in ignition. *Whom*, the engine, newly tuned, started like a giant bird and we were away. Back a foot to give myself room. Then *whom* into the street.

As I was coming out a van drew out of a parking space three cars in front of me. It was facing my way, and I had to brake. But the van came on. It hit the Ferrari on its offside wing and crunched me against the steering wheel. The crash seemed as loud as a grenade.

Two seconds' silence. A man getting out of the van. Two more from the pub. Pains in my chest. So this was it. Sense of guilt mingled with the blazing, killing anger. Deserts. Somebody would get his deserts.

Pick up the bottle from the seat and get out. Wondered if any of my ancestors had been in the Charge of the Light Brigade.

First man incautious, came at me on his own, stick raised. I got in first and he yelled, dropped his truncheon. I hit him again as he fell; great joy. This was all that life was for now. Something hit me on the side of the jaw, almost knocking my head off; fell against the car, clutching, still clutching the bottle; up with it, crash in a man's face; something kicked me in the stomach; no air, no air, I'm going to die. I hit the third man as I fell; broke his wrist, I think, hope. Down, crash into the road, rolling over, trying to get up. Still no air, no air.

Then it was just a question of boots.

CHAPTER THIRTY-ONE

I Four weeks in hospital doesn't take long to say. It's a lot of time if you're in there, even if the first week you're mainly on pethidine.

The hoodlums had done a good job, but the car crash had attracted too much attention for them to finish it off—or finish me off, if that had been their aim in life. But I think it would probably satisfy Roger in far off Costa Blanca. Fractured jaw, three broken ribs, a ruptured spleen. They'd get their pay.

And I'd got mine. It was quits. Bloodletting all round. No, it wasn't suicide but it was as if I had been fighting myself, injuring myself, trying to kill myself. As I'd been doing all my life. Roger had provided the instrument.

At times in that first week I must have raved a lot. Someone had put some fruit by my bed and I thought it was Erica staring at me out of the orange; and my father peering over her shoulder, laughing, sneering. Teeth were everywhere. And bodies and raw butchered flesh and cosmic froth. And God knows what else that I prefer to forget. There'd never been a time when humanity seemed so obscene.

Yet when Shona came I behaved like a tame sheep; and she came regularly. The company of Shona Ltd. had been floated on the stock exchange and the shares had been six times oversubscribed. And then my mother came, and I carried on the politest conversation. Mother thought it was all the results of a car crash, and lectured me on driving too fast. I knew there were all sorts of things I wanted to say to her, lots and lots of interesting things, but I was too tired and weak to begin. So she went away unmolested, promising to return, as I knew she never would. I wondered sometimes if she was the not-quite-innocent cause of it all. And then Alison was there and sat by my bed and held my hand and whispered things to me, and paid me three visits before she returned to Kirkcudbright.

And none of it meant anything—yet. Shell shock, delayed concussion, battle fatigue, accident trauma.

I only wished the nights were as easy. Then the skin peeled off and everything was monstrous and visceral and bleeding and tumorous and unbearable.

Derek never came. Perhaps you could hardly blame him. Perhaps he jumped at shadows when he went home at night. My one real contact with what you could call normality was Van Morris. He came twice a week, and toward the end of my time brought Essie with him. He'd arranged with the insurers for the car to be repaired. The damage was not as bad as I'd thought, and he said it would be ready for me as soon as I was allowed out. He told me his pay had been doubled, and when Shona came next I thanked her for it.

She said, "It is nothing. But I am concerned about you when you are discharged. They say you must be convalescent for at least another month. I do not think you should drive that fast car."

"I shan't. I'm going to fly off somewhere, sit in the sun for a bit."

"Barbados?"

"Ah, no. Just somewhere local for the time being. Greece or Italy. I might try Spain to see how Roger is going on."

She said soberly, "I trust you are joking."

"Reckon so. I shall leave that part to Chalmers. He was in here to see me yesterday."

"Will they catch him?"

"He doubts it. We've no extradition order with Spain, and it's only fraud Roger is wanted for. If it was murder they would stand a better chance."

"It nearly was," she said.

|II| In the end I went no farther than Taormina. The autumn lingers on in Sicily, and although it was painful to swim I swam. I also sat for ages on the raft in the middle of the bay and thought. Looking back, what I thought is a blank, but it certainly filled the time.

One or two girls tried to get to know me at the hotel but it didn't work. I was still a walking zombie. Yet toward the end of the fourth week a few things had become clearer and a shade—believe it or not—more peaceful. Somebody quite recently said that experience is what used to be called the soul. At this stage I differed from this view, because I could stand back and look at my experience, my faults, my inept dumb actions, my misdeeds, if you like, and see them as detached entities. So who was looking at them in this way? Merely something that was the sum of those deeds? Not so.

I flew back on a Friday but never left Heathrow. I put up at one of those deadly hotels which surround the airport like toadstools, and the next morning flew to Inverness. There I hired a little Ford Cortina and drove to Wester Craig.

By now the late November mists had come down, and every other day a gale stalked the hills. At least the roofs didn't leak this time. The long darknesses were a change from the temperate autumnal suns of Sicily, and I walked a fair bit and got wet a fair bit and read a fair bit, and, once again, thought. I made no attempt to get in contact with Lochfiern House, but after I'd been in residence a week Alison turned up.

Coppell was out with McVitie so I opened the door myself. She stood on the bottom step smiling quietly up at me. I took her hand and drew her in.

"You said you'd tell me. In the hospital you said you'd let me know."

"I didn't make up my own mind until the last moment, and then I thought you were at Castle Douglas."

"I was. Until Mary rang yesterday."

"So you've only just arrived. You've grown your hair."

"A little. Do you like it?"

"I like it any way."

I took her right up to the bedroom. There was no need for polite talk or will-you-won't-you hesitations. It was as if we'd never been separated.

Afterward I told her about the perfumery forgeries, the way we had tracked them down and stumbled on something bigger, the flight of the man behind the racket, the scene outside the Lamb and Flag. I had been too tired to say much in the hospital and she had not wanted to approach Shona. Alison had seen the reports of Erica's death in the papers and swallowed the verdict without a second thought. A tragedy for everyone concerned. I did not mention my father. Only three people knew about that: Shona, my mother and Kenneth Kingsley. It was enough.

At least until I turned Catholic and confessed it to some spotty priest.

She told me what there was to tell in her own life. Catriona was not with her; she had started nursery school in Kirkcudbright.

"So you will want to go back there soon?"

"Not soon. My mother is very happy to have Trina. I can stay a week or two."

So she stayed. Not with me, but she might just as well. You can't hide something that won't be hidden. I saw the Abdens a couple of times; their welcome was equivocal. I had just lost my wife in the most tragic circumstances. I'd had a severe motor accident—just like their own son—which had crippled me for two months. I was having an affair with their daughter-in-law/sister-in-law and barely preserving the decencies. If eventually I married her—allowing a proper interval following my first wife's death—it would probably be as good an arrangement for everybody as could be. But this disagreeable modern habit of jumping the gun was not popular in the Highlands and was not easy to ignore. Lucie and her mother were guarded, Mary breathily welcoming.

Weather heavy all the time; broodingly dark, enormous clouds blanketing the sky, so that daylight seemed a temporary event; you were always just pulling the curtains back as it appeared over the spiked skyline or drawing them across as the last remnants drained away. The wind howled like runaway dogs. There were no lights outside at night; you peered through black panes that reflected your own face. I wondered if the absolute blackness outside equaled the blackness of my soul.

Cold drafts everywhere, even in the bedroom—drafts like cold thoughts pushing their way into the sham coziness and warmth of the shared bed. Some fires smoked. Never in the history of the house had there been so many fires burning—even the two in the ancestral hall. Early on in my stay I'd tired of sputtering logs—half the wood round here was resinated—and ordered a ton of coal. Surprisingly it arrived next day, and we burned this with the profligacy of the short-lived. Sometimes timbers creaked as if you were on a ship.

Gulls, sea duck, scoters, blew in flurries across the brief windy daylights, waves on the loch threatened the shaky quay I had repaired, mountainous seas bursting endlessly on distant rocks sent spray up to join the driving mists.

When we were alone together we talked a fair amount and smoked a little and ate and drank a little, and sometimes sat in total silence listening to the quarrelsome gales. We talked of theaters and books and gardens and sunshine and families and fishing and shooting. She said she often went shooting at home with her brother.

"You *enjoy* shooting birds?" I said. "Very strange."

"Not so strange. Not when they're bred for the purpose."

I said, "They say about the English upper classes, don't they, that when they wake in the morning they say, 'What a lovely day, let's go out and kill something.' Are the Scots as bad?"

"You're one. You ought to know."

"A town-bred one. But I think of all the birds that have become extinct in the Highlands in the last eighty years—so maybe the answer is yes."

"Animals too: I could mention half a dozen without stopping to think . . . But yes, I enjoy grouse shooting, pheasant shooting. As I say, they're bred for this only. So I am only taking away from the countryside what has been specially added to the countryside."

"But when you see one fluttering down suddenly deprived of flight, its wing broken, doesn't that take away from the thrill of the shot?"

"You mustn't be sentimental, David. You are not a vegetarian. You shut your eyes to the murdered sheep, the bullock under the axe, the strangled chicken. A shot is usually at least as humane a way of bringing the food to the table."

For once in her life she'd spoken sharply, and after a minute I said, "Touché. Who am I to gag at killing off a bird or an animal considering that I seem to enjoy killing people."

She sat up and looked at me, eyes intent, steady. "What on earth do you mean?"

"Off-color joke," I said. "But you know it isn't given to every man to stab his wife to death in a fencing duel."

"I hope you're not telling me you found pleasure in it!"

I put my lips to her arm. "Not in those words. But sometimes I wake in the night and think how much I'd come to dislike her.

Then I say, why did I not sidestep and parry, why did I just stand and meet her charge?"

"But you couldn't have *known* this would happen! The protective clothing!"

"No . . . I couldn't have known."

"Then is there any need to ask such questions?"

"No. No need. But sometimes they rear their ugly heads."

"Don't let them."

She slowly lay back on the pillow, her urchin cut, grown longer, feathering about her head.

She said, "I sometimes think you don't tell me the whole truth."

"About what?"

"Your thoughts. Your feelings. Your understanding of yourself."

"Nobody can, Alison. There's no such thing as the whole truth. There's only ever a partial account of a partial reality."

"Sometimes you frighten me."

"*I*—frighten *you*? Come off it. I'd think that impossible."

"Why?"

"Because you would never be frightened of *anything*. You're so stable, so enduring."

"That's not much of a compliment."

"It's meant to be." I again kissed her arm, but higher up. "But why do I frighten you—always supposing I remotely do?"

She shivered. "You're tickling me."

"Never mind. It's in a good cause."

"You seem," she said, "sometimes you seem not to have your whole attention on what you're saying. Maybe observing what you should be taking part in."

Oh, God, I thought, was this the same old charge? "Don't say I'm not taking part in you."

She smiled privately. "No, David, it is not in the big things. It's in the little things. You are far the best lover I have ever had."

"Among many?"

"No. I was too well brought up. But no man has ever paid me the attentions you do. Physically you are all that a woman could want."

"Physically only, I see. My broken ribs have created a mental blockage."

"No, don't joke, sweetheart. But sometimes after it is all

over—an hour after when I am driving home perhaps—I wonder if I have been pleasing to *you.*"

"I can only answer that, my love, by beginning all over again."

"Please do. Now. Please. Please do."

But already I was beginning to feel there was no future in it for me.

 She left on the following Monday, after three weeks. Trina was breaking up from school any day and she wanted to be back then.

We'd never had a cross word, Alison and I, and now never would. We separated with every evidence of loving regard. I said I was still convalescent—at least that I still felt a sense of shock which would take a time to wear away. I hadn't even decided whether to leave Wester Craig or to stay over Christmas. But as soon as I'd decided I'd let her know. Of course I'd write often. She said she could bring Trina for Christmas at Lochfiern—or somewhere else if I preferred. I said fine; take care, my love, there's snow forecast, we don't want another motoring casualty.

After the little yellow Mini had disappeared round the fold in the land I walked slowly back to the house. It was a rare fine day, with a pale sun shining on white water and black rocks and sugarloaf peaks and hillsides brown with bracken. Although the battering winds had been so cold, we'd not had a single frost yet.

Coppell was standing in the doorway, shading his eyes and staring up toward the hills.

"What are you looking at?"

"I think it is a black guillemot, sorr. You see them but seldom now. He's a lovely wee chap. See him there turning into the sun."

"Do you shoot birds for pleasure, Coppell?"

"Oh nae, sorr, not that sort. Of course when Mr. Malcolm was alive we had regular shooting parties, but usually they would drive east to one of the grouse moors. Round here I would shoot only the eagles."

"Don't you think they're entitled to a lamb or two?"

"McVitie wouldna think so. It is all a ma'er of opinion."

"Yes . . . yes. So much in this world is all a matter of opinion."

I stayed another week. Physically I seemed absolutely OK after the incident outside the Lamb and Flag. Spiritually (or morally or whatever you like) I was less OK about the episode in the Knightsbridge flat. But my spilled blood had in some way helped.

On the day before I left I wrote to my beautiful mistress:

Dearest, dearest Alison,

This is the most awful letter I've ever had to write, and I pray to God I'll never write another like it. Because it's to tell you that our love affair is over. We said good-bye on Monday with loving promises, and that's how it should be. Because the desire hasn't gone. Only the reasoning mind behind the desire.

I know I'll never marry again. Things in my own past, far past, reinforced by the calamity of Erica's death, make it pretty plain to me that I'm not the one to pass on my own peculiar genes to yet another generation of Abdens. And if I just remained your lover it'd be wildly unfair to you and still more to Trina—who badly needs a father. You're so beautiful, and young enough to marry again properly and settle into some good Scottish laird's home and raise a family, become a personality in the district and forget the Abdens of Wester Craig and Lochfiern. It's not for you to stick around as the mistress of a rackety, unstable and disorderly baronet.

We've had a great and glorious time together. You've been wonderful to me; your body has been wonderful to me. I shall always remember these weeks with immense delight. Thank you, thank you, dear Alison.

I'm leaving Wester Craig tomorrow and may not come back. It's impossible to see anything clear at present. Even at thirty-seven, life seems to stretch a hell of a long way ahead. I only know what I know.

And because I know what I know I am writing this letter of good-bye. To you, my dear, all my love and loving wishes for a happier future than you'd ever find with me.

Ever your
David

Parts of the letter were a lie, but they were lies in a good cause: trying not to hurt more than I could the feelings of someone I really cared about.

Before I left I gave Coppell and McVitie a check for £1000 each. Said it was a once-only Christmas present to supplement their wages. Before I came back, if I came back, I'd ring or write to them.

I didn't go to Lochfiern. There was no natural conversation I could carry on with them.

I drove the little hired car to Inverness, checked it in and caught the plane to Heathrow. It was another fine day, and when I got to London the damned shops were already trumpeting Christmas. I wondered why I liked Alison and disliked Erica but had been able to live permanently with neither of them. The answer was clearer in my mind than it had ever been before. It was not Erica's death that lay between Alison and me. It was not the sword. It was not the iron handle of the Aga. It was not even dislike of passing my own particular genes on to another generation. There was simply the one woman who had ruined any hope I'd ever had of falling in love with either Erica or Alison. Because I'd cared too much for her. But she'd slipped away into the past where I couldn't ever reach her again. Where I couldn't reach *all* of her. Not as I remembered her. Not as she had once been. Not as I wanted her still. Time had taken half of her away. Forever. Forever.

It was seven when I checked in at the Berkeley and bathed and changed. By then the business day would be over, so I took a taxi to South Audley Street.

A voice answered the buzzer but it was not Shona's. When I got up, a small good-looking girl opened the flat door and said, "I'm Cherry. I'm really the daily help but I've stayed on this evening to get Mme. Shona's supper, as she isn't feeling too well."

Escorted by her I got to the bedroom door, where Cherry discreetly faded out. Shona was sitting up in bed in a scarlet silk bed-jacket, her hair tied carelessly back with a scarlet ribbon. She didn't look much different from when I'd seen her last, her fine pure skin with its yellowish tinge, great eyes slanting at me.

"David! This is a surprise."

"Yes. What's wrong with you?"

"Very little, I'm glad to say. But the specialist is trying a course of injections which are supposed to work miracles but do not have a happy effect at the outset. I have to stay in bed three days."

"And this is the first day?"

"The third. I am now already feeling better, and shall be up tomorrow. And you?"

"I'm feeling better," I said.

"You have come from Scotland?"

"From Scotland."

"To stay a little while in London?"

"A little while, yes."

"Well, do not stand in the doorway, my dear. Let us talk in comfort."

So I went across and drew up a chair beside Shona and took her hand.

ABOUT THE AUTHOR

Born and raised in Manchester, England, WINSTON GRAHAM moved at age seventeen to Cornwall in the scenic western highlands that would be the setting of many of his novels. Mr. Graham, whose works have been translated into seventeen languages, received the Order of the British Empire in 1983. He now resides in Buxted, Sussex, with his wife, Jean.